Soul
of my
Soul

LISA HELEN GRAY

FAMILY TREE
(AGES ARE SUBJECTED TO CHANGE THROUGHOUT BOOKS)

Maverick & Teagan
- Faith engaged to Beau
-Lily
-Mark
-Aiden is with Bailey

Mason & Denny
-Hope
-Ciara
-Ashton

Malik & Harlow
-Maddison (Twin 1)
-Maddox (Twin 2)
-Trent

Max & Lake
-Landon (M) (Triplet 1) is with Paisley
-Hayden (F) (Triplet 2)
-Liam (M) (Triplet 3)

Myles & Kayla
-Charlotte
-Jacob

Evan (Denny's brother) & Kennedy
-Imogen
-Joshua

HAYES FAMILY TREE
(Eldest to youngest)

-Jaxon
-Wyatt
-Eli
-Reid (Triplet 1)
-Luke (Triplet 2)
-Isaac (Triplet 3)
-Paisley
-Theo (Twin 1)
-Colton (Twin 2)

Soul

of my

Soul

PROLOGUE

JAXON

THE FIRST TIME I MET LILY CARTER, I was twelve years old. It was our first day of high school and the halls were bustling with people. Some I recognised, some I didn't. I'd been trying to find my locker when the crowd parted, and there she stood in all her beauty. She was glancing down at a piece of paper clutched tightly in her hand, her lips moving as she read from it, and although I couldn't hear her, I knew she'd have the voice of an angel. Kids had pushed and shoved into me, rushing to find their lockers, yet they all avoided the girl in front of me. It was like they knew she wasn't to be touched. I couldn't look away from her. She just stood out from everyone else, and not because of her looks—though admittedly, she was the most beautiful girl I'd ever laid eyes on.

Then she looked up and took my breath away. The sun blaring through the wide double doors not far behind her cast a glow around her, and I whispered to myself, "She really is an angel." Her sandy-blonde hair, which fell down around her waist, blew lightly in the breeze, making her look like a goddess.

I was enthralled, enamoured with her. Her big brown eyes were wide with people got too close. I wanted to go to her, to yell at everyone to stand back. I started to, but a hand clamped down on my shoulder and my best friend, Kurt, was grinning at me and telling me how cool high school was going to be. By the time I turned back, to get one more look, one more fill, she was gone.

But I knew I had to know her.

Just knew it.

My drink sloshing all over my hand brings me back to the present. Glancing to the left, I glare at my brother Wyatt. Wyatt is the second eldest in our large group of siblings. We look more like twins with our same height and facial features. The only differences really splitting us apart are the number of tattoos and our personalities. Wyatt only has a few pieces of ink, whereas I'm pretty much a guinea pig for our other brother Reid, who loves designing and tattooing. Wyatt has laugh lines, and I can't remember the last time I laughed. At twenty-four, I'm feeling more like eighty-four.

"Seriously, bro, did we really need to come?" he growls, pouting into his own drink as he scans our surroundings.

I sigh, scrubbing a hand down my face. We've not long arrived at an engagement party we were personally invited to by our neighbours, Faith and Beau. Our neighbours who also happen to be a member of a family we've had an ongoing war with up until recently.

The Carter's.

The Carter's are a massive family, and I say this only because I thought ours was big. What started off as five brothers, ended up with offspring, who we happened to grow up with.

Their dads, however, are kind of legends around our part of town. Everyone knew them and wanted to be them. I grew up with my dad telling me stories of the trouble and mischief they'd get up to. There was also loads of crap put into the papers, but he would never mention what it said to us. Said it wasn't his business.

Then we met the Carter's in high school and shit just hit the fan. Everything and anything would get blown out of proportion and shit would escalate quickly. I couldn't even tell you what started the feud between our two families. Fights would break out, girls' hearts would get broken, and when we grew up, pubs got destroyed. I can't even begin to count the places we're barred from, or have to make a deposit when we enter in case we get into a fight and break something, or be turned away at the door if more than one Carter is already inside. There's only one place in town that will let our families in together and that's The Ginn Inn. And only because we all chip in when things get broken.

Then recently, my sister shacked up with the worst of the Carter's: Landon. He's ruthless, cunning and quiet. He has a way about him that makes people pay attention and grown ass men avoid him. He also had a sharp left hook. Trust me, I'm the only one out of my siblings who is evenly matched against him, so when a fight breaks out, we always go head to head.

A sigh escapes my lips because as much as it pains me to admit it, I'd rather my baby sister be with the likes of Landon Carter, who I know adores and loves her, than Maddox Carter, who is a male whore.

He's also almost always the instigator of all our fights. He's a fucking shit stirrer and loves to wind people up.

Now that Landon's living with Paisley on our farm, we have to do shit together if it means keeping our sister in our lives. She's not the baby of the group, but she may as well be. She's the only female, except for our mum. Since our dad died in a boating accident, we've looked out for her more than she found acceptable.

The only reason I've moved passed my issues with Landon is because of her love for him. A few months ago, I let my mouth run off before thinking. I let my anger keep speaking for me, and I said some things that were unforgiveable. I went weeks without Paisley talking to me, and it killed me. I don't want that to happen again. We have always been the closest out of the nine of us.

"Are you going to fucking speak or keep spacing out on me?"

I scrub a hand along my jaw. I need a fucking shave. "Sorry, what did you say?"

He scoffs, shaking his head as he downs his drink. "I don't see why we had to come. No one fucking else has, except Paisley, and look at her. She's having the time of her life."

I do, glancing over at the bar where she's cuddled up to Landon, laughing at something Hayden Carter—who is Landon's triplet—is saying.

"Because she wanted us to try and make more of an effort with the family. Plus, could you say no to Faith? She looked determined to have us here."

He grunts. "Fuck no. Her bloke didn't look happy about us coming here, either. I guess I should find satisfaction in that."

I chuckle under my breath before bringing my cold glass of whiskey to my mouth. The cool liquid touches my lips just as Lily Carter and Charlotte Carter walk inside. I choke on my drink, coughing up a lung.

"Holy shit!" Wyatt whispers.

He can say that again.

Lily is wearing a blue, tight-fitting dress that looks painted onto her skin. I can see every curve of her luscious body. Her tits are practically popping out of her top and the bottom of the dress is rising up, barely covering her arse. I've never seen her dress like this. Fucking ever.

My dick gets hard as I scan her legs, which look fucking long wearing those fuck-me-heels.

"Fuck!" I rasp out.

She looks uncomfortable as shit as she tries to pull it down, bringing a grin to my face. She's fucking hot.

"If I didn't think every Carter would incinerate me, I'd totally tap that."

A noise rises from the back of my throat as I glare at my brother. "Shut the fuck up!"

He looks at me, smirking. "Aw, Jax, why so mad?"

It's not something I talk about, but my brothers goad me at every chance. The first day I met Lily, I went home and told my mum. I filled her in on everything Lily, telling her I found the girl I was going to marry when I grew up. My brothers have never let me live it down. They didn't know it was Lily at first, but it wouldn't have taken a rocket scientist to figure it out. I watched her all the time at school. It was hard not to. As we grew older, my obsession for her became worse, and one night I got drunk, took a girl home, and called her

Lily. She made sure the whole house heard.

"Fuck you," I snap out, my attention going back to Lily. She's saying something to Charlotte, who I notice is also dressed to the nines. She looks uncomfortable with the blatant stares they are getting but, in the end, sags her shoulders and nods at whatever Lily is whispering to her. I watch them walk off into the crowd, towards the hallway where I know the toilets are located. My gaze zeros in on Lily's tight, round arse and stays there until she's out of sight.

Fuck, I need to get laid.

I swallow down my drink, ignoring Wyatt's booming laughter. "Brother, you are so fucked."

I glare at him as I slam my glass down on the table, earning a few curious stares. "Shut up!"

He laughs louder. "They'd literally feed your balls to *our* pigs."

"I'll feed your fucking balls to the pigs if you don't shut it," I snap, before storming across the room to the bar.

He follows, still laughing his head off.

Fuck if he isn't right though. It wouldn't be a Paisley situation. Yeah, we were all pissed when we found out about her sleeping with Landon. Furious even. But with Lily, it wouldn't be about brothers protecting their sister. It would be about an entire family protecting precious cargo.

And who could blame them.

People don't talk about it, but Lily Carter has demons. Something terrible happened to her, and instead of infecting her, making her jaded and filled with hatred for the world, it made her something else. She's rare, and there aren't many souls like hers in the world anymore. She might be withdrawn, but she's loving and filled with so much kindness it can make me feel sick sometimes. But I'm drawn to it. There's something about her that would make anyone jump in front of bus to save her.

I'm a selfish bastard to want all of that to myself.

However, something tells me if I were to pursue her, the Carter's would rain hell down on me.

I just don't think I give a fuck anymore.

I've wanted Lily Carter since I was twelve years old. That feeling has only intensified as I've watched her grow into a sexy as hell woman.

My brother's hand on my shoulder stops me before I reach the bar. He takes one look at my face, and his lips twist.

"Fuck!"

"What?" I snap, pushing his hand off me.

"Look, I get it; she's hot. But she's not worth the shit it would cause. Don't ask me how I know it, but something tells me if you touch that girl, we will never see you again."

I scoff. "I'm not going to touch her," I lie.

I will. Just when the time is right. Fucking faceless girls and wishing they were her is becoming tiresome. She's the beginning and end.

"She comes with too much baggage," Wyatt tries, reading my lie. "Do you really want to deal with that?"

My hands clench into fists at my side. "Do you like your two front teeth?"

His lips tighten as I draw my gaze away. I'm scanning the crowd near the hallway she disappeared through, hoping to catch another glance. She's untouchable, always has been. There's not one Carter who will let you near her, even if you don't pose a threat. And I'd never fucking hurt her.

The crowd begins to clear around the hallway, and there she is.

Fuck me!

Lily looks more comfortable when she steps out with Charlotte not far behind her. She looks stunning, dressed in a long-sleeved, mint green dress that flares at the bottom. The dress is longer than the other, nearly touching her knees. However, she's never looked more sexier than she does now. She has her own style, and although it can be old-fashioned at times, she owns it.

Her sandy-blonde hair is pulled back in two braids and twisted in some fancy do at the nape of her neck.

Wyatt clicks his fingers in front of my face.

"What the fuck is your problem?"

"You have drool on your chin. Fuck a different girl and get over it."

"There's nothing to get over," I lie, wishing he would just drop it. The more he talks about her, the harder it's becoming not to go find her and turn the charm on. This happens when I know she's close. It's easier to control myself when she's not around. An out of sight, out of mind kind of thing.

His eyes close briefly after taking a good look at my expression. When he opens them, they're hard and cold. "If you cause a fight tonight, not only will Paisley and Mum kill you, but so will I. I've got a fucking date tomorrow with some class A chick. Turning up with a black eye won't turn her on like it does the others. And if you fuck it up for me, I'll fucking drown you in the creek."

I roll my eyes. "I need a fucking drink."

"Fucking hell!" he groans, but I tune him out as I step up to the bar.

I guess tonight I'm gonna have to control myself further. From the corner of my eye, I can see her hips swaying towards her parents.

Fuck, I need another drink.

CHAPTER ONE

LILY

Laughter fills my classroom as I finish the puppet show I put on for today's craft lesson. It's a lesson where we can just relax and have some fun. My other students loved it, and now my new students do too.

Mr Hartman, our school principle, made a lot of changes this term, which is how I ended up teaching year three instead of year five. I had been teaching year five for three years, and I didn't think I'd adjust to the change. But I've come to be grateful for it. I've fallen in love with them and it's been fun teaching a new age range.

"Miss Carter, can we sing some songs now?"

Sammy's face lights up with glee when I turn my smile to him. He's one of my special needs children and I just adore him.

"Of course. Do you have any recommendations?" I ask softly.

He nods eagerly. "Yes. 'Rewrite the Stars' from *The Greatest Showman*," he yells excitedly.

Warmth fills my soul at the sound, and I nod. Everyone else cheers, although a few boys groan, too cool to sing along to songs. It makes me giggle.

"One song, then it's home time."

We learned 'Rewrite the Stars' for Children in Need. We sang it in the school hall in front of all the parents on Monday.

I walk over to the laptop attached to the screen on the wall, click on the link I saved to the front screen and let the music play. The children don't take long to join in.

All except one.

Star Merin.

Star Merin started St. Martin's in September and has been on my mind ever since. The first time I met her, she hadn't even worn school uniform—which is required here at St. Martin's. Instead, she wore clothes that were far too small and had clearly not seen a washing machine.

Ever since that day, every time I look at her, my heart breaks a little more inside. Something inside of me is twisting my stomach in knots and making me dizzy with worry. It's safe to say I have a soft spot for the little girl.

She's tiny for seven years old and way behind when it comes to her education. But it's not that which has me worrying. It's her behaviour. She doesn't interact with other kids—although she did try when she first arrived. But kids can be cruel, and even though I have lovely children in my class, some in the others can be mean. I've seen and heard kids calling her names and have taken them to the school principle myself.

But it's not just that. It's the way she flinches when someone gets too close or yells too loudly. I've spoken to not only Karen, the support worker here at the school, but Mr Hartman too. Neither have been able to do much without damning evidence. I asked if they could speak to her parents, get a feel for them, but nothing ever came out of it. I've planned to stop one of her parents after school or before, but the only person I've ever seen pick her up or drop her off is her older brother, who must have to get to school himself.

Once the song is finished, I smile broadly at my class and applaud them.

"Well done. You guys sounded beautiful," I tell them. I watch as a few students sit straighter in their chairs, grinning from ear to ear. "Why don't you get your coats and bags ready for the bell."

Hearing them all shuffle out of their seats, I turn my gaze back to Star, who hasn't moved from her seat. She pushes her thumb through the hole in her cardigan, looking around the room nervously.

"Hey, Star," I greet softly, bending down in front of her table. "You not going to get your coat?"

She removes her chewed up sleeve from her mouth to answer. "I lost it."

"Have you not got another one you can wear?" I ask softly, worried for her health. It's freezing outside and soon the ground will freeze. After all, December is only a few weeks away.

She shakes her head. "No. But Miah said he will get me one."

No mention of her parents, I note. The girl is really breaking my heart. She looks so sad, so devastatingly sad.

"He sounds like a real good brother," I tell her.

She smiles at me, and I melt at the missing tooth. "He is. The best."

"You finally lost your tooth? Did the Tooth Fairy come?" Last week she was unsettled as it was really loose and hurting.

Her smile falls into a frown as she bends forward. "Daddy said she isn't real. I didn't get anything under my pillow, and I looked. A whole lot."

I take her cold hand in mine, feeling the tension in her arm. "Well, I think she must have got the wrong address," I whisper so the other kids don't overhear.

Her eyes spark with hope as she leans in closer. "She did?"

"She did, because this morning I found a bag of new school clothes that have your name inside. Would you like them?"

I've already checked with Karen if this is okay. She said she called Star's parents, told them we had some school wear donated, and asked if they'd be interested in having them for Star. It was the nicest way we could broach the subject. It's clear Star's parents have fallen on hard times. Her uniform barely fits her and has stains and tears. Karen didn't tell me much, but she did say she got a grunt from the dad and was taking that as a yes, they would accept the uniform. She also didn't inform them they were bought by me.

"Would I!" she squeaks, nodding enthusiastically. She claps her hands in excitement, then winces. My forehead creases into a frown when she rubs her shoulder.

"Are you okay?"

She sucks her bottom lip into her mouth, looking nervously outside. "I'm okay," she whispers, and it's a blatant lie.

Michelle, my T.A, begins to call out the names of the children whose parents are outside waiting to pick them up. I know Star's brother will be late, so I press further.

"You don't seem okay. Would you like to show me where it hurts?"

Her hazel-green eyes flash to mine, and I suck in a breath. There is no denying the fear lurking in them. My breath becomes hard to catch.

"Star, we have to go," Miah snaps, walking into the room. I stand up straight, feeling my heart begin to race. I hadn't even heard anyone come through the door.

Michelle is glaring at his back. He clearly pushed through as we don't allow family members back here unless invited.

"Miah, you're early," she squeals, jumping from her chair.

His expression softens as he looks down at his sister. "I finished early. I fou—bought you this," he explains, holding up a red coat with a white ring of fluff on the hood. It doesn't look brand new, but it's in better condition than her last one.

Tears gather in her eyes, and as I watch her, it brings back painful memories, ones of a lady bringing me a coat when I didn't have one—had never owned one. Memories I wish I could forget because I don't like reminders of the time I didn't have those things. My eyes begin to burn as she hugs his legs.

She takes the coat before turning to me, and I suck in a breath at the bright smile she gives me. This one is genuine, filled with so much happiness my chest begins to ache.

"Look what Miah got me. Isn't it boo-tee-ful?"

I bend down once more, taking the coat from her hands. "It's a beautiful coat for a beautiful princess," I tell her hoarsely. I help her pull her arms through and zip up the front of her coat. Smiling, I take her hand and say, "Twirl."

She giggles, twirling. I stand and watch her entire face beaming with pride. Such a small thing to some people, but huge to someone like Star.

My gaze goes back to Miah, who is watching his sister with a soft expression. It hardens when he sees me watching him.

I notice bruising around his neck, and once again, my breath hitches and that sick feeling in the pit of my stomach comes back.

I need to help them.

I need to help them like Dad helped me.

"What?" he snaps roughly, glaring at me.

Taken aback, I rest my hand on my chest. "Can we talk for a moment?"

A look of panic flashes across his face before he masks it. "No, I've got to get Star home for her dinner."

"You don't want to talk to Miss Carter?" Star asks.

He takes her hand. "We have to go. Dad is waiting," he tells her, but there's a warning in his tone that I don't like.

"Please," I plead. "I can help you."

"Look, lady, I don't know what it is you want to talk about, but you can't help me. Look at you. You look like you belong in a Disney movie," he scoffs. "Now, I've got to go."

He pulls Star behind him as he rushes out the door. Once they're gone, Michelle turns to me, her face pinched with worry.

"I'm sorry, but someone needs to report those kids. I know it's wrong to gossip, but look at the state of them. They need new clothes—*clean* clothes—and to be given a bath. And is it me or is that boy looking skinnier by the day?"

Michelle means well, I know that, but it still hurts to hear her describe them like that. I bite my bottom lip, worried for the siblings.

"I've tried talking to Principle Hartman. He said he will speak to the parents."

She shakes her head. "There has to be something else we can do. They aren't being looked after."

I have a million things I should be doing, but all I can think of is Star and Miah. "I'm going to try one more time. She was hurt, Michelle."

"I saw she was favouring her other arm. I didn't want to say anything in case I was wrong."

"That's okay. But you can feel free to tell me anything, even if it might be wrong."

"Thank you."

I nod, mad I didn't see she was favouring her other arm. "If you like, you can go. I'll clean up after I've finished talking to Principle Hartman."

She waves me off, already heading over to the puppet box we made. "I've got this; you go sort those children out."

Grabbing my bag and coat, I head out of the classroom and make my way through the maze of hallways to the principal's office.

I knock twice when I reach it. "Come in!"

Stepping inside, I find Mr Hartman sitting behind his desk. "Hello," I greet softly, fiddling with the edge of my coat. Mr Hartman always makes me nervous. He's a pudgy man, bald and loud-spoken. At sixty-two years old and having been a principle for twenty-nine of those years, I think Mr Hartman dislikes his job. And me sometimes.

"What do you want now, Ms Carter," he sighs, blowing out a breath. The way he says my name sends a shiver up my spine. He never addresses any of the teachers by their name, always by our surnames. I should have gone to Karen, but she doesn't work Fridays.

"I've come about Star Merin, Mr Hartman," I explain.

He looks up from the pile of paper sitting in front of him, puffing out a large breath, looking annoyed. "Again? I've been through this with you, Ms Carter. Star Merin is fine. You shouldn't judge people by their appearance."

My heart sinks. "That's not what I'm doing."

His thick, grey, bushy eyebrow raises questioningly. "You're not? Then tell me what it is you're doing, because it seems to me you're being uptight over a low-income family. You see a girl in the only clothes her parents can afford and assume she's not looked after."

My eyes begin to burn once more as I clasp my hands in front of me. I'm not doing that, am I? "But that's—"

"That's exactly what you're doing. Now, good evening, Ms Carter. I have work to do before I go home to my wife. Who, may I add, will be waiting to serve me dinner."

I nod, my throat tightening. "Okay," I let out on a mere whisper, standing in the doorway, watching him go back to his work.

This isn't in my head. It isn't. Something is going terribly wrong for Star Merin and her brother, Miah, at home.

"Why are you still here?" Mr Hartman booms.

I jump, a squeak escaping my lips. I don't waste time getting out of there, rushing past the receptionist and a few other teachers.

"Lily?" I hear shouted, but I ignore them, rushing out as tears begin to flow. They can't see me crying. They'll know I'm weak.

My car is parked out on the road instead of the school carpark. My old parking spot is now used as a space for the bins, and Mr Hartman wants to keep them there so the bin men don't have to go down the small road at the back of the school where they used to be. It's just another thing he wouldn't talk to me about. I don't like walking out onto the street where there aren't any streetlights. When I work late this time of year, it's dark. And with only a few townhouses on the street, it's pretty vacant. It's scary.

I wipe my nose before reaching into my bag to pull out my keys. My hands shake, and I drop them. Frustrated, I take a deep breath and pick them up. Once I'm in the car and have turned the ignition, I sit and wait for the heaters to warm up. My mind soon wanders back to Star and what I can do to help her—both her and her brother. There must be something.

"Uncle Myles," I whisper into the empty car, more determined to get someone to listen to me and actually hear my words.

Uncle Myles is a social worker. If anyone can help, it's him.

PULLING UP OUTSIDE my uncle Myles and aunt Kayla's house, I notice my dad is here. My entire system calms somewhat.

A knock on my car window makes me jump, a small startled scream escaping my lips.

I shut off my car as Hayden, my cousin, opens my door, her long wavy brown hair curtaining her face.

"Hey, what are you doing here?" she asks, then takes one look at my face. Hers hardens. "What the fuck? Who the fuck upset you and who do I have to kill?"

"No one. Is Uncle Myles inside?"

"Who upset you?" she demands, stepping back so I can get out of the car.

I slam the door behind me and lock the car. She steps up beside me as we walk up the steps to Myles' house.

"I'm fine," I tell her, avoiding her gaze.

"Just so you know, I don't believe a word of it. Charlotte's inside; maybe you will talk to her."

Charlotte is my other cousin, daughter of Myles and Kayla. I'm surprised she's here though. It's Friday and she normally works until six. She owns the library she renovated not long ago. She's made it thrive and even does kids' parties. Her home is not far behind the huge building, just at the back of my house.

"I just need to talk to Myles," I assure her.

Instead of knocking when we reach the door, we walk straight inside. Benefits of being such a close family.

"Hayden, Lily," my aunt Kayla greets. Her dark red hair falls heavily down her back. She's beautiful, always has been, but her soul is another matter. She's pure goodness. Just like her daughter.

"Hello, guys." Charlotte waves. Her hair is a darker shade of red than her mum's but is just as vibrant. Both have smooth, creamy skin with ruby red lips. The only difference between the two is Charlotte has deep dimples when she smiles.

"Is everything okay?" Charlotte asks warily, looking to Hayden beside me.

"I need to speak with Uncle Myles," I tell Aunt Kayla.

"He's with your father in the living room," she says, her gaze going over my shoulder to Hayden. I ignore the look she gives her and head into the living room.

Dad's face lights up when I step inside, and he gives me a huge smile. I reciprocate, only mine doesn't reach my eyes like his does.

"Is everything okay?" he asks, placing his cup of tea down before getting up from the sofa. At twenty-four, I still need him, and I'm not embarrassed to admit that. He saved my life when I was four years old. Many kids wouldn't remember that stage in their life, but I remember every second of it.

Dad might not be my biological father, but he's the only father I've ever known. He's the only man I've ever loved. You see, we had a shitty mum. After she had my dad and his four brothers, she left them with their sick father and never looked back. Fast forward twenty years and she had me. I was abused from the day I was born. I was neglected, beaten, and traumatised by the men she brought through whatever home we lived in at the time.

Then one day, something happened. Men and women came charging into the home I was in and took me to the hospital. That day, I met my eldest brother, but he became my dad the second he took me home. A dad I loved more than anything and who has protected me since the day my life began in that hospital room. Every demon I've had, he's slayed. He's beaten away so much darkness and fear that he's my go-to person whenever I feel scared or lonely. He might not be able to protect me from my nightmares and the past I had before him, but he will try.

We never talk about my adoption; there's no need to. For me, for him, and even my uncles, I am my father's daughter. I'm loved and cared for by all of them.

He's the strongest and noblest man I know.

"Princess?" he calls.

I shake my head and turn to Myles. "I need help. There's a little girl in my class. She wears dirty clothes that are far too small and is very rarely clean. I've never seen her parents either, but I don't need to. I know something is wrong at home. I'm not judging her by her appearance. I promise. I just know, and no one is listening to me. No one will hear me when I say something isn't right. And it's not right, Uncle Myles. It's not. I'm not seeing things because of my past. I'm not," I rush out, feeling my chest begin to tighten. I try to calm my breathing, practicing the techniques my psychologist taught me when I was younger.

"Lily," my uncle Myles begins, but I place my hand up to stop him. My eyes close when I feel my dad come up behind me, pulling me into his chest.

"I'm not seeing things. You need to listen to me. Even today, she was hurt. I know it. She was going to tell me what happened, but her brother came in to get her and stopped it. You need to believe me."

"Lily, I don't—" he starts again, but panic rises inside of me.

"No, you have to listen," I yell.

"Lily," Dad soothes.

I look to Dad, knowing he will believe me. "Someone is hurting her, Dad. I can *feel* it inside," I plead. "Her brother, Miah, had bruises too. Please, the school principal won't do anything. He said I'm being judgmental because of her appearance. But I'm not. I wouldn't do that. Ever."

"Calm down. We believe you. But we need you to start at the beginning," he tells me, steering me over to the sofa.

Numbly, I take a seat next to him and gaze up at him. "You believe me?" I whisper, relief seeping through me.

"Of course," he tells me softly.

"I'll go make us all a cup of tea," Aunt Kayla announces, sharing a look with my uncle.

Uncle Myles has been a social worker since I can remember, and he's good at his job. It's why I've come to him. I know if anyone can help with this, it's him.

"I'll come," Charlotte says politely, tears gathered in her eyes.

When they give Hayden a pointed look, Hayden ignores them. She shrugs. "I'm not going anywhere. I want to hear the rest of what this prick of a principal said about Lily."

I chuckle under my breath. Sometimes I wish I could be more like Hayden. She's fierce and doesn't let anyone mess with her. I've seen her cry only twice in her whole life, and one of those times was when she thought she lost her brother Landon in an attack that left him fighting for his life.

It feels like I've cried the majority of my life.

I turn back to Dad, feeling hope for the first time. The longer we leave those children in the care of abusive parents, the worse it will be for them.

"You really believe me?"

"Even if you didn't have the past you do, I would still believe you. You'd never tear a family apart if you weren't so sure, princess."

I close my eyes briefly before something occurs to me. "Wait, do you think I'm seeing things because of my past? Do you think Mr Hartman is right and I'm seeing things that aren't there?"

He takes my hand. "Fuck no! We didn't have the best start in life, Lily. It's not a nice truth, but it's *the* truth. Because of that, we see things differently to others. We see behind the fake smiles and lies. If anyone can see if someone is being abused, it's you."

"Mr Hartman doesn't think so," I tell him, breathing evenly now.

Dad's jaw hardens. "Mr Hartman needs to be paid a visit."

"Dad," I whine, rolling my eyes, knowing he's being silly. He wouldn't really do that. I think.

"Well, he does. Have you reported anyone else in your class for suspected abuse?"

I shake my head. "I haven't, no."

"Because none of them are being abused. My girl has light in her eyes, but when we first met you, there was only shadow. You can see the same shadow in other people's gazes, sweet girl."

"Why don't you start with the girl in your class," Myles says.

Aunt Kayla times her entrance perfectly, walking in and handing everyone a cup of tea. I take mine, the heat warming me.

After taking a sip, I dive in, explaining everything from the very first moment of meeting Star; her brother always dropping her off and collecting her, the clothes I bought her, and today.

By the time I'm finished, I feel like a weight has been lifted.

CHAPTER TWO

LILY

Hᴀʏᴅᴇɴ ᴀɴᴅ Cʜᴀʀʟᴏᴛᴛᴇ ʙᴏᴛʜ catch a ride back with me after leaving my aunt and uncle's house.

The worry for those two children is still there, but I know Uncle Myles will help them. And he won't mess around and spend months doing it. He's the best at his job, even won an award for helping so many kids.

"I'm not drinking fucking wine. It tastes like piss and vinegar," Hayden snaps at Charlotte from the front seat.

Charlotte huffs in the back. "It's all I have, Hayden."

Hayden turns around in her seat. "What do you get for Landon? I'll drink that."

"Landon doesn't have time for me anymore," she tells her, and I can hear the sadness in her voice.

Landon, Hayden's brother and our cousin, recently moved in with his girlfriend, Paisley. Before Paisley, Landon was always with Charlotte; they were inseparable and best friends. It's been an adjustment for her not having him around. She wants him to be happy, so she'll never tell him it hurts her that he doesn't hang out as much.

Sensing how upset the subject will make her, Hayden keeps quiet, so I decide to speak up, my voice low. "I have some beer in my garage. It's Maddox's so he won't mind if you take some."

"Thank you," Hayden tells me. "See, sorted. We're gonna have fun, ain't we, Charlotte?"

Hayden might be hard on the outside, but she has a heart of gold.

"We are," Charlotte answers, sounding happier now.

I pull up outside my garage. I never actually use it to keep my car inside. I've been driving three years, and even though I'm a safe driver, I'd still scrape the sides of my car trying to get in and out. It's safer to just park outside on my drive.

We jump out, my gaze immediately going to the house to the right of mine. I smile and wave at my new neighbour, Barry, who is out sitting on his deck chair.

Barry moved in a few weeks ago and we became fast friends over the Harry Potter movies. He's an older gentleman, with a rounded belly and thinning grey hair. He kind of reminds me of a giant teddy bear, just like my granddad who passed away last year.

I've also told him to stop sitting outside in this weather before he catches a cold.

"Hello, Mr Barry," I call, waving.

"Come 'ere, girl. Look what I got today," he calls, the chair underneath him creaking.

Me, Hayden and Charlotte walk over. "What did you get, Barry?"

He opens his front door and grabs a shopping bag from inside. I smile at his enthusiasm as he pulls out a rectangular box.

"Only ordered me a Harry Potter Cluedo board game," he says giddily. "My granddaughter taught me how to use The Amazon."

"I think you mean, Amazon," I tell him softly, smiling.

"Want to play?"

"Already know who did it. It was Mr Mustard in the library with a candle stick," Hayden says, making us all laugh.

Just then, the door down from Barry's opens and out walks Blanche, a lady in her sixties.

Blanche isn't as social as Barry and has lived on this block for years on her own, without making friends with anyone other than me.

The street was falling apart until my dad came in and renovated and sold off most of the houses. Now, with the library on the corner, new houses built up along the street, it's liveable. I love it here.

"Good evening, Blanche," I greet softly. It took time, but I won the old lady over. She can be quite grumpy, but I never let it get to me. Inside, I know she's a loving, kind person.

"Hello, Blanche," Hayden calls, far too loudly before muttering, "Witch," under her breath.

"Hayden," I whisper, staring in shock.

"Whore," Blanche snaps, shoving her glasses up her nose. "What have I told you, it's Mrs North to you."

"Maybe if you got some you wouldn't be such a grumpy old witch," Hayden snaps back.

"Maybe if you kept your legs closed, STDs would stop spreading," Blanche sasses back.

"Oh dear," I whisper when Barry looks to me, enjoying the fun. Sadly, this happens every single time these two see each other. I'd think Blanche secretly liked Hayden if it weren't for the doll cushion I found her sticking pins into while hissing Hayden's name. I didn't tell Hayden, afraid she would retaliate.

"They might not have had them in your day, Blanche, but we have condoms to prevent that. It's called safe sex."

Blanche gasps. "Does your mother and father know you speak to your elders like this?"

Hayden snorts. "Please, my dad would be egging me on. And you're ancient, not an elder. I don't think the museum has artefacts as old as you."

Blanche looks to me. "I'll be talking to your father about her. She needs controlling. Maybe he can talk sense into her parents."

"I'm s—"

"Don't you dare say you're sorry," Hayden insists before glaring at Blanche. "My parents can't control me either. Now run along and stir your cauldron."

"Well, I never," Blanche gasps, eyes wide.

"I'm sure there's nothing you've never done at your age," Hayden comments, grinning.

"Slut!" Blanche hisses, storming back inside her house.

I turn to Hayden, hands on my hips. "Do you really need to antagonise her every time you see her?"

Hayden just keeps grinning. "Please, she saw us pull up and wanted the spar. I think the little old lady gets a kick out of it. Plus, I've still not forgiven her for calling the police on me."

"She thought you were breaking into my home," I remind her softly.

"I wasn't. I was looking through your window because you weren't answering. I didn't need to be jumped by two policemen and tackled to the floor."

"You ran away," Charlotte adds. "After kneeing one in his genitals."

Hayden glares her way. "They scared the shit out of me. It was dark. And if this one," she says, shoving her thumb in my direction, "was home when she said she'd be home, none of it would have happened. And let's not forget you had asked Miss Nosey Pants to look out for me because you went to the shop."

I bite my bottom my lip, because she has me there. I did tell Blanche, who was watering her flowers at the time, to watch out for Hayden's arrival.

I jump when Barry begins to hoot. "Girls, I thought life would be boring without my Callie, but you girls bring youth back to my soul."

"Want to do shots?" Hayden grins.

He laughs, hooting loudly once again. "Why not. We can play Cluedo. Never played me some Harry Cluedo. My Callie loved Harry Potter."

Callie was his late wife who died some time ago. I see the loneliness in him every single time I see him. It's why I like to come sit with him for a little while. I don't see him get visitors. It's no hardship either as he's a great person to be around.

"As much as I'd love to join you, I promised this one we'd watch a movie," Hayden explains gently, tipping her head to Charlotte.

His attention turns to me. "What about you, missy? You got plans?"

After the day I've had, Cluedo is just what I need. I think Barry wants the company too. Since he's moved in, I've not seen any family members visit him. Although, he has spoken about grandkids a lot.

"I'd love to," I tell him softly. "Let me just run home and get into something comfy."

"All right, darlin'. I'll put the kettle on. Do you want to play out here or inside?"

The wind picks up, answering for me. "Inside. I've told you, you will catch a cold sitting out here."

"Blood is hot as hell, girl. Ain't no way I'm getting a cold," he warns me.

"We'll speak to you later," Charlotte tells me, and I know they're going to use my garden to get to her home. Our gardens join, yet the entrance to her home is around the side of the library.

"See you both later. Have fun," I tell them, then quickly turn to Barry. "Be five minutes. Want me to bring snacks?"

He grins big, a tooth missing, which makes him look more adorable. "Girl, you don't need to ask me twice. Get your booty back over here."

I giggle and run across the front garden to mine. I let myself in, quickly heading to the kitchen to feed the cats.

Willa, my one-eyed cat, hears me, meowing at my feet the minute I hit the hallway. Peggy, my other cat who has three legs, toddles in after her and both weave in and out of my legs, meowing.

"It's okay, Mummy's home to feed you," I giggle, placing the bowl of wet food down. They dive right in, sounding like they've not been fed in years.

After checking they have enough water in their bowl, I head upstairs to my room. I live in a three-bedroom cottage that was renovated before I moved in. It was originally a two-bed, but thanks to my dad the entire loft was converted into a bedroom and en-suite. It's the only room upstairs with a large walk-in wardrobe.

Picking up my fluffiest pyjamas, I put them on, along with my Tinker Bell dressing gown I bought on a whim when Hope and Ciara, my other two cousins from Uncle Mason and Aunt Denny, took me shopping. It's another thing I hate doing. It's always crowded, and people push and shove like there's a zombie apocalypse going on outside.

After pulling on a pair of thick socks, I struggle with what to put on my feet. It seems silly to put on a pair of boots when I'm so comfy. Instead, I dig out the new slipper boots my mum bought me last year. They have a big unicorn horn at the front, which I adore.

Once I'm ready, I race back down to the kitchen, petting Willa and Peggy once more before grabbing some snacks.

When I step outside, I can smell rain coming. Barry is at the door before I can knock, beaming with excitement. He limps to the kitchen table, his walking stick in hand. He had a fall not so long ago and needed something done to his hip. He never really went into detail, and I guessed he had his reasons. Personally, I think it's a pride thing as he went on about nothing putting him down right after.

"Milk and sugar?" he asks, stepping over to the kettle.

"Just milk, please," I say, looking around once again at his cosy, quaint home. His small one-bed bungalow is perfect for him. It has a kitchen area that fits a kitchen table and then opens into the living room. At the back is a bedroom and another door that leads to the bathroom.

I like how all the houses on the street aren't the same. I know Mrs North has a two-bed home, but hers also has a cellar. I'm glad I didn't get one of those. Cellars freak me out.

Then there's Mr and Mrs Spencer. They have lived here five years, and even though I've never been in their home, I know by talking to them it has a conservatory, a games room in the cellar, and a living room, dining room, and three bedrooms.

"Sweet," Barry mutters.

"Pardon?" I ask, my voice soft as I shake out of my memories.

"You. You're sweet enough. You don't need sugar, darlin'. Be good for one of my grandsons if they ever get their heads out their arses. Told their mamma not to let them go galivanting around town, picking up random women. Would she listen? No. A couple of 'em are trouble. Not good enough for someone as special as you," he says as he bangs around the kitchen.

If only he knew. There's nothing special about me. I have demons and secrets just like anyone else.

"I've not seen your grandsons here," I comment, hoping I'm not being rude.

He looks over his shoulder as he continues to stir the tea. "Couple of 'em are scared to come here. I'm still pissed at them for raiding my liquor cabinet years ago. The others come by; mind you, you're at work then so you wouldn't have seen them."

"I'm glad you have them though," I tell him. "They seem like they missed you."

And they did. He spoke about them all the time.

He shrugs. "When my Callie died, I was left in that big farmhouse alone. I guess they felt sorry for me. Didn't want to burden them though."

"I don't think they'd think that, Barry," I assure him, taking the tea he offers me.

He takes a seat opposite me. When he takes out a bottle of whiskey, my entire frame freezes. He pours a hefty amount in his tea before catching my eyes. "Put hairs on my chest that will. Warm me right up."

"T-that's okay," I tell him, feeling my legs begin to bounce and sweat drip down my back.

Please, not here. Not now.

It goes unnoticed as he opens the boardgame. I'm too afraid to tell him I don't like alcohol. It's not even the alcohol. I can have it in my fridge, but I don't like being around people when they're drinking it. Or more likely, when men are drinking it.

I might feel safe with Barry, but there's no telling how he will turn when he's had a few drinks. I know all too well that people can change once they've had a sip. My mum's stream of boyfriends was proof of that. I remember the beer cans, bottles of whiskey just like the one Barry has, and then the smell of it as they yelled at me, hurt me.

I scrunch my eyes closed tightly, willing the memories of Mum's past boyfriends drinking to disappear. The pain, the humiliation, the fear of what came after. Sweat beads down my back and my hands are clammy.

The front room door bangs open, making me squeal and jump. My eyes fly open, but they don't move from Barry, who is sitting in front of me, still unaware of the turmoil going on in my head.

"What the fuck?"

I know that voice.

I'd know that voice anywhere. A shiver runs down my back, and slowly I turn my wide gaze to Jaxon Hayes, standing in the doorway with his brother Reid.

Jaxon and I went to school with each other. All the girls talked about him, about stuff they really shouldn't talk about.

What always drew me to Jaxon was his protectiveness. My family are protective of each other. Jaxon, however, I noticed just downright hated bullies. And I was a magnet at school for them.

One day, a girl and all her friends cornered me in the bathroom. I'm not good with surprises or being touched, so when one of them grabbed me from behind, I had one of my episodes. I was trapped in a sea of horrific memories, some new, some I already knew, and it was like I was being tortured all over again.

Jaxon, somehow, must have heard me. He carried me out of those bathrooms and protected me. He didn't let me go until I was safely in the arms of my father.

I've never even thanked him, too scared in case he thought I was a freak. He's never looked at me like I am, or even made me feel like I was.

I snap back to reality when they step further into the room.

What is Jaxon doing at Barry's house?

"Lily?" he calls, seeming just as shocked to see me as I am him. He looks to Barry, then to the table, and then back to my face. His jaw tightens as he walks over and takes the bottle of whiskey in one swoop.

"Granddad, Lily doesn't like being around alcohol," Jaxon tells him, his voice sharp. He grabs the bottle, shoving it inside the first cupboard he opens.

The Hayes are his grandkids? What?

Now I kind of want to know which one of his grandkids stole his booze. If I were to guess, it would be Reid. I feel guilty the second his name enters my mind. There could be a simple misunderstanding.

"What? How do you know sweet Lily?" Barry asks, his gaze going from me, to Jaxon, then back again.

"This will be good," Reid says, a smirk on his face. He takes a seat next to me, his lip curling at the table. "Harry Potter Cluedo? This was your fun night, Granddad?"

I still can't believe Barry is their granddad.

How bizarre is that?

"Fun to me, boy. No lip or you'll get a clip around the ear. Now, tell me, what is this about my booze and how do you know Lily?"

"Don't sound so shocked, Granddad." Jaxon smirks, his eyes on me. The intensity has me looking down at the table. "I went to school with Lily. And as for the alcohol, I don't know. I just know she takes great measures not to be around it. Her family are the same when it comes to her."

My lips part in shock and I watch him. I hide my fear of alcohol, really well. He must have been watching closely to pick up on it. Really closely, because my family would never disclose that kind of information.

This time he's the one to look away, like he just let out a big secret. I find myself fidgeting nervously.

"I didn't have the best upbringing for the first four years of my life," I whisper, feeling ashamed. It's hard to admit, but he also has the right to know if he's okay with Jaxon putting away his whiskey.

Barry's eyes harden. "Who the fuck would hurt you? You look like a fucking fairy princess," he booms.

I smile shyly at him. "Um, thank you?"

"Your fucking family hurt you?" Jaxon grits out, his voice deadly.

Nervously, my eyes flicker back to him, finding it hard under his scrutiny. "Of course not," I rush out, not wanting him to think badly of my family. They mean everything to me. I look warily to Reid, hating they're all here. I feel like I'm being pressured, even though they aren't demanding anything.

"It's okay, Lily," Jaxon says softly, clearly sensing my panic.

"No, it fucking isn't. I want to know who hurt this girl," Barry booms.

"You didn't say you were having a party, Barry," Hayden calls out as she walks through the open door. She takes in the room, then her eyes come back to me. "I forgot to get Maddox' stash out your garage."

"You've been here five minutes and you make friends with the Carter's," Reid booms, slapping his thigh whilst laughing.

"Shut the fuck up, Reid," Hayden snaps, sitting down next to me. "What's going on?"

"I'll shut the door," Charlotte sings.

"You really need to kill that cat," Reid tells her. She gasps, her eyes watering. Everyone who is anyone knows about Charlotte's misfortune when it comes to pets. At the moment she has a cat called Kat-nip, and it attacks her every chance it gets. Which is why she's covered in cat scratches.

"Reid," Hayden snaps again, her eyes flicking from Jaxon to me. "What's wrong, Lily?"

Before I can answer, Barry does. "She was telling me which one of you hurt her as a baby," he snaps.

Hayden's face hardens at first, ready to bite his head off. I can see it before she even takes her first breath. I reach for her hand and squeeze, so her gaze comes to me. Her expression softens and she squeezes my hand back. "Were you telling them, Lily?"

I force out a nod. "Kind of. Not all of it. Jaxon put the alcohol away."

Realisation dawns. "Ah," she murmurs, then turns to Barry. "You don't have anything to worry about, Barry. Lily wasn't hurt by any of us. It was all before she came to live with us. It's not alcohol itself, it's people drinking around her. It doesn't matter that you remind her of a soft, cuddly teddy bear; she doesn't trust people drinking it."

My eyes widen at Hayden for going into that much detail.

"What the fuck? But she looks like all of you," Jaxon announces, confusion written all over his face.

No one outside our family knows about my past. They don't know about my adoption, or that my dad is biologically my brother. It would only confuse people and it's pointless information since Dad has and will always be my dad.

"That's 'cause she is one of us, dickhead. She doesn't like talking about it, so if you want the story, you will have to ask her, but that's all you're getting from me," she tells him, then turns back to Barry. "No one in our family has ever hurt Lily. We'd all die to protect her."

"Good. She's like a fairy," he booms again, softer this time, before taking a large gulp of his drink.

"I need a drink. That has boggled my mind completely," Reid says.

"A fairy," Charlotte whispers, staring at me intently. "You really do look like a fairy princess. Not like Tinker Bell—way prettier than her. Maybe Perri Winkle?"

I giggle at her expression. "I don't look like a fairy," I tell her.

Reid snorts, and my attention turns to him. "If this Perri whatshername is hotter than Tink, then yeah, she's right. You do look like a fairy."

"The pyjamas do fit," Charlotte laughs out. And want to curl into a ball of embarrassment when I remember my outfit. What must Jaxon and Reid have been thinking, seeing me in my nightwear in their granddad's house?

"This is weird," Hayden groans. "So, why are you two here? Robbing the joint?"

Barry laughs. "They're my grandkids. Are you single?" he asks her. "Jaxon, she could give you a run for your money."

My chest tightens a little and I don't know why. I rub it, glancing away, but not before I notice both Jaxon's and Hayden's eyes widen in horror.

"Fuck no!" Hayden snaps. "The Hayes brothers are in the no-go zone."

"Says a Carter," Reid snaps back.

"Like you have a chance with any of us," she sasses back at him.

"Like I'd let you," he growls.

Fluttering her lashes, Hayden leans around me to see Reid. "If I were to flash a little boob, show a little leg, run my finger down your chest and whisper sweet nothings in your ear, you'd be on the floor panting like a dog."

"Wait, a Carter? Isn't that the kid shacking up with my grandbaby?"

"That's Landon, my cousin and best friend. He's also Hayden's brother. They're triplets. You'll probably meet Liam at some point."

Barry's eyes widen a touch. "Sheeet, do you not have televisions? There's loads of you."

I giggle. "We are a big family."

"He a good kid?"

"The best." Charlotte beams at him, bouncing in her seat.

"The worst," Reid mutters, but I notice Jaxon has kept quiet. My gaze flicks to him, and I blush slightly when I find him watching me, his eyebrows drawn together like he's trying to figure out a puzzle.

"Fuck you, Reid," Hayden snaps. "Unless you want to pick your teeth up from the floor, be careful what you say about my brother."

"Fuck!" Reid groans. "I'm kidding! We have a mutual understanding with Landon and Paisley. We like our balls, and Paisley said she'd rip them off if we did anything. Even though you deserve payback after what you did to our van. And we promised Landon we wouldn't fuck with him when he was on Hayes turf. Which is all the fucking time."

Hayden scoffs. "It was scrap metal and you know it. If you weren't so dumb, you'd know he switched them out."

"I thought it looked cool," Charlotte adds.

I giggle because I remember the photos she sent me of the prank my brothers and cousins did to the Hayes Removals van. It was in retaliation to the Hayes brothers slashing Maddox's tyres, instead of Landon's.

"Are you sure I can't sway you into dating one of my boys? What about Wyatt?"

Hayden's lip curls. "No offence, Barry; you're cool and all, but your grandsons are jackasses and could in no way handle me."

Reid snorts. I don't know whether the sound is from agreeing or disagreeing with her.

Barry grins, taking another sip of his drink. I find myself not caring, my hands no longer shaking.

And although I want it to be because I know he's a good man, I know it's not because of that. It's because Jaxon is in the room. He's always had a way of making me feel safe. It's not his big presence or huge muscles, or his strong will. It's just him.

"Don't say another word." Barry grins. "Change your mind and want to play Cluedo?"

Hayden sighs, looking around the table. "Go on then. But just so you know, if Reid doesn't stop staring at my tits, it will be him murdered in the kitchen with a butcher knife, and I did it."

Barry bursts out laughing, slapping the table. I smile at his happiness, feeling it within my soul.

"Hayden, you aren't really going to stab him, are you?" Charlotte whispers, causing me to giggle.

And that is how our night went; playing Cluedo with two Hayes brothers, their granddad, and Hayden and Charlotte. By the end of it, we had so much fun Hayden threatened to rip Reid's balls off if he told anyone about it. He threatened the same back, but I don't think either of them meant it.

Spending the night distracted, having a lot of fun, made me forget all about Monday and what it could bring.

CHAPTER THREE

JAXON

Work on Sundays is normally slow, which is why we usually only work half the day. Now it's getting late into the evening and we still have a bunch of new promotional ideas to go through.

Lately, work has just been slow and it's all down to a new company, Big Move, that moved in at the beginning of the year. Slowly, the guy—Andrew Black—who owns it, has been poaching our customers, stealing new clients before we have chance to sign and basically just fucking things up for Hayes Removals.

Today was just another clusterfuck. The prick had the nerve to show up here and make us an offer. Didn't matter that we turned down the three other guys he sent, emails and phone calls. He still thought we would buckle under pressure.

He wanted everything, even our international removals and storage units. Our storage units are top of the range and we had wealthy people who rented them. Our storage units are the only thing keeping us afloat at the moment. If we didn't have that income, we would have had to dissolve the business by now, thanks to this moron. He's doing everything to make sure there's nothing left of our business to save.

"Bro, we've got to do something about this," Wyatt groans from his desk near the large window.

The old cattle barn was renovated five years ago. It was rotting and falling down in places. The large area where the barn was located was prime retail though. It was perfect for what I had in mind when I finished school. While I went to college for my business degree, I had the place rebuilt to be what it is now. Hayes Removals.

It has a large loading bay area where we've kept our offices instead of storage boxes. The storage boxes we keep in the back room where the offices were originally located. I never suspected business would boom the way it did, so when we hired more staff and more of my brothers finished school and started working here, we moved to the loading area. It's great in the summer, but during the winter, not so much. It gets cold as a brass monkey.

At the back is an extension where I sleep. I could have stayed at home, which is only walking distance away, but I found sleeping here became easier when I worked late. It also gave me peace from my brothers. So the extension was added and a bed, bedroom furniture and a small kitchen area was put in, making it liveable. Luckily, I have toilets in the building, just outside the room. I did have a shower installed, but one of my brothers broke it, so I head over to Mum's since I eat there every morning anyway.

Today, I was wishing I lived away from it all. From Mum's, from the business. I just need the fucking peace. Peace to think, to plan, to come up with something that isn't going to bankrupt us. I've already had to let three guys go this month. I don't want to let any more go. They were hard workers, good men.

"Jax," Wyatt snaps, getting impatient.

"I just need a minute," I growl.

"This is the third offer in person, bro. Him coming here? He's getting impatient. He's gonna step up his game," Eli, the third eldest, says. Getting up from his desk, he grabs his guitar. His chain rattles at the side of his leg, his baggy trousers hanging off his arse. "I've got a gig to get to. Call me if you need me."

I give him a chin lift, knowing Eli needs his pub gigs to relax.

"He's right," Wyatt tells me.

I lean back in my chair, taking note of the empty room. Everyone else has left for the night. We've been trying to go over strategies to get more clients. Then dickhead turned up and interrupted. The triplets, Luke, Reid and Isaac left when he did, more to make sure he did leave than to actually leave us to figure shit out.

"I know. I just have no fucking idea what to do. He's a corporation, big money. I don't understand what he wants with us. We might not be a small business, but we aren't big either. We do alright."

Wyatt pulls out a bottle of Jack and two glasses before walking over to my desk. He pulls Reid's chair close and takes a seat, kicking his feet up on my desk.

"That's what I don't get. There's more to it. Did you see the way his eyes hardened when you asked how he knew about your international clients?"

After taking a hefty swig, I answer, "Yeah. Another thing that doesn't feel right. Mr Yang is our highest profile client, who hires us for international removals. He's a fucking billionaire, and if he gets wind of this, we might lose him. We lose him, we're fucked. He throws too much business our way."

Wyatt looks doubtful. "I don't know. It still doesn't sit right. We have a lot of high paying clients. Look at that housewife chick. She stores her jewellery in our containers. I still think the bitch is robbing it," he says on a grin. He couldn't be more wrong. The woman was burgled a few years back and doesn't feel safe keeping it at home anymore. Before I can speak, he carries on. "He could just be after them to make his profile bigger. We don't use them the way he will, and they'll know that. We don't share who we take on as clients. For fuck sake, we have a rock legend storing his guitars here."

He's right. We do have a lot of high-profile clients. But the containers we rent and the confidentiality we are strict on, is what they come here for. They know we can't afford to ruin the business they put our way. They also know someone won't come looking here for their belongings.

We are actually due a security upgrade, which is something else to put on my to-do list.

This isn't about the containers though. I don't think it's particularly about our clients. I hope. I have an inclination it's something to do with our international routes. We move items overseas, making sure they are handled with care and arrive safety. This part of the business is mostly done through word of mouth. We don't advertise it as we're not the ones who personally deliver it. We just make the arrangements, pack and deliver the goods to the plane they are loaded on. We're paid a good amount to do it, too.

"Whatever it is, he isn't getting it. I'm not fucking selling."

Wyatt holds his glass up. "Cheers to that."

Shaking my head, I glance at the stack of papers on my desk. I should be going over tomorrows schedule, making sure it's all in order, but I need to get out of here.

"I'm going out," I blurt out suddenly, getting up.

Startled, Wyatt gets up. "I'll come with you."

I hold my hand up. "No. I need alone time. I'll check in with you later, alright. Make sure you check the containers and lock up before you leave."

He nods, concern written all over his expression. I grab my jacket and keys and leave. Hopefully he doesn't forget to do the primary search of the building, making sure it's all good.

Since I sleep there, there's no need to have a security guard for the containers. And since we hired a guy called Liam to install our security system, there's no way someone can get in without being seen. He's good, really good, and everyone wants him to install his security. But that was four years ago. It needs updating, and he said it would need doing annually. We just haven't gotten around to doing it. He's also pricey, but to keep my business afloat, I need to put the money in.

Getting in my car, I have no idea where I'm heading. It isn't until I pull up on a familiar street that I startle.

Either my mind is seeking my granddad, which is doubtful, or the pretty blonde who lives next door to him.

Seeing as I'd most likely get my head torn off for even knocking on her door, I pull up on Granddad's drive. If anyone can give me advice on my business, it's him.

Swinging out of the car, I check the quiet street and close my eyes. It's going to rain again tonight, and it's meant to freeze tomorrow. The stillness of the dark street is what I need to let everything go.

I'm just walking up the path to Granddad's when I hear a scream so loud pierces my ears.

Lily.

Paling, I jump and slide over the bonnet of the blue Mini parked right against the garage door.

When I reach her front door, I start banging, but the screams become louder.

"Fuck!" I hiss, looking around the empty street again. There's no one a-fucking-bout.

I put my hand on the door handle and push down. My shoulders tense when it clicks open. A part of me is angry as fuck she'd leave her door open like this, but the other is thanking my lucky stars I didn't have to kick the door down. I run down the hall, following the screaming, and come to a sudden stop in the kitchen doorway.

Water is everywhere and Lily is holding a towel over the tap, which is just making the spray worse.

And yet again, she's wearing nerdy fucking pyjamas but is sexier than a Victoria Secrets model. These ones have tiny bunnies and stars on. She looks cute as hell.

"Can I help?" I ask, my voice deeper than usual as I step further into the room.

She jumps, letting go of the tap to face me, her screams louder. She slips on the water, and before she can hit the floor, I move, catching her under her arms. Her entire body tenses, freezing in place.

The water continues to spray everywhere, all over the counters, all over the floor and all over us.

As much as I want to stay where I am, my hands holding her ribs, just below her breasts—which I now have a clear view of since her white T-shirt has gone see-through and her nipples are showing—I don't.

"Fuck!" I hiss when the tap makes a gurgling noise.

I bend down, throwing bottles of bleach and what-have-you out from under the sink. Lily becomes unstuck and moves slightly away from me.

I quickly shut off the water and hear her sigh of relief. "I think I broke it," she murmurs softly.

I chuckle, getting up, water dripping down my hair and off my face. "I think you did. What happened?"

She sucks in her bottom lip, her attention on the taps that have now stopped flowing with water. "I turned it on, and it started making funny noises. When it does that, I usually just give it a tap and it's fine. Maddox said he'd fix it, but he's been really busy with work."

"It wasn't fine," I guess correctly, struggling to stop myself from laughing. She looks adorably devastated.

Looking at me, she shakes her head. "It made a louder noise and it was like it burst. Water was everywhere and I tried to stop it, even tried turning the taps off, but, well, you know the rest," she says, her cheeks turning pink.

My gaze moves back to her chest, and I grit my teeth, finding it hard not to pull her to me and lift her on top of this counter.

"Want me to look at it?" I offer.

I watch her struggle to decide, crossing her arms over her stomach protectively. "You don't need to do that. You've done enough," she tells me, then in a cheerier voice, says, "I'll call Maddox."

Her tits bounce in her top and I groan. Her nipples are hard, poking through the thin, wet material.

"Please go put a shirt on," I groan pleadingly.

A dark blush rises in her cheeks as she looks down at her top.

"Oh no!" she moans.

It happens quickly, like she forgot there's water all over the floor. She slips backwards and I reach out. I try to steady her, but my feet slip out from under me and I fly forward. My head bounces off the counter as we go down. Not wanting to crush her when we land, or cause her to bang her head, I quickly twist us, my back slapping hard on her kitchen tile, my T-shirt soaking up the water.

I groan, feeling a pounding begin at the front of my head. Blinking, I stare up at Lily who stares back, her lips slightly parted.

"You're bleeding," she whispers, staring at the top of my head.

Her voice, so soft and alluring. I can't look away, can't blink. Her lips form a pout, and all I can do is stare. She's watching me back, her gaze on my mouth now, staring with utter fascination.

Her breath hitches and she tenses above me. Her eyes dilate, and I know she wants to kiss me. I can see it on her face; it's written all over her.

Her body might want to kiss me, but she's not ready. Nowhere near ready. I'm not even sure if she's ever been kissed. I know she's never had a boyfriend, never gone on a date, so the likelihood of her kissing someone is nil.

She blinks and becomes focused, like she's seeing her surroundings for the first time. "You're bleeding," she repeats softly.

I clear my throat and slowly start to sit up. Startled, she begins to rise, causing me to groan when she slides down my body, her knees resting on the floor either side of me. I sit up, clutching my head when a wave of dizziness hits me.

My hand comes away with blood on it.

"Shit! I really am bleeding," I mutter.

"Let me get a towel," she rushes out, squeezing my knee. She's bent over in front of me now, and I get a clear view down her top.

"Lily, please go and put a clean top on," I murmur gently.

The pink in her cheeks is back, and she nods quickly, scrabbling up off the floor and out of the room.

I groan as I get up from the floor, looking around the place for a dish towel. I search through drawers, finally finding one and pressing it against my head. I think it's stopped bleeding already, and there's definitely an egg of a lump already formed.

Just perfect. Now I'll have to explain where and how I got it to my family.

When Lily walks back in, her steps are uncertain, wary. I'm glad to see she's got a black T-shirt on this time, this one reading 'I love Christmas'.

"Are you okay?" she asks, and there's no mistaking the shakiness in her voice.

"I'm good, babe. Are you okay? I didn't hurt you when we fell, did I?"

Her gaze softens, and I didn't think that was possible. "You didn't hurt me, Jaxon. Do you need to go to the hospital?"

"It's just a scratch," I assure her.

She plays with the hem of her T-shirt, looking unsure. "It looked pretty deep."

"Head wounds always bleed more than normal. I'm good. Promise," I tell her, then look around at the destruction. Her kitchen floor is soaked. "Babe, get your mop bucket and start getting some of this water from the floor before it starts to seep under and mould. I'll go grab my tools and a clean T from my car, then I'll come back and fix your sink."

"You don't need to—"

"Babe," I warn, giving her a 'don't argue' stare.

She bites her lip but nods obediently. I reach the kitchen door when her soft voice stops me.

"Jaxon, how did you know I needed you?"

My heart stops at those words. I don't even think she realises what she just said. Most men wouldn't give a fuck, would probably run a mile if a woman said they needed them. But hearing it from Lily… It's like a fucking gift.

I look over my shoulder, masking the emotions running through me and answer with a grin. "Babe, you were screaming the street down. I'm surprised the neighbours haven't called the police."

She giggles timidly and it brings a grin to my face. "Thank you."

"Pleasure," I tell her, then continue out the kitchen. Then a thought comes to me, and I backpedal into the room. "Babe?"

She jumps, startled. I grin. She's fucking cute when she's skittish. "My name's Lily, Jaxon," she reminds me softly.

My grin spreads. "Next time you come in, lock the door after you, yeah?" Her brows scrunch in confusion, so I continue. "I'm glad I didn't have to kick your door down. I thought you were being hurt. But even so, next time, lock it. There have been a lot of break-ins around here."

I watch as she melts, leaning heavily against the mop handle. "Okay, Jaxon."

God, when she says my name, I feel it in my dick.

I give her a chin lift and make my way back outside to my car. I lift open the boot, grabbing my gym bag. Fortunately, I washed it last night and threw it back in my car ready for the gym tomorrow after work. I grab my vest then search for my hoodie I know I left in the back of my car. Once on, I grab some tools from my boot and go to take a step towards the house.

Granddad is standing between their driveways, his beefy arms crossed over his chest, watching me with a look I can't read.

"What?" I snap, hating the look he's giving me.

"Pretty little thing, ain't she, boy?"

I close my eyes before meeting him up the garden. "Granddad," I warn.

"What? She is. Perfect she is. But, boy, I've heard of your exploits. She don't need that in her life, and as much as I love you, I won't let her be another girl to you. She don't need hurt in her life. Not anymore."

My gaze hardens on the man I respect more than anyone, anger fuelling my veins. I thought he knew me better than that.

"Does Lily look like someone who I'd fuck around with?"

His jaw clenches. "I don't know, Jax, is she?"

I rear back, my teeth snapping together. "She's not that kind of girl. The fact you'd think I'd do something to her is one thing, but for you to think she'd let someone get that close to do that to her, is another. Not feeling real friendly right now, Granddad."

"All right, boy, all right."

"No, it's not all right. I get where you're coming from. I really do. She has that way about her," I tell him, my gaze going briefly to her house. "Everyone around her wants to protect her. Even people she meets briefly. Teachers at school, lads… fuck, even nerds with no hope of winning a fight stuck up for her against the bitches at school. They were jealous as fuck of her."

"Boy, I get it," Granddad says softly.

"I won't hurt her," I declare.

"I was wrong," he admits.

"Yeah, you were. I heard her screaming and went in. She's broken her taps. You don't need to stand guard out here."

Another grin forms. "I'm seeing a different side to you."

"Granddad," I warn again, my voice low.

He holds his hands up. "Just saying. Didn't think my boy had it in him. You know, to settle down, have a girlfriend, make me some great grandbabies. Now, I'm thinking he does. I'm thinking he has a hard-on for the girl next door and he's too scared to do anything about it."

I groan, wishing the ground would swallow me up. "It's not like that."

"Doesn't seem like that to me."

"What are you lurking around outside our Lily's for?" a voice snaps. I look to the right of me to find Blanche, a grumpy old lady who lives next door to Granddad. He told me all about her the day after we moved him in. "I'm calling the police."

"Blanche, he's my grandson. You've seen him before."

Her watchful gaze comes to me, and her eyes slither into slits. I can feel my balls shrivelling up from the hard stare. "I'm just fixing her sink, Blanche."

"It's Mrs North to you," she snaps, gripping the door. "And I heard screaming."

I roll my eyes. I've had enough of being put down. "If you heard her screaming, why has it taken you fifteen minutes to come and check on her?"

Her head goes back and she opens her mouth, but no words leave. I've shut the old bat up.

"Hi, Barry, hi, Blanche," Lily greets, and when I turn my attention to her, she's watching me shyly, a light blush to her cheeks.

"He bothering you? I could phone the police," Blanche happily volunteers.

"He's my grandson," Granddad groans.

Lily giggles. "It's fine, Blanche. Jaxon saved me from ruining my kitchen. He's fixing my tap."

Blanche huffs before storming back inside. The sound of her front door slamming makes Lily jump.

She smiles and it lights up her whole face. "I think she likes you."

I raise my eyebrow at her. Has she gone mad? "She threatened to call the police on me."

She clasps her hands together, not losing her smile. "Yeah, but she actually called the police on Hayden. I think that says a lot."

I shake my head at the crazy conversation we're having. "Let's get your sink fixed."

"I'd offer you a coffee or tea, Barry, but I don't have water at the moment."

Granddad smiles gently at her. "It's all right, princess, I've got one brewing as we speak. Want me to make you one?"

Her warm eyes soften further, like she's not used to the kindness. It's bizarre, because apart from the bitches at school, I've never seen anyone be mean to her. In fact, everyone goes out of their way to be nice to her. It makes her more of a mystery. How can someone, whose life is so clearly jaded, who has a lot of emotional scars, be as kind and considerate as Lily. Why, when everyone is so pleasant and giving, does she treat each act of kindness like it's the first. She's truly remarkable.

And I still haven't forgotten about Hayden's comment from the other week. *It was before she came to live with us.*

She pretty much disclosed Lily wasn't theirs. But Lily looks a lot like them. She might have blonde hair, whereas pretty much everyone else has brown, but the eyes… she has the same big, brown, doe eyes as her dad, uncles and most of her relatives.

Will Lily Carter ever stop being such a fucking mystery to me?

A truck pulling up in Lily's driveway has us all turning. I inwardly groan when I notice Maddox's truck, his logo printed on the side.

Lily steps down, a new light in her eyes as she rushes down to greet him. I tense when she flings herself into his arms the minute he gets out of the car. His hardened eyes meet mine over the top of her head and narrow dangerously.

"Well, this will be interesting. Didn't know she had a boyfriend," Granddad whispers.

"He's her cousin," I whisper back, my voice harsher.

Granddad chuckles.

"What are you doing here, Hayes?"

There's no mistaking the venom in his tone, and I straighten, glaring back at him. "Coming to see my granddad," I tell him, which isn't a lie. I notice Lily relax somewhat when I don't mention her sink.

"Nasty cut you got there. Walking into walls again?" he asks, relaxing—probably because I'm not here for Lily. But if only he fucking knew.

"Barry," Granddad says when I don't answer, holding his hand out for Maddox. Maddox grins, stepping forward and shaking it.

"Maddox," he introduces. "Lily said you're the shit with Cluedo."

My body tenses and my gaze flicks to Lily. Did she tell them she played with us? We might be on good terms with Landon because he's dating our sister, but it doesn't mean the same rules apply to the rest of their family. Maddox, out of all of them, knows how to push our buttons, and in return, we can rile him up. Although, it's very rare he gets pissed. The only time he gets truly angry is if Lily is mentioned. Since the two are extremely close, I can see why this would be his trigger point.

"Sure am," Granddad announces proudly.

Maddox nods, giving Granddad the seal of approval. It makes me want to vomit. Then his attention comes back to me, to the bag I have in my hand.

"Fixing something?"

I look to Lily and watch as she stiffens. "Um, Jaxon was just, um…" she starts, rambling and looking nervous.

I step in. "Her tap burst. I was at Granddad's when she came to ask for help. I was just about to go in and look."

"We don't need your help," he grits out before looking down at Lily. "Why didn't you call me?"

"It just happened. There was water everywhere," she explains.

"Shit! I need to go turn the water off before it seeps into the floor," he mutters, but she pulls him to a stop.

"It's already turned off," she whispers, not looking at him. She's not outright lying to him, but I can see what it's doing to her by not confessing the whole truth.

"How'd you know how to do that?"

She shrugs, and I can see the blush rising up her neck to her cheeks. "Um—"

"We'd best go inside then, Granddad. Leave Maddox to fix the tap," I yell, and Maddox's gaze comes to me, watching me warily. He's not buying anything, but for Lily, he's going to keep his mouth shut. He doesn't need to say anything though. I can see by the way he's looking at me that I'm being warned.

Whatever.

If he thinks he can scare me, then he's as stupid as everyone thinks he is.

"See you around, Lily."

"Thank you," she replies softly. "For—you know, nearly fixing my sink."

My lips pull into a small smile. "Pleasure, babe." I don't look away, afraid this might be the last time we share a moment like this.

"Lil, why don't you go inside. I'll be with you in a sec with my tools," Maddox orders gently.

She nods, giving me one last glance before waving goodbye to me and Granddad.

Maddox steps up close, the good-natured look gone and one in place that I've seen all too much on his cousin Landon's.

"Stay the fuck away from Lily," he warns, his tone deadly and quiet. "I might be a ray of fucking sunshine a majority of the time, but do not mistake me, Hayes. I will rip you a-fucking-part if you go near her."

With that, he walks back to his truck. Granddad heaves out a breath. "Welp, that was interesting," he says, and I roll my eyes at him. "Now, come inside and tell me what brought you to this side of town to see me."

"Can't I just want to spend time with my granddad?"

Granddad stops just inside of his door to look at me, raising his eyebrow. "Boy, don't try to be funny 'cause you ain't. Now, stop beating around the bush and tell me."

I nod sharply and follow him inside. I spend the night drinking whiskey and talking about the new company moving in on our territory, and how he wants our business. I listen as he tries to find solutions but, in the end, the only thing we can agree on is that this man isn't going to go away unless we play dirty.

Granddad's only questions was: "How dirty are you willing to get?"

With the business and the hot blonde next door on my mind, I kept drinking, hoping it would help me forget. It didn't until fell into a drunken slumber on my granddad's sofa.

CHAPTER FOUR.

LILY

Monday is my favourite day of the week. The kids come in with more energy than I've seen in anyone, and that's coming from someone with a big family who have tons of energy. The children come in full of fun stories of their weekends and aren't shy in telling me. And I love hearing them. All of them.

For the first time, I have a story of my own. One I can't really share or talk about with anyone. Faith would listen, but she wouldn't understand.

Last night, Maddox wouldn't leave, even though he wanted to. I was used to him staying over, but last night he stayed because Jaxon's truck was still in his granddad's driveaway. It was gone when I woke up this morning, same with Maddox's.

So, after he settled in the spare bedroom downstairs, I went up to bed and went over everything from the sink bursting to Jaxon walking in and scaring me. I reflected on the fact I didn't freak out when I saw it was him standing in the doorway. In fact, I felt something inside of me soothe, and I calmed my breathing.

Falling into his arms and then on top of him was another story. I imagined kissing him. Can you believe that? I've never fantasised about a male. Ever. Of course, Jaxon has always had this effect on me, but last night, it was different. I felt him everywhere and could smell him long after he left.

However, I kept replaying that scene of us on the kitchen floor, soaking wet, over and over. I changed it. In my mind, I leaned down and kissed him like I knew what I was doing, and he kissed me back.

In my mind, I played it cool, made him laugh, and he stayed.

Albeit, it *was* in my mind and it never played out like that. It's not like anything could really happen between the two of us. I might not be there when the fights break out between my family and his, but I hear the PG version of what happens and it's not pretty. I wish they'd move through their differences and become friends.

Jaxon though… I think I'm having my first real crush. I may have already been crushing on him, but last night it became more.

Maybe talking to Faith would be a good idea?

"Earth to Lily," my TA, Michelle, calls, clicking her fingers in front of me. I hadn't even realised the kids had walked in and were busy hanging their coats up. He's fogging up my mind.

I blink, smiling sheepishly. "Sorry, I spaced out."

She grins, wagging her eyebrows. "Good weekend, huh?" I giggle, feeling the blush rise in my cheeks. "Oh my god. Did you meet someone?"

"What? No! I, um, I… My sink burst."

Her shoulders slump, and she looks at me, adorably confused. "That made you blush?"

I shrug, looking out the window when I see Star and her brother, Miah. "Um, can you settle the children for a second, please? I just want to speak to Miah."

Michelle looks out the window, her expression worried. "Lily, don't. Let the school handle it."

I ignore her, continuing to the door that leads out to the playground. Miah is bent down on one knee in front of Star and seems to be comforting her. She nods, still looking down at her feet.

My breath hitches when she quickly wraps her arms around his neck. I watch him close his eyes like he's in pain.

I push down on the bar and step out into the cold. Even in black, thick tights and my grey dress jumper, I'm cold.

"Miah, could I talk to you?" I call out. I hate that I'm delaying him getting to school himself, but I need him to know I'm going to help them. I might not know the facts, but in my gut, I know I'm right about their situation.

He jumps, his gaze hardening on me. "No. I'm late," he snaps, then looks down at Star. "Go inside. I'll see you later, yeah?"

"Okay, Miah," she whispers softly.

He turns and walks out of the playground, and my eyes revert back to Star, who's walking stiffly towards me. I notice she's wearing her new school clothes that, thankfully, Michelle remembered after I left the classroom Friday and raced home. She's also wearing the new coat Miah got her.

"Did you have a good weekend?" I ask, taking her hand when she reaches me. Silence. She doesn't answer or even look at me. My heart constricts. I can sense the emotional pain rolling off her. She's hurting, and from what, I don't know. I hate not being able to do something right now.

"What about Miah, did he have a good weekend?"

Silence.

I sigh sadly, feeling lost as she lets go of my hand and walks to her coat peg. She's not talkative on a good day, but I've got a feeling something happened over the weekend. Something bad. She's never been withdrawn from me.

Small arms wrap around me, and I look down and smile at Jake. "Morning, Miss Carter."

"Morning, Jake. Did you have a good weekend?"

"I had the best. My brother slept at his friend's house, so I got to play Fortnight for two days," he screeches, seeming excited over it.

Having got an Xbox due to Maddox always staying over, I'm lucky to know what game he is talking about.

"Isn't that a little violent?"

He laughs like I said the funniest joke, but I'm being serious. It has all sorts of weapons on it.

"It's the *coolest* game *ever*, Miss Carter."

I smile down at him, patting his head. "I'm sure it is."

"Morning, Miss Carter, look what I made you," Sara, a cute red-headed girl says, and walks closer, holding a box. I take the box, my eyes widening with glee.

"You got me a present?" I gasp, grinning wide.

She nods with so much enthusiasm my heart spasms. She looks so happy. "It's cupcakes. We put fairies on them. Mum said I could bring you some because you remind her of a fairy princess."

I giggle, having heard that a lot lately. "Thank you so much. I can't wait to eat them."

She crooks her finger at me to come closer. I play along, looking around as I bend down. "What?" I whisper.

She leans in further. "There was five, but Daddy ate one. He said you couldn't give someone something that wasn't an even number."

I gasp in horror. "*He didn't?*"

She nods, a cute little frown marring her face. "Yeah. He said he'd give me *five* pounds if I didn't tell Mummy."

I chuckle lightly. "Did you tell her?"

She gives me a 'duh' look. "Yes. You tell us all the time that lying is bad. And Mummy gave me an extra cupcake for telling the truth. It was a *big* win."

I giggle again, holding the box to my chest. "I'll make sure no one else eats them."

She licks her lips as she eyes the box. "If you want, you can share with me. I don't mind."

I nod, then put my finger over my lips. "Don't tell anyone else."

Her eyes widen and she nods furiously. "I won't. Pinkie swear."

She runs back to her desk, a bounce in her step. My kids are simply adorable and so kind-hearted. I place the cupcakes on my desk, and in doing so, look across the room towards the desk at the window. Star is looking out, her expression sad and lost. Tears clog my throat. She hasn't acknowledged anyone else in the room, and that tells me she's truly deep in thought, and those thoughts aren't good.

I'll keep watch on her the rest of the day, see if she perks up. If not, I'll contact my uncle Myles again and see what he says.

Who am I kidding. I'm going to contact him anyway.

It's been twenty minutes since school officially finished. All the kids are gone but Star. Normally, we send them down to reception and wait for them to be picked up. It's not uncommon that a parent is late. Everyone does it.

Star Merin, on the other hand, doesn't have parents picking her up. She has her older brother, who is still a kid himself.

"Would you like to help me put away the paints, Star?" I ask softly.

I've been keeping an eye on her all day, and she's become more withdrawn with each hour that passes. I watch her nervously watching the clock on the wall, and I already know she can't tell the time. Not because she's thick, but because no one has taught her. She's seven years old and struggles with her ABC's. It's heart-breaking, and all I want to do is give her all of my attention so she can learn all the stuff she's missed.

Star lifts her head from the desk at my question, then her eyes go to the paint box, an activity she didn't take part in. No, she sat and stared out the window, and I felt like she needed that, so I didn't push.

"Okay," she answers quietly, her voice tired and sad.

My throat closes, and I lean down and grab the first box, the heavier one, while Star grabs the other. She cries out, dropping the box, and a startled gasp escapes me. I drop the box on the table and kneel in front of Star.

"Star, what's wrong? Where does it hurt?"

She's clutching her stomach, her face pale and scrunched up in pain. My stomach turns at the idea and my heart begins to race.

She's hurt.

This has been on her mind all day. I've let her sit in my classroom, even during lunch, and she was in pain. She'd been suffering and never said one word.

I let her suffer. I knew something was wrong and I didn't push her for answers.

Tears fill my eyes as I gently pry her hands away. She sniffles, and I move slower. First, because I don't want her to startle and run off. And second, because I don't want to hurt her. The idea my touch right now could be causing her pain brings bile to my throat.

Her arms drop to her sides, slapping against her thighs. She sniffles again and the sound makes my heart stop.

"Lily?" Michelle calls, and I hear the concern in her voice. I don't stop, not taking my eyes from Star. She's looking down at the floor, her entire body frozen.

Flicking my gaze down, I suck in a breath and fall back on my heels.

"Oh my God," Michelle breathes out in horror.

Her voice trails off as she speaks quietly to Star. I can't hear her, can't reach the surface to hear if Star replies or not. I clutch my head as a pain like no other ricochets through my brain.

Images. Feelings. More images and worse feelings flash through my mind.

I clutch my head tighter, and it takes everything in me not to scream out, to release the horror, the pain and torment, to let it all free.

I'm shivering in the corner of the small room. I'm always in the smallest. It feels like the cupboard that Mummy locks me in. It's cold in our new flat, noisier than the last one too. All I have is the blanket I use to sleep on the floor. With no carpet to make the floor softer, I have to use it otherwise it hurts.

"Lily!" the voice booms.

Mummy's new boyfriend, Richard. He scares me more than the others. He's mean. Really mean. Mummy's mean too, but sometimes, when I'm really, really good, she lets me have dinner. She doesn't forget.

"Lily, get in here, right fucking now!"

I know it will be worse if I try to hide. And with nowhere to hide since we don't have much in the new flat, he will find me quicker.

My body quakes in fear as I slowly push down the handle of the door. My bare feet slap against the dirty floor, and I want to cry when I see the mess.

Mummy is going to be so mad.

I walk into the living room, and on the sofa is Richard. He has a rounded belly, greying hair, and hair all over his face.

They've been together a real long time, but she always gets a new one. She says the last one was a waste of space, and she uses words that are naughty. The nice lady who lives next door to us keeps telling Mummy to stop saying them. It causes more shouting.

"Child," Richard snaps, pulling me roughly by my arm. I cry out and bite my lip to stop the tears that threaten to fall. When I cry—and I cry a lot—it makes them madder, or when they drink the blue cans, it makes them laugh.

"What did I tell you about making noise?" he yells in my face.

I don't speak, too afraid. I found out early they don't like me speaking.

"That busy-bee next door is sticking her nose in, said she could hear you crying. You want something to cry over?" he yells again, spitting in my face.

His hand comes out, and my cheek hurts so much when he knocks me to the floor. I knock over one of the blue cans and look up, my bottom lip trembling.

His face gets scary and angry, and he steps forward, kicking me in the stomach until I roll over.

"Good for nothing little bitch," he yells.

My gaze comes into focus, and I see Star and Michelle still in front of me. I rush up to my knees, taking Star by the arms. I know I'm beyond hysterics. I know I need to calm down, but she's hurt. Those angry red, blue and purple bruises could only have been inflicted by an adult. I'm sure one is the shape of the tip of a boot.

"Star, I will help you," I rush out.

"Lily," Michelle calls, and I look to her, feeling tears fall down my cheeks.

"I'm helping her," I tell her, feeling my heart race faster.

"Lily, we need to report this, let it go through the proper channels," she warns me softly.

"No! I'm helping her!" I scream, startled at the sound of my own voice. I never raise it. Ever.

"Have you been to the hospital?" I ask Star, even though it's a stupid question. She looks frightened; frightened of me? I'm not sure.

"Lily, we will help her," Michelle tries again, but I've gone past listening. I can feel the boot kicking into my side, can remember how it felt to breathe afterwards and how I wished I could die. I learned about death so early in life. My mum would tell me she wished I was dead because I was worthless, I was a brat, spoiled and needy.

"Get away from my sister," Miah snaps, barging into the room. He looks more intimidating looming above me.

Despite his anger, he handles Star with care, taking her hand and beginning to pull her away.

My heart starts pounding at a rapid pace as I run in front of him. His glare hits me in the gut. "Please don't go. I can help."

"We don't need your help. And you shouldn't be lifting little girls' tops alone in the classroom," he snaps angrily.

"Hey now," Michelle starts, stepping up beside me.

Wetness splashes against my cheeks when he moves around us. I grab his arm. "You can't leave. I'm going to phone the police," I rush out. An unsettling thought begins to well inside of me. If I let him leave here, he might not bring her back. He could tell whoever is hurting them that I know, and they could run.

Haunted eyes snap to me, widening in panic and fear. "No. You can't phone the police. They'll split us apart. I'm looking after her," Miah growls, taking two more steps around me. He's nearly at the door so I do the only thing I can do. I grab his arm, pulling him.

"No, I'm not letting you go back to them."

He shrugs my arm off roughly, but I grab him again. "Get the fuck off me, lady."

"Lily," Michelle calls sharply, but I don't loosen my hold.

I can't breathe.

I step back in front of him, hands to his chest. "Don't. Please, I'm begging you. You can trust me."

"We can't trust anyone," he mutters, pushing past me.

My shoulder jams into the door, and I wince at the pain. It's going to bruise.

My fingers press lightly into his bicep. "Don't take Star back there."

"Miah," Star calls, her voice trembling.

It's hard to focus on her when tears blur my vision. She's scared.

"Star, come with me, please. I can help you," I tell her, calming my voice.

She looks up at Miah. She's torn. I can see it, and I hate that I'm doing it. But I'm the adult. They're the children. And I'm doing what is best for them.

"What is going on here?"

Yes!

"Mr Hartman, you have to stop him from leaving," I plead. "Star has bruising on her stomach."

"Is this true?" Mr Hartman asks, and my breath hitches. Why isn't he doing something?

"She lifted my sister's top. It's creepy as fuck. And everything is fine," Miah snaps. "And she manhandled me, put her hands on me."

Mr Hartman's eyes practically bulge out of his head. "You did what?" he asks, his voice hard.

I rub my chest, gasping for air. "Please, she has bruises. They need help, Mr Hartman."

"My office, now!" he demands, pointing to the classroom door.

I shrink into myself, folding my hands over my stomach to try and ease the cramps. "She's hurt, Mr Hartman. It's your duty as a school headteacher to report it."

"You put your hand on a child, Miss Carter. I suggest you keep your mouth shut and go to my office. I'll deal with this."

"You'll help them?"

He shakes his head, his lip curling. "Office," he snaps, then turns to Miah and Star. "Go home, kid. It's getting dark. I'll look into this with Miss Carter. Please, have your parents call me."

"What?" I yell. "No. Help them."

Mr Hartman's hard eyes come to me. "Leave. Go grab your stuff and leave. I'll talk to the schoolboard about this, but from here, you are suspended until further notice."

"What?" I whisper, tears streaming down my face.

"You put your hand on a child, Lily, hurt him," he snaps.

My attention turns to Miah and Star walking out the school gates. I shake my head, disappointed once again in the school system.

I had a teacher when I lived with my birth mum. I don't remember much about her, but I do remember she was kind. She was gentle, and she made me feel loved. She promised she would get me help, until she didn't. She kept saying it, but that help never came. Until my mum said she was a nosey bitch and we had to leave. I never saw her again. But I knew… I knew growing up I wanted to be that teacher. I wanted to make kids feel the way I felt when I went to school.

If I don't have that, I don't have anything.

I nod mutely, feeling my shoulders sag. I wipe at my eyes, looking up at him. "That little girl is being hurt, Mr Hartman. She's getting psychically hurt. You can sit behind your desk and do nothing, or you can ring the right people and help her. You could change that little girl's life. Both of those kids' lives. It's what you agree to when you become a teacher. You're their guardian when they're at school. You teach them. But what are you teaching them? That hitting people is okay? That trusting adults will get you nowhere?"

"Lily," Michelle whispers, stepping towards me, but I hold my hand up while wiping my tears away with the other.

Keeping my voice low and soft, I continue. "I was Star once. I had adults constantly letting me down, time and time again. If it weren't for my dad, I would have continued to not trust anyone in life. He showed me what love was. He showed me there were good people in the world, people who cared whether you ate, whether you had a bed. You will never understand the feeling of going to sleep scared out of your mind that someone will wake you up and beat you. You have no idea what it's like for little girls like Star. No idea whatsoever," I tell him, then take in a deep breath. "But you have the power to help her get a better life. You have the power to place her into the care of people who will do everything that is best for her. Don't let her down."

With that, I walk over to my desk, bend down and grab my bag and coat from under it.

"Lily," Michelle calls, but I ignore them, heading outside. Rain begins to trickle, washing away my tears as I head to my car.

CHAPTER FIVE

JAXON

"**D**IDN'T WANT TO BRING THIS up in front of your mum, but did you sort out that jackass messing with your business, yet?"

Shifting into second, I turn onto Granddad's road. We've just come back from spending the day with Mum, getting an early dinner.

"We're planning. You were right. We needed to do some research first, find out facts. We're still getting it coming in. Got a friend who's good with computers."

"What's he found?"

I pull into the driveaway and lift the parking break. "A lot of companies, even small ones like mine, go bust when he's around. He comes in and gets a bargain at either auction or because sellers need the first offer he gives to pay for the setback he's cost them."

"Shee-it," Granddad mutters. "Can't stand men like that. Born with a stick in their arse."

I chuckle under my breath. "He should have done a deep background check into us, not the business. He'd know that he's fucked with the wrong family."

"Sure fucking has," Granddad snaps out, pushing open his door.

Pushing out a leg, I step out of the car, looking over the top at Granddad. "Thanks for not bringing it up in front of Mum. We don't want her finding out."

"Probably for the best, Jaxon. She'd eat 'im alive."

I laugh at that, my eyes glancing down the path where Granddad's bin is still out. "I'll grab your bin. Want me to hang out before I get back to work?" I ask, my eyes glancing over at the house next door.

Granddad follows my line of sight and begins to chuckle. "She'll be at work for another hour."

I heard Lily was a teacher. For what age, I have no clue. I can't see her teaching teenagers; they'd eat her alive and spit her back out. I think in all the time I've known her, I've never heard her raise her voice. Not once. Not when the girls at school picked on her, not when her brothers or cousins got into fights, not ever. I'd be shocked as fuck to find out she taught high school kids. Then again, if she were my teacher when I was at school, I might have fucking enjoyed it.

"Yeah?"

Granddad gives me a knowing grin. "Yeah."

Granddad's gaze goes over my shoulder, his eyes drawing together. I look over my shoulder and see Lily's blue Mini Cooper swerving slightly up the road.

"What the fuck!" I growl, stepping down the drive.

"She's not gonna slow down," Granddad warns, stepping beside me.

Fuck, she's not. I quickly rush to the end of the drive and wave my arms in the air for her to stop. She doesn't, and I can see why when I get a glimpse of her face through the windshield. She's crying.

Fuck!

"Lily," Granddad shouts when she slams on the breaks too late, hitting her bin in the process.

I run past Granddad and over to the car, throwing open the car door. "Lily, are you okay? Fuck, are you hurt?"

"Jaxon?" she whispers, tears streaming down her face.

This is fucking killing me, seeing her like this. "Lily, talk to me."

"I tried to help them," she says, her voice still low and shaky.

"Help who?" I ask, keeping my voice steady. I want to grab her, wrap her in my arms, but I'm worried it might set off a trigger.

I feel Granddad step behind me as I kneel down into the car. I look up, shaking my head at him when he goes to talk.

"I tried. I don't want them to be hurt again. Someone is hurting them."

Fuck, I think she's lost it.

"Who, Lily? Who's hurt?"

Her expression when she finally turns to me sucks all the air out of my lungs. She looks fucking destroyed, ruined.

"Lily," I whisper, leaning forward and cupping her jaw. "Let's get you inside."

She nods, her eyes still distant. "I need my uncle Myles. I need my dad. They'll know what to do."

"We'll call them," I tell her gently, helping her out of the car. I turn to Granddad as I hold Lily against my chest. She sags into me, and it takes little effort to help support her weight. "Sort the car, Granddad. I'm gonna take her in."

He nods, his worried gaze on Lily. "Make her a cuppa, that will have her calming in no time," he tells me, and I nod. A sniffle comes from Lily, and I don't know if she knows she's doing it, but she's clinging to me like I might disappear, her face shoved into my chest.

Fuck, she's tiny.

"Wait," Granddad calls, and I look back to him walking up and handing me her bag. "Call her folks."

I nod, helping Lily up to her door. "Are your keys in your bag?"

"I need to help them," she whispers.

Definitely in shock.

"Baby, keys," I say gently, stroking her cheek.

She blinks up at me. "Keys?"

"Yeah, we need to get you inside."

She shakes her head then looks around and down to the bag in my hand. She opens the front pocket, pulling out a set of keys with a rainbow keychain.

I take them from her grasp, slow so I don't spook her. I open her door and the second we step in, two cats come flying down the stairs.

I do a double take when I see one only has three legs and the other only one eye. What the fuck?

I keep an eye on them as they begin to meow and shut the door to, in case she doesn't let them out. I didn't see them when her sink burst. Most likely hiding when they heard their mum screaming like a banshee.

We step into the front room and I place her down on the sofa, kneeling down in front of her with my hands on her thighs. "Lily, I'm gonna go and make you a cuppa. Granddad will be back in a second, okay?"

"I couldn't help them. They're going to get hurt."

I still have no idea what she's talking about, and as much as I want to hold her, I know she needs her family. I've seen the connection they share, more with Lily and Charlotte than anyone. But I've noticed they spend more care around Lily than Charlotte. With Charlotte, they avoid everything, not wanting to hurt her feelings. Girl is whacky as fuck but has a heart of gold. You'd have to be a fool not to see it.

I lean forward, pressing my forehead against hers, and cup the back of her head. "Everything is going to be okay."

Her breath hitches and her eyes finally focus on me. "Jaxon?" she whispers, but it comes out as a plea.

Fuck if it doesn't do something to me.

"Yeah, baby, it's me."

Her eyes fill with tears once again before she bursts out crying, wrapping her arms around my neck. "My heart hurts so bad."

Her words are gut-wrenching. "Baby…"

"I feel like I can't breathe," she sobs out, clutching me tighter.

"I'm going to go make you a cuppa, then come back and we can talk. Maybe I can help you, yeah?"

She pulls back, blinking up at me. God, she's so fucking beautiful.

"You'd help me?"

I tuck a strand of hair behind her ear. "Yeah, Lily, I would," I tell her, feeling my throat tighten. She has no idea that there isn't anything I wouldn't do for her. "Now, you gonna lie down so I can put the kettle on?"

She nods, her red-rimmed eyes watching me with hope. "Yeah."

"Good," I whisper back softly, pulling a pillow out and helping her lie down. The minute she's down, she tucks her knees to her chest, her eyes filling with tears once again. I sigh, watching her for a moment longer before grabbing her phone out of the bag.

Granddad's walking in when I hit the hallway. "She okay?"

I shrug. "She's a mess. Something's happened and she's just rambling. Her car?"

"Just a little scrape at the front. Done more damage to the bin."

"I'm gonna go put the kettle on. You want to help, or you want to watch Lily?"

"I'll go sit with Lily," he tells me, and I give him a chin lift before heading down the hall. I scan through her contacts, pressing call when I come to 'Dad'.

"Princess, you good?" her dad answers immediately. I close my eyes, hating that I have to give him bad news.

"It's not Lily."

"Who the fuck is this?" he growls, his panic clear over the phone. There's no mistaking it, and I can hear him barking orders and people in the background.

"It's Jaxon Hayes."

"I swear to fucking Christ, you hurt my girl and they'll never find your body."

I believe him too, and it hurts like fuck to know he thinks I'd hurt any girl, much less Lily. "Sir, if you'd stop, I'll explain."

"Then fucking explain," he growls, and I swear I hear a car starting.

"I don't know if you know, but my granddad moved in next door," I start, but he cuts me off.

"Of course, I fucking did. I'm the one who owned the house."

I sigh. Of course he did. There isn't much around here the Carter's don't own.

I clear my throat as I flick the kettle on. "We were outside when Lily got back. Her car was swerving a little, then she crashed into her bin."

"What?" he yells, and I hear someone ask him what happened. "Shut up, Max!"

"You need to come here," I call loudly down the phone when he begins arguing with the person on the phone.

"If you stop yapping shit to me, I'll find out what's wrong with my daughter," Maverick snaps. "Jaxon, is she hurt?"

"No, sir. She's a mess though. She's not making sense, keeps going on about not helping someone and them being hurt. She's not stopped crying."

"Fuck," he growls down the line, then I hear him tell Max to phone his twin. Which means Lily's uncle Myles.

"We're on our way. We're thirty minutes out. I'll call her mum; she'll be able to get there sooner."

"I'll stay with her," I mutter, even though it's no hardship. I wasn't planning on leaving.

"Yeah, I bet. Thank you for calling."

"Put your goddamn foot down," I hear yelled, and I pull her phone away from my ear.

"I swear to God, Max, you don't shut the fuck up, I'm gonna throw you out of the car without stopping to pull over. I'm going ten over already."

"I'll let you know if anything changes," I call out.

"Thanks again."

"No problem," I tell him before ending the call.

The cats begin to meow around my feet, so I look through the cupboards, finding cat biscuits. When I see their water bowl is empty, I fill that up too, then go about finishing Lily's cup of tea.

Once I'm done, I move through her house, noticing all the photos of Lily and her family. I pause at one just outside the living room. It's all of them surrounding an older couple sitting in some garden chairs. They're either smiling or laughing in the picture, but when I locate Lily, I pause. She's in her teens in the picture, and I remember her vividly from that time. The same sadness in her eyes, the same forced happiness. There was always something blocking her from fully being happy, and I know it wasn't her family. When she was with them, she seemed more relaxed, more genuine with her smiles and laughter. But there were times when she wasn't, like she felt out of place in a huge family she hardly knew. It was just another of many mysteries when it came to working Lily out. I've begun to wonder if anyone can work her out.

She's standing at the end of the group, Maddox slightly behind, not that much younger than her. Her dad is beside her, and she's tucked under his arm. But she looks withdrawn from them, her blank expression staring beyond the camera rather than at it.

Hearing another sob coming from the living room, I move away from the photos and into the living room. She's still curled into a ball on the sofa, Granddad sat next to her, trying to console her.

He looks up when he hears me walk in, his lips tight. "I think we may need to call an ambulance. She's delirious and clearly in some sort of shock or transfixed on somet'."

I set the cup of tea down on the coffee table, smirking when I see the 'Every animal needs love' placemat.

"Her parents are on the way," I tell him. "I went through her shit in the kitchen. She has some coffee if you want to go make one. Her dad will be a while, and he said he'd ring her mum."

He still doesn't look any better at the news. "Hopefully sooner. She's not good, boy. I'll go make a coffee." He looks at the table as he gets up. "Want one?"

I nod, anything to have a moment alone with Lily. He gives me a chin lift and steps out to give us privacy.

"Lily," I call out, bending down in front of her. I place my hand on her shoulder, and she jumps, startled.

Did someone hurt her? Is that what the ramblings are about?

"Jaxon?" she whispers hoarsely, blinking up at me through wet lashes. Her hands are tucked under her cheek and the sadness lurking in her eyes is gut-wrenching.

"It's me, baby. I need to know if you're hurt. Can you do that for me?"

She blinks again, still looking dazed. Her eyes and nose are red from all the tears. "I'm not hurt."

"You said someone was hurt; who is it?" I ask soothingly, moving as close as I can without invading her space. When I see her begin to close down on me, I smooth my thumb across her cheek. "Baby, stay with me."

"Stay with you," she repeats, nodding like she wants that. Fuck if her expression doesn't say she wants that. At the minute though, I don't think she even knows what day it is.

"Yeah, baby, stay with me. Can you tell me who is hurt?"

Her hand moves, grabbing my wrist with a strength I didn't think she had. "They're children, Jaxon. Just children. I know what they're going through, not having anyone to help you. She was hurt so badly, and no one will listen to me," she rambles frantically, getting hysterical again. I quickly stand and shift her legs, pulling her into sitting position. I wrap my arms around her, hugging her to my chest as she continues. "He suspended me. I don't know what I'm going to do. I just wanted him to help them. *I* wanted to help them."

"Who, Lily?" I ask, bending down a little so I can see her face.

Something bad has happened, something that has brought back bad memories for Lily. If someone has hurt her, they won't have the Carter's to worry about. They'll be worried about me coming for them.

"Star, a little girl from class. Her brother is older, but he knows, and he's not protecting the person hurting them. He's protecting him and Star. I see it when he talks to me or Star. But I grabbed him, Jaxon. I grabbed him and I think I hurt him. Mr Hartman said I hurt him."

Jesus! I pull her tighter against me, closing my eyes briefly when her hand fists my T-shirt. She's clinging to me like she depends on me, and the fucked-up part of it is I'm glad it's me she's holding onto.

"Lily!" a frantic voice calls.

A woman with light auburn hair and hazel eyes comes barrelling into the room, skidding to a stop in front of me and Lily.

Her mum.

She looks nothing like Lily. She doesn't have the same heart-shaped face, bow lips, or big doe eyes like Lily does. I know she's her mum because only a mother would look like she does. I've seen it plenty of times with my mum.

"Lily, what happened?"

"Mum?" Lily calls, sitting up a little. Her bottom lip trembles and she throws herself at her mum.

"Oh, Lily," her mum whispers, and it's filled with pain.

Lily pulls back suddenly, nearly pushing her mum over. "You can help me. We need to save them, Mum."

"Save who, darling?"

"Star and Miah Merin. Someone is hurting them. Someone bad, Mum. I think it's one of their parents, and I keep seeing it and telling Mr Hartman, but he won't listen."

"Slow down," her mum says, placing her hands on Lily's knees.

Lily reaches down, whether she knows she's doing it or not, and grabs my hand in hers.

"Mum, you can help. You helped me. Dad helped me. We can help them," Lily rushes out, her voice rising.

"Where's my daughter? Who are you?"

"I'm Barry, her neighbour," I hear my granddad call. I close my eyes before looking at the door where Maverick Carter, Lily's dad, walks in. Max, Landon's dad, steps in behind him.

Maverick's gaze narrows on mine when he sees how close I am to his daughter. He soon forgets about me when he takes a look at Lily.

"Lily, princess, what's happened? Are you hurt?"

A frustrated growl bubbles up her throat, filled with more tears. She slaps the sofa with her free hand and the one holding mine squeezes tightly. "Listen to me! Please, one of you listen to me!"

Maverick bends down, and I quickly glance at his brother, Max. He's standing near the fireplace, his gaze watchful but also calculating. If I were to guess, he's picturing who he has to kill first.

"Princess, I am listening. Now, why don't you tell me what's happened?"

Lily goes to open her mouth but a commotion at the door startles her. "What the fuck have you done to my cousin?" Maddox growls, barging into the room.

"Hey now," Granddad calls, clearly not used to the Carter's.

I start to stand, but Lily holds me tighter. Maddox sees and his gaze goes glacial.

Shit!

Maddox storms over to his uncle and aunt, knocking them both down to get to me. He grabs me and I stand, giving Lily no choice but to let go.

"Maddox," Lily screams.

"Maddox," Maverick warns.

"Just like his dad," Max mutters, sounding amused.

"What the fuck have I told you," Maddox snaps, pushing me out of the room. I catch my feet, moving quicker.

"I swear to God, Carter, you touch me one more time, and I will fucking hit back."

He smirks, following me out. "Yeah? You think? I've told you before and I'll tell you again, stay the fuck away from Lily."

He has told me before, plenty of times. The time I saved her when she was being hurt by the girls at school and a lot from then until now. I also remember him threatening me at Faith's engagement party, but it's a blur. The whole night is.

By the time we're outside, I'm surprised I haven't tripped over my own feet.

"He hasn't done anything but help me," I hear Lily scream.

My jaw tightens, wanting to go to her.

"Jax, let's go home," Granddad says, watching Maddox like he's a ticking time bomb.

"Good idea," Maddox snaps. "And stop sniffing around my cousin. I find out it's you that hurt her, I'll fucking bury you."

I move forward, getting in his face. "I'd never fucking hurt her, or any female," I snap.

"You wanna pray that's what happened. You've got a reputation," he goads. He knows for a fucking fact I've never touched another woman in anger. Ever. He must read my mind because a cruel smirk lights up his face. "If you can fuck over your own sister, you'll have no problem with Lily."

Fuck this shit. I pull my fist back, ready to punch. Maverick steps in between us, his face a cloud of thunder.

"Stop!" he roars.

"Not me who started it," I snap back. "I was helping Lily. Nothing fucking more. I don't appreciate being accused otherwise."

"Like you don't want to get in her pants," Maddox growls, trying to shove his uncle off.

Maverick turns his glare to his nephew. "I said stop. I wasn't talking to him," Maverick warns, his voice deadly. He turns back to me, scanning my face. "I'm grateful. So fucking grateful you were here for her. It goes without saying, kid. She's special, always has been, but she's also sensitive. Glad you were here."

I nod and move back to my granddad before Maddox says anything else to kick things off. Granddad pats my back, his eyes narrowed on the Carter men.

"Come on, I'll make you a drink till you've calmed down, then you can head home."

I give him a tight nod, too angry to talk.

"Jaxon?"

Hearing my name called, I inwardly groan and turn to Maverick. "It also goes without saying, if your intentions are more, it will be you being buried. Lily doesn't need someone like you in her life."

Gritting my teeth, I let Granddad pull me back, hearing his whispers of not to listen to them. But it's fucking hard not to.

He doesn't know what the fuck Lily needs, and if he stopped babying her for five minutes, he'd see that. Hell, see she's capable of making smart decisions on her own.

Fuck!

Any ideas I had of being with Lily just went out the window. Even if she were able to step out of her little bubble and take a chance on me, her family won't allow it. And the fucked-up part of it is, they won't get anyone who'd protect her like I would.

CHAPTER SIX

JAXON

S WEAT RUNS DOWN MY BACK and forehead as I lift another box from the back of the van. It's the third job today and, thankfully, we're ahead of schedule. Good news for the business and good news for the boys who want to get off early.

Tim, a lad who started not long after we first started up, steps out of the house, his face a cloud of thunder. Reid follows behind him, a smug grin on his face.

"What did you do?" I ask, dropping the box back down in the van. I don't have the patience for his shit today, not after the other day. My mood after getting accused of being the one who hurt Lily hasn't improved. I just can't get her out of my mind. She's constantly there, her voice echoing with those painful words. I could feel them like it was me pleading.

"I didn't do anything," Reid tells me as he grabs his water bottle from his bag.

"He was fucking the daughter in the downstairs toilet," Tim growls, glaring at Reid.

My eyes narrow on Reid. "What the fuck!"

Reid sighs, looking at me like I'm being an unfair parent. But he wasn't the one who had to deal with the last woman he fucked on the job. No. It was me and Tim.

"Bro, she's hot."

"One, you're fucking working. Two, have you not learned your fucking lesson?"

He rolls his eyes, not taking me seriously. "She was begging for it, bro. She kept touching my dick and whispering dirty shit in my ear."

"So, you fucked her in the loo?"

The 'duh' look he gives me gets my back up. "Couldn't do her upstairs; her mum is up there still crying about her husband leaving them."

"Please tell me she's an adult," I plead.

"Yeah, she's twenty-two, doesn't even live at home."

"If I get punched again because you can't keep it in your pants, I'm quitting," Tim snaps, grabbing a box.

"You 'ent quitting," I tell him.

He looks at me, raising his eyebrow. "If he doesn't sort his shit out, I will."

"Don't tell me where I can stick my dick," Reid growls.

Tim rests the box on the wall just outside the door. "I'm not. I'm telling you not to do it at work because it affects us all."

"What, you can feel me and her orgasm?"

Looking disgusted, Tim throws up his hands. "Do you take anything seriously?"

"Yeah, your mum when we're in bed together."

Tim steps menacingly towards Reid. I intervene, pushing Reid in his chest. "Go get fucking busy, and I swear to God, you speak to an employee like that whilst working, I'll be firing you," I snap.

"I own a part of the business," Reid says, looking at Tim over my shoulder.

I grab him by his fleece coat, shaking him hard. "Don't fucking test me, Reid. I'm fed up of your shit. Either get it together or find another job. I'm done fucking babysitting you."

He lets out a whistle between his teeth. "Fuck, alright. I was only playing around. Soz, Tim."

"Whatever," Tim mutters, grabbing the box. "Don't say shit about my mum again either. She's dead."

"Fuck, Tim, I'm sorry," Reid tells him, taking a step towards him. He runs his hand through his hair, guilt written all over him.

"Whatever!"

Tim leaves us both standing on the street outside. I look to Reid and slap him upside the head. "Bro," he snaps.

"Don't fucking 'bro' me. Get your shit together," I growl.

"I will. I didn't fucking know about his mum. Sorry, I thought fucking blondie would relax me."

I open my mouth to answer when my phone rings. Since I transferred calls to the office to my mobile, I can't leave it.

Pulling it out, Mum's name flashes on the screen. "Mum, you okay?"

"Jaxon, you need to come home!"

The panic in her voice has me standing at attention. Reid, feeling the tension stands straighter and steps closer, his face unreadable.

"Mum, what's happened. Are you okay?"

"No, it's Paisley," she manages to get out, sounding panicked. Fuck, my sister suffers with diabetes and has been treated for it for as long as I can remember. Which means, she's been in the hospital more times than I like to admit.

"What hospital are you at?"

"We're not, dear. We're at the farmhouse. She's been hurt. She was getting the bedside tables she left in her container and saw someone trying to break in to the containers. He attacked her. She's banged her head."

"Where the fuck was Wyatt? He was meant to be loading his truck. And why haven't the alarms gone off?"

Reid goes on alert and gives me a look, wanting answers. I shake my head and move over to the truck that's already been emptied.

"I don't know. And Wyatt already loaded up the boxes and has left to pack up the house. She's really shaken up, Jax. You need to get home."

"On my way."

"What's happened?" Reid asks, not wasting any time.

"Tell you on the way," I tell him. "Fuck!" I turn back to the house just as Tim comes back out. "Tim, I need you to be in charge. We have a family emergency at home."

He wants to ask, but instead nods, knowing we often have to leave due to Paisley. "Of course. Call me and let me know everything is okay."

"Will do," I tell him and lift myself into the truck. On the way, I run down everything Mum said on the phone.

Reid looks at me. "Fuck! You know who's done this."

"Yeah," I say, not having a good feeling.

"Black," he bites out.

"Yep," I mutter through gritted teeth.

I'VE BARELY GOT the van into park before we're both out and rushing up to the house. The front door opens to Mum's worried expression. She's been crying and her hands are shaking.

"She's in the living room. Landon is on his way. He and his cousin were on their way to get some supplies for the spa."

The spa she's talking about is the building—or hut, as Paisley wants to call it—where clients can come for spa treatments. She really wants to make the place feel therapeutic, and what better way to do that than build a place to relax.

"We've got this, Mum. Did you call Wyatt?"

She nods, leading the way into the living area. "Yes. He and an acquaintance of yours are in the barn right now. They got back two minutes ago."

I nod, and when I walk in, Paisley has an icepack on her hand and a cloth on her head that I can see has blood already seeping through.

Shit!

Shit, shit, shit.

I kneel in front of her, gently pulling away the cloth. I suck in a breath. "It doesn't need stiches, but I can't be certain. You feeling okay?"

She sniffles, shaking her head. "My wrist hurts."

I let her put the cloth back on her head and move down to her wrist. I wince when I lift the towel of ice off her wrist. Already the swelling is bad, and bruising is appearing.

"I think you may have broken it," I tell her.

She clears her throat, and I know she's trying really hard to be brave. "Mum said it was sprained. Landon is going to be so pissed."

"He's not the only one. As soon as he gets here, we'll take you to the hospital. Something tells me he'll be pissed if we leave without him," I tell her, and she nods. "Can you talk me through what happened?"

She nods, putting the ice back over the swelling. "I remembered I still had those side tables in the container. Landon kept saying we needed something to put our drinks and remote on. Rex and Midnight keep knocking our drinks over on our coffee table," she starts, and I nod, because Rex, when he's with Midnight, can be a little hyper. He's a good dog though and the guests love him.

"Okay, so you went to get them?"

"Yeah. Landon said he would later, but we've been so busy with the bed and breakfast and him starting the spa. He wanted to get enough done before the weather turns bad. We've not spent much time together. I wanted one less thing for him to do, so when it was quiet, I decided to go over."

"Then what?" I ask when she starts to look dazed.

She shrugs. "I don't know. I put in the outdoor code and it wasn't working. I just thought someone was in there or you had turned it off. I didn't even think," she tells me on a hiccup. "It was the same with the main door. The system wasn't on. I should have called one of you. I'm so stupid."

"Hey, you weren't to know. It could have been anything," I tell her. I don't like seeing her worked up, and I hate that she's blaming herself. It's also not good for her health.

"I should have known," she repeats, stronger this time.

We have backup power on that side of the building. She wasn't to know that.

"What happened then?"

Mum walks back into the room, a cup of tea in her hand. She sits down next to Paisley and holds the cup out to her while holding the cloth with the other. "The bleeding has stopped. Try to drink some of this."

"Thanks, Mum," Paisley whispers.

Reid moves from my side and takes the seat on the other side, moving in close. "Tell us what happened next."

"I walked down to the end of the first hallway and turned right. As I reached the bit where I usually go left, I heard a noise down the right hallway. I looked down there but couldn't see anything. The lights were out," she tells us. "God, it's like a classic horror movie. You don't investigate the noise and you most certainly don't go down a dark hallway after hearing said noise. I was so fucking stupid."

"Why did you go down there?" Reid asks, and I know he's holding back his anger. Not because he's angry at Paisley, but at the situation.

"I was being nosey," she admits, her shoulders sagging.

"Being nosey?" I ask incredulously, then frown at her. "Please don't tell me you went down there to see if it was a celebrity."

Reid growls. "No," I whisper harshly.

Paisley blushes, leaning into Mum. "I'm sorry. I worked for years at Hayes Removals and you never told me who rented them due to confidentiality. I thought if I bumped into one, it'd be okay."

"Paisley," I sigh.

"I know; I'm sorry," she yells. "How was I meant to know someone was down there. And I didn't do it on purpose."

"All right, calm down and tell us the rest. You heard a *noise* and went to investigate."

Her eyes narrow on me. "I walked down there, and I heard metal clang on the floor. It could have been anything. I thought someone couldn't see so I turned on my phone light. I shouted, "Hey", in greeting and then the man looked up. I yelled it again but this time because I knew he was breaking in. He looked harmless. He was skinny, had glasses on, and was covered in acne. I didn't think. He went to run, and I grabbed his arm, trying to stop him."

"Paisley, why would you do that?" I say, stopping her.

"That was stupid."

She goes to move her hand and winces. "Trust me, I know. I'm sorry. He pushed me, harder than I thought he would. I banged my head on one of the container doors and fell on my wrist. I called Mum, and she came over. You know the rest."

"Did you recognise him? Maybe a guest at the bed and breakfast?" I ask.

She shakes her head. "No. Never seen him before."

A car door slams outside and Paisley looks up, her eyes going to the window. I watch in amazement as her entire body relaxes and the scared look on her face disappears. "Landon's home," she whispers.

"Paisley," Landon yells, running into the room. He takes one look at her and his entire expression hardens. His gaze comes to me. "You want to sort whatever is going on with your business or I fucking will. And if you find this guy, I'll deal with it."

"She's my sister and it's my business," I snap, standing up.

"Yeah? Then why the fuck is her head bleeding? Why is her wrist pressed against her chest? I know someone is fucking with you. Some fancy dickhead trying to take over. Why you haven't dealt with it, I don't know. But it ends now. Either by you doing it, or me. And you don't want that."

"Don't tell me how to look after my business and family, Landon. I won't give any fucks about showing you how much I don't like it."

"Like you could take me," he growls.

"Landon, Jaxon," Paisley calls, pain her voice. We both step away from each other and look down at her. "Please don't fight. This is my fault. Now, can you please take me to the hospital? My wrist really, really, hurts."

Landon gently helps her to her feet. "I'll take you. My car is outside."

"I thought you were with Maddox?" she asks him.

"I was. I drove because I needed to make a stop on the way back. He needed to get to another job."

She nods then turns to Mum. "Thank you so much, Mum. I don't know what I would have done if you weren't here."

I feel like I've been stabbed in the back. I should have been here. Fuck, my security shouldn't have been off. I should have had an alarm sent through to my phone. If I had upgraded when I was supposed to, then this might not have happened.

"Let me know when you're back," I tell her, kissing her forehead. Landon glares, but I ignore him, like always.

"Want me to come with you?" Reid asks.

Landon sneers at him. "No! You can wait here. I'm not waiting around while you find a nurse to fuck. You can see her when she's back."

"Fuck, man, she's our sister."

"She's my world," Landon roars back. "And I had a phone call with her sobbing and telling me someone hurt her."

"All right," Reid says quietly, stepping back.

Paisley leans further into him. "Landon," she whispers quietly. "I'm fine."

His expression softens when he looks down at her. "No, you're not. But you will be."

"My hero," she whispers, smiling dreamily at him.

I gag, looking away. "Just get to the hospital. Let us know what they say, and we will see you when you get back."

"I will. Thanks for coming back."

"Any time," I mutter and watch Landon lead her out.

They've not even made it to the car when Liam and Wyatt walk in, Wyatt's face tight.

"What you got?" I ask, getting straight to the point.

"Man, I wish it was under better circumstances. Whoever it was knew that system and bypassed it as easily as if he had a key to it all. He managed to turn off all the cameras, fucked up on the hallway lights, but not sure if he was meant to do that or not. He turned everything inside off. He got into two containers, just left them open and was working on the third when he was interrupted. Nothing has been taken, though you need to double check that. If

I were to guess, he was waiting until he had a few more open and was gonna take a couple of valuables out of each."

"How the fuck did he get through all of that? You said it was hard to breach."

"Mate, that was years ago, and I told you then that you'd need it upgraded every year. New tech, new methods, and better equipment. That dude has had years to learn that system. My guess is he's had a lot of practice at hacking into it."

"So, you're saying I fucked up?" I ask, wishing I could catch a break.

"Wouldn't put it like that. This guy… he knew what he was doing."

"Did you get anything to help us find him?"

"Not on the cameras I installed, but I noticed your old cameras on the house are facing the barn. Are they still connected?"

"Yeah," I tell him. "It's all stored downstairs."

"Go through today's tape. It will be on there. It had to have caught something. He walked right through the front door and left in a rush."

"Thank you."

"No problem. But, uh, he's fried your system too."

"How soon can you get one installed?"

He pauses, thinking it over. "I had a cancellation which is why I'm free now. Want me get started?"

"I'd owe you one," I tell him, meaning it.

"This one won't need updating for a few years. It's the best one I've ever used."

"Thanks."

"Mrs Hayes," I hear shouted.

"I'll let you sort that out," Liam says.

"I'll come with you," Wyatt tells him, and Liam gives him a chin lift.

"Mrs Hayes!"

Mum sighs in exasperation, glaring at the doorway as Earl, who owns the farm attached to the back of ours, walks in. He has to be in his eighties. He's been old for as long as I can remember. And is a mean son of a bitch.

"Mr Harvey, what can I help you with today?" Mum asks, pasting on a smile.

"What you can do is control those boys of yours. They've stolen my Pearl's Jeep."

I glance at Mum before watching Earl. "You saw the twins?"

The twins, Colton and Theo, are known to get into trouble. But it's rare they skip school. Since they started their new school for advanced kids, they've been enjoying the new challenges it's given them.

"Well, no, but those two are good for nothing. Always up in my farm causing mayhem. Hooligans is what they are."

"Now, Earl," Mum says in her 'mum' voice.

He doesn't look at her, so I step forward. "Earl, the twins are at school. They'd never skip to steal a car."

"It was them. I was checking the fence lines and I saw one running towards the farm. They broke my fence and smashed the Jeep's window. Then drove off."

I glance at Reid, and we both share the same look. It has to be the person who broke into here.

"Earl, do you have cameras on your farm?"

"Of course I don't. If I did, those boys would have been arrested."

"Fuck!"

Feeling the tension, he turns to Mum. "What's going on?"

"It wasn't the twins, Earl," she whispers. "Someone tried to break into the containers here on the farm and hurt Paisley when she caught them."

His face immediately hardens. "Low lives. I hope you called the police."

"Yeah. They're going to be by later to take Paisley's statement."

"All right. Sorry for the disturbance. I'd best go report my car missing."

I jerk my head in a nod. "We'll let you know when we find anything."

He lifts his chin. "Thank you."

"Why don't I walk you out," Mum tells him.

The minute they clear the room, I whirl on Reid. "Get everyone, including the twins, and try to find out who this person could be."

"The twins?" he asks in horror.

Yeah, the twins can be unpredictable at the best of times. "We need their computer skills. Maybe they can find out who he is."

"Then we fuck him up?"

"First, we need answers. If we're gonna get proof this is Black, we will need it."

"You aren't going to the police with this are you?" he asks, the word 'police' coming out like a bad taste in his mouth.

I grin at him. "Fuck no. But if I'm going to fuck someone up, I want to make sure it's the right person."

"Shit yeah." Reid grins, then rushes out to do as instructed. I kiss Mum on the cheek before heading over to Hayes Removals.

CHAPTER SEVEN

LILY

Mʏ ʜᴀɴᴅs sʜᴀᴋᴇ ᴀs I ᴅʀɪᴠᴇ ᴅᴏᴡɴ the lane towards the Hayes farmhouse and Hayes Removals. I passed the bed and breakfast and saw Landon's car in the mini carpark out front. I'm hoping he's too distracted to look out the window. I don't want him to spot me here. I know he won't like it.

However, I couldn't go another day without coming to say thank you to Jaxon. Twice in the past few weeks he's helped me. Both times he could have ignored since he and my family have differences.

But he didn't, and after hearing Maddox say those mean things to him, I know I need to do something. Maddox apologised to me, but it's not me he needs to say sorry to. It's Jaxon.

I'm nervous though. So nervous I feel like I'm going to hyperventilate. As I pull up outside behind a moving van, I put the car into park and shut it off. I grab my bag and the cake I baked from the passenger seat before getting out of the car.

I take a deep breath, looking at the huge building.

What am I doing? What if he isn't here? What if he doesn't want me here after everything that happened the other day?

I turn around, going back to the car. I can't do this.

"Lily? Is that you?" Wyatt, Jaxon's younger brother, calls.

I smile and greet him. "Hey, Wyatt."

"You leaving?" he asks, his eyebrows raised.

I look at my car, then back to him. "Um, yeah?"

He grins. "So, you pull up, then leave straight away? And is that a cake?"

I look down at the chocolate fudge cake in my hand, sucking my bottom lip. "Yeah."

"For me?"

Oh God. I shouldn't have come. What if he takes the cake before I have a chance to give it to Jaxon?

You aren't even in the building to give it to him.

I pull my shoulders back and shake my head, forcing out a nervous giggle. "No. Um, actually, I was wondering if Jaxon was here."

"Lucky fuck," he mumbles under his breath. "He's in the office, just through that door."

I look to the door he's pointing to and nod. "Thank you."

"Well, I'd best be off. Mum has finished dinner. Jaxon's working overtime. He has invoices to finish or something."

"Doesn't he have a receptionist?"

Wyatt grins. "Yeah, she quit and now owns the bed and breakfast."

I laugh and nod in understanding. I remember Maddox telling me about the fight at breakfast where Paisley quit. Or she quit before. I'm not sure. Why he was at breakfast with the Hayes family is beyond me. He came home with a black eye that day.

"I'll let you get dinner," I murmur.

"Nice seeing you."

"You too," I whisper back and stare up at the door, still unsure.

"You gonna stand there in the cold all night?" he asks from behind me, making me jump.

"Does he hate me?" I blurt out.

Confused, he shakes his head. "Lily, I don't think there's anyone on this earth who could hate you."

"Okay," I whisper.

"Go on up and get out of the cold," he tells me.

I take the first step, air filling my lungs. Opening the door, I step inside, finding a wide-open space with a huge window on the far end wall; squares of glass in a rusted frame. I don't know why but I find it beautiful. There's just something about it. And I bet it looks cool when it rains.

"Lily?" Jaxon calls, and I jump, forgetting why I was here.

I turn my head in the direction of his voice to find him getting up from his chair at a large desk. He looks tired, stressed.

Maybe now isn't the right time.

"Um, hi, I um…" I pause, taking in a deep breath. "I baked you a thank you cake."

His eyes warm and his lips pull into a smirk, but as quickly as it appeared, it disappears. "You didn't let Charlotte bake it, did you?"

I giggle, relaxing. "No. I want to say thank you."

"True," he mutters, eyeing the cake. "Would be hard if you killed me as a thank you."

I giggle again and hand him the cake. "I'm sorry about the other day. You were trying to help, and he said all that mean stuff to you."

Gently, he places the cake down before giving me his full attention. "You don't have to apologise to me. Ever." The fieriness in his voice has me nodding in agreement. Seeming satisfied with my reaction, he continues. "Are you okay? After the other day I mean?"

Feeling my cheeks heat, I admit, "Kind of. If anyone asks, I'm hunky dory."

"If anyone else asks?"

Feeling nervous, I begin to walk over to the window, running my finger along the edge. "Yeah. They love me and they mean well, but it can be too much sometimes."

I feel him rather than see him step up behind me. "And you don't want it to be too much," he guesses.

"No. They have done so much for me. All of them. And they continue to do it. I just don't want to be a burden." My eyes widen at what I just revealed. "I'm sorry. That was way too much information."

He takes my hand and goose-bumps rise on my arm, and my stomach flutters. "Baby," he murmurs softly, and those flutters go wild at hearing him call me that, "you could never be a burden. And you can talk to me about anything."

I glance at him from the corner of my eyes, blushing when I see him focusing intently on me. "Thank you."

"You didn't say. Did you get it sorted, whatever was wrong?"

I take in a deep breath and face him. "No—maybe. I don't know. My uncle Myles is looking into it."

"Are you okay with telling me what it was about?"

I deflate when he lets go of my hand to lean casually against the window. "There's a little girl in my class—Star. She started in September, and there's just been something about her. Call it good instinct, call it intuition, or call it knowing from my own experience. I just knew she was being hurt at home. At first, it was little things I'd pick up on; her reluctance to make friends, behind in her education and always withdrawn and distant in class. Then it was because her brother was the only person I saw drop her off or pick her up. He'd turn up with bruises all the time. I reported it to the headteacher, but he said I was being judgemental. She was wearing dirty clothes with holes in them. They were far too small, so I asked permission to buy her new ones as a donation."

I wipe under my eye, pausing before I make another fool of myself.

"It's okay," he tells me gently, taking my hand once again. It gives me strength to continue.

"I noticed she was hurt so I went to him. When I got nothing, I went to my uncle Myles."

"What did he say?"

"That he'd look into it," I tell him, shrugging. "But on Monday, her brother was late picking her up. Later than usual. I got her to help me pick up toys because she had been more withdrawn than normal from the beginning. Every time I looked at her, she would look close to tears. Anyway, she cried out when she tried to lift a box of paints, and I lifted up her top to reveal her stomach. She had huge bruises. One was the tip of trainer print."

"Fucking hell," Jax whispers harshly. "Let me guess, the headteacher ignored it again, and because you laid a hand on a kid, even if it was out of concern, you got into shit."

My eyes fill with tears because he gets it. "Yes."

"Dickhead."

Shocked, I begin to giggle. "I wouldn't ever call him that, but between you and me," I tell him, before leaning in and whispering, "he is one."

He laughs, pulling his hand back, and I miss it. I miss the warmth and how it makes me feel.

"You'll get it sorted, Lily. Your family would do anything for you."

I soften my features. "I know."

From the corner of my eye, I notice the clock on the wall and realise the time. Sugar. "I'd best be going," I tell him, not really wanting to go.

"What are you doing?" he asks suddenly, then looks embarrassed he asked. "Sorry, too nosey."

I giggle and shake my head. "It's not. I'm going to get some food and then watch a movie. I find not working is boring. I didn't know what to do with myself all day, so I decided to treat myself."

"On your own?" he asks, shocked.

Slowly, I nod. "Yes."

"I'll come with you."

"You will?" I squeak out.

"Yeah. I'll follow you back to yours in my car, and I'll drive."

I bite my lip and look away. "I don't know," I tell him, dragging my words out.

His hand squeezes my bicep. "Hey, no one will know. Come on, what better way to thank me than to let me take you to the cinema? In fact, I can't remember the last time I went. Mum makes us have movie nights at home. Does that count?"

Gasping, I look up at him with wide eyes. "It's completely different. Totally different. They have these cool chairs now that recline so you don't get back ache."

"Or bum ache?"

I giggle, yet nod, because he is not wrong. "Yes. And you get popcorn, iceblasts, the works."

"Sounds like a deal then."

"What about my family?" I blurt out.

His expression softens. "They don't need to know, Lily. And if by any chance they see us, I'll duck for cover. I know you don't like conflict."

"I don't. I hate hearing the stories about you all fighting."

He grins. "Don't be. They keep life interesting."

"You really want to come?"

"I really do," he tells me, and his eyes dilate a little when he says it. More flutters, more goose-bumps.

"Okay then. I'll go wait in the car."

"Be out in five."

I walk back to the door, excited and a little scared about spending time with him. With my hand on the door handle, I remember why I came.

"Jaxon?"

"Yeah?"

I glance over my shoulder at him. "Thank you. Not just for the other day, but for the kitchen sink. And for lying to Maddox. You knew he'd cause a scene and you lied for me."

"Lily, I'd do anything for you," he tells me heatedly, then turns back to his desk.

Stunned and somewhat confused, I head outside. What did he mean by that? And why is my heart racing so much?

I look back towards the door, my lips parted in surprise. "I wasn't hearing things. He really did say that," I whisper to myself.

My phone chimes in my pocket, and I pull it out.

MADDOX: Movie later?

I bite my lip, contemplating what I should do. I glance back at the door, seeing Jaxon through the small window. I want to spend time with him, but I also don't like lying to my family or letting Maddox down. He's my best friend, aside from Faith. If he found out, he'd be so mad at me.

It's Jaxon though.

For once, I'm going to take a chance. A chance on Jaxon, a chance on life.

ME: Feeling a little under the weather. Tomorrow?

MADDOX: I'll make you soup.

ME: It's that time of the month.

I bite my lip harder. If there's one thing that can clear Maddox from a room or shut him up, it's the 'time of the month' talk.

MADDOX: Just remembered I promised Madison I'd spend time with her.

Madison is his twin sister. Both are polar opposites but the best people I know, and he loves spending time with her.

It still doesn't make this any better.

"You ready?" Jaxon calls, swinging his keys around.

Feeling off balance, still shocked I'm going out with Jaxon Hayes, I can only nod.

"We should get food after. It's late, so last showings will start soon."

I hadn't thought of that. "Okay, Jaxon."

He opens my car door for me, his warm eyes meeting mine. "Jump in then."

My muscles feel stiff as I bend down into the car. "You'll follow me home?"

His gaze softens. "Yeah, baby."

With a nod, he steps back, and I shut the car door. I turn the car around and wait for him.

I'm grinning from ear to ear.

THE PARKING LOT has emptied somewhat since we arrived, yet people are still parking up and heading off to who-knows-where. The night is cold and a layer of ice dusts the screens of the cars. I'm grateful Jaxon came now. I hate driving in snow or rain.

I cast a look at Jaxon and a giggle slips free at his expression. He pouts—

yes, pouts—and lightly bumps his shoulder with mine.

"Don't laugh. Next time, I'm picking the movie."

My heart jumps at his claim that there will be a next time, and my stomach flutters because it's something I really, really want.

"It was a good movie," I tell him, trying to keep the laughter from my tone but failing.

"It was Mary Poppins, babe," he mutters dryly.

I giggle again. "And it was good. Not as good as the original, but still good nonetheless."

He grins and shakes his head. "Got a dick, babe. If my brothers find out I just spent two hours watching that, I'll get shit. For the rest of my life."

"No, they wouldn't. I bet if they watched it, they would love it," I tell him.

He throws his head back and laughs. "Babe, you're funny."

"I wasn't joking."

He takes one look at me and laughs harder. "Come on, let's get something to eat."

I look up at the restaurant we're about to go in, only to find it closed. "It's closed."

"Crap! I should have checked what time it closed," he says, looking around the area. There's a lot of places here. The cinema, Nando's, a bowling alley and a few other restaurants, all of which must have closed at ten. It's now eleven.

"It's okay. We can just go through a drive-through," I assure him.

We walk over to his car, and he stops at the passenger door. "Wait, the pizza place in town is open till three in the morning. We can grab something from there."

Oh no! I know which pizza place he's talking about and it's right next to a club.

"Um, I'm sure the drive-through is closer."

"Come on, it's only five minutes away."

Not wanting to put a downer on the night, I slowly get into the car, my palms already beginning to sweat.

This is not good.

CHAPTER EIGHT.

LILY

I THOUGHT I COULD DO THIS, but I can't. Jaxon turns onto the road I know the pizza place is on. It's also on the same road as one of the busiest clubs around here.

I see them the minute we hit the street. Loads of lads and men staggering, shouting and singing. One falls into the road.

I inhale through my nose, trying to calm my breathing. My vision begins to blur and dots dance in front of my eyes.

Please, not now. Not here.

Blinking, I start to focus. A guy shoves another guy into the road and those black spots dance in front of my vision.

"Can we go?" I whisper, but Jaxon doesn't hear me. He's concentrating on not running anyone over.

A startled scream escapes me when someone taps on my window, laughing at my reaction. I lean forward, gripping my hair as a headache starts to form.

"One, two, three," I chant quietly, breathing through it, but it's no use. Memories surface and distantly, I hear my name called.

At first, I thought it was fun. He sat me in the chair and began to spin me. I squealed out, thinking he was being nice. Then he started spinning me faster and it scared me. I clung to the chair, my arms hurting.

"Stop, I don't like it."

He laughs, drinking the horrible tasting drink again. Suddenly, he pushes the chair over to his mate, who laughs hard. He's drinking water, but still acts like Richard when he drinks those cans.

"Drink this, sweet girl," he murmurs, and the back of my neck prickles. It's the way he always watches me; it makes me scared. He scares me.

When I don't take the drink, he squeezes my cheeks together and tips the liquid into my mouth. It burns my throat, and I start to cough.

He and Richard laugh harder. "Martin, spin her again," Richard hoots.

I feel dizzy, the room spinning around me. Martin pushes me away, and I come to a jolt next to Richard. He forces his drink down my throat and I gag, right before I vomit all over him.

"You silly fucking brat," he yells, smacking me off the chair. Pain radiates through my cheek. He gets up and I crawl away, crying. "You need teaching a lesson."

"Put her back on the chair," Martin snaps, and before I have a chance to move, his hands are under my armpits and he's sitting me in the chair. "Watch this."

"Fucking bitch has ruined a good T-shirt," Richard snaps.

"Please, no!" I plead when he forces me to sit, slapping my legs.

"Stay there or I'll make it worse," Martin snaps at me, and the hardness in his eyes and his tone has me listening. I don't want it to be worse than this. This is already worse. I want my teddy. I want my blanket on the floor.

He walks around to the back of the chair and rocks it back and forth. I feel dizzy and sick again. I grip the arms of the chair, and when he lets go, after pushing with so much force I feel my hair blow back, I cry out.

Richard and Martin start laughing again, and I can see why when the chair crashes down the step. I fly out of the chair and onto the hard floor, and I scream at the pain in my arm.

"Lily!" is screamed in my face, hands shaking my shoulders.

I blink rapidly and find myself still in the car but no longer in the passenger seat. I'm cuddled up to Jaxon. Heat rises in my cheeks.

Outside the window, I notice we're no longer on a busy street but in an empty carpark.

"Where are we?" I rasp out, my throat feeling raw. Embarrassment washes over me, and I timidly look up at Jaxon. "I was screaming, wasn't I?"

His face is pale, and his hold tightens on me. "What happened back there? What did I do?"

"It was nothing you did," I tell him quietly, going stiff in his arms.

I feel his attention on me, but I can't bear to look at him. "It wasn't me. But it was. It was me driving down town to the pizza place. All those drunk people," he whispers harshly. "Fuck!"

It takes some strength, but I manage to turn in his arms. "Jaxon, this wasn't your fault. It happens. More than I like. I should have told you why I didn't want to go down there."

"Yeah, babe, you should have. I don't ever want to see you like that again," he tells me, his voice rough.

It hurts hearing that and my stomach sinks. "Jaxon, it happens all the time. I can't stop them."

"What is it?"

I shrug, looking down at my lap. "Flashbacks. PTSD. It could be a number of things that trigger it."

"Flashbacks?" he asks, sounding unsure.

"From before I moved in with my mum and dad."

"Babe, you're gonna have to explain."

"I never talk about it," I tell him quietly.

He cups my cheek, tilting my head so I'm facing him. "You don't have to tell me anything you don't want to. But, Lily, I want you to. Not because I'm nosey, but because I want to get to know you better."

"You want to get to know me better?"

He grins, tucking a stand of hair behind my ear. "Yeah, I want to get to know you better."

"And what if you don't like what you find?" I ask him honestly. It's one of my biggest fears; that someone will realise how broken I am and then won't want anything to do with me. I'm worried they'll see I'm not worth the effort.

"Take a chance, Lily. Take a chance on me," he tells me in an almost demanding way.

I inhale and square my shoulders. "What would you like to know?"

He scans my face before relaxing. "Tell me what you mean about your mum and dad."

"I'm adopted," I admit, watching his face turn into shock. I give him a small smile. It's the expression I always imagined people would have at the news.

"Explain a little bit more, babe, because you look just like your dad. I don't get how you could be adopted."

"And uncles," I finish for him, giving him a pointed look.

He shakes his head, not getting it. "Still unsure of where this is going."

"Dad is actually my brother, so are my uncles, obviously," I share, hoping I'm doing the right thing by confessing all of this to him. I don't like sharing personal business. "It's something I really don't want to get into, not in detail, but they didn't know about me. When they did, Dad saved me right away. He and Mum adopted me, and ever since then I've been his daughter and my uncles' niece."

I say it so plainly, like it's no big deal. And it's not to me. Other people might find it hard to wrap their head around, but to me, it was the best thing to ever happen to me. I needed them in my life, and I would have taken them as brothers, uncles or my dad. I was just lucky enough to get them as my dad and uncles.

"Um, that's... wow," he stutters. "How? How did things not get confusing?"

"I don't know. I was young, but I felt double my age. I had gone through things, knew things no other kid that age should." Seeing the look on his face, I continue. "I had a long adjustment period, but it wasn't because of them. It was because of me and my past. It took me a while to believe I belonged. Dad gifted me with a family, so I took it."

"But you were already family," he points out, his tone gentle. "Was it not weird at all?"

I smile at him. "Yeah, we were, but I never had a mum or a dad. My birth mum wasn't a nice person, and I never knew who my biological dad was. Dad gave me everything. He gave me four strong, loyal uncles who would lay down their life for me. They never failed to make me laugh and, in the beginning, it was hard to even smile. I was too scared.

"Dad gave me a mum who was gentle and kind. Before bed, she would brush my hair, read me a book, then tuck me in and kiss me goodnight. She would ask me what I wanted to eat, if I was thirsty, and check if I was warm enough. And then there was Faith," I tell him, feeling a soft smile play at my lips. "I didn't even realise how much I needed someone like her in my life until I met her in the hospital. She was banged up from an accident that happened the night the social workers rescued me, but she was so cheery and full of life. She gave me her toys and told me all about the prince she was going to marry when she grew up. She described in detail every little thing we would do together. She gave me hope. So, it wasn't weird. It was never forced on me and no one blinked or agued when Dad said he was adopting me. Although, I did hear later that my uncle Max asked why it couldn't be him."

"And does all your family know you're adopted?"

"Yeah. My past—even though I don't talk about it—is something everyone needed to know. There were times I couldn't handle being around certain people, and as they grew older, they never understood why. They didn't get why I was scared of alcohol, why I couldn't stand doors being shut or why I freaked out when someone touched me unexpectedly."

When I'm done, I look up at him. I'm struck by the way he's looking at me. Not with pity or horror, but something else, maybe in awe?

"Why are you staring at me like that?" I ask on a shaky whisper.

"You really are the purest soul I've ever met, Lily Carter. I can't imagine the life you led before if it means your face gets soft because someone put a brush through your hair. Everything running through my mind is bad, but something tells me what I'm thinking doesn't even come close to what you went through.

"I see the sorrow in your eyes. I see the pain you bear as if your mind is speaking those thoughts out loud to me. And yet, here you are; soft-hearted, generous, and warm. So if you're wondering why I'm looking at you the way I am, it's because I'm staring at a unicorn. You, Lily Carter, amaze me in the best possible way."

Warmth fills my chest at his words.

"Jaxon," I whisper, too stunned to say anything else. I struggle with what to do. I'm still lying across his lap, my head resting against his arm and the window.

He kisses my forehead, his lips soft yet pressing hard against my skin. "Do you want to talk about what your flashback was about?"

Ice fills my veins. "My childhood before being adopted wasn't good, Jaxon. I really don't like reliving it in my memories, and I can't talk about it without it bringing more memories back."

"Okay, baby. I get it," he says softly, rubbing his hand up and down my arm. "But can I ask you to think about something?"

"Think about what?" I ask, catching my breath when his gaze turns intense.

"I want you to think about telling me," he says, and I open my mouth to refuse but he places his finger across my lips. "I don't know if you're cottoning on to what is happening here between us, but I want you to be able trust me enough to talk about anything. I want to be the person you can confide in."

My lips part. "What are you saying?"

He looks down at me, running his fingers through my hair. "I'm saying I want us to get to know each other."

"As friends?"

His lips pull into a smirk as he leans down closer, his breath fanning across my face. "No, Lily, not as friends."

My eyes widen and my entire body freezes. He wants to be more than friends. What do I say to that? When he leans down further, my eyes widen for another reason and I pull back, banging my head on the window.

Ouch!

He was going to kiss me.

I think.

"Sorry, Lily," he says, his expression apologetic.

"I don't know how to kiss," I practically yell in his face. I don't want him to feel guilty for wanting to kiss me. Not when I want him to. I'm just scared.

I groan, burying my face into his shirt. I cannot believe I just said that out loud.

His body begins to shake, and I pull back, feeling close to tears with embarrassment when I see him laughing.

I go to get off him, but he pulls me back against him. "Kind of figured that out, babe. But you didn't need to scream it at me."

"I'm so sorry," I stress, feeling hot all over.

"It's not rocket science," he tells me.

"What isn't?"

"Kissing," he replies, then leans in closer. "I can teach you."

I want that more than anything. I've never imagined kissing anyone, never crossed my mind. Jaxon, however, makes me want everything. I want what Faith has, what Aiden and Landon have. And I can see me having that with Jaxon.

I never understood what I felt all those times in his presence until he showed up in my kitchen to help with my sink. I liked seeing him there, in my space, which is very rare. After that day, I couldn't stop thinking about him. Then he held me that day after the incident at school happened. What I felt for him… it was like it expanded. Now I think about him all the time. In the shower, in bed, making breakfast, even when my parents are talking to me. He's constantly on my mind.

"Okay," I whisper, feeling my stomach tighten with nerves when he moves closer. My eyes flutter closed when he's a mere breath away.

"Just follow my lead," he whispers against my lips.

His lead? We aren't dancing. And what if I get it wrong? What if I stick my tongue in too far and make him choke? Or God, worse. What if I have bad breath? I did eat a lot of popcorn at the cinema.

All thoughts flee when I feel his lips pressing against mine. My entire body goes solid, but his hand at my waist begins to rub small, smooth circles.

"Relax," he whispers, pulling back a tad.

Cautiously, he presses his warm lips against mine once more. I thought books exaggerated about how good it feels to be kissed, but blood heats through my veins, my stomach does somersaults, and my heart races a mile a minute. I gasp and grip his shoulder when his tongue runs across my bottom lip, my taught body relaxing. I pull back, my lashes lowering as I take in his sensuous mouth.

This time, I move, braving our first kiss. I know it's more than this. I'm not that naive. I've watched movies and read a lot of books. I follow his lead and lick his bottom lip like he did mine. He makes a noise in the back of his throat and tingles spread down to my core.

I gasp in shock when his tongue caresses mine. It's not gross like I thought it would be. Our tongues entwine and he presses his lips harder against mine.

His hand is warm and gentle when he cups my jaw before running his fingers up into my hair.

A noise escapes up the back of my throat as he deepens the kiss. Just as I think I'm beginning to get the hang of it, he pulls back, breathing heavily. My heart is just as bad, my chest rising and falling.

Slowly, I open my eyes and stare into the depth of his forest green ones.

"Wow," I whisper, and his face softens.

"Yeah, wow."

I know my smile is big because my face begins to ache. I want to do it again. And again. Okay, maybe all the time. Who knew kisses could be like that?

"Let's go get a McDonalds, then I'll drop you home," he tells me, his voice quiet, like he's scared to ruin the moment.

"I could eat McDonalds," I murmur, not looking away from him. I'm still in shock, I think. I kissed someone, for the first time. I kissed Jaxon.

Oh God.

I kissed Jaxon Hayes.

My family are so going to kill me.

"What's wrong?" he asks, sitting us up straighter.

"What are we going to do? My family will go mad," I tell him, feeling emotion clog my throat.

"Let's take one step at a time. This has just begun," he soothes.

He's right. And I'm acting like we're getting married tomorrow. But I want this. I want to be with him. I didn't know I wanted or was ready for this kind of relationship. But I don't want to give it up. I'm excited for what our future holds. What my future holds.

"One step at a time," I repeat, realising everything has happened quickly.

"Why don't we start off as friends. Get to know each other," he offers, reading my expression wrong.

"But still kiss?" I blurt out, not hiding the hope in my voice.

He chuckles deep. "Yeah, we can kiss."

I relax against him. "Then I'm okay with getting to know each other."

"Let's go get some food," he says and helps me off his lap and back into the passenger seat. I can't stop smiling, and I have the urge to get my phone and text Faith. She will know what I should do next.

I lose my smile for a split second, worried she won't take it well. She'll worry and talk me out of it, but in the end, I know she will be happy for me.

With that thought in my mind, I text her and tell her to come to mine after she finishes work tomorrow. She will know what to do.

CHAPTER NINE

LILY

A SMILE LIGHTS UP MY FACE WHEN MY phone beeps. I race over to my kitchen counter to open up the text message.

JAXON: Hey, beautiful, you still on for later? X

Jaxon and I exchanged numbers last night when he dropped me off. As soon as I got into bed, my phone lit up with a message from him asking to see me today.

LILY: Of course. Did you want to go out or eat in? Xx

JAXON: As long as I'm with you, I don't mind what we do. X

A low squeal escapes my lips as I read his reply.

LILY: I'll cook dinner. Xx

JAXON: Please don't take this the wrong way, but you can cook, can't you? You don't get your skills from Charlotte, do you? Because she gave me food poisoning one year at Family of the Year. X

I burst out laughing because I remember that year. Everyone had tried to avoid Charlotte's dish, but one girl thought Charlotte's looked better than hers, so she swapped their dishes. It didn't end well for anyone.

LILY: I can cook. I promise. Xx

JAXON: See you later, baby. I need to get back to work. X

LILY: Have a good day. Xx

JAXON: I will now I've spoken to you. X

I sigh, placing my phone down on the counter. He's coming here later. Here, in my home.

"You're just jealous you don't have my tits. They don't hang south like yours, Blanche."

My eyes widen at the sound of Hayden's voice. I run down the hallway and open the front door.

"Hayden," I greet, noticing Faith behind her, shaking her head. She's amused.

"Hello, Miss North," she greets my neighbour.

Blanche grunts and heads back inside. I panic about Hayden being here. I should have told Faith I wanted to speak to just her.

My hands begin to sweat as I think of something else to bring up in conversation. I can't talk to Faith with Hayden here, not about Jaxon.

"Hey, you coming for lunch too?" I ask softly.

Hayden turns away from Blanche's home and my eyes widen a touch at the top she's wearing.

"Hayden, would you like to borrow a jumper?"

She rolls her eyes and pulls up her low-cut tank top, her boobs nearly popping out. Her leather jacket reaches just below her breasts and the sleeves only reach her elbows. She must be freezing.

"No. I popped by quickly to see if you had any instant pasta I could have," she asks.

"Sure. But why do you want some?"

"Charlotte wants me to go to the library for lunch. Something to do with meeting the new girl she has on trial. Wants me to feel her out."

Faith chokes, looking at Hayden in horror. "And she asked you?"

Hayden narrows her gaze on Faith, and I gulp, stepping back. "And why wouldn't she?"

"Um, I don't know, because you'll scare the girl half to death."

"No, I won't," she snaps.

Faith rolls her eyes. "Yes, you will. You scared away all your babysitters, Hayden."

"No, I didn't. Dad did."

"Really?" Faith asks in shock.

"Really. And yes, maybe we played a few tricks on them, but Dad scared us into it. He said they kept checking him out and Mum would have to watch her back. Then there was the time one ate some chocolate bars and he lost his shit. The next time she came he told us she wanted to eat all our treats."

I look wide-eyed to Faith. Uncle Max really took babysitting seriously. "I'll go get your pasta," I tell her and gesture for them to follow me inside.

"Does Charlotte not have food in the library? Why won't she go into the coffee shop; she owns it?" Faith muses out loud from behind me.

"She's banned from the coffee house. Apparently, the smell of coffee and freshly baked scones makes her think she's Gordan Ramsey. She nearly burned it down last week," Hayden informs us. I remember the message shared about that news. It makes me worry for Charlotte being alone with kitchen appliances. "And I'm not eating anything she cooks. If I bring something with me, I can tell her I'm craving it."

I reach up into the top cupboard and pull down a pack of pasta you cook in a cup. "Here you go."

"Thanks. Sorry I can't stop. I really do need to get going. I'm already a little late," she tells us.

"Have fun," I offer.

"Catch ya later."

My phone beeps from the kitchen side, and I rush over to it, smiling wide when I see it's another text from Jaxon.

JAXON: Do you want me to bring something with me? I forgot to ask earlier. X

LILY: No, just yourself. Xx

JAXON: I can't stop thinking about you. X

I melt at his words. I can't stop thinking about him either. Do I tell him that, though? I don't like the thought of him not knowing. What if he thinks I don't like him or think of him either? What if he thinks I'm being too forward? Some guys tuck tail and run when a girl expresses her feelings.

Going with my gut instinct, I text him back.

LILY: I can't stop thinking of you either. Xx

He sends back a love heart, and I hold my phone to my chest, treasuring it.

"Okay, girl, spill. What has that big smile on your face?"

I jump, forgetting Faith was still here. "I met someone," I blurt out, coming to stand closer to the round counter that sits in the middle of my kitchen.

Faith looks shocked, her mouth opening and closing.

"I really like him," I tell her when she doesn't say anything.

"Who?"

I quickly move over to the fridge and grab us both a bottle of water. When I turn back, she's watching me curiously.

"I don't want to say who just yet. I don't want anyone else knowing either," I tell her, giving her a pointed look.

She tilts her head to the side. "I won't tell anyone, Lily. There has to be a reason you're hiding this from the family."

"There is," I rush out, but then hold my hands up to stop her when she goes to say something. "And it's nothing bad. I just want this for myself. Just for the time being."

"How long has this been going on?" she asks, stunned.

"A day," I admit sheepishly.

Her eyes practically bug out of their sockets. "A day? Lily, how did you meet someone in a day? I think we should tell Aiden and Mark. They could look into this guy."

"No," I squeal, placing my hand on hers when she goes for her phone. "It's Jaxon!"

"Jaxon?" she asks, then shakes her head. "Jaxon Hayes?"

I bite my lip and pull my hands back. "Yes. And please hear me out. I really like him, Faith. Like, *really* like him."

She doesn't look convinced. "I guessed you had some sort of crush on him at school, and I've seen the way you watch each other when we've bumped into them."

"He watched me?" I ask excitedly.

"You really do like him?" she breathes out.

I nod in delight. "I do. Faith, he barged into the house when I broke my sink, thinking I was hurt. He didn't care that he was breaking and entering. Then he helped me. And the other day when I had that incident after work… He was there. He was so attentive and caring. Then yesterday, I went to thank him, and we ended up going to the cinema and McDonalds. I've never had so much fun in my life, Faith. And I had an episode and he didn't look at me like I was a freak," I rush out, and watch different emotions run over her face.

"Lily," she drawls out, like she's trying to think of what to say.

"He kissed me," I whisper, sighing dreamily. "Time froze for me, Faith. It was tender yet demanding. Soft yet hard. It made me feel like I could fly. And he liked it too."

"But… Jaxon Hayes?"

"He's not what you guys make him out to be," I say, feeling a little hurt she'd think otherwise.

She places a hand over mine. "I'm not saying he's a bad person, Lil. I'm just worried what will happen when everyone finds out. They won't take the news well."

"But they will when they see how happy he makes me," I tell her, praying I'm right.

"It's been a day, Lily. Not even that. A night. And how do you think you can hide this from everyone?"

I can feel frustrated tears rise to the surface. "I just know. I feel it inside here," I pat my chest. "I know this is right," I tell her, feeling hysteria rising in my throat. "I've never asked for anything. Anything, Faith. I'm asking you to trust me now."

"I do trust you."

"No, you don't. Because you'd realise not once have I ever given anyone a chance before. No one besides family. I never let people get close."

"You have friends, Lily."

I shake my head. "No, I don't. I know people, yes, but have you ever seen any of them come to my home? Do I go to theirs?"

"You went by Gina's a few weeks ago," she mentions.

Gina was someone I went to college with. We happened to be in the same study group. "I was taking her a gift for the baby. It would have been rude not to bring them something."

I can see it's sinking in. "Lily," she says softly.

"I told him a bit about my past," I tell her.

She rears back in shock, looking at me in a new light. I've never really spoken in detail to Faith about it. Maddox knows a little more, but it's only Dad and Mum who know it all.

"You told him?"

"Not all of it. Not even a blip. But I still spoke to him about it."

"Are you sure about this?"

Nodding, I squeeze her hand. "I am. I never thought of a relationship before. Look at how many times I was asked out during school and after. I didn't say yes to any of them, did I?"

"True. I'm just worried. This is Jaxon we're talking about."

I give her a small smile. "Faith, we had so much fun together. And he texted me as soon as he got home to say goodnight, and again first thing this morning. He agreed to keep it quiet until I'm ready. He said we can get to know each other first."

Her face scrunches up. "What does he mean by get to know each other? I hope he doesn't mean he can come around whenever he likes, do the, uh, business, and then leave. I'm not cool with that and you shouldn't be either."

I laugh yet feel my cheeks heating. "He means getting to know each other, as in, getting know each other. Not that other stuff." I can feel my cheeks become hotter before the next words even leave my lips. "And I'm not ready for, um… that part of a relationship. Like you said, we're a day old," I tell her playfully, using the same words she used earlier.

She laughs, then pulls me in for a hug. "You're teasing me. You never tease me," she says, then pulls back to look at me, really look at me. "You really do want this."

I nod and quietly reply. "I do."

"Hag, I don't got time for this," we hear yelled.

"Wait!" we hear Blanche screech, and the sound of panic in her voice has me running to the curtain.

I look out, and the instant it registers what is going on, my entire body tenses. Star and Miah Merin are outside Blanche's house. Star looks shaken up and is clinging to her brother's leg. He looks just as bad, and his face is bruised and swollen.

"Oh my God," I whisper, and before Faith can stop me, I run out of the house. "Star?"

Star glances at me, her eyes widening with surprise. "Miss Carter."

"Fucking great!" Miah hisses, turning his angry scowl my way.

"Miss Carter?" the man they are with slowly grits out, his voice sending a shiver up my spine. His gaze runs over every inch of my body as he takes a drag of his fag. I rub up and down my arms, feeling dirty and unclean. "You're the uptight bitch I have to thank for this shit?"

"What's going on?" I ask to anyone, then look down at Star. "Are you okay?"

"How do you know these children?" Blanche asks me. I look up to find her pale and shaken.

"Star is my student," I inform her. She nods, still in a daze.

"Like I said, I need the money," the man snaps, looking at Blanche now. His dark hair is thick with grease, his clothes not much better than the kids'. His teeth are rotten, yellow, and his skin worn and wrinkled.

Faith stands beside me and squeezes my hand.

"I don't have any money, boy, and even if I did, why would I give it you and my daughter. You took her away from me fifteen years ago."

He snorts. "Your waste of space daughter is fucking dead. Has been since she gave birth to brat two."

I gasp at his harsh words, tears filling my eyes when Blanche wobbles on her feet. "Blanche," I call out, reaching for her.

"Nelly? My Nelly? She's dead?"

"Look, bitch, I got to get out of town. I need the fucking money. I got two kids to feed and Nell always said you were good for it."

"Nellie," Blanche whispers, clutching her chest.

"Like you feed us," Miah snaps.

"You mouthing off?" the man growls, taking a step towards Miah, his hand raised.

Oh no.

I move quickly, hearing Faith call out my name, but I ignore her warning. He is not going to hurt these kids again. I won't let him.

My feet slide on the grass as I step in front of Miah. The back of their dad's hand connects with my cheek, and I fly backwards onto the floor.

Too familiar angry vibes fly at me, and I cower backwards, knocking into Miah's legs. I struggle to breathe, looking up at the menacing man above me.

I can't breathe. I gasp for air and vaguely feel Faith bend down beside me. She's saying something, but I can't focus on anything but the man in front of me, looming above.

His head jerks, and I imagine he scoffed or snorted. He looks at me like I'm something he stepped in before flicking his fag at me.

I scream. I scream so loud I feel it all the way down the back of my throat and in my chest. It burns and it's raw.

But memories I know all too clearly come flying back, and I roll to the ground on my side, clutching my head.

I whimper and cover my ears as the music in the next room blares, hurting my ears. I don't feel well. My tummy hurts and I feel dizzy.

The door bangs open, cracking a hole in the wall. I jump, sitting up and wrapping the blanket around me.

"Mummy?"

She's not walking straight. She has a glass bottle in one hand and something that smells funny in her mouth. Usually when she has that, she's kind of nice. She leaves me alone and laughs a lot with Richard.

"Get up. A friend wants to see you."

"Mummy, I don't feel well."

Her eyes narrow on me as she stomps over and slaps me around the face. "Don't call me mummy. Not at home. Only in front of those fancy suit people."

"I don't feel well," I cry out as she drags me up off the floor.

"You'll do as you're fucking told," she screams, and before I can tell her I will do anything, she puts the thing in her mouth on my back. I scream, crying out in pain as my skin burns. She pulls me up, dragging me out of the room. "You need to toughen up."

"What's going on here?"

I freeze when I hear Richard's voice and try to cower behind Mummy. She doesn't let me, pushing me in his direction. His grips my arms painfully, and I bite my lip to stop myself from crying out.

"Misbehaving again. Taught the girl a lesson," she tells him, sitting down between two men. They both watch me, their eyes looking at me all over. I don't know why, but I know these men are worse. They'll hurt me more.

"What'd you do?" Richard asks, his beady eyes never leaving mine. I cower and glance down at my bare feet.

"Put me spliff out on her back. Won't fucking moan again," Mummy laughs.

"Did you like it?" Richard asks me, blowing the same foul smoke in my face. I cough, making him laugh. "Maybe she wants some."

"It will calm her down," the new man speaks up.

I shake my head when he brings the white paper to my lips. "Take it," he yells. I keep shaking my head. I don't like it when they blow it in my face. I'm too scared to do what they tell me to do. I don't like how the drinks they make me drink taste either.

He backhands me to the floor before leaning over me, grinning. "You'll pay," he says, and I crouch into a ball just as he brings the burning paper down on my back.

CHAPTER TEN

JAXON

"I DID TELL YOUR MUM NOT TO bother you, that you were busy working," Granddad mutters, squeezed in at the end of the van by Reid. Wyatt snorts next to me. Mum wouldn't care if I was in the middle of CPR. If one of the family needed something, we had to be there.

"She doesn't care, Granddad. And we had another last-minute cancellation anyway. It's all good."

While they chat about ways to get more business, I tune them out, my mind wandering to Lily. I'm hoping to get a quick glimpse of her before tonight. I just need another fill. Tonight can't come quick enough. It's not classed as stalking if I just happen to bump into her. I mean, my granddad lives next door.

Last night was one of the best nights of my life. I keep seeing her big, doe eyes staring up at me. Her voice, her laugh, and the sweet scent of her skin.

I hadn't even meant to kiss her, but it was like time froze when she stared up at me. That one look held so much trust. She was stunningly beautiful, and I had to kiss her. I was drawn to her.

A small chuckle escapes my lips—slipping the boys' notice—when I think of how she moved away and blurted out that she couldn't kiss. I wasn't expecting it. At first, I thought I was being rejected. She's always been too good for someone like me and it was like a harsh reminder for that split second. Then those words slipped free and I couldn't have been more relieved in my life.

Fuck, she was sexy as hell when she was being cute. I could still taste her on my lips when I woke up this morning. I've not had a moment where I've not been thinking about her. I even fucked up a time stamp for a removal that, luckily, Wyatt caught on to. My head hasn't been in the game all day. I was glad when Mum called to take Granddad home.

"What on earth?" Granddad booms out. I concentrate on the road ahead, and fury boils through me when I see Lily on the floor outside Granddad's neighbour's house.

That's when the sound finally registers, and I know it's her screaming on the floor.

Faith is yelling at a man looming over them and two kids are looking on, wide-eyed yet standing out of the way.

The tyres screech on the tarmac, and I don't even shut off the car before I'm flying out.

"Lily," I yell, and Faith's gaze meets mine. I see the relief in her eyes.

The guy she was yelling at turns around, and his lip curls. I don't even think. I throw a punch straight to his jaw.

"What did you do?" I roar.

He steadies himself, wiping blood from his lip. "None of your business. It's between me and my kids."

I look over my shoulder and notice Faith is trying to cup Lily's face. I see red at the light bruise already forming on her cheek.

"Did he hit her?" I ask when Faith looks up. She nods, her eyes filled with tears.

The man doesn't have any warning, but I do see his eyes flash with fear when I go at him. I grab his ratty coat when he tries to run, and my lip curls at the smell coming off him. My knuckles crack when I punch him in the nose. Seconds later, blood begins to pour out.

"You like hitting girls?" I bite out, pushing him away.

Taking two steps towards him, I don't let him steady himself before punching him again, this time in the jaw.

"Fuck you!" he growls, holding his palms up to ward me off.

"Not only girls by the looks of it," Reid bites out from somewhere.

Out of the corner of my eye, I see him looking at the two kids. I didn't pay attention to anyone but Lily before, but now looking closer, I notice the older one is covered in bruises. Some old, some new.

Low life scumbag.

"Think you're a big man, do you," I yell, punching him until he falls to the floor. I kick him in the stomach with my steel toe cap boots. He curls over, clutching his stomach as he wheezes through the pain. "Does it make you feel like a man beating on innocent kids and women?"

"Jax," Granddad starts, pulling me off. I try to shrug him off, but Reid steps up and pulls me back.

"The dickhead ain't worth it, bro," he snaps in my ear.

"I've called the police," Granddad's bitchy neighbour yells.

"You did what?" the guy yells, looking at the old lady with hard eyes. He gets up on his knees, spitting out blood. "Are you fucking stupid? Nelly always said you were a dumb old bitch. Kids, come on, we're going. I made a fucking mistake coming here."

"No!" the old lady shouts.

"Get here, kids," he bites out, keeping one eye on us, the other glaring at the kids.

The boy pushes the scared little girl behind him, his expression hard. She's whimpering, her gaze fixed on Lily, who sounds like a wounded animal, lying on the floor. I badly want to go to her; however, I want to make sure this guy isn't a threat anymore. She's still crying out, clutching her head.

"No," the boy says, standing up straighter. Something tells me this is new for the kid.

When, who I presume is the dad, moves towards them, Wyatt, Reid and I step between them.

"The kid said no," I warn.

"They're my fucking kids. If that silly little slut hadn't stuck her nose—" he doesn't get the rest out because I move towards him, ready to kill him when his beady eyes glance down at Lily.

"Stop," Wyatt snaps, pushing me back. "Go to Lily. We can sort this out. The police should be here soon."

"Lily, come back to me," I hear Faith whisper, tears in her voice.

I glare at the guy before rushing over to Lily. Her cheek is already turning purple, but luckily it hasn't swelled. Gently, I lift her off the grass and cradle her in my arms. Immediately, she burrows herself into my hoodie, her cries turning into whimpers. I look down, watching as she fists my shirt like she can't get close enough.

"Shush, baby. It's okay. Everything is okay," I soothe, keeping my voice low so my brothers don't hear me. I feel Faith watching me and meet her gaze.

I know Lily didn't want anyone knowing, but right this minute, I couldn't give a fuck who finds out. She needs me.

"You really do care," she whispers, also keeping our conversation between us. I watch her for a minute before looking back down at Lily, kissing her temple. "Don't break her heart. I don't need to warn you I have access to sharp instruments." Giving her a tight nod, I hold Lily closer.

"Where the fuck do you think you're going?" Reid asks.

"I don't need this fucking shit. I want my fucking kids and to get out of here."

"We aren't going," the boy tells him, trying to sound strong, but I can hear the defeat in his tone. "I heard them outside. They were going to take us."

"I'm the adult. You'll do as you're told."

"She's an adult," he tells his dad as he points to the old lady. I forgot her name. It's easier to remember her as either old lady, bitch or, well, evil bitch. "And you said she's our nan, so we can stay with her. We don't need to be split up."

"Yes, you can," she agrees, stepping up beside the two kids. Her hands shake but she manages to place them on the kids' shoulders, steeling her spine.

"Fuck this. Don't make me come over there, boy," he growls, and the little girl whimpers, clinging tighter to her brother's legs.

"We can wait for the police if you like," the boy says suddenly, a small smirk playing on his lips.

The dad throws his hands up. "Fuck this shit. Stay here, see if I fucking care. I've got police sniffing around and you two good for nothing brats aren't worth going to prison for. But don't think you'll be loved," he laughs. "You'll never be loved. Not by anyone."

"Yes, they will, Seth," the lady tells him.

"Fuck you. All of you. You'll pay for this," he says, his eyes glancing at each of us.

"Stop him," I yell when I see him moving to bolt.

Wyatt moves quickly, too quickly, and ends up tripping a little. Seth is gone. He's fast for a skinny guy who has clearly drunk and done drugs way too much.

Faith begins to cry, still hovering over Lily. "Reid and Wyatt will catch him." My voice is rough and startles her a little.

"I've texted my dad. I think. I don't know. My hands were shaking too bad."

"I'm so sorry," the old lady speaks up, still standing by the side of the kids. She looks shaken, pale, and I pass a look to Granddad. He gets my meaning and moves closer to her.

"It will be okay, Blanche. Why don't we get these kids inside?"

I look up when Reid and Wyatt run back up the path. "Fuck, I'm out of shape. How am I unfit? I lift fucking furniture for a living," Reid pants.

"We lost him as soon as we hit the next street," Wyatt explains.

"Are you serious?" I growl, livid.

Wyatt steps forward, catching his breath. "Bro, he was gone. I swear."

I give them a sharp nod.

"What was that all about?" Reid asks, and I look up to see he's asking the kids.

"Faith, go grab a blanket for Lily. I don't think she will let me move her yet."

Her wet eyes meet mine. "I'll try Dad again," she tells me and gets up to run into the house.

"Why should we tell you?" the older kid snaps.

"Be nice, Miah. They scared Daddy away. He can't hurt us now," the little girl says quietly.

The air turns tense at her words, and Reid bends down to her. "He hit you?"

She looks up at Miah for permission to answer. The poor kid has probably been groomed not to tell an adult what happens at home and to hide her injuries.

Miah sighs. "Yeah, he does. But I got it handled. When I turn sixteen, I'm taking Star and running away."

Realisation dawns at hearing their names. "You're the kids Lily has been worrying sick over."

"She shouldn't have stuck her nose in," he says sharply, but there's no denying the worry in his expression when he looks down at her.

"Watch it, kid. She's doing everything to help your situation. She fucking cares."

"What would she know about our situation?"

I glare up at him. "Kid, fucking look at her. Does she look like someone who doesn't know about your situation? She's lived her own hell, so watch what you fucking say."

"Bro, calm down," Wyatt coaxes.

"And maybe watch your language," Reid whispers, leaning down.

"No," I snap, then turn to Miah. "Explain what happened. What brought you here?"

His attention turns away from Lily. "He's a drug dealer. He gets us to sell his stash or have us take it on the train somewhere. He says people won't search us. When she—Lily—reported our situation, he become antsy. A social worker was trying to see us, but he didn't answer, pretending we weren't in. He wouldn't let us go to school either. Then the police came knocking yesterday and he flushed his stash, thinking they would break in. Whoever he works for are pissed and out for blood. He needs money to pay them back. Which is why we are here."

"And the bruises?" Reid asks.

Miah gives him a dry look. "He likes to tickle us. What do you think?"

"I'm so sorry," Blanche whispers quietly.

Faith comes running back out, placing a blanket over Lily. Lily shies away from the touch, clinging tighter to me.

"Whatever," Miah mutters, not looking at her.

"I didn't know about you," she tells him.

"How?" Reid asks, looking between them. "How could you not know you had grandkids?"

"My daughter was a good girl. Never had a problem with her until she met that man. She rebelled and started using drugs. Not even a year later they were married, and I couldn't stand by and watch her flush her life away. She moved away and I've never seen nor heard from her since. I can't believe she's gone. My baby."

"The police are here," Wyatt murmurs.

"Why don't you get the kids inside. I'll stay with you," Granddad tells Blanche.

"I think Hayden exaggerated. She doesn't seem that mean to me," Reid whispers, and I push him away from me.

"Dad's here," Faith murmurs. She gets up and runs to the car blocking Lily's drive. "Dad!"

"What happened?" he asks, and I don't hear her reply because my attention turns back to Lily.

"Jaxon?" she whispers, blinking out of her haze.

"It's okay. Everything's okay."

"You? Again?" Maverick growls, looking livid.

"Dad, he helped her," Faith gets out, coming up fast behind him.

The police begin to talk to Blanche and Granddad. When one of them asks if Lily's okay, my brothers step in, explaining she is.

"Let's get her inside," Maverick murmurs, bending down to pick up his daughter. She clings to me tighter and his jaw goes slack, but then his gaze narrows on me, like he can read my mind.

"Lily, your dad's here," I tell her, gently prying her fingers from my hoodie.

"Bro, we're gonna get the lady and kids inside. Be back out in a second."

I'm torn, not wanting to leave Lily but knowing I have to. Another car pulls up, and before I know it, Maddox is storming across the gardens.

Fucking hell.

"Warned you," he murmurs quietly, bending down in front of me. He gently pulls Lily into his arms. She goes, clinging to him as he stands up. Maverick steps back, and I get up, ready for a spar if it comes to it.

"Jaxon," she whispers sleepily, her eyes closing.

The veins in Maddox's neck bulge as he glowers at me.

"Let's get her inside. It's going to rain," Faith orders. Both men send me one more glower before walking over to Lily's.

Faith stands beside me, both of us watching as they carry Lily inside. Once they're out of sight, she turns to me. "Thank you for being here. I don't know what I would have done if you hadn't turned up when you did."

"No need to thank me."

"I'll tell her to call you when she's more with it. She probably won't remember that you were here," she tells me, crestfallen. "She never remembers much of what goes on outside of her mind. But whatever plays in her mind continues on a loop for hours."

My stomachs twists into knots at her words. I look away from Lily's front door, down at Faith. She's the complete opposite of Lily, appearance wise. Faith is dark to Lily's light, but I can see why they are sisters. Both have big hearts.

"She won't remember?"

"No," she says, shaking her head sadly.

"Will you tell her—that I was here? I don't think your dad or Maddox will appreciate you reminding her about my involvement. And I don't want her to know to earn brownie points. I just need to hear from her that she's okay. If that makes sense."

"It does. I'll tell her, I promise."

"Thank you."

"Just—I mean, just… please don't hurt her."

"I won't," I vow.

"Bro, we've got to go," Wyatt says, his voice tense. Hearing it, I go on alert and give him a chin lift.

Faith forces a smile. "I'd best get inside before they drive her nuts."

I want to say something, anything, but nothing comes out. She walks off, and I watch her for a moment, really wanting to check if Lily is okay. It's killing me being on the outside. I want to be in there.

"Bro," Reid calls out, his arse getting in the van.

"What's going on?" I ask, walking to Wyatt, who's waiting for me at the end of the path.

"We got a location on the dude who broke in."

My head jerks to him, wondering if I'm hearing him right. "Good, I'm in the mood to let off some steam."

"I'll drive," Wyatt tells me, and I nod, too riled up to drive. My phone goes off as soon as I get in the van.

LILY: Please come back later. I'm sorry. Xx

I want to text and ask her to explain what happened, but I want to see her face to face.

JAXON: Not even your family could keep me away. Text me as soon as the coast is clear, and I'll be back. X

"Everything okay?" Reid checks, trying to read my screen. I slide it on silent and put it in my pocket.

"Yeah, just in the mood to teach someone manners."

Reid grins and sits to face the front.

"YOU SURE THIS IS IT?" I ask Wyatt as we step out of the lift. The place stinks of piss and beer. Needles and rubbish litter the entire building, and I'm pretty sure someone jacked off in the lift a few times.

"Yeah. Found out his name is George Snotts, and that he lives here," Wyatt replies, looking down at his phone.

"Snotts?" Reid snorts.

"What I don't get is why someone who can do what this guy can, lives in a shit hole like this," Wyatt comments, curling his lip at the woman stepping out of the flat to the left. He steps aside, not wanting to touch her. She's wearing a short leather skirt and a tank top that reaches below her tits, letting her overly large belly hang out. She wipes her mouth as she watches us walk past. The big guy standing in the door, his shirt undone, flashing his beer belly and unbuttoned trousers, slams the door when he sees us.

Clearly, they are used to trouble here.

"This is it," Reid whispers, looking down the hallway both ways. He bangs on the door and immediately someone begins cursing on the other side. I give the others a side-glance when we hear things begin to drop.

Reid knocks again, tapping his foot impatiently.

"Hold on!" a voice that sounds like it belongs to a boy yells.

"Are you sure?" I voice again to Wyatt. I'm not down with hitting a kid. I might scare him a little but where's the fun in that?

Wyatt doesn't answer because the door opens, revealing a face I've memorised from the cameras.

George Snotts.

He's definitely not a kid. Just a man who hasn't hit puberty. He's got to be in his early thirties. If he's younger, he sure as fuck aged well.

Fire lights up through my veins. George's eyes widen, and he goes to slam the door on us. My foot blocks the door from shutting in our faces. I slam it in his face, knocking him back into the room.

"Hey, what do you think you're doing?"

I grab him by the face, walking him backwards fast, and just before I reach the wall, I turn him slightly, smacking his face against the wall with a sickening thud.

I lean down, whispering, "Payback," in his ear. I shove him further into the room, away from all doors. Seeing the blood dripping from his mouth and nose brings me sweet satisfaction.

My brothers fan out, circling the weak man who moves to lean back against the sofa, whilst I walk back towards the door.

I do a quick scan of the room and notice all the computer equipment. How the fuck he works in here is beyond me. The place fucking stinks of rot and mould and every surface is covered in takeout or junk food.

"This can go two ways," I start, turning my back on him. I slowly close the door. The sound of the lock clicking in place has the tension in the room skyrocketing, and when I hear George whimper, I grin.

George audibly swallows, his expression frantic when I turn back around, my movements controlled, steady.

His head looks like it's about to spin as he tries to keep track of all three of us. Wyatt and Reid keep circling their prey, and fear strikes in the scrawny man's eyes.

"I think you've mistaken me for someone else," George squeaks.

"I don't think we have," Reid drawls lazily.

"You have information we want," Wyatt tells him, giving him a warning glare.

"And you can give it to us in two ways. One: we can beat it out of you. Or two: you can happily tell us and then we beat you. One will just take longer. For both of us," I explain.

He turns his head left and right, his gaze scanning for a way out of it. I smirk, stepping further into the room, and crack my knuckles.

"I didn't do nothing," he snaps, moving away when Reid steps closer.

"Hayes Removals ring any bells?" I drawl, ducking my head to keep eye contact when he flinches away. "Yeah, I can see it does."

He spins fast, grabbing the lamp off the side table. He rips it out of the socket and begins swinging it side to side. Reid steps back, dodging the lamp, and starts laughing.

It takes George off guard and he eyes Reid like he's crazy. "I've not done nothing to you." I take a step forward, ignoring the lamp he swings my way. "Stay back."

"Swing that at me again and you'll be eating through a straw," I warn, my voice deadly and stern. "You broke into our warehouse." His eyes widen and my smirk kicks up a notch. Yeah, he's getting it. "You pushed our sister, broke her arm and made her bleed."

"I'm sorry," he yells, swinging the lamp frantically. "I was paid. You don't need to do this. Stay back!"

"That's where you're wrong. Who sent you?"

We know; we just want it confirmed. But he doesn't need to know that. And seeing him sweat is making this more fun.

"Nope, he'll kill me."

I've had enough with this circus show. I wait for an opening before jumping forward, grabbing the lamp and throwing it across the room. In seconds, I have my fingers digging into the back of his neck and I'm slamming his face down on the side table. He grunts, gripping the table to try push and himself back up.

"Who sent you?"

"He'll kill me."

Reid laughs and leans down, going face to face with George. "You need to be more worried about what we will do if you don't answer. My bro there might have given you two choices, but I just added the only one that is gonna matter. If you don't tell us what we want, we will make you wish you were dead. Tell us and we will leave you with the beating you deserve."

"You're lucky it's just us three. Our other brother, Eli, always leaves people who fuck with us a gift. You know, to teach them a lesson," Wyatt murmurs cryptically.

I watch George close his eyes tightly, slamming his lips shut. I grin at Wyatt before grabbing George by the neck and storming through the room to the computers. I slam his face down on the keyboard, taking him off guard. I hear the crunch of his nose as it smacks against the keyboard and find satisfaction in it.

"You ready to talk?" I ask, my voice low. I want him to defy us, badly. He deserves a world of hurt after what he did to my sister. We don't usually gang up on people, but when it comes to our sister, none of us get the short straw. We all fuck them up.

Reid looks at the screen that flicks on, and on it are pictures of us. "Fuck!" he whispers.

George looks up and whimpers, closing his eyes once again.

So he knew who we were. Interesting. He's a good actor. I genuinely thought he had no idea when we walked in. I believed it was our appearance that scared him enough to slam the door in our faces.

Wyatt grabs him and slams his fist into his face. "What is this?"

"It's my job. To watch you. To find everything there is to know about you."

"Dude, you could have got my good side," Reid comments, flicking through the images. One of me, Lily, Maddox and Maverick in her driveway pops up and Reid's questioning gaze meets mine. I shake my head, warning him not to bring attention to the photo. I don't want this fucker anywhere near her.

Wyatt shakes him, cursing. "Tell us."

"For a fee," George tries to bargain.

Any control I have is gone when he has the nerve to try and broker a deal. "You think you can fucking play us?" I growl, picking him up and throwing him over the desk, onto his back. A few of the computer screens fall to the floor at the back, the rest crunch under him.

"I won't talk," he tells us, thinking he has the upper hand. He's scared shitless though. My gaze lands on a Star Wars paperweight on his desk. I lean over, picking it up.

"Lay his hand flat," I order Reid, testing the weight in my hand. It's heavy and perfect for what I have in mind.

"What are you doing?" George screeches. "That's a collector's item."

"This?" I ask, and he nods.

I nod to Wyatt, who steps forward and pins down George's shoulders.

He's not even struggling over what is about to happen, too bothered about the piece of crystal in my hand.

I lift it up and slam it over his pinkie finger. He struggles to make a sound as he reddens from the pain. He gasps for air, and when he gets a lung full, he cries out in pain.

"Tell us," I demand.

I slam it back down on his index and middle fingers. He cries out once again, struggling to cradle his hand. Reid has his wrist pinned to the table and his other hand is gripping George's chin, warning him with actions not to move.

"You broke into our business, hurt our sister. We don't mind being here all night," Wyatt warns him.

"Maybe someone needs to feel how she felt," I murmur quietly. One of his fingers is bent out of place and already swelling. But as I grab his wrist away from Reid, I yank and twist it backwards before slamming it hard on the edge of the desk.

He curls up on his side, his knees pushed to his chest as tears stream down his face.

"Andrew Black," he screeches. "Please, stop!"

Wyatt grabs the weight from my hand and smacks it across his head, right where Paisley was bleeding. Reid, not wanting to be left out, picks him up by his T-shirt before punching him in the stomach, over and over until the guy's head drops forward.

"What the fuck is that smell?" Wyatt asks as Reid pushes George away. He rolls to the floor, groaning in pain.

"He fucking pissed himself," Reid snaps, looking down at the man in disgust. "Why do they always fucking piss themselves?"

"Get everything off his computer. Then wipe everything. Even his backups must have backups. Make sure it's all gone and then smash the lot up," I order, and Reid gets straight to work.

"Wasn't as much fun as I thought it would be. Kind of pathetic really," Wyatt whines, scrubbing his palm along his jaw.

I look down at George, who has passed out, kicking him with the toe of my boot.

"No, but we still have to figure out a way to deal with this Andrew Black guy. He won't back off if we threaten him, bust him up a little. In fact, he'd probably use it against us."

Wyatt considers that, then nods, agreeing. "We will sort it. We just need to be clever about it."

Reid stands up straighter from the main computer. "I'm starving. Want to grab some pizza?"

"You done?" I ask.

He grabs a bottle of Coke from the side and pours it inside the docking station. Steam begins to rise as sparks fly, and he steps back, nodding. "Who's gonna do the honours of smashing it up?"

I smirk, and Wyatt throws the paperweight towards one of the screens. It sails through the air before cracking through the screen. It literally smashes through it, cemented into the screen.

I rip one off the wall as the other two do the same, all of us making sure nothing is left for George to salvage.

Before we leave, we all manage to land one more blow to the man on the floor, leaving him curled up in a ball, stewing in his own piss.

CHAPTER ELEVEN

Mum, Dad, Faith and Beau are helping me settle the kids in at Blanche's house. I still feel a little shaken up, but it's nothing I haven't been through before or can't handle.

The police had come and gone and informed us they were yet to locate Seth Merin. Dad stressed at me until I pressed charges against him for hitting me. It didn't take much convincing. As much as I like to see the best in people, I don't see good inside Seth Merin. I didn't see much of anything when I looked at him. He's soulless, just like the men my mum brought home. And it hurts that the world still has people like him in it.

My cheek still stings, reminding me that his hit wasn't intended for me but for Miah, who is still glaring at me from across the kitchen table.

Everyone in my family, at some point, had turned up to check if I was okay. They didn't stay long, and when I told Mum and Dad that I was fine, they tried to get me upstairs to lie down. I refused, telling them I wanted to check in on the kids, to see if they were okay. What they saw must have been terrifying for them. They had to have been scared about meeting a grandma they never knew they had. I desperately wanted to go over and check if there was anything I could do. Dad had seen the determination and offered to come with me, which led to everyone else coming with me.

I also wanted to check what the police were doing on Blanche and the kids' behalf. I only knew what would happen for the assault on me.

Then there were social services. I didn't know a lot of how it works legally, so I was worried that with Blanche's age and the fact she only met them that day, they would be gone. So, we raced over here as quick as my dad would let me. Fortunately, the kids were still there, and I began to relax. I wanted them to have a good home and be able to stay together.

Blanche hadn't looked good when we arrived and wasn't taking the news of her daughter's death well. She looked frail and vulnerable for the first time since I moved in. Gone was the sassy remarks and bad temper. I kind of wish Hayden was here so she got that spark back, and if anyone could bring the old Blanche back, it would be my cousin Hayden.

We decided to stay after that, seeing as she needed us for at least a little while. While we made things comfortable for the kids, we let Blanche absorb everything and get herself together.

Dad and Beau are in the cellar, looking to make sure the space is suitable for a teenage boy to live in since the kids couldn't share a room forever and Blanche only had two bedrooms. Blanche said it looks like every other room except it isn't decorated and only has one light.

Star seems happier than I've ever seen her, really enjoying her chats with Faith, who is sitting at the table with her and Miah.

Mum tried to get her to leave with Charlotte and my uncle, but she opted to stay, and I know it's because of me. It hurts her to see me have an episode. In her mind, I've not gotten over what happened to me. I have. And it's all because of her and my family. Faith never gave me a chance as a kid to fold into myself. She was always there, being her normal, cheery self. And I loved hearing her stories about her Prince Charming and everything she had seen and done.

However, it's my consciousness that won't let me forget my past. It's there, weighing me down to the point not even a psychologist can help me anymore.

It doesn't make it any easier on my family though, which is why they are so protective of me. They want me to know they are there and nothing bad is going to happen. I love them for it. I do. But I hate that they worry about me.

Barry left not long ago, informing Blanche he would be back in the morning and that if she needed anything, to yell. It was incredibly kind of him to stay with her, but I could see it was making him uncomfortable. He looked relieved when we knocked on the door. I wanted to laugh when I saw him.

"You okay, baby?"

Taking in my mum's tight face, I can tell she's still concerned for me. She hasn't stopped hovering, and I love her for it. But I do wish she wouldn't worry as much. However, I know what it's like to have someone not care if you wake up in the morning, so I can take the overprotectiveness from my parents.

"I'm fine, Mum."

"How is your head?"

"Good. Headache is nearly gone."

"I'm glad. I really wish you'd come stay with me and your father tonight."

"Mum, I'm fine," I promise her, resting my head on her shoulder.

"I'm worried about them," she whispers, changing the subject, and I lift my head up. "Mrs North is still in shock and Miah looks angry at everyone."

"They've been through a lot," I remind her gently.

She hugs my side. "I know. I just wish there was more we could do."

So do I, Mum. So do I.

I finish dishing up their dinner before taking the plates over to the table. Miah continues to watch me. I'm unsure whether he hates me or is trying to figure me out. There's none of the usual hatred and anger I see when I catch him looking at me. Instead, there is something else, and its stewing inside his mind.

Having him hate me, even if it's only a guess, hits me harder than I thought it would. I desperately want him to trust me so I can help them.

"It's only spaghetti bolognaise, but it's all we could cook up on short notice. If you don't like it, I can always find something else. I'm sure I have some nuggets at mine," I tell them honestly and gently.

"This looks amazing," Star breathes, looking down at the food in wonder. Tears gather in my eyes at the sight of her. It's like she hasn't seen food before.

"Yeah," Miah mutters as I place his in front of him.

"Miah, you get to eat," Star tells him, her eyes lighting up with hope.

My stomach sinks as I look at Miah.

"Star," he snaps, turning bright red.

"But you get to eat. You don't need to give me yours," she whispers, struggling to keep her pasta on the fork.

I want to reach over and hug him. He gave up his food to make sure his sister had enough.

To keep myself busy and stop myself from hugging him, I quickly grab a spoon from the drawer and head over to Star.

"Here, twirl the fork like this." I show her how to twirl the pasta and then press it against the spoon. "Now it won't fall back off."

"Thank you, Miss Carter."

"Call me Lily," I tell her softly, and then look at Miah. "I'm really sorry for what you've been through."

"Faith, why don't we go see if Mrs North will eat something," Mum coaxes. "Lily has done her a plate."

Faith nods and gets up to follow Mum into the living room. Once they're gone, Miah turns to me.

"You caused this," he accuses, narrowing his eyes. My heart sinks as I drop down into a chair opposite them. He really does hate me.

I blink away tears and clasp my hands in my lap under the table. Maybe if they knew more about me, they'd know I'd never do anything to hurt them, that I only want to help them.

"My mum and her boyfriend's beat me," I rush out, desperately wanting him to trust me. His eyes widen, flashing to the living room where Mum and Faith are before coming back to me. I know where his mind went. "Not my mum. My biological mum," I whisper, feeling my throat tighten when his expression hardens.

"Why are you telling me this? I don't care," he snaps, shovelling a fork of food into his mouth.

"Miah," Star whispers, her voice trembling.

"I'm telling you this because I want you to know you can trust me. I was young when it happened to me, younger than most can remember. But I do. It was the norm for me, and I didn't know I could be treated differently. It's the same with you and Star. He's not allowed to hurt you. You've done absolutely nothing wrong, and even if you did, you still don't warrant that kind of treatment."

"Yeah?"

"Yes," I tell him gently.

He slams his fist down on the table, making both me and Star jump and the plates rattle. "Did you have a brother or sister?"

"I didn't know about them until I was taken from my birth mum," I admit, not wanting to go into detail. I notice Dad and Beau come up the stairs from the cellar, and both freeze at the top.

I know Faith has told Beau a little about me, but she would never confide any details of what happened. Surprisingly, I don't mind him knowing. He'll be married to my sister soon and he's already part of the family.

"So, you don't fucking understand," he retorts sharply, pulling my gaze away from Beau. "I had it fucking handled. I was making sure she had the things she needed. I was going to get a job when I left school and look after her. I was going to get us both out of there and because of you we will be separated. She could end up with anyone thanks to you."

I rub at my chest as I struggle to swallow past the lump in my throat. "I—I'm so sorry."

Fat tears drop on the table beneath me.

"You're fucking sorry?" he growls, shoving his food away.

"You need to eat," I whisper, deflated.

He laughs with no humour. "Like I could eat. I can't stand the sight of you. It's making me sick to my stomach."

"Now that's e-fucking-nough. Don't talk to my daughter like that," Dad growls, walking around to stand beside me. He places his palms on the table and leans towards Miah.

"Dad," I whisper, putting my hand on his arm.

He doesn't spare me a glance, his glare still on Miah. "She got you out of a fucked-up situation, one neither you nor your sister deserved to be in. I've been where you are, kid. Exactly where you are. I had four brothers to protect, four brothers I raised, and I was too scared to speak out to anyone in case they separated us. Our granddad took us in and raised us. I get you're having a bad time of it, kid, but there's no fucking need to take your problems out on someone trying to help you. Someone, I might add, who had it worse than you and me could ever fucking imagine."

Miah looks to me, and I can see the guilt flash in his eyes. Dad's words stay with me and it hurts to hear them.

"Dad," I whisper, squeezing his arm.

"What's going on?" Mum asks, stepping into the room.

None of us move our focus from Miah. After a few minutes of silence, he leans back in his chair.

He looks at me, and my heart constricts when tears fill his eyes. "I'm sorry. I'm really sorry, but I can't lose her. We are all each other has. I won't let them take her. I'll run before it comes to that."

"No one is going to take you," Blanche says, her voice strong. She has more colour in her cheeks and looks more present.

"How do you know that? No offence, but we don't know you. And you're old. Why would they let us stay with you?" he asks, his lips twisting.

"Because I'm your grandma, that's why. And never call me old again, boy. I have years left in me."

"Please don't leave me," Star pleads, and for the first time, my gaze goes to hers. Tears are streaming down her face and she's looking up at Miah, petrified.

"Hey," I coax, moving over to her. I kneel by her chair and take her face in mine. "Miah isn't going to leave you. Blanche, your grandma, will look after you."

"But Miah said social—"

"Forget what your brother said," Dad tells her gently. "Let us adults sort it out. What you need to worry about right now is eating all that yummy food before I eat it."

Star opens her mouth in awe at Dad, before a shy smile lifts her lips. "Would you like to share?"

Dad chuckles. "I'll let you eat this one. But next time, we can share."

I watch as Mum walks over to Dad, and he tucks her into his side.

"We're back," Charlotte cheers, walking in and carrying a ton of bags. "Mum and Dad are grabbing the rest."

"What on earth is all that? And please tell me that troublemaker hasn't come with you," Blanche asks, looking around Charlotte.

"No. Hayden is busy today, but she'd love to see you," Charlotte informs her. "And we thought the kids might need some supplies. Clothes and bedding and stuff. Isn't it great? I picked all of Star's clothes. I *can't wait* to have children."

"Let's not tell your dad that," Mum warns, her lips twitching in amusement.

"How do you know she's talking about Hayden?" Faith asks, reaching for some of the bags.

"Mrs North and Hayden don't get along, but I think they secretly like each other," Charlotte replies absently, dropping some bags onto the table. "Want to see what I got you?"

Star doesn't even reply. I'm pretty positive she doesn't know Charlotte is talking to her. Charlotte pulls out a pink unicorn top with frilly lace at the bottom and a denim skirt.

"Those are for me?" Star asks in awe, before bursting into tears. She throws herself at Miah, who winces in pain. He doesn't even seem uncomfortable with a crying girl in his arms. He gingerly picks her up and holds her to his chest.

"Isn't that nice of her?" he asks, his voice hoarse.

"You should see what we got you!" Charlotte yells with so much enthusiasm, I'm surprised the windows don't rattle. "We were going to get you a phone or something, but Mum and Dad put their foot down. Mrs North doesn't have a television so I brought over my spare that you two can have."

"Ooh, I have an Xbox you can play on," I tell them, clapping my hands. I want them to be comfortable here. And it won't hurt to show social services they are loved and cared for.

"Isn't that Maddox's?" Faith asks, biting her lip.

"He won't mind. He will want to help," I explain. "I'll grab it later."

"Ooh, I love this outfit," Charlotte murmurs, holding up a pair of dungarees with a red and black striped top underneath. It has a big love heart on the front pocket.

Myles and Aunt Kayla walk in loaded down with more carrier bags full of stuff. As soon as Myles puts them down, Mum claps her hands and orders everyone to work.

I put a hand out on Myles' arm to stop him from following. "Did you hear anything?"

Blanche must feel the tension because she steps closer. "Is everything okay?"

I take a quick look at the kids, noticing they have finished their food and are now heading out the room with the others.

"This is my uncle Myles. He's a social worker," I explain.

Her hands begin to shake. "Will they take them away from me?"

Myles gives her shoulder a squeeze. "I won't be fully briefed on what will happen until tomorrow when I speak to everyone involved. We don't make a habit of taking kids away from their family if it can be helped. I will be honest and say they might class the kids as being 'at risk' living here. They are not safe to go back to their father. We also don't know if he will come back for them."

"I won't let him take them."

He smiles gently at her, but I know it's because he's trying to go easy on her. "He's not a weak man, Mrs North. We will discuss this more tomorrow morning, but until then, you are guardian of those two children."

"If they see you are making a home for them, they might ignore all the other stuff," I tell her optimistically. "They already have new clothes and bedsheets. And you saw how excited Star got over food."

Her face is still pinched tightly. "I don't want them going into care. They're my grandchildren. My daughter might have made some wrong decisions, but I loved her, and I know deep down she wouldn't want this for them."

"I know, Mrs North. Tomorrow, yeah?" he tells her gently.

She nods, then looks to me. "Thank you, girl. You've got good folks."

I beam. "They're the best."

Dad steps up behind Blanche, making his presence known. "Hi, Mrs North. You were right about the cellar. It's been damp-proofed and made liveable. It needs some heating down there and maybe a couple more light fixtures. I'm gonna have my nephew come around tomorrow after your interview with social services and take a look. Until then, he will need to sleep up here. They mentioned earlier they share a bed at home, so they're used to sharing a room, even if it isn't advised at their age."

"I have a camp bed in the car," Myles rumbles, not sounding pleased at the news Dad shared. I bite my lip. "If Maddox can get that done as soon as possible, that would be great. Ideally, the two aren't allowed to share a room. But for tonight he can sleep in the bed and Star can sleep on the camp bed. It's big enough for her but might be cramped for Miah."

"Great," Dad replies. "It's getting late and the kids need to get to bed soon. I'll get everyone to finish up and we can do the rest tomorrow."

"Thank you," Blanche tells him, yet she still looks worried.

"I can stay," I tell her. "I can even stay on the couch."

"Lily," Dad calls softly, and I know that sound.

I blink up at him. "She might need help."

He smiles down at me, cupping the back of my neck. "Yeah, and you live next door. The kids need to get used to being here with Blanche, get to know their grandma."

He's right.

"Okay," I breathe out, before turning back to Blanche. "Would you like me to come around for the interview tomorrow?"

"I think your dad is right, Lily. I need to sort this out. But I will keep you informed." She looks back at the front room where the kids are looking through bags. "Give us a day to get settled, then you're more than welcome. Anytime."

"Okay. And no matter the time, if you need me, come knock on my door. Okay?"

She smiles warmly at me for the first time. "I will."

"I'll go get the others," Dad mutters before moving through the room.

CHAPTER TWELVE

JAXON

After cleaning George's grime off me, I sat around catching up with invoices while I waited for Lily to text me. I had begun to think she'd changed her mind, when she texted me, saying she was back at home and it was clear to come over.

I'm not gonna lie and say I wasn't worried when she said she was back home. Flashes of my sister being in hospital came to me when she said it, and then all I could picture was Lily lying in a hospital bed, and I wasn't there for her.

I regretted leaving her. I could take the Carter fury, but what I couldn't handle was Lily getting it. There's no telling how they'd react towards her if they found out about me. I don't want them upsetting her, family or not.

I texted her back saying I'd be over in ten and headed straight over.

Which is where I am now, parking my car down the road, out of view of the house. I don't want to risk one of her family members passing by and seeing it. Granddad wouldn't care if I parked in his drive, but if the Carter's see my car parked there all the time, I know they'll start asking questions.

The sneaking around shit is something I've not done since school. It's not amusing, but for Lily I'll do it. I'd do anything for her.

I note her back garden needs some fresh grass laid as I step up to her backdoor. Hopefully it's something I can do for her when the weather picks up.

I knock twice and wait for her to answer.

The relief on her face when she opens the door reminds me why all of this is worth it. She surprises the hell out of me when she wraps her arms around my neck.

"You keep helping me," she whispers.

Holding her waist, I relish in the feel of her pressed against me. "He laid a hand on you."

"He did, but I'm okay. I promise."

I pull back, scanning the light bruise on her cheek. It could have been worse, a lot worse, yet it doesn't stop me from wanting to go find the fucker and kill him.

"You said you just got back," I mention, stepping inside after her. A cat comes running in, sliding on the laminate flooring and smacking into the cupboard.

Lily giggles, straightening the cat before it shoots off again. "Sorry, we were playing with the laser and catnip. I think I overexcited them." She stands up and looks shyly at me. "And I was at Blanche's house with the kids and my family."

I nod, understanding. "All right. Before we talk about all of that, why don't we order some food and watch a movie."

Her smile is blinding. "I'd love that. But, um, can we, uh, watch it upstairs? I don't want someone to drive by and see the tele or lights and think I'm still awake. They'll knock on the door to see why I'm still up and if I'm okay."

"Babe, it's nine," I tell her, amused she goes to bed early. I shouldn't be surprised.

"I sleep early on a weekday. I have to be up at half five—well, I did before. It's been hard to adjust, but I still keep getting up early."

"Half five? What time does school start?" Jesus. When I was at school it started at quarter to nine.

"Half eight, but I sometimes open up breakfast club, which starts at seven. It takes me a while to wake up."

I grin at the faint blush on her cheeks. "Good to know."

"Would you like a drink? I have fizzy drinks, tea, coffee, water."

"Coke if you have it, babe."

I lean back against the counter, watching her move. I love the dip at the bottom of her back. It makes her arse look rounder. Images of bending her over and running my hand down the bottom of her back have me biting back a groan.

"I have a few movies upstairs, but I have Netflix too," she tells me, handing me a can of coke.

"I can Netflix and chill." I nod, liking the sound of it after the day I've had. She giggles. "Netflix and chill?"

"Isn't that what all the cool kids call it?"

Giggling harder, she nods. "I guess."

"What takeout do you want? I'll order it now."

"Do you like Indian?"

"Love it. I'll call and we can go pick a movie while we wait."

I THROW THE rubbish from our takeout in her bin, leaving the leftovers on the side before heading back upstairs. I nearly trip over Willa, one of her cats she introduced earlier. One-eyed Willa. Go figure.

Lily is now lying in her bed and it's a sight to fucking see. We've just finished watching some click flick I didn't pay attention to. I was too engrossed in everything that is Lily.

"What?" she asks when I continue to stare.

I grin. "Didn't think I'd ever see your room, babe. It's you," I tell her. She has more photo's, more knick-knacks and more girly shit lying around. Even her bed set screams girl. She has a grey and pink flowered bedsheet and a dozen or more pillows.

"What would you like to watch now?" she asks, fiddling with the sheet.

I get back onto her bed, wishing I could get under those sheets with her, but something inside of me knows she would freak. Or I'm scared that is what her reaction to me will be. With Lily, I never know. And it's one of the many mysteries I love about her. I'm more than happy just being next to her, so there's no point in risking it.

"Tell me how the kids are instead."

She leans forward, her eyes crinkling at the corners. "I think they have a long way to go, and with Blanche looking after them, they'll get there. Miah, the boy, is angry. At his dad, at me, at the world."

"At you?"

She crosses her arms, a cute line creasing her forehead. "I think he hates me for all of it. I think he was hurt again by his dad because I opened my mouth," she whispers and sounds like she's struggling to breathe.

"Hey," I whisper, pulling her against me. She rests her head against the nook of my neck. "They were being hurt before you got involved. If anything, you've stopped any more beatings. Next time could have been worse. He could have killed one of them. That girl was tiny."

"I know. I'm just so sad for them. It hurts me so much inside that I can't catch my breath or my thoughts. I just wish there was something more I could do to make their lives a little bit better."

"What do you think would make it better?"

She shrugs. "Not belongings. However excited they were to receive all the gifts they got from my family, it's not that they want."

"So?" I volley.

"They just want to be loved. They want to feel safe enough that they can close their eyes at night and not worry if they ate food that was meant to last them. Maybe a new bed for Miah," she says absently, more to herself than me. "Yes, tomorrow I can go get him a new bed."

"New bed?"

She tilts her head to look up at me. "Yeah. Dad looked at the cellar and said it's good to turn into a bedroom. Just needs some heating and a little more light. Maddox is going over tomorrow to take a look. But he still needs a bed and his own room. He can't sleep on a camp bed, which is what Star is sleeping on tonight as they've had to share a room, and the camp bed is tiny. And uncomfortable, trust me."

"You slept on it?" I grin when I see her cute little pout.

"Yes. We went camping last year and it was great, but so uncomfortable. In the end, Maddox threw the beds out and we slept on the spare sleeping bags."

My body shakes with laughter. "Babe, I promise to make it better for you next time."

"Next time?" she asks, her jaw slack.

"Yeah. We can go when summer starts up. You don't work in the holiday's, right?"

"I don't," she says, her lips twisting into another pout. "Will we still be friends then?"

Tipping her chin up with my finger, I briefly touch my lips to hers. "Baby, by summer we will be more than friends."

Her lips part. "We will?"

"Definitely," I admit, fucking sure of it. I've had a taste of her now. There's no way in hell I'm letting her go.

"I really like you, Jaxon Hayes."

I grin when her eyes go round. She hadn't meant to blurt that out. "I really like you, too, Lily Carter."

I kiss her again then settle back down on the bed. She snuggles up to my chest, her hand placed over my heart.

"I'll bring the boy a bed tomorrow. I have one in Paisley's container that hasn't been used since I was a teen and got a double bed. It was gonna be skipped, but Mum talked me into keeping it. Glad she did."

"Really?" she asks, looking up at me with wide eyes.

"Really."

"You really are the best. I don't get why people say mean things about you. They wouldn't if they knew you."

I try my hardest not to grin at her sticking up for me, but I do. She's so cute. If only she knew. I've done some shit in my time that might put Lily off, stuff her family could use against me. And if that time ever comes, I want Lily to know the real me. I want her to love me enough to not care that I've done some unmerited shit and slept around.

"I bet."

She lets out a yawn. "They wouldn't."

"Before I leave to let you get some rest, what caused the episode earlier? Was it because he hit you?" I ask gently, not wanting to dredge up bad memories for her. But I need to know. Not because I'm nosey, but because I want to figure her out, know everything about her.

She inhales a deep breath, blinking up at me through those ridiculously long eyelashes.

"No. It was the fag," she murmurs, so quiet I almost miss it.

"Fag?" I question, wondering where that came from.

"After, he, um, hit me, he threw a fag at me."

I grit my teeth together, making sure to remember to burn the fucker when I find him. "Did he burn you?"

"No, it must have flicked right off me," she tells me, but she seems distant.

"There's more to the fag, isn't there?" I guess.

A slow nod before lowering her head. "Yes. I was burned a lot as a kid. On my back mostly, but I do have some on my feet and hands," she says, then I look down at her hands and notice she's running her finger across a silver scar.

"Show me."

"What?" she breathes, blinking up at me.

"I want to see them," I tell her. If she has lived it, then I can see it. "Can I?"

Reluctantly, she nods and gets out of bed. As she stands, I move over to her side, sitting on the edge of the bed.

I can see her hands shaking as she grabs the bottom of her T-shirt. I place a hand on her hip, halting her, and she jumps, gasping.

"If you don't want to, Lily, say no," I tell her, my voice filled with emotion.

She doesn't speak, but her hands lift her T-shirt slowly up her body. She keeps the front down as much as she can. My attention is riveted by the scars on her back. I clench my teeth, feeling for the little girl who endured them. What she must have thought and felt.

Lifting my hand, I run a finger over the first scar, this one the worst. It's raised, puckered, and it makes me wonder if there is more to this one than a cigarette burn. The hitch in her breath is audible as her shoulders rise and fall.

"Jaxon," she breathes, her voice low and husky.

Moving forward, I press my lips against another scar. "These scars don't define you."

Her chin drops into her neck. "I know."

Once I've kissed every last one, she's hyperventilating, so I slowly lower her T-shirt, covering all that creamy skin and stand up behind her. My fingers caress her hips and then slowly move to her stomach.

"Jaxon."

I kiss the side of her neck, unable to stop myself. All that smooth, creamy skin is begging to be kissed.

"I'm sorry this happened to you, baby."

She turns slowly in my arms, looking up at me. "You don't need to be sorry, Jaxon. It happened and it's over. I've got the best life. I have great people in it. Yes, I'm haunted by everything, and if I could switch it off, I would. The only time I think about it is when I have one of my episodes. It's like I get lost in my mind and can't find my way out." She pauses to inhale a deep breath. "However, I don't want people to feel sorry for me. I really am okay. I couldn't have been given a better upbringing."

"All right," I whisper, leaning in to take her lips, but a loud bang echoes through the house.

"Go to your bathroom and hide," I whisper.

"Lily? You ate all this food without me?" a deep, slurred voice booms. "Woah, there's a lot."

"Fucking Maddox!" I grumble.

Lily giggles but then sobers when she realises what this means.

She wrings her hands together. "Oh my god."

"It will be fine. He won't come up here, will he? Get rid of him," I tell her, watching the door from the corner of my eye.

"Lily! Where is my Xbox? It's gone."

Does he even realise he sounds like a high school girl who just met Justin Bieber?

"Oh no," she whispers, closing her eyes.

I look down at her, finding her biting her lip. "What?"

"I gave Miah his Xbox."

Shit! That should piss him off. I can't help but chuckle.

"You gave away his Xbox?"

"It's a spare. Who needs two really?" she says, but she doesn't believe her words.

"Wow, you had Indian and only saved me a bit?" Maddox yells upstairs. "Lily?"

When we hear his voice coming closer, Lily begins to panic.

"You need to hide," she whispers.

I look around the room, wondering where the fuck she wants me to hide. "Where?"

"Under the bed," she says, trying to shoo me towards her bed.

"Babe, one, it's too low for me to fit under, and two, even if I could, it's filled with boxes."

She bites her lips, her eyes going around the room. "You can't hide in the bathroom. He uses my shower."

"Lily? Shit, who put that step there," Maddox curses. "Have you been moving the house around?"

I raise my eyebrow towards the door, but Lily begins to pull my arm. "You have to jump out the window."

"Jump... out your window?"

I don't even have time to think before she's pulling the window up.

"Lily, I think I'm drunk," Maddox yells. "And your cat is being mean, glaring at me with his one eye. Go stare at the wall, furball."

"You're disturbing cat nap time," she yells softly back, her eyes widening. "Oh no. Now he knows I'm awake. Go!"

"I'm not jumping out the window."

Her eyes plead with me as her gaze rocks back and forth between me and the door. "Please. I don't want to lose you. I really do like you, Jaxon Hayes."

Softening at her words, I nod and duck through the window, swinging a leg over.

Great, the garage roof is there so it's not as high up as I thought.

"I think you've been broken into and the only thing gone is my Xbox," Maddox says, just as I go to turn back inside to give her a goodnight kiss. "And maybe my half of the food."

Her wide eyes meet mine, and she pushes me, her hands flying to her mouth after. I fall backwards, landing on the garage roof with a grunt. I roll to my side, inwardly laughing.

Lily Carter just pushed me out her window.

"Someone out there?" I hear from close by.

Groaning, I roll closer to the house, so my back is against the cold brick. "Nothing. Just looking at the stars," Lily replies, her voice high-pitched.

"Xbox, food, and shower," Maddox sings. "Not in that order."

"Why don't I go make you some food while you take a shower."

Make him food? He's a grown arse man. He can make his own fucking food. I grunt, hearing the window shut.

I jump down onto the bins, feeling muscles ache in my back. Fuck, that landing hurt.

I'm heading down the drive, rubbing my hands together to ward off the cold since my coat is still inside Lily's, along with my shoes, when the door behind me opens.

At first, I think it's Maddox, that he found my shit, but it's Lily, wearing her slippers and racing down the path towards me with my stuff.

"Are you hurt? I'm so, so, so sorry."

I chuckle. "Babe, I'm good. You okay?"

"I thought I killed you," she breathes out.

I cup her jaw, leaning in. "Kiss me goodnight."

Her eyes dilate with hunger. "I can't. He's in the shower and will be out in a minute."

"Babe, kiss me," I rasp.

"Okay," she whispers.

Leaning up on her tiptoes, she presses her lips against mine. They're as soft as I remembered, light in touch. She even tastes fucking good. She hums into the kiss, making me grin. I pull back, kissing her once more before taking my things.

"Don't make him food."

"Who?" she asks, swaying slightly. I chuckle, shoving my feet into my trainers before reaching for her.

"Maddox. Tell him to cook his own food."

"I like doing things for him."

I sigh, knowing this is something we will need to talk about down the line. "All right, but don't let him treat you like a slave."

"All right. Good night, Jaxon," she whispers, kissing me again, her cheeks and nose bright red.

I grin. "Sweet dreams, Lily."

CHAPTER THIRTEEN

LILY

ICAN'T KEEP THE SMILE OFF MY FACE as I stare down at the message I received before I woke up this morning. It was waiting for me to read it when I woke up, and I think he planned that after finding out how early I wake up. This morning I did sleep in though, but still, it was a nice thing to wake up to.

JAXON: Good morning, beautiful. X

He thinks I'm beautiful. And he kissed me again last night. My lips are still buzzing, and I can't wait to do it again. I never want to let go of this feeling inside.

I spent most of the night tossing and turning, my mind on everything Jaxon. His presence, his voice, his lips. Then my mind went wild with future possibilities, things that might not even happen between us or for us. But I thought about it anyway. I want everything with him.

One thing I did dwell on was Jaxon's reputation. Apparently, he is worse than Maddox—according to a few in my family. I don't mind that he has had other girlfriends though. I just don't like what it means. He has experience where I don't have any. I guess I don't want him to be disappointed in me when he finds out I have no idea what I'm doing.

Would he leave me if I do it wrong or I'm not very good at it?

The thoughts swirled in my mind until I couldn't take it anymore and put on a film to fall asleep to.

I didn't know what today would bring. I knew what I wanted it to bring, and that was for Jaxon to be in my life. I've had just a tiny piece of him, and I feel like I've missed out my whole life on something that could be spectacular and magical.

No one has ever drawn my attention the way he has. They've never made me think of a relationship beyond friendship until him. Now I feel like I'm rushing into things, getting ahead of myself when he might not want the same things. My feelings are already growing, too invested in something that has just started.

I'm sure there is a name for girls like that. I'm pretty sure the boys have named a few girls it, and they didn't look happy about it when they said it.

I don't want to be that girl, to force Jaxon into something he doesn't want to do. But if we are going to keep kissing, if I'm actually considering taking it all the way, then I want to make sure he's on the same page, that he really is the one. It's all I've ever wanted really. I was a lot like Faith in that way, wanting the right person to give myself to in every way. It was old-fashioned, but it was me. I didn't mean sex before marriage, but for it to be with the one I knew I would spend the rest of my life with. It was something I felt strongly about, and I hope Jaxon feels just as strongly about me to understand what I want.

My phone rings, and I dash to it, hope blossoming in my chest at the thought of talking to Jaxon. Maddox is still here, snoring in the other room, so I won't have to worry about him overhearing me.

The number is one I don't recognise, yet I answer anyway due to the police saying they would phone.

"Hello?"

"May I speak with Miss Lily Carter."

"This is she," I reply, biting my thumbnail.

"Hi, this is Louise Davis. I'm calling on the behalf of the school board for St. Martin's."

"Um, hello. How can I help you?"

"We've gone over the complaint made towards you, and after new evidence coming to light, we would like to apologise on behalf of St. Martin's. We were informed of an investigation pending with the Merin family after you voiced your concerns about them, and then yesterday evening, the schoolboard was informed of the wrong-doings going on at their home."

"Yes, I reported the children being mistreated myself," I explain, my heart sinking. This doesn't sound good at all. "Am I fired?"

"No," she rushes out. "Not at all. We are extremely disappointed in the manner Mr Hartman dealt with the matter. We had no report filed about this situation by the school, but a TA, Michelle Lemon, made a statement that you filed a report more than once. Is this correct?"

"It is," I manage to get out slowly, wondering where this is going. If I'm not fired, what is going on?

"Mr Hartman has been dismissed for his transgressions and we'd like for you to start back at the school. Once again, we apologise for everything and can see that you were trying to help the children."

Shocked is an understatement, and I can't help but feel bad about Mr Hartman being made unemployed.

"Would you like me back right away?"

"Well, we were told you were attacked by the children's father, and I know this must have scared you. If you would prefer, you could return when the term starts back up in the new year."

I can't help but smile. "Thank you so much. Yes, I would love to come back."

I can hear her exhale a relieved breath. "This is great news. We will be in touch. And once again, we apologise."

"It's completely fine. You were all doing your jobs."

"Well, some of us were," she mutters. I don't say anything, too happy I've got my job back. "I'll let you go. Thank you for taking the time to speak with me."

"You're welcome."

We end the call and I can only stare down at my phone in shock. I have my job back. They aren't firing me. I squeal, jumping up and down, and bring up my last message to Jaxon. I can't wait to tell him.

"Turn the noise down," is groaned, and I stop what I'm doing.

There's a knock at the front door just as the door to my spare bedroom opens and Maddox steps out scratching his bare chest, wearing only a pair of grey boxers.

"Um, can you cover that up?" I ask him, looking away.

He grins. "And disappoint your neighbours when I open the door? Nope."

"You want Mrs North to see you?"

His grin spreads, and he wraps his arm around my shoulders. "Everyone wants this. It can't be helped. I'm just that good looking."

I giggle and stay wrapped under his arm as he pulls the door open. He groans, looking at our uncle Myles.

"It's too early. I didn't do it."

I blink up at Maddox, confused, but then Myles speaks, sounding amused. "I didn't know you were here, but I should have guessed. Madison is annoyed with you."

Maddox groans when Myles mentions Madison's name. "I was seriously drunk."

"You pissed up her dress."

Maddox glares harder at Myles when I gasp. "Maddox, why did you do that?"

"It was a dress she bought for a date," Myles adds, his lips twitching.

"Madison is going on a date?" I squeal, excited.

"I thought it was the shower," Maddox explains, ignoring my excitement.

Myles blinks. "It was hung up on the bathroom door."

"Like I said, I was drunk."

"Why were you even in your sister's bedroom?"

Maddox groans. "Because I heard the wanker talking about going on a date with her to all his friends in town."

"He was bragging?" Myles asks, his voice hard.

Maddox sighs, his shoulders sagging. "No. But he acted like the big man and I didn't get a good feeling about him. I couldn't let my twin go through a date with him. What kind of brother would that make me?"

"That's so sweet," I muse, then pause, looking up at him. "Wait, so you got drunk over it and went back to Madison's? I don't understand." And I don't. If he was there, why did he come back here?

Maddox squeezes my hip playfully, winking down at me. "No, I got drunk because I posted my table number at Pennies on Facebook and said the first girl to buy me a drink could take me on a date. I ended up getting more drinks than I bargained for. And food."

"You can do that?"

He nods. "Yeah. It's for table service so you don't have to go to the bar. You order on their app and pay for it there and then. They bring it over."

"Wait? Food? You said you were hungry when you got back."

He grins. "I burnt most of the food off when I took a blonde out of the bar."

"Surprised you could get it up with the amount you apparently drank," Myles mutters, making me blush. "And pissing on your sister's dress?"

Maddox holds his free hand up. "She hates it when I turn up smelling of chicks that can't afford decent perfume, and she hates it when I smell like a brewery, so I went to take a shower. It was an accident. I thought it was the shower curtain and I always pee in the shower."

Ew.

Myles shakes his head, not believing him for a second. He must have been really drunk to mistake a dress for a shower curtain though.

"I'm going to go get some bleach and clean my shower," I mutter, moving to go do that, but Maddox laughs, pulling me closer to his side.

"I've come to talk to you," Myles tells me gently.

I nod, knowing this is about Star and Miah. I desperately wanted to go over this morning, but I knew they were right in saying they had to get to know their grandma.

I open my mouth to offer him inside when another car pulls up. Aiden, my brother, steps out, waving his arms around in greeting.

When he pulls Sunday, my niece, out of the back, a wide smile spreads across my face. She's beautiful and so much like her dad. I love her to pieces.

He jogs up the path with Sunday in one hand and three changing bags in the other. She's already gotten so big and now moves along the floor. Before long, she'll be walking, and I can't wait to see it.

Aiden got some girl pregnant and didn't know until the day the hospital called to tell him he was a dad and the mum had sadly passed away during birth. It breaks my heart every single time, but Sunday is loved by all, especially her father. He really stepped up and became a brilliant father. It's also good his girlfriend, Bailey, is in the picture. Sunday might have grounded my outgoing, ex party animal brother, but it's Bailey that soothes his soul and keeps him sane.

"Da, da, da," Sunday mumbles, smacking her dad in the face with her toy.

He grins at her, winking. "Yeah, baby girl, da, da."

I lift my arms out, reaching for her, and she comes willingly, also calling me da, da. I giggle, snuggling my face into the little girl's neck and breathing in her baby smell.

"I need a favour," Aiden starts, dropping the bags next to me.

"Of course I will," I tell him, glad I can spend some time with her.

"I've not even asked you yet," he says, grinning at me.

He doesn't need to. I will always say yes to looking after my niece. She's no hardship, and it's a miracle he's even letting me. He was so protective of her, wanting to do everything by himself when she was first born.

Looking back, it was only me and Bailey he didn't mind holding Sunday, other than himself. All the others he would quickly take her back and do it himself. But not once since he brought her home has he ever asked me to hand her back to him.

I also love that he trusts me with her, even knowing how I can get with my episodes.

I blow a raspberry at Sunday, making her giggle, before turning back to Aiden. "Go. We are going to have a fun day together."

He grins, leaning forward and kissing my forehead. "Love you, sis." He pulls back, puckering his lips at his daughter. She giggles before opening her mouth wide, slobber and all, and throwing her face against his, her mouth all over his. I giggle, watching his eyes light up with happiness. "Great kiss for Daddy, baby girl."

"She just slobbered all over your mouth," Maddox points out, before stepping away and gagging. "Oh God. She has a runny nose too."

He gags again before rushing down the hallway to the downstairs bathroom. I laugh, shaking my head.

"Is Uncle Maddox a wimp? Yes, yes, he is," Aiden coos at Sunday. "I'll be back at five to pick her up."

"Okay. See you later," I tell him. "Can you say, bye, da, da?"

"Da, da," Sunday yells, waving goodbye to her dad.

Myles has a faraway look in his eyes before meeting my gaze. "Never thought I'd see the day you guys would start having kids of your own. Definitely didn't think it would be Aiden and that he'd be so damn good at it."

"He's the best," I whisper, stepping aside to get us both out of the cold.

He shuts the door behind him and takes in a deep breath. "They've granted Mrs North temporary custody of the kids. They'll be kept under close supervision, so I'd expect a visit once, if not twice a week from social services."

"That's great news," I breathe out, feeling my eyes well with tears.

He strokes my cheek before heading over to the kettle. "It is."

I look down at Sunday who is back to playing with her toy. "It's good news all around today, isn't it?"

"What other good news did you get? It's half ten."

I laugh and open the kitchen cupboard to grab the spare high chair I have for Sunday. I place her in it, before grabbing three cups off the shelf. "I got a phone call from the school today. I'm allowed to go back. They heard about yesterday so they said I could have some time off and go back when the new term starts back up."

"Oh, Lily, that's fantastic news. We should go out tonight and celebrate. I know your mum and dad were worried about you. They're going to be thrilled when they find out."

I can feel my face pale. I can't go out tonight. I made plans with Jaxon after he finishes work.

"I can't tonight."

"Do what tonight?" Maddox asks, walking in with fresh clothes on.

"Celebrate. Lily got her job back."

Maddox grins before walking over to me and lifting me off my feet. "That's great news. I'm happy for you."

"Put me down," I giggle, swatting him playfully.

"But why can't you tonight?"

Not wanting to lie to Maddox or my family, I give in. "Okay. We can do something tonight."

"What was you going to do?" he presses, watching me carefully. I look away and start making drinks.

"Catch up on soaps?"

"Hadn't you better get to work?" Myles asks Maddox, and I sag with relief at the change of subject.

"Yeah. I need to go fire some men."

I turn around with wide eyes. "Why? Is everything okay?"

He takes his cup of coffee with a shake of his head. "No. Fuckers have been stealing timber from the yard."

"That should get them fired," Myles mutters before thanking me for his drink.

"Hope you have a good day," I tell him.

He kisses the top of my head before putting the half-drunk cup on the side. "Will do. I'll see you later. And thank you for letting me crash again. I swear, I'm gonna get my neighbours evicted by summer next year."

"They can't be that bad," I tell him, but secretly, I hate he has noisy neighbours. He tells me all the time how they throw parties and argue non-stop.

"He just hates that he never gets invited," Myles comments.

"That's exactly it." Maddox grins, shaking his head. He finishes pulling his coat on before bending down to Sunday, blowing a raspberry on her cheek. She giggles, fisting his hair. "Bye, squirt."

"Wait, do you need lunch?" I call out before he reaches the door.

"I got it," he yells back, swinging his keys around his fingers. "I'm going to get Paisley to cook for me. It pisses Landon off."

I giggle whilst rolling my eyes. Landon won't be happy if he finds out Paisley cooked for him again.

"I'd better get going. I've got a house call to make," Myles informs me, kissing my temple.

"Bye, Uncle Myles. And thank you for coming to fill me in on everything."

"Anything for you, sweetheart. Take care of yourselves and I'll be back later. I'll text your dad to let him know."

"Okay."

When he's gone, I look down at Sunday in her chair and clap my hands. "Shall we get messy? Shall we bake some cakes and get flour everywhere?"

She bangs her toy against her tray, excitement filling her eyes. I take that as a yes and start pulling out ingredients.

SUNDAY IS FULL of energy and has given me no time to text Jaxon to cancel our date tonight. We've just finished making cupcakes when I hear a van pull up out front. Peeking out the window, my heart speeds up at the sight of the Hayes Removals van.

"Jaxon," I whisper. Moving faster than possible, I grab Sunday's coat and quickly pull it on her. She claps her hands excitedly, probably thinking we're going on a trip.

We step outside just as Jaxon pulls a headboard from the back of his van. He notices me and a wide grin spreads across his face.

He drops the headboard on the ground, leaning it against the van, and walks over to me.

"Hey, beautiful," he greets, and my darn heart skips a beat once again. Sunday giggles, throwing herself forward.

He quickly steps forward, taking her from me. In a daze, I watch as she smacks her open mouth against his face. He chuckles, looking down at her.

"Hey, tiny." He looks to me, a twinkle in his eyes. "I guess this is Aiden's kid and you're babysitting?"

I take Sunday's hand, letting her grip my finger instead of his hair. "She is. Jaxon, meet Sunday. Sunday, meet Jaxon."

"Mi," she babbles out, resting her head against Jaxon's shoulder.

I giggle. "I think she likes you."

"Is she the only one?"

"No," I admit earnestly, watching him under my lashes.

He grins. "Good."

When Sunday's lids begin to droop, I step forward. "Here, let me take her."

Sunday doesn't cause too much of a fuss when I take her away from Jaxon. She happily snuggles into my neck, sticking her thumb in her mouth.

Everything around me blurs away when my gaze locks with Jaxon's. The look he's giving me steals my breath, and I find it hard to look away.

"What?" I ask, finding myself breathless. How can he do that with just one look? Make me feel lost yet found. He takes my breath away yet gives me life.

He's enough to send any girl crazy.

Jaxon takes a step closer. "I could watch you all day, Lily Carter. You're the most beautiful woman I've ever laid eyes on. But right now, I'm imagining you waiting for me to come home from work with our daughter in your arms."

I struggle to catch my breath. It sounds like a fairy tale, something too good to be true. He wants all of that and with me. *Me.*

"You are?" I ask breathlessly, taking a step closer.

"I am, and it's a beautiful sight," he confesses, taking another step closer until we're a step apart.

"Hey, peeps," Charlotte yells, and both Jaxon and I jump apart, turning to find her walking towards us.

"Landon popped by earlier and mentioned you had Sunday for the day. Thought I'd come join you for a bit whilst the library's quiet."

"Isn't it always meant to be quiet?" Jaxon rumbles.

"Well, duh, yeah. But, like, there's no one there." Charlotte grins, then it's like she notices him for the first time. "Wait, are you here to see your granddad or get abused by one of our family members?"

I can feel heat rising in my cheeks, and I look away when Jaxon doesn't answer.

"Wait, is that a bed?" she asks, looking at his van.

"Yeah, for the kid. Um, I thought maybe they didn't have one and we had one spare," he explains, falling over his words.

I smother my giggle. "Aw, that is so sweet. I'll make you some muffins as a thank you."

Wide-eyed, he looks to me for help. I clear my throat and feel myself becoming flustered.

"Um, I already baked him some cupcakes. I was going to drop them off at your granddad's."

"You did?" Charlotte asks me, seeming to deflate.

"Yes. I'll just go grab them," I say, ready to turn in.

"No, I'll get them. You two looked like you were having a conversation."

Oh no.

"We were talking about the bed," Jaxon quickly puts in.

"Cool." She beams, but then as she steps off, I hear her muttering, "I could have baked some muffins."

I giggle and turn back to Jaxon, just as he exhales a huge breath. "Thank God you didn't take her up on her offer. Sorry, Lily, but Charlotte's cooking is a deal breaker for me. Never make me eat it. I still can't eat a muffin because of her."

"I'll protect you."

He grins, and that soft look he reserves only for me is back. "Yeah?"

"Yes," I tell him, feeling goofy for the smile on my face.

"I can't wait to see you tonight. I thought we could go ice skating."

I love ice skating.

I lose my smile as I shift Sunday higher up my chest. "Jaxon, about that…"

He frowns, losing his smile. "Have you changed your mind about us?"

"What? Of course not," I practically yell out. I clear my throat, shaking my head. "I was meant to text you, but I got carried away making a mess with Sunday, so I was going to wait until she had her nap before texting you."

"What were you going to text me?"

I don't like the look on his face. My heart squeezes almost painfully, and I take a step toward him, putting a comforting hand on his bicep. "I got my job back. I start back after the new year."

He grins wide. "That's huge. I'm happy for you, baby. We should celebrate."

I melt at knowing he wants that. "That's why I was texting you. My uncle Myles was here when I got the news and has arranged for us to go out later," I tell him, then look down at my feet, hating the next words that come out of my mouth. "I would invite you—"

"Hey," he interrupts, his voice low. "It's fine. You go out and celebrate with your family. I'll come by after and watch a movie or something. That sound good to you?"

My heart warms. "Are you okay with that? I feel terrible I've had to let you down."

"They don't get to find out now, baby. We can tell them when we are ready."

"Tell them?" I ask, trailing off. This is what I've been wanting to know, what has plagued my mind since things progressed. Is this what I think it is between us? Is this something he sees a future with? I want to know everything, so I don't get my hopes up.

"That you're mine, and I'm yours."

I melt, a soft smile on my lips. "Yes!"

"Got 'em," Charlotte yells.

I giggle at Jaxon's crestfallen expression. He winks down at me, mouthing, "Later," before walking off to grab the bed.

CHAPTER FOURTEEN

LILY

I HARDLY ATE ANYTHING AT DINNER. Jaxon said he didn't mind that I'd come out to celebrate with my family, but it didn't stop the guilt eating away at me. I didn't like that I had to hide him from my family. I love them. They're the most important people in my life. Jaxon, however, has wormed his way into that zone without even trying. He's just there, in my heart.

Everything he said earlier had been magical. He saw a future with me, like I did him. He called me his. *His*. I knew what that meant, and I was totally on board with it.

My future has been planned out. I like order, hate change, and never saw past my job at the school and my time with my family. Now I have Jaxon, and those few moments we shared were special and made me want more from life. He is my more.

Lying to my family, even though it's not a direct lie, is something I've never done before. I hate lying. It gets you nowhere in life, and in the long run, it makes people miserable. I've seen it time and time again with the people around me.

"You okay, princess?" Dad asks, watching me with worry.

I force a smile even though my emotions are all over the place. "I'm fine, Dad. Just tired."

"Sorry about that," Aiden comments, wincing as he hands Sunday another chip. The rest of us have finished our dinner and dessert, but Sunday only woke up thirty minutes ago.

"It's not Sunday. We had loads of fun today," I tell him, easing his mind. "I just didn't sleep well last night."

"You didn't look tired when you were talking to Jaxon," Charlotte helpfully comments.

My pulse spikes when all eyes come to me, Faith's widening. I can feel the heat rise up from my neck.

Everyone stares, waiting for me to say something. I don't, looking away and down at the table.

"Jaxon Hayes?" Maddox asks, his jaw clenching.

"She baked him cookies," Charlotte boasts. "He loved them."

"I bet he did," Dad growls.

"Dad," Faith warns slowly, her voice gentle.

"Why the fuck is he hanging around?" Landon asks, and I divert my attention to him. He's asking Paisley, who's watching me. She ducks her head when our gaze meets and shrugs at Landon's question.

Does she know?

"He brought a bed for Miah," Charlotte tells everyone, happily sipping her wine.

"How did he know the kid needed a bed?" Maddox asks, watching me now.

"I told him!" Faith blurts loudly.

"When did *you* see him?" Beau asks accusingly.

Oh god, this is going terribly.

"When everything happened?" Faith answers, but it comes out as a question.

Maddox snorts. "Probably hanging around Lily. He's always had a thing for her."

He has?

"Like she'd fall for that di—um, head," Aiden muses, then winces across the table. "Sorry, Paisley."

"It's fine," she says on a sigh, used to the banter between our families. I never really understood how she felt about being in the middle until now. It must hurt to have the man you love and the family you love be constantly at odds.

"Let's not talk about this," I say softly.

"Yeah, let's talk about something else. It's not like you'd let him get near you anyway, and he doesn't have the balls to cross us," Maddox boasts.

"Hey!" Paisley snaps.

"Sorry, Paisley," Maddox offers, then glares at Landon. "This is your fault."

Landon doesn't answer, snuggling into Paisley's neck and whispering something to her that makes her giggle.

"Actually, I'm going to go. I'm really tired," I tell them.

"It's only half six, baby," Mum comments, placing the back of her hand on my forehead. "You don't have a temperature."

I give her a soft smile. "Just tired, Mum."

"I'll walk you out," Dad says, and I nod, grabbing my bag from under the table. I start to say my goodbyes, kissing everyone on the cheek. When I get to Maddox, he leans back in his chair, his brows scrunched together.

"Lil, before you go, I forgot to ask this morning; where did you put my Xbox? I wanted a game last night and couldn't find it."

I bite my lip, looking at Faith a few chairs away from me. She giggles, leaning her head against Beau's shoulder.

"What?" he asks, looking at everyone around the table.

"It's not missing, if that's what you're worried about," Charlotte tells him.

He raises his eyebrow. "So where is it?"

"Um," I mumble, not too sure how he's going to take this. If I tell him gently, he might take the news better.

"She gave it to Miah," Charlotte blurts. Landon laughs. "What? It's sweet. He didn't say it, but I could see he was really excited to have it. His entire face lit up. Although, some of those games were questionable. Did you see that one game? It had guns, Maddox. Really, Maddox, guns?"

Slowly, our eyes meet, and his jaw slackens. "Please tell me Charlotte drank the fruit juice again and doesn't know what she's talking about."

"Hey, I've only had a bottle. And I didn't dream it. I was there. I think," she says defensively.

"Maybe you should have water, darlin'," Myles tells her.

"All right," she agrees.

"He's never had a computer before, Maddox. They'd been through so much and I wanted him to have something good," I explain before he can get mad.

"My Xbox though, Lil?"

"I just wanted to make him happy," I mumble sadly, looking down at my feet.

"Hey, it's fine. It's cool he has something in that old bat's house. He'd be bored as hell."

Hope blossoms in my chest. "You're not mad?"

He stands up, pulling me into his arms. "How could I be mad at you for being so darn caring. I'll go out and buy another to keep at yours. It's no trouble."

"I could buy it," I offer.

He knocks his fist under my chin. "I've got it. I'm just glad the kid has something."

"You're such a good person," I tell him, feeling stupid now for worrying. I should have known he'd want to do something good for Miah.

"Come on. I'll walk you to your car," Dad says.

I pull back from Maddox, feeling much better. "Night, guys."

Everyone shouts their goodbyes as Dad and I walk out. It's freezing when we step out, the ground shining with ice.

"Better not snow," Dad warns, looking around the carpark.

"I love snow," I whisper.

He chuckles. "I know you do. I still remember the first time we let you play out in it. You were so happy, mesmerised by everything and loved building that snowman."

"It was a great snowman," I tell him, remembering the time he's talking about. We went out as a family and built the biggest snowman on the street. That was after I spent twenty minutes just admiring the snow, touching it and trying to catch the snowflakes on the tip of my tongue. My biological mum had never let me play outside, and I don't think Dad realised at the time that it was my first time seeing it.

"You'd talk to us if something was bothering you, right?" he asks out of nowhere.

"Of course. Why would you ask that?"

"You seemed distant at dinner and hardly touched your food," he tells me, leaning back against my car.

"I'm fine."

"Princess, you can't lie for shit. Something is bothering you."

I feel tears gather in my eyes. I hate that I'm lying to him and now he knows it. "Are you disappointed in me?"

He reaches out to grasp my shoulders. "Never! But I am worried about you. You've never lied, even though that wasn't a straight out lie. You are tired, but that isn't why you left."

He's right. I am tired, but that isn't what's bothering me. "Can you trust that I know what I'm doing? And when I'm ready to share, you and Mum will be the first people I talk to? This is just something I need to keep to myself for a while."

He grins, kissing the top of my head. "That I can do. I might worry every waking moment, but I love you and trust you to make the right decisions. But just know, you can come to me about anything. *Anything* at all," he says, emphasizes the 'anything'.

The way he's looking at me is like he knows. I struggle not to tell him. To not tell him everything and how it's weighing on me. I want to share how happy I am, but how torn I am because of the conflict between the two families.

"Thank you, Dad."

"Get in your car. It's cold out."

I smile, leaning up to kiss his cheek. "Love you, Dad."

"Love you more, princess," he tells me, a tender look in his eye.

I get in the car, glad it's not frozen enough that I need to scrape ice off my windscreen. Dad waits by the door of the restaurant until I drive off.

The guilt I feel inside isn't eating away at me as much. Now my dad knows I'll come to him when I'm ready, I feel a lot better inside. He knows there's something going on, so when it does come out, it won't be such a big surprise.

I pull over when I'm out of sight of the restaurant and text Jaxon that I'm on my way home, then I pull back out and drive the rest of the way with a smile on my face.

I'M HOME FIVE minutes when I hear a tap on the backdoor. I grin, rushing to the door and pulling it open.

"Jaxon."

"Beautiful," he murmurs with a gentle expression. He grasps me around the waist and lifts me backwards into the house. He deposits me down, reaching for my lips.

"Hm, you taste like chocolate."

I lick my lips, sagging against him. "Chocolate fudge cake. My favourite."

He grins. "Good to know."

"What have you been doing all night?"

"Waiting for you," he tells me, still holding me against him.

My face drops. "I'm so sorry about today."

He runs his fingers through my hair. "Don't be. I'm here now, aren't I? That is more than I could ever ask for."

"My dad knows something is going on," I tell him.

His eyes widen a fraction before he covers it. "About us?"

"No, with me. He understands I'm not ready to talk about it."

"It will all work out in the end. Once they see how happy we are, they'll be okay. But we need to get us in a place we're good at before we tell people."

I place my hand on his chest. "I know. I just don't like keeping you a secret. I don't know, it feels—"

"Sordid? Dirty? Sexy?"

"Jaxon." I giggle, smacking his chest lightly. He places his hand over mine, bringing our bodies flush together.

"I'm joking. Don't let it trouble you. You're happy, right?"

"Very," I admit quickly.

His eyes crinkle as he smiles at me. "Me too. Do you think your family will be happy when they found out?"

I'd like to think they'd be happy for me. I really do. But I also know how protective they are of me. I thought I was getting ahead of myself this morning, but after hearing him call me his, I thought more on it. I've come to the conclusion that they might make me stay away from him. And I've never gone against my family. They mean so much to me. It's killing me inside that somewhere down the road, I might have to choose. It's making my insides twist upside down.

"I don't honestly know," I answer him after a minute.

His gaze softens. "They'll probably get mad, baby. It's me. And if they do, you need to remember it's because of me and not you. But we will go through it together when the time comes."

"All right."

"Now, I've been looking forward to you snuggling against me and watching a film all evening."

A grin spreads across my face. "Me too."

He steps up behind me, placing his hands on my hips. "Lead the way," he sing-songs in a deeper voice, making me giggle. We reach the front entrance where the stairs are, when there's a knock on the door.

My heart races as I pull open the door under the stairs and push Jaxon inside. He frowns, looking dazed before realisation dawns across his face.

"Sweetheart? Really? First the window and now the cupboard."

I can't help but giggle. "I'm sorry. Let me check who it is."

He sighs, but then another knock comes, and he shuts the door on himself. I straighten down my top before stepping over to the door. I open it, surprised to find Blanche, Star and Miah at my door.

"Blanche, hello. Come in out of the cold. Is everything okay?"

"Hi, Lily. I'm really sorry to bother you so late in the evening, but I need your help."

"Hi, Star. Hi, Miah," I greet, closing the door when they're all in before turning to Blanche. "What can I help you with?"

She looks down at Star, her lip curled slightly. Star is itching her head furiously, her lips puckered in a pout.

"I think she has headlice. I have no idea how to get rid of them. My Nellie never had them."

"That's okay. I know how," I tell her gently, trying to hide my smile when she pulls away from Star. "Do you have them?"

Miah looks at me with a sneer. "No!"

"All right," I tell him, smiling in amusement.

"I couldn't find it," Jaxon suddenly says, stepping out of the cupboard. I bite my lip at how ridiculous the scene is; him walking out of a cupboard I hang coats and keep shoes in.

"What were you doing in there?" Star asks, looking around him and into the small cupboard.

"Lily is missing her shoe," Jaxon answers, coming to stand by my side.

"I have nits," Star tells him, seeming more confident in herself. I can't help but smile as I lean against Jaxon. They're already improving and seem so much happier.

"Guess what?" he says in a loud whisper.

Star leans forward. "What?"

"I'm a pro at getting rid of headlice. We can evict them in no time."

"Evict?" she asks with a cute pout.

I giggle and answer, "Evict basically means to remove. He'll get rid of them for you."

"You can do that?" Star asks, her voice soft.

"Anyone can do that," Miah snaps, leaning against the wall with a bored look on his face.

Jaxon ignores his attitude, which makes me like him more. "Do you have any stuff?"

Seeing the question is directed at me, I nod. "I do. Are you really going to do it?"

He shrugs like it's no big deal, but it's the sweetest thing in the world. "Yeah, I did Paisley's as a kid."

"Is she your daughter?" Star asks, staring wide-eyed up at Jaxon with hero worship in her eyes.

"She's my sister."

"And you got rid of hers? Because it itches real bad. I don't like it."

He chuckles, bending down to her level. "I bet it does. Want to come into the kitchen while Lily finds the stuff so we can get started?"

"Yes."

I watch, feeling my throat tighten when he takes her hand. I clear my throat, addressing him before he leaves.

"The stuff is in the middle drawer in the kitchen. It has to be left on for fifteen minutes before you do anything," I tell him before turning to Blanche. "We'll go through it once it's been on long enough then leave it on for the night. I'll come over in the morning and go through it again. You'll have to keep doing it until all the eggs have gone."

"I will. I just don't know what I'm doing," Blanche says, looking uncomfortable with Jaxon in the room.

I hide my smile as I turn to Miah. "Want to watch a movie in the front room?"

"Whatever," he mutters, then his eyes go to the stairs. "That cat only has one eye."

I turn to look at Willa, who is looking at us through the bannisters.

"That's Willa," I tell him.

"Cool!" Star yells, looking at my cat.

"You go in the kitchen whilst I set the TV up for Miah," I tell them, and Jaxon walks down the hallway with Star in his grasp, Blanche reluctantly following. "How are you settling in?"

"Why, you want to report that to your uncle too?" he asks snidely, and I frown, hurt he'd think that of me.

"I just want you to be safe and happy."

"Whatever."

I switch the TV on and hand him the remote. "I have all the movie channels so pick whatever you want."

"What the fuck! Has that cat got three legs?"

"Don't swear," I tell him, then pick up Peggy. "Her name is Peggy. She was a rescue cat who had been run over."

"You really do like helping people, don't you," he says out of nowhere. When I look up, he's watching me with an expression I've yet to see on him.

"Yes. Everyone deserves to be helped, to have someone on their side. The cats have me and you have Blanche."

"I guess so. She's grumpy though."

I chuckle, feeling my chest expand. He's talking to me. "She just takes a while to get comfortable. She seems to really like you there."

"Yeah, she does fuss a lot, but she hates it when Star messes with her stuff."

"It's an adjustment for her too. She's not only found out her only daughter is dead, but that she has two grandkids she never got to see grow up. It must be sinking in."

"Dad told us she didn't want to know about us," he tells me, and I don't say anything, hoping he'll share a bit more. "I'm, um… I'm sorry I yelled at you the other day."

"It's fine. You were going through a lot."

"What your dad said… Is that true?"

I sit down on the arm of the sofa, letting Peggy down. She hops over to Miah, sniffing him for a few minutes before she finds it acceptable to lounge next to him.

"Yes, everything he said was true," I admit, not wanting to go into detail.

"And he let it happen?"

"We didn't know about each other. It's a long story. We're actually biologically siblings with different fathers. We didn't know about each other, but the second he knew, he came looking. I was saved, and he adopted me. He'll forever be my dad, and same with my mum."

"You don't think about your biological mum?"

I look to the floor for a moment. No one has ever asked me that before. "Not in the way people might think. I only think about the terrible person she was, someone I aspire to never become, but other than that, no. My mum now is my mum."

He seems to think about it for a moment. "I don't think you have to worry about becoming her. You've not got a bad bone in your body."

I giggle. "I get that a lot."

"I bet you do," he tells me with a small smile, but then he frowns, looking deeper in thought. "Do you think I'll be like him?"

"No," I tell him quickly, placing my hand over his. "You protected your sister."

He removes his hand from under mine and stares at the television. "I would imagine hurting him, hurting his friends who came into the house."

"That's normal," I explain gently.

"What? Sticking a knife in his throat is normal?"

I'm shocked by his honesty. "Do you still have these thoughts?"

"When it comes to him, yes. All the time."

"But no one else, right?"

"No, but sometimes it scares me. I mean, is that how he started off, picturing hurting us when we made too much noise?"

"I can't sit here and tell you why they do the things they do, because I don't know. I lived it and still can't understand it. I lived thinking it was me, that I was a bad girl. Then it just became normal. I thought all parents did it to their children. But they don't. It was never about me, not really. It was just who they were."

"Yeah," he murmurs.

"Would you like a drink or something?" I offer when he doesn't say anything else.

"If you have any Coke, or any fizzy pop, I'd love one. Blanche doesn't keep them around, says they're bad for us."

"They are," I admit, lightly laughing.

His eyes harden on me. "But I won't die tomorrow from it, like she seems to think."

I laugh now, hard. "No, you won't. I'll sneak you a can of Coke."

I'm by the door when he calls out to me. "Thank you."

"It's only Coke."

He shakes his head. "Not for that, though I appreciate it. I'm saying thank you for everything else you've done. Star really loves it there, and I suppose it's not so bad. We're finally safe, and I don't have to worry as much that he'll hurt Star. I still worry he will come back."

"He won't hurt you again," I tell him. "And you're welcome."

I rush from the room when my throat begins to tighten and my eyes glaze over with tears. I stand there in the hallway, trying to catch my breath. His words mean everything.

I made him safe.

When I'm sure I won't burst into tears, I head into the kitchen to grab his drink.

CHAPTER FIFTEEN

JAXON

Breakfast time is now always interesting with Landon around. We might tolerate the fucker being with my sister, but it doesn't mean we have to like him enough to give him a free pass. Which is why my brothers love to wind him up. Trouble is, he likes to do the same, especially with Reid.

"So, you think Hayden will pop by and see me later? A sister for a sister and all that," Reid taunts.

I inwardly groan, knowing where this will lead; to Reid lying on his back across the table, complaining about how Landon broke his back. He's never brought up Hayden before though, it's usually just lighter banter.

"Reid," Mum snaps, wiping her mouth with her napkin. "Can we eat one breakfast in peace?"

Landon just smirks at Reid. "You really think you have a shot?"

Scoffing, Reid throws his napkin on his finished plate. "Please, she's so hot for me she could melt an iceberg."

"Let's find out," Landon states calmly, pulling his phone out of his back pocket.

Reid is still grinning, but I can see the uncertainty in his expression. Paisley leans against Landon. "What are you doing?"

He kisses her and a growl erupts from every male in the room.

"I just fucking ate," Wyatt snaps.

Putting his phone on the table, he clicks the loudspeaker and ringing echoes around the kitchen.

"Bro, it's fucking eight in the morning. You really do have a fucking death wish," Hayden snaps into the phone, her voice filled with sleep.

"She sounds like sex and orgasms," Reid exclaims with a grin.

Landon narrows his eyes, but it's Hayden who answers.

"Please fucking tell me you didn't ring me for that dickhead to speak to me. I swear to God, Landon, I will—"

"Hayden!" Landon rumbles, his lips twitching.

"What?" she snaps, louder this time.

"We were just having a discussion. Reid here thinks he has a chance with you. I quote, you're so hot for him you could melt icebergs. Thinks he can talk smack about you and I'd retaliate. I think he forgets who you are."

Laughter. Loud, boisterous laughter erupting from the phone fills the room. Everyone just stares at the phone, but looking at Reid, I can see he's lost his confidence and is glaring at the phone, pissed off.

"Wait!" Hayden cries through laughter. "I take it back, bro. You can wake me up any time if I get a laugh like this."

"You're on loudspeaker," Landon replies, leaning back with a smug expression.

"Good, so the dickhead can hear me when I say, I'd rather rot in a ditch with ants and snakes eating away at my flesh while only having my own piss to drink than ever be hot for him."

"She's in denial," Reid snarls.

"Nope, that's you, sugar plum. Now go play on the motorway. I have to get some sleep."

The call ends without a goodbye to her brother, and we're all riveted by the expression on Reid's face. Then he smirks, getting up. "I have the biggest boner after listening to her morning voice. I'm going to tug one out."

That's when it happens. Mum screams when plates get knocked off the table, cursing about how they are her best set. Paisley, used to it after growing up with us, just calmly slides her chair away from the table.

I jerk my chin at Wyatt. While he grabs Reid, I grab Landon, pulling the two apart. "That's enough," I yell, throwing him onto the kitchen counter. He goes to take a shot at me, but Paisley steps up, wrapping her arms around his stomach.

"Come on, I've got to get to work. I've left them to do breakfast by themselves."

He takes one more heaving breath before looking down at her, his expression softening. "Come on then."

Alarms blare and all of us look to each other before pushing our way through the door. We get outside just as a dark green car with no plates speeds off, kicking dust up on the way.

"Fuck!" I curse, turning towards Hayes Removals. The lights on the vans are flashing, the alarms ringing in my ears.

"Shit!" Wyatt yells as we get closer, and I see what he's done. The windows on every van have been smashed and the tyres have been slashed.

"Who the fuck did this?" Eli snaps, just as his phone rings. "It's Tim. He's out on a job."

Well, at least we have one working van.

"I'll call the police," Mum sighs, patting my arm as she passes.

"Thanks, Mum."

I look at the carnage, shaking my head. We'll have this on camera, and there's no way some fucker could hack the feed again. Still, these are damages we can't afford to have right now, nor vans out of commission.

"Do you think it's the same person who pushed me?" Paisley asks, tucked into Landon.

I look at Landon and wince. I'd forgotten to tell him we found the guy who hurt her. He must read it because he grinds his teeth together.

"No, Paisley, it's not."

"But—"

"If he says it's not, it's not," Landon says gently. "Why don't you go up to the house and I'll help these clean the glass up."

Paisley beams up at him. "You are so sweet."

"I know." He smirks, and I clench my jaw. Fucker doesn't want to help; he just wants to grill me.

Wyatt sidles up next to me. "This wasn't George. One, he doesn't have the strength to do this, and two, he was pretty fucking scared before we left him."

I nod, but Eli spinning and meeting my gaze has the hairs on the back of my neck standing on end.

"What?" I ask him, but he ducks his head, finishing off his conversation.

"Yeah, we'll be out soon. Cheers. Bye." He steps over to us and takes in a deep breath. "Tim got barricaded in the house he was working at with Newman. The van has been vandalised. They got out about fifteen minutes ago but have been talking to the police."

"He's going to pay," I growl, moving around the vans to my car. Landon puts a hand to my chest. "Not now, Landon."

"No. I told you he was mine. He touched Paisley. You've dealt with him, haven't you?"

"Yes," I snarl, pushing him back. "But we have enough going on right now. We don't have time to coddle you. I forgot, okay. Now fuck off so I can go finish this."

"Let him go, man," Luke says, coming to my side.

"I want to know who the guy is," Landon growls at Luke. "He can go, but you and me are going to pay someone a little visit."

"Whatever," I say, and take the keys out of my back pocket. Wyatt catches up to me, opening the passenger side door. "I need to do this alone."

He doesn't listen, shutting the door behind him. "We're not only family, but partners. We all have stakes in Hayes Removals. We're doing this together."

With a sharp nod, I twist the key, starting up the engine.

Fucker needs to learn who he's dealing with.

WE PULL UP OUTSIDE Big Move, and I can't help but once again be baffled as to why he wants our company. The place is clearly bigger than ours. There are twice as many vans, and the building where the offices are is a lot bigger too. To the side is a warehouse with the metal rolling doors rolled halfway up.

Forklifts are moving loads in and around the warehouse, something we don't do or are equipped to do.

"This really doesn't make sense, man. He has a good set up here. And he must do good to stay in business."

"I know. I'm taking a wild guess and saying this is personal to either one of us or to a client of ours."

"Yeah, me too," he murmurs as he steps out of the car. "But none of us know who he is."

The office is a smaller building next to the warehouse. We head over to the door, pulling it open and letting the cold air breeze through.

The receptionist looks up, a smile on her face. "Hello, welcome to Big Move. How can I help you today?"

Wyatt steps forward. "Hey darlin'. What's a pretty little thing like you doing in a place like this."

The girl blushes, dropping her pen at his compliment. "I, um, it's just until I find something else."

"I bet. How long have you worked here?"

"I moved here with the company when we opened not long ago. Mr Black needed someone who was already trained."

"How come they moved here?" Wyatt asks, pretending to be interested, yet not too interested in her answer. "I mean, the place has other branches. Why another one here?"

Her face lights up, and she leans forward. "Don't tell Mr Black I told you this because he'd fire me, but when his dad made him director of the company, he told him he had to get profits up by so much before the end of next year or he would be cut off."

"How's he doing with that?" Wyatt asks, dipping his voice a little.

She scrunches her nose up. "Well, not so good. We've actually lost a little business since he started over. A lot of the old clients don't want to be involved. He did try to hit up this art dealer or someone big, but the guy turned him down. And not nicely either," she explains. "Wait, are you potential clients?"

When she looks close to panicking, Wyatt reaches out, tugging on a piece of hair. "Darlin' we just came in to see Mr Black. Glad we got you though. So glad," he drawls.

She blushes further, and I'd groan if it weren't for the fact we just got something.

"Who was the client he approached?" I ask curiously.

"What are you doing, Jessica?" Black calls sharply, before he steps out of a doorway.

He looks up and sees us, his expression hardening. "Hayes."

I grin. "Black."

"Um," Jessica murmurs, looking from him to us. She's probably pissing herself for giving us so much information.

"You've come to accept my offer?"

Slowly, I take a few steps towards him. "No. What I've come to say won't take me long."

"It won't?"

"It won't," Wyatt states, his voice hard. His easy-going attitude gone.

I clench my jaw before leaning forward a little, letting him see how serious I am. "You will leave our business alone. You will stay the fuck away from this day forward. We aren't going to change our minds, and you won't run us out of business. Don't fuck with us, Black."

An arrogant smirk lifts at his lips. "I have no idea what you are talking about, Mr Hayes. But if someone is sabotaging your business, wouldn't it be best to sell now whilst there's a business to buy?"

"No," I tell him curtly, my eyes narrowing into slits. "Whoever is doing it should know they messed with the wrong family."

"Have they?" he asks, trying to act innocent in front of his receptionist, who I presume he's kept around less for her experience in filing and more for her experience in fucking.

"Oh yes," Wyatt says, his cheerful tone fake. "I mean, it's good it's not you doing it, right?"

"It is?" Black asks, his expression hardening now. He hates to be made a fool of, that's clear to see. "Why don't you go make me a coffee, Jessica."

"No, she can wait here for one more minute," Wyatt says.

"Now!" Black orders.

"I, I..." Jessica stutters, looking kind of pale now.

Wyatt positions his body in front of her exit, and I can see Black fuming in anger. He's got to be going on forty. For daddy dearest to make him wait this long to run the business must fucking suck.

For him.

"What do you want?" Black snarls, showing his true colours because Jessica pales further, looking up at him open-mouthed.

"You know why we're here," I sneer.

"Because someone is messing with your business. That isn't my problem."

I tilt my head. "Clearly. Which is good, because it means we don't have to tell you that we've not retaliated once. We've let this play out, hoping the other person would be a man, not a little boy." The veins in the side of his head pulse, and I know I just hit a nerve. I grin wider. "Wouldn't want us to start fucking things up for them. I mean, we're a lowly business. We do well, but when we fall on hard times, it's easier to pick back up. But I mean, a business like this wouldn't be, would it? All that machinery, that much staff and upkeep of vans."

I shrug, like it's no big deal.

"But it's good it's not you, right, man? You wouldn't want to fuck things up for your company, would you. Might make Daddy mad," Wyatt goads.

"Have a nice day," I say, then stop at the door. "Before this mess gets bigger, the person might want to think about sending a cheque to make up for the repairs we've endured. If not, it's blood for blood."

We exit the building, letting the door slam shut behind us.

"We need to find a connection to him and one of our clients," Wyatt whispers.

"Yep. And find out who his dad is."

our relationship a secret has made it difficult to do that.

Then yesterday, I read an ad on Facebook about an ice-skating rink that was opening close by, and it reminded me of our plans that were cancelled not long ago.

I knew I couldn't take Lily to the one close by due to the off chance of bumping into a member of her family. It didn't stop me from googling other places that were further out of town.

For the hour drive we talk about our days. She's been helping a lot with Star and Miah, and I know she's becoming overly attached to them. I love hearing the adoration and excitement in her voice when she talks about them. They're great kids. Aside from the night I spent combing nits out of Star's hair, we've spent a night watching them for Blanche until she got back from her night out at bingo. They're special kids and it's been great sharing that with Lily.

"I've not been ice-skating in years. I'm really excited," Lily tells me as we get out of the car.

I take her hand in mine, pressing my lips to her knuckles. "Good. I've never been."

She gasps. Disbelief is written all over her. "You've never been ice-skating?"

"No." I shrug. "How hard can it be?"

She tugs her bottom lip between her teeth, watching me from the corner of her eye. "Um, not much? I'm sure you'll be fine."

I don't like the lack of confidence in her tone. We step inside and kids are everywhere. I look around, wondering where all the adults are. There must be thirty to forty kids here and only a handful of adults sitting to the side.

"Can we have two adults and skate hire?" I ask through the pay window.

The woman behind the counter pops the lollipop out of her mouth. "It's closed for a kid's party."

"What?"

"It's okay. We can do something else," Lily speaks up softly, pulling my hand a little.

"We've come for a date. This is our first official date," I tell her. When will we get a break? We've spent a lot of time together, but I've yet to take her out on a real date and she deserves to be taken everywhere. I've had this planned for two days. Nothing was supposed to mess this up. This can't be happening. I groan. "I messed up our first date."

"You can come to my party," a little girl around the age of eight says, answering all my prayers.

Ah, so someone *was* listening to me. I look down at her, smiling. "Thanks, kid."

"We couldn't," Lily tells her gently.

A middle-aged woman spins around, taking her daughter's arm. "Sorry. She'd invite the entire town if she could."

Lily laughs. "It's okay."

"Their date is ruined," the little girl says. "Can they come skate, Mummy, please?"

The mum doesn't look convinced, so I put on my best pout when she looks at me. She laughs, shaking her head at her daughter. "All right. That's if you don't mind skating with a bunch of kids."

"We couldn't impose," Lily tells her gently.

"We'd love to," I say at the same time.

The mum laughs. "I'm Danielle, this is my daughter, Alex. She's eight today."

"Happy birthday," Lily cheers, smiling down at her.

I pull my wallet out of my jacket, grabbing a few twenties and handing them to her. "Happy birthday, and thanks for inviting us to your party."

The little girl's eyes widen with excitement, and she snatches the money out of my hand. "Thank you!"

"We couldn't," Danielle starts, leaning in to take the money back, but the girl spins out of her grip.

"Nope. You have to say thank you graciously and accept all of your presents, remember, Mummy."

Danielle pauses for a minute before laughing. She turns to me and Lily. "Are you sure?"

"She's doing us a favour," I tell her, shrugging.

"Have fun then, I guess."

Me and Lily follow the little girl into the main skating arena. She points to another booth not too far away. "Go grab your skates and come have fun."

I chuckle and step up to tell the lady our shoe size. By the time we're ready to go, Alex has rounded up a small group of her friends. She's whispering and her friends begin to giggle.

"I think she likes you," Lily muses, a soft look on her face.

"I like *you*," I declare, leaning down to press a kiss on her lips.

The girls begin to squeal, clapping their hands. "Do you love her?"

I pull back, rolling my eyes at Lily, who giggles, her cheeks turning pink. She's still getting used to kissing me, I know, but she fucking rocks at it.

"Who's ready to skate?" I yell, and all the girls throw their hands up. I take in a deep breath, watching one do a spin as she moves out of the group.

Maybe I should have practiced or something. I swallow, clutching Lily's hand tightly. "If you fall, I'll catch you."

It really doesn't look safe, I muse as another girl speeds off, nearly tripping over her feet.

"Thank you," Lily replies, a small smile tugging at her lips.

She goes first so I can keep a steady hand on her, but one foot on the ice and it's like my feet are being zapped, sliding here, there and everywhere. I fall on my arse and a grunt escapes my lips.

The girls laugh, and when I look up, Lily is holding the side, trying to cover up the fact she's laughing with them.

"I'm okay," I tell them, but I end up slipping over once again.

We should have just gone out to eat.

On all fours, I crawl over to the blue wall and pull myself up. Once I'm up, I begin to feel better, but as soon as I try to move, I'm falling again. I grip the wall before I can land, groaning.

This is humiliating. I'm practically doing the splits.

"Come on. Keep your feet apart like that and when you go to push off, think of window screen wipers. Go from the inside out and keep doing it like that, in the motion and shape of your wipers."

The girls are full on laughing now. "You're old and can't skate?" Alex taunts loudly.

I glare at her. "If you want to keep your birthday money, zip it, kid."

She laughs harder, shaking her head. "You really should have done something else for your first date. You look silly."

"I think he's brave," Lily says gently.

I puff my chest out and stick my tongue out at Alex. I focus back on skating, or more to the point, standing upright. It's useless. As one foot goes out the other wanders and begins to slide. It's like there's no balance in my body.

"Show me how you do it," I order Lily, watching her eyes spark. She's just been standing there, skating along while I struggle to hold onto the wall.

"Are you sure?"

I gentle my voice a little, trying to sound less out of breath. "Yes. I want to see you skate."

She pushes off backwards before fluidly spinning until she's facing the direction everyone seems to be going.

I nearly slip again when I pay more attention to her than actually holding on. But she's so mesmerising, so elegant and graceful I can't seem to take my eyes off her. She holds out her hands as her speed picks up, lifting her face up to catch the breeze.

The moment she faces my way again, there's a wide smile on her face. Her hair is blowing back, her cheeks are pink, and she looks sexy as hell in every fluid move she makes.

I begin to panic when she doesn't slow down, heading right for me. I let go of the wall, feeling my entire body freeze at the thought of her getting hurt. But at the last second, she bends her knees slightly, tilts her body, and ice scraps off the floor as she comes to a screeching stop in front of me.

Standing straight, her face is filled with happiness. "That was so much fun. I thought I'd forgotten, but it's like riding a bike."

It most certainly isn't liking riding a bike. Maybe a bike with one wheel, on ice, with oil spread all over the ground. Maybe then it's like riding a bike.

"You looked beautiful," I croak out hoarsely.

Her smile is breath-taking. "Thank you. And look at you standing up."

Alex, who is still skating around me with her friends, snorts. "Yeah, he's a big boy now."

Lily giggles and takes my hand. "I'll crush you if I fall," I warn, trying to pull back, but she holds on tighter.

"Just hold onto the wall with one hand and me with the other. Just get used to where your feet go and the movements."

I'm so glad no one who will see me again are here.

We move around the rink slowly at first, but the more time passes, the easier it gets for me and the less I think about where to put my feet.

Towards the end of the night, Lily begins to teach half the group how to do some spins. Even the boys have come over, telling her she's cool.

She's brilliant with kids, amazing really. She was born to be a mum. I've never feared becoming a parent. I actually looked forward to the day I had kids, as long as it was with the right woman.

Having helped raise Paisley for most of her life, I knew it was something I'd never fear. My brothers, on the other hand, dread the day and are always careful it never happens. I would even go as far to say Eli hates kids. He always looks constipated if one gets close.

Lily with a child would be a sight to see. She looks truly happy and in her element teaching these kids.

Alex and her friend Ellie squeeze my hands. We've been skating in a smaller circle, the girls teaching me to turn without falling over.

It's been an experience, that's for sure.

A buzzer rings and all the kids begin to groan. Parents start walking over to the barrier, calling their kids over.

Lily looks up, her cheeks pink and bits of hair sticking to her face. She skates over, taking the hand Ellie dropped to help Alex pull me over to the exit.

"Thank you so much. You've made my girl's day," one mum says, and I expect her to be looking at Lily but find her talking to me.

"Me?"

She laughs. "Yes, you. I think she has a bit of a crush on you. She's loved teaching you."

Rubbing the back of my neck, I reply. "You're welcome, I guess."

Lily giggles as Alex's mum and dad step into our group. "Thank you so much, you two. The kids have really enjoyed it. They're all talking about Lily teaching them a *cool* trick."

"It's been so much fun," Lily tells her.

I look down at Alex, who is still holding my hand. "Thanks for the invite, kid. I had fun too, I guess."

She tilts her head and taps her chin with her index finger. "Maybe I'll go bowling next year, do something easier. That's if you think you can lift a bowling ball," she teases.

I twist my face up in a mock scowl and stick my tongue out at her. "Maybe I'll roll *you* down the bowling alley."

"You could try, big guy. You'd probably still miss the pins."

I laugh and look to her parents. "She really is something."

They pull their daughter into their arms affectionately. "That she is. I'm Matt, this is my wife, Danielle, who you met earlier."

"Nice to meet you. I'm Jaxon and this is my girlfriend, Lily." After a pause, I continue. "We'd best be going. Thanks again."

We're about to take our skates back when Alex's body slams into my legs. She hugs me tightly, and when I look up to see if it's okay with her parents, both are holding each other with tears in their eyes.

Alex hugs Lily next, who doesn't tense up like she does when other people touch her unexpectedly. She hugs her back, giving her a kiss on the top of her head.

"Bye. It's been so awesome. I can't wait to tell everyone who didn't come what they missed."

"I've had fun too," Lily tells her.

She races off as fast as she can, still in her skates. "Until next year," I joke to the parents, trying to ease the tension.

Danielle sobs into her husband's chest, and Matt looks ready to bawl himself. *Did I say something wrong?*

"Is everything okay?" Lily asks gently.

"Alex has leukaemia. She starts treatment next week. We're trying to stay positive, hoping we get to see her ninth birthday."

Holy fuck.

I fall back a step, unsure of what to do with the news. She's eight today. Fucking eight. She has her whole life ahead of her. It's wrong and unfair, especially when so many cruel and twisted people walk this earth.

"Oh my God," Lily breathes, clinging to me.

"She doesn't even seem ill," I murmur, looking over at Alex, who is standing with the remaining kids, talking.

"It's in the early stages. She has her good and bad days," Danielle explains sadly. "She's been trying to put on a brave face in front of her friends, but we could see how scared she was. *Until* you two walked inside. I saw my daughter's spark for the first time in months. Alex has been truly happy tonight and it's thanks to you two."

I don't know what to say, too choked up. I didn't even know. She's beaming with so much energy and life.

Now, taking a closer look, she is paler than the other kids, and her frame skinner than what is considered healthy. I didn't notice before. Her forward personality blinded me from it.

"We're so glad we could do something," Lily whispers, sounding sad herself. I wrap my arm around her, pulling her close.

"My mum owns a farm," I blurt out, before giving them the address. "She doesn't have a lot of animals left, but any time you want to bring Alex down, feel free. She can help my mum feed them and stuff. Mum would love it too. My sister also runs a bed and breakfast on the same land. You could stay there for free while she visits."

Danielle places her hand over her heart. "That's really kind of you."

I shrug, uncomfortable at the gratitude shining in her eyes. I didn't offer it for that. I did it because I'd feel shit if I left this place and never knew what happened to her. She's a good kid and she'd love the farm.

I can feel Lily's eyes on me, but I don't look down.

"She'd really like that. We will see what the doctors say first and let you know," Matt says.

I pull my wallet out of my back pocket and take out a business card. "If you ring the number on the top, that's my office number. We can arrange something when you're ready. The offer doesn't expire. You will always be welcome."

"Or call to let us know how she is," Lily rushes in, making me hold her closer. She has a heart of gold.

"Cheers." He takes the card from me, placing it in his own pocket. "We'll call."

Lily and I walk off to the booth to get our shoes and return our skates. We say another goodbye to Alex once again as we leave, and this time I notice something different. She's exhausted. I can see by the light blue bags under her eyes.

Stepping outside, the wind blows us back a step. It's freezing, and I pull Lily closer as we head back to my car.

We stop at the passenger side and I have the car door open when Lily stops to look up at me.

"You really are incredible, Jaxon."

"I aim to be," I joke, still torn up over the little girl inside.

She stands up on her tiptoes, wrapping her arms around my neck and pulling me down a little. She shakes her head, and the warmth flowing off her wraps around me like a blanket. "No, don't do that. What you did for her was amazing."

"You did it too," I argue, grasping her hips.

She smiles slightly. "I had fun, but Alex was all you. You made her night, Jaxon. That is something you can't deny. She was happy with her birthday money," she jokes, giggling a little. "But spending time with her while she skated was probably the best present she received. She loved every minute of it. And she's going to love going to the farm."

"I can't believe she has cancer," I rasp.

Compassion fills Lily's eyes and they begin to water. "She's so tiny."

"That's what I was thinking," I admit.

"Hopefully her parents will call with updates," she says, then bites her bottom lip, looking away briefly. "Will you tell me if they call?"

"Of course I will. And if they come down, you can spend the night at mine. It's not much and it's cold as hell." I pause, not liking the idea of Lily in my warehouse. Not because I don't want her in my bed, but because she deserves to be filled with luxury and my room at the warehouse isn't even close. "Maybe I'll get us a room at the bed and breakfast."

She giggles, stepping closer until our bodies are flush. "Thank you for bringing me here today. I've loved every single minute."

"You mean I didn't completely fuck up our first date?"

She runs her fingers through the ends of my hair, making me groan. "No. I don't think it could have gone any better. You, Jaxon Hayes, are on the verge of making me fall for you."

My ears perk up at that, and I move in closer, bringing my head down to meet hers. "Just on the verge?"

She smiles a little wider. "Yes. That doesn't scare you?"

"No, because I've already fallen, Lily. I've been waiting for you to catch up."

Her lips part and a silent breath escapes. A grin tugs at my lips, right before I lean down and press them against Lily's. She sighs into my mouth, caressing her tongue against mine.

Fuck, she tastes good, like bubble gum tonight.

She's a natural kisser, so fucking good it's hard not to blow my load in my jeans. I could kick myself for not making her mine sooner. I've missed out on this for years. On her. She's beautiful inside and out.

I rest my forehead against hers, breathing heavily.

"Don't ever leave me," I demand quietly.

Her hands are cold when she cups my jaw. "I won't. I promise."

I kiss her once more, holding her close. "Do you want to grab some food here or at your house?"

She blinks up at me, still dazed from our kiss. "I don't mind as long as I'm with you. I'm not ready to end our night."

Her honestly has my knees knocking together. I know she's not ready for more than kissing, but every time she says something like that to me, I want to slide inside of her.

She'll be the end of me.

Or the beginning.

CHAPTER SEVENTEEN

LILY

Babysitting Star and Miah has become one of my favourite things to do. I've always loved kids, which is why I chose it as a career. Everything about them makes my day. The way they speak, the way they light up when they've learned something new or found out a cool fact that has been around for generations. I love singing choir hymns and organising the Christmas play. I'm sad I have to miss this year, with Christmas just two weeks away.

Miah and Star are different. We share a connection I've never felt with another student.

I love them. Just like they are a part of my family.

Which is why when Blanche asked if I could watch them while she visited a friend who was in a home, I said yes. She would have taken the kids with her, but she said they were bored out of their minds the last time they went.

I've seen such a massive change in Blanche's attitude. Not towards Hayden, but to everyone else. She's more approachable, and I even saw her smiling at Star the other day when she practiced her lines for her school play.

Today, though, was spent going out and getting Blanche a Christmas tree. It makes me sad that she doesn't have one in storage, not even an artificial one. My heart hurt when she explained she didn't have a reason to do it.

"I think it's only right Star puts the angel at the top of the tree," I muse, looking down at Star next to me.

The bright white lights reflect back in her eyes as she stares in awe up at the tree. "It's so beautiful," she whispers. "Miah! Isn't the tree just beautiful. It looks like the ones from the television."

Miah looks up from his homework, grunting at his sister. But I can see the surprise when he sees the tree for the first time. He's been so busy doing his math homework he hasn't looked up once.

He clears his throat. "Yeah, it does."

Star clasps her hands together, but then her bottom lip begins to tremble. I bend down, gently placing my hand over her arm. "What's wrong?"

She leans into me, looking so sad I want to cry. "I'm never going to reach the top to put the angel on."

She is just the cutest. I look over my shoulder at Miah, who is still staring at the tree, just as mesmerised as his sister. "Maybe your brother will lift you up so you can reach it."

Her lips part when she turns to me. "He is really strong." Spinning, she faces her brother, back to being filled with happiness. "Would you, Miah? I'll let you eat the extra chocolate."

I giggle, waiting for Miah to answer.

He rolls his eyes as he gets up, causing Star to squeal. "And there isn't a spare chocolate. You and Lily ate it before you started putting the tree up."

Star giggles, lifting her arms in the air for her brother. "Sorry. I'll give you a little piece of one of mine."

"I'm good," he grunts, swinging her up on his shoulders. My arms reach out quickly in case he drops her. When I see he's good, I hand her the golden angel.

"Put it on this one," I direct, holding the bottom of the branch it's going on. She leans forward, one hand on top of Miah's head, the other on the angel, and places it on the branch.

She claps her hands. "I love it!"

The door opening has us all greeting Blanche. "Surprise!" Star and I shout.

Blanche looks shocked for a moment before her eyes begin to mist over. She places her hand on her chest.

"I hope you don't mind, but I found some decorations in one of the boxes ready to go in your loft."

Since the cellar is now Miah's room as of a few days ago, she had to clear the boxes out. Jaxon said he'd come over tomorrow to take them up. He's so kind and generous with his time.

"I don't mind at all, child," she tells me, taking a step forward. She takes an old clay ornament, twisting it left and right. "Your mum made this when she was in year one at school."

"She did?" Star asks, interested.

Miah puts her back down on the floor, and although he tries to act bored, I can see he really wants to know more about his mum.

"Yes. And this one she made in nursery," she tells us, taking the one with a small handprint on it.

"Can you tell us about her?"

Sadness fills Blanche's eyes. "I'm sorry. I didn't even think. You probably have loads of questions about your mum."

"Yes. Was she a beautiful princess?"

Blanche laughs, a softness reaching her facial expression. "She was. She looked just like you as a little girl."

Miah clears his throat, stepping a little closer, and I feel like I'm intruding. "Do you have pictures of her. Our mum I mean."

Tears gather when she clears her throat, struggling to get it together. I want to go to her, but this moment is just for them. So while they share that moment, I grab my bag and coat.

"I've got loads. Let me go get an album."

"I'll get going. You have a lot to talk about," I explain softly.

"Bye, Lily," Star yells, hugging my waist. I smile down at her, kissing the top of her head. "Thank you for an awesome day."

"You're most welcome," I tell her through a chuckle.

"Thank you for watching them again, Lily."

I turn to Blanche, my smile spreading. "I'll always be here when you need me. I love watching them."

"You're a real gem, child."

I blush at the compliment and wave goodbye to everyone before letting myself out. My phone rings as I step outside, so I don't pay attention to my surroundings. By the time I reach my house, I've located my phone and keys.

I answer when it starts to ring again, seeing Faith's name. "Hello. I'm so sorry. I was just on my way back home."

"Have you been with Jaxon again?" she asks.

I sigh, shutting the door behind me, my phone tucked between my ear and shoulder. I drop my bag as soon as soon as Willa and Peggy come to greet me. I reply as I pet them. "No. I was babysitting Star and Miah. Why, is everything okay?"

"No. I'm just worried about you. You've been spending a lot of time with him. The family are starting to ask questions."

I straighten, biting my bottom lip. "Who?"

"Maddox for one. He said the deadbolts are always on the door when he tries to come around and sometimes you don't answer at all. Mum is also worried, wondering if something has happened and you're pulling away."

My heart sinks as I drop to my sofa. "I don't mean to make them worry."

"Hey, I'm not having a dig," she replies softly. "I'm just letting you know that you and Jaxon need to decide when to tell people."

"We're waiting."

"For what?"

I look down at my lap. "I think I love him, Faith. Really love him. He makes my tummy flutter and my heart race. I get so excited when he texts, calls or comes to visit. And when I see him…" I inhale before letting out a soft breath. "I just want to be in his arms. I could listen to him forever."

"Oh, Lily. I don't think there's any thinking about it. But are you sure? This is Jaxon, and he and our family don't really get along."

Tears gather in my eyes as I stand back up. "They don't know him like I do. He listens to me. He's drank beer around me, and do you know, not once did I flinch or even think about it. It didn't even register. Our first proper date, over a week ago, was spent at an ice rink. It was closed for a private party. The little girl whose birthday it was said we could go in. He gave her a lot of money to say thank you because he thought he ruined our date. He couldn't even skate, but he didn't complain once, and we had so much fun. Then we found out the girl has cancer and he offered for them to stay at the bed and breakfast for free so Alex could see the animals on the farm.

"The other day, we ordered sandwiches and they put egg on mine. He gave me his so I wouldn't have to go without. And he doesn't even like egg himself. He's kind, funny and so incredible, Faith."

She interrupts me when I go to list off more reasons why they don't know him like I do. "I get it, Lily. I really do. I'm just worried about you. This can't be good. I know how you get. I bet it's killing you to hide this from everyone."

I rub my chest as I stare aimlessly out of the window. "It is. It really is. But I'm scared that if I tell them, I will lose him. What if they tell him to leave and he does?"

I struggle to breathe at the thought, never wanting it to happen.

"Calm down. We will sort something out, okay." I take in a steady breath, and she waits patiently for me to do so. "Now, can I at least know if you're being careful?"

"Yes, we're making sure the doors are locked when he's here and we go out of town for our dates. Although we have met up close by to have lunch a few times."

She giggles through the phone, confusing me. "No, Lily. I mean sex. Are you using protection?"

I nearly choke on saliva. "We've not had sex."

"You've not?" she asks.

I giggle at the surprise in her voice. "No. He said it's too soon for us, that we will wait until I'm ready."

"Um, I, well... Crap! He really is different with you," she lets out on a stutter.

I smile into the phone as I scan the street. A green car is parked across the road, one I've never seen before.

Someone is sitting there, but I ignore it for a moment, answering Faith. "He is. And he's so gentle and patient with me."

"I should hope so." She pauses for a breath. "I need to go. Beau is back, but you really should think about telling Mum and Dad at least."

"I will. I know it's selfish to keep him to myself. I didn't mean to worry anyone."

"Lily," she whispers gently. "You are the most selfless person I know. Just because you want something that is just yours, it doesn't make you a bad person. It was the same with me and Beau remember. I wanted us to have our time before all our family got involved and tried to scare him away."

I giggle, remembering our time camping. They didn't like that the two were sharing a tent together. "He was such a trooper."

"That he was," she says on a laugh. "Just think about it. Talk to Jaxon and see if he's ready to let the world know."

"I'm not ready," I admit before she can say goodbye. "I just need time."

It's definitely a man in the car, I muse, squinting to get a better look.

"All right. I'll drop it. I love you and I'll speak to you tomorrow."

"Love you too," I tell her, a little distracted now.

I can't tell if he's watching this house or next doors. It's bizarre. Faith ends the call and I slowly bring the phone down. It's stupid, but I feel if I make any sudden movements he will come and get me. That's how much it's giving me the creeps.

"I should ring Jaxon," I mutter, feeling stupid for worrying. He's coming over tonight anyway.

I unlock my phone just as I hear another car. I look up, seeing Jaxon's car drive past. I'm a little stunned when the car in the street drives off, its tyres skidding on the tarmac.

I begin to pace. Maybe I should have called the police. What if he's trying to burgle one of the houses? There's been a stream of break ins around the area. It was my lame excuse as to why I kept bolting my door. I went to bed each night going over and over the lie I kept telling Maddox. I hated that I was hiding something from him, especially when we've been close for most of our lives. He's always been my rock. And I know he's going to hate me when he finds out. It's another reason I haven't told him about Jaxon. I can't lose him. But I can't lose Jaxon either.

Maddox spent most of his late teens until now hating the Hayes family. He mostly talked bad about Jaxon and Reid. I know he doesn't like him, and I'm not ready for the emotions I'm going to feel when two of the most important people in my life hate each other.

Jaxon keeps scanning the street as he jogs up my path. Usually he'll do this to look out for my family, but the look on his face concerns me. If I were to guess, he saw that car too and thought it was out of place.

I head into the kitchen and meet him at the backdoor, unlocking it. "Did you see the car?" I ask in greeting, stepping into his arms.

He kisses my forehead, a frown marring his forehead. "Yeah, baby. Did you manage to get a number plate?"

"No, why?" I ask, taking a step back.

He runs his fingers through his hair. "Fuck!"

"You're scaring me," I tell him on a shaky whisper.

He pulls me into his arms, rubbing his hand up and down my back. "I'm sorry. That car is the one that raced away after the van windows were smashed."

"Wait, your windows were smashed?" I ask, wide-eyed. I grab his hands, scared for him. "What happened?"

He quickly runs through everything that happened, and my heart is racing by the time he's finished. "That man won't hurt you next, will he? Does he know you're here?"

He bends down until we're level. "I'd never let anyone hurt you, Lily. Ever. And no, I don't know what's going on, but I saw the driver of the vehicle. It was the kids' dad—Star and Miah's. He saw me at the same time I clocked onto him, and he drove off."

"It was Seth Merin? Do you think he's here to take the kids? Wait, he smashed your windows?" I clutch my head when a headache begins to form.

Placing me on the kitchen side, he steps between my legs, pulling me flush against him. "Stop worrying."

"He's ruining your business because you helped me. I'm so sorry, Jaxon."

He strokes my cheek, a tender look in his eye. "This isn't on you. I don't know how he's involved, but I'll find out. It sure isn't because of you. Don't worry about this, please."

"Is that why you've not told me? Because you were worried?"

He smiles now and it reaches his eyes. "No, baby. I haven't told you because it's not important right now. Business will pick up soon. And when I'm with you, it's you I want to get to know. It's *you* I want to hear talk. It's the best part of my day."

I melt against him, my heart skipping a beat at his words. "What are you going to do?"

"Well, I'll call my brother in a second. He knows someone who can help us find Seth," he explains, before pressing a kiss to my lips. "First, though, I need to run something by you, and I don't want you to get mad or upset, okay?"

My stomach rolls. "Okay."

"Mum found out about us."

"What?" I ask, panicked. No, no, no. I'm not ready. Not yet. I haven't told my parents or figured out *how* to tell them.

"Calm down. She was cleaning the office when you called earlier. She saw your face pop up, and I couldn't lie to her. I'm sorry," he says, kissing me again. "She's promised not to tell a soul but has asked if you'd come for lunch tomorrow."

"Lunch?"

He chuckles. "Yes. Lunch. Everyone is out on a job at that time. And she wants to meet you. If you're not ready, it's fine. She won't be offended."

I can't say no. I don't want to hurt their feelings, and I'd be lying if I said I didn't want to meet his mum. "Okay."

His smile spreads across his face. "Great. I'll call my brothers and then let her know. I'll warn you though, she can be really in your business."

Seeing him this happy warms me. I lean forward, kissing him, glad it was me that made his face light up like that. He can be so serious at times, but I like that about him too.

"All right. And I don't mind."

CHAPTER EIGHTEEN

JAXON

L ILY IS RUNNING LATE. NOT THROUGH any fault of her own but because my brothers took ages to leave for a job they were on.

Things are running smoother now Black has quietened down. However, the company we were relocating this morning were over an hour late to open the building, then continued to make life difficult for us when we were there. I was ready to say fuck it and drive off, but we needed the business. At the time we did anyway. Why we bothered, I have no idea. We got back to the offices to have Eli inform us they left a really bad review.

Wyatt suggested it was Black's doing, yet we had no proof. The guys we were working a job for were general assholes. That said, it might be something to do with him as the move was booked last minute. We were also informed it would be a quick, easy move and it wasn't.

Hence the reason we were running behind, which didn't make us look good to customers waiting for us to arrive. It made us look like we weren't capable of doing our job, and we get business by how quick and efficient we are.

"Are you sure this is okay?" Mum asks, wiping her hands down her apron.

I roll my eyes as I check my phone for any messages. Lily said she was on her way over thirty minutes ago.

"Mum, the food is great. Lily will love it no matter what."

"Oh no. So she could completely hate it and not even tell me?"

I chuckle under my breath, getting up from the large kitchen table. I grip the top of Mum's shoulders, leaning down to look in her eyes. "Lily's going to love you. Will you stop worrying."

She blinks up at me, trying to hide how emotional she is. "She's the first girl you've brought home to meet me. I'm allowed to make sure everything is perfect."

She cooked frittatas, salad and chips. Pretty sure she has nothing to worry about. It's one of Lily's favourite foods, and fortunately for her, Mum's frittatas are the shit.

"I'm just going to head outside and see if she's here."

"All right. I'll put the kettle on."

Mum's answer to everything is to put the kettle on. Having a bad day; put the kettle on. Feeling depressed because your pet died; put the kettle on. Death in the family; put the kettle on. Celebrating a birth; put the kettle on.

I pat her on the shoulder before heading out, leaving her to do what she does to make herself calm down.

My entire body tenses when I see Lily sitting in her car outside, staring blankly ahead. I panic and head around to the passenger side and get in. She jumps, her startled expression meeting mine.

"Hey, what's happened?" I ask, wondering if something happened with the kids. Since I saw Seth, their dad, sitting outside their house last night, I've been worried. He's the same person hanging around our jobs, and the one who smashed our windows.

We're currently looking for him, and I have no doubt we'll close in on him soon. So far, we've only been able to find other people looking for him. He owes a lot of money to a lot of bad people. Men you don't mess with. We're hoping we get to him before they do because we want answers.

Lily's hands begin to shake, and I take them in mine. She's cold, shivering. "Talk to me."

"What if she doesn't like me?"

I laugh, wondering where women get this shit. "Lily, how can she not like you?"

She looks up at me, the tips of her lashes wet. "Because I'm broken. What if she wants someone better for you, someone who is strong? I'm not that person."

I sober, resting my forehead against hers. My heart beats rapidly hearing her talk about herself like this.

"Lily, you're not fucking broken. I don't think you see how strong you truly are."

"But I freak out. You can't have a normal life," she argues softly.

"Why wouldn't I?" I ask, keeping my voice low. She's breaking my heart.

"What if you want to go to the pub to have a drink? I can't do that. I've tried. You saw me at Faith's engagement party. Even after she only invited people I knew and kept it low-key, I still had to leave because it became too much."

"Lily, I don't care about any of that. If I want to go for a beer, I'll go have a beer. You don't need to come with me."

Her cheeks redden. "I know. I didn't mean I'd go with you all the time."

I chuckle at the insecurity in her tone. "I didn't explain that right," I tell her, then take a deep breath. "Let's put it this way. Would you make me do something you liked doing, but knew I didn't?"

She looks hurt I'd even suggest it. "No, of course I wouldn't."

"Exactly. Which is why I won't mind if you don't want to hang around drunk people. In fact, it eases my mind that you don't."

"It does?"

"It does," I tell her, tucking her hair behind her ear. "Now, do you feel better or is there something else?"

"You really don't think I'm broken?" she whispers, her voice shaky.

"Lily, far from it. I've never met anyone as strong as you in my life. Most would crumble with what you've faced. Not you. You channel it into being a better person for those around you. Look at Star and Miah. Look how far they've come. I'm pretty sure Miah smiled at me the other day."

"What if your mum sees me have a freak out and then wonders whether it's safe for you to have a child with me. I've always worried about it. What if I'm not strong enough to deal with a flashback while I have a child in my arms? It scares me. I don't want to put you through that."

She turns back to the front of the car, wiping her hands down her jeans. I take her in. Lily's thoughts go deeper than anyone can imagine. It's like she's taken every future possibility and conjured up every negative scenario that could happen.

"Baby, I have no doubt in my mind that when we have children—and yes, I mean that—you'll undoubtedly make an incredible mother. There are no what-ifs that it will be with me either, because we will spend the rest of our lives together. I can promise you that." I take a deep breath, debating whether to say the next part. It's now or never though. "You have such a big family. A protective one. And I'm sorry, Lily, but they've not helped you by smothering you."

She turns open-mouthed, hurt flashing across her face. "They're my family."

I squeeze her hand. "I know. And they love you. I've never seen another family love like yours except ours. It's a bond well beyond blood ties. It's deeper than that. If you were to hold our child in your arms, and some drunken fool came stumbling past, I don't think you'd freak out. I think your mind would rewire itself to protect our child. You can't stand hurting the people around you. I've seen how upset you get even when you try to hide it after Maddox calls or texts. You can't stand the fact you might hurt his feelings by ignoring him.

"Then there's Charlotte. You love her so much you can't even tell her that her cooking fucking sucks. Instead, you look for the positive and comment on how pretty it looks. Give yourself a chance, Lily. Give us a chance."

"You really do believe that?" she asks, her eyes wide and hopeful.

I nod. "I do. I've never met anyone else like you. You are everything that is good in the world and you are fiercely protective of everyone around you. You love everyone to be happy and loved. Why would it be any different for a child, our child?"

She melts back into her seat. "I think I'm falling for you."

I grin, leaning down to give her a peck on the lips. "Good. Just know that when you've fallen, I'll be here to catch you. You were made for me, Lily. You're the other half of my soul."

Her eyes go all misty. "Jaxon," she whispers.

"And Mum will see that too. She's going to love you as a person no matter what, because you're Lily. She's going to be over the moon that I've got someone as special as you in my life."

"If you're sure," she says softly, her gaze on my lips.

I'm grinning when I lean down to steal another kiss. My girl loves her kissing. She sighs in contentment, kissing me back.

Blinking up at me, she rests her palm above my heart. "Shall we go and meet your mum? I brought her some flowers. I got wine and chocolates too. I was nervous and didn't know what to bring so I brought some more flowers in case you didn't like the first ones I picked."

I chuckle and then twist in my seat, and sure enough, two large bouquets of flowers sit in the back, along with a gift bag with a bottle of wine and a box of Cadbury's chocolates.

I twist back around and burst out laughing, dropping my face into the crook of her delicate neck.

"Baby, you are nuts."

She giggles, tapping my shoulder for me to get up. After pressing a brief kiss to her neck, I lift, our gazes meeting.

"Which flowers should I take in?"

I tug her lip out from her teeth and kiss her once more. She's just too fucking cute sometimes. "Just take the red ones in."

"Should I take the wine and chocolates?"

I shake my head. "No. You won't need to. We'll eat the chocolates later when I come over."

Her eyes heat, which I love. "Okay," she tells me breathlessly.

"Let's go then."

We both straighten, and as Lily sorts her bag and keys out, I wait and watch until she's ready. I move to the back door, grabbing the red bouquet of flowers from the back seat, chuckling at the sight of the others.

We walk up to the house hand in hand, and Mum is there to greet us, tears swimming in her eyes. She still has on her pink frilly apron that reads, 'I love to cook' on the front.

"Don't you two look perfect together," she gushes loudly. I groan, looking up to the sky. "I'm Liza, Jaxon's mum."

"Hi, Liza, I'm Lily. Thank you for inviting me to your home."

"Pleasure is mine."

"Lily got you these, Mum," I tell her, handing her the flowers.

"My cousin arranged them for me. I hope you like them."

Mum leans back on her heels, looking at Lily like a proud mum. I roll my eyes. "You are a sweetheart. Thank you. Come in, come in. I've cooked some frittatas. Do you like frittatas?"

"I love them," Lily answers, following my mum into the house. She seems more relaxed now, but there's still tension in the way she carries herself.

I thought it would be Lily's parents who found out about us first. I'm hoping Mum knowing before them doesn't set us back. I know not telling any of them is beginning to get to Lily. And honestly, I'm ready to tell them all. I want the world to know she's mine. It's also getting old sneaking into her house, especially when we are adults.

I pull out a chair at the kitchen table, letting Lily take a seat. Mum sighs dramatically, like it's the first time I've shown manners. Not that I can say I've pulled a chair out for a girl before.

"Thank you." Lily's voice is soft, a hint of nerves back. I take the seat next to her, letting Mum finish the dinner.

"How was your morning? Was Star okay getting to school?" I ask. Star, for the past few days, has been getting picked on. They break up in a few days, yet she refuses to go to school, making it impossible for Blanche to get her there on time. She said some of the boys were picking on her.

Lily's expression saddens. "She cried the whole time. Apparently, a boy pushed her into a puddle yesterday after school. I dropped them off with

Blanche this morning. It was hard to walk away. I don't know how parents walk away."

My body tenses hearing a boy got physical with her. I'm about to tell her I'll be going down there, but Mum speaks up, probably saving me from making a fool of myself.

"Trust me, they do it because they need the break," Mum adds, before banging around with the plates. "I used to run as fast as my legs would take me when I dropped the boys off. Paisley, on the other hand… I never wanted her to leave my sight."

Lily giggles, ducking her head while I narrow my eyes at Mum.

"What about Miah?" I ask instead. The kid is quiet, nothing like how I was at his age. He seems to have a good head on his shoulders. For the most part at least.

"He wanted to go in with her and get her to tell him who was picking on her so he could sort them out," she says reluctantly.

"He sorted it then?" I ask, relaxing. I really don't like the thought of someone hurting her. She's so tiny.

Lily's eyes go round. "No! I sent him to school and told him sternly that under no circumstances does he threaten a young child."

I grunt. "The kid pushed her into a puddle, baby."

She places her hand over mine. "I know. Star was really upset, and we did have a word with Michelle, who has taken over my class until I'm back. She said she will speak to him at break time. You have to be reasonable about these things. There's no excuse for his behaviour, I know, but I don't like upsetting kids."

I blink. She really does believe that. "Miah sounded reasonable to me."

Mum drops a plate of wraps on the table and begins to laugh. Both Lily and I pull apart to watch her. Once she's pulled herself together, she addresses Lily.

"He would do it all the time when Paisley came home upset. He'd go into that school and scare the boys until they wet themselves."

"You didn't!" Lily gasps, gripping my hand. "Jaxon."

"They were picking on her. I wasn't having that. Don't tell me your family didn't do it for you."

She bites her lip, glancing away. "Maybe."

I laugh, pulling her close so I can kiss her. "They did, Lily, because I was threatened on a weekly basis by a bunch of scrawny kids younger than me. And I never even bullied you. Hope must have told them I watched you a lot."

"You watched me?" she asks, sounding a little breathless.

"Baby, I could never take my eyes off you. You were the prettiest girl I'd ever laid eyes on. You still are."

Her cheeks tinge pink as she leans in to me. "You shouldn't say really sweet things in front of your mum."

I grin and shrug. "Why?"

A dreamy sigh escapes her. "Because I really want to kiss you," she whispers, leaning in closer.

My grin spreads, and I lean down, capturing those lips with mine. A moment later, Mum clears her throat. She's grinning from ear to ear.

"Dinner's ready."

Lily jumps away, sitting straighter in her chair. "Thank you, Liza. It looks so good."

"You are most welcome."

Once we fill our plates, Lily turns to me. "Did my cousins really threaten you?"

There's sadness in her voice when she asks. "It's fine. They were what, ten at the time? Maddox turned up a few times with your brothers, who were just as small."

"I'm sorry."

I shrug. "Don't be. I'd have done the same if it were Paisley."

"Wasn't it Max and Maverick Carter who scared you that bad you ran home?" Mum asks after finishing a bite of her food.

I glare at her. Why did she have to bring that up?

"Dad? Uncle Max? What happened?" she asks, sounding panicked.

Great, just great. Any progress I had in getting her to tell her parents might just go out the window.

"It's nothing."

"It wasn't nothing," Mum helpfully adds.

"Please tell me," Lily pleads, but I shove food into my mouth so I don't have to answer.

Mum however…

"It was the day after Jaxon helped you with some girls in a bathroom, I believe," she starts, taking a sip of her tea. "You weren't at school the next day, but your dad and uncle were waiting for Jaxon after school."

"To thank me," I half lie, giving Mum a warning look to shut up.

Mum laughs like she's remembering it. "Yeah, that Maverick might have said thank you, but it didn't stop him setting Max onto you."

Lily groans. "What did he do? He means well, I promise. Dad said he was dropped a lot as a baby."

Mum begins to cackle. "Mum, let's eat dinner. Lily didn't come to hear this."

"I don't mind," Lily says gently, rubbing my thigh.

Well, shit.

"Anyway, your uncle was telling Jaxon all the things they were going to do to him if he didn't leave you alone."

"Leave me alone? You never spoke to me before that day," she says softly.

I force a smile. It's hard knowing she never noticed me before now. It is. But I also know it wasn't done out of entitlement. Lily just lived in her own world. I, however, more than noticed her. I found myself finding ways to be around her, even if it meant being in the library, watching her in class, or sitting close in the dinner hall.

"Like I said, I was always watching you."

"Wyatt said he practically stalked you," Mum informs her.

"Awesome, Mum. Awesome."

"Stalked me?" Lily asks, her face lighting up.

"I just happened to be in the same place as you." Mum snorts at my lie.

"What did my uncle say exactly?"

"He told Jaxon what happened to boys who looked at a Carter girl. I think that kind of cemented the war. The boys found out and straight off, they wanted to get revenge. Jaxon wouldn't hear of it. I think he was too embarrassed that he ran all the way home, scared they would remove his eyeballs and hands."

"It wasn't. It was her dad telling me he'd break every bone in my body if I ever went near her again. I didn't really take Max seriously. He just seemed like he was on day release. Your dad, though, scared the shit out of me. Everything about him screamed to run."

"He's a big softy," she giggles, rolling her eyes.

I bet he is when it comes to the women in his family. Men outside, not so much. I'm still shocked Beau survived. It gives me hope though. Out of all the Carter's, Maverick is the only one I worry about. There's just something about him. I'd happily take on any of the others, even Landon, but there is no way I'd be able to take Maverick on without shitting myself in the process. I'm man enough to admit that.

"Were you okay?" Lily asks, biting her bottom lip worriedly.

I grin. "Yes. Everything was fine then, and it is now."

"Are you ready for Christmas?" Mum asks, and I relax back into the chair at the change of subject.

"I am. We decorated our trees yesterday. The place looks incredible. It's one of my favourite times of year."

"Ours too."

"That reminds me," Lily says, placing her napkin over her plate. "I got you a present."

I finish the last bite of food before addressing her. "You got me a present?" I'm surprised. I got Lily's the other day. I got her a few things since I couldn't choose just one.

"I did," she says, clapping.

"Wait, when did you get this? I thought you finished Christmas shopping ages ago."

She beams up at me. "It's not much. It's only something small."

"I'll love anything."

Mum's phone beeps and she pulls it off the kitchen side from behind her. "Jesus!" She begins to laugh, getting up and clearing the table.

"What's wrong?" I ask, grabbing mine and Lily's plates.

"Rex has chased the duck into the bed and breakfast and now Paisley has scared children screaming."

"You have ducks?" Lily asks, surprised.

"Duck," Mum replies, then looks at me. "Yeah, we had someone come drop her off. They wanted us to watch it for a bit until he's safe to go home. He seems to be happy though."

"That's so sweet."

I bite my bottom lip to keep myself from laughing. "What Mum isn't telling you is that Charlotte got drunk one night and stole it. She thought it was being bullied, but if I were to guess, or care, I'd say that thing was the bully. It's forever scaring the animals and guests. It's only Rex who doesn't run away from it."

"Aww, maybe he just wants someone to play with," she tells me, then her eyes widen. "Wait. My Charlotte?"

I laugh, nodding. "Her and Madison, I think, got drunk and walked home through the park."

She seems to think about it for a moment before shrugging. "That's okay. It's not as bad as the time she got stuck up a ladder because she thought she saw someone robbing a house."

Mum pauses from her washing up, looking over her shoulder. "In her house?"

Lily shakes her head. "No. It was the house across the street from where they lived. I believe she thought the couple were on holiday."

"Was anything taken?"

Lily smiles at her. "No. It was actually the man having an affair and she caught him in the act through the window."

I burst out laughing, pulling Lily into my arms. "Your cousin is nuts."

"She's the best person I know," she admits.

I shake my head, looking down at her. "No one comes close to you."

"Right, I'll leave those dishes to soak. Your sister really needs me to go get that duck. Landon threatened to cook it for dinner if it came in again."

Lily gasps while I chuckle.

"All right."

"It was so lovely to meet you, Lily. I'll look forward to meeting your parents. Max and Lake, Landon's parents, are a hoot," she tells her. "Wait, maybe when you two start to tell people we can get the family all together. I still feel terrible I couldn't go to Faith's engagement party."

Lily tries to hide it, but I can see my mum's comment has upset her. "They will really love that, Liza. And it was lovely meeting you too. Jaxon speaks about you all the time. All of you."

"All good things I hope?"

"Yes," Lily tells her, relaxing a little. Whatever was going through her mind has gone. For now, I'll leave it, but later, when I go to her house, I'll get it out of her.

Mum steps forward and pulls Lily in for a hug. Lily hugs her back just as tightly.

"Come around again soon. I'm sorry I have to shoot off."

"It's okay. We have all the time in the world," Lily declares.

Mum's eyes begin to go misty when they land on me. "And you're not bursting into flames at the hint of commitment. I'm so proud of you."

"Please don't hug me again," I tease.

She slaps my shoulder and heads out the kitchen, calling, "Soon!" over her shoulder.

"I really like your mum."

I pull her into my arms. "I'm glad. I'm sorry it wasn't a long visit."

Her gaze softens. "I've loved it," she admits. "Let's go get your present. You can't open it until Christmas day though."

Rubbing my hands across her lower back, I smirk down at her. "What if I take a peek?"

"Then you'll go on Santa's naughty list and won't get any more presents."

Her teasing makes my dick hard, especially hearing *naughty* spill from those lips. "Ah, we wouldn't want that. Would you like yours?"

Her lips part. "You got me a present?"

I swing her up in my arms, her arse in the palms of my hands. I lean in, taking those lips I can't get enough of.

"Yes. Did you think I wouldn't?"

She squirms in my arms. "I wasn't sure. Thank you, Jaxon."

"You're welcome, Lily."

CHAPTER NINETEEN

LILY

J AXON TAKES ME IN HIS ARMS again as we reach the front door. It feels like he's using all his strength to be gentle with me, especially when his lips claim mine. Every caress, every touch, is a step closer to a part deep within myself being healed. It's a part I never knew needed to be healed.

I get just as lost in him as I do listening to the sound of rain hitting my window.

Being with him is a new experience every single day, and each and every moment is one I'll forever treasure.

Tentatively, I reach up to cup his face, and his fingers flex at my hip. I moan. I love it when he touches me like this. I get electric shocks that feel delicious all over my body.

Feeling bold, I press my body closer to his. He moves us back towards the door and gently rests me against it. I tilt my head up to meet his, feeling dizzy and off kilter.

I'm so lost in the sea of sensations running though my body that the feel of his tongue entwining with mine has me swaying.

We've kissed a lot over the past few weeks. Sometimes for so long my lips feel bruised and swollen. But it's never been like this. The electrical current running through us can't be anything but filled with sparks.

There's a soft demand as he cups my jaw, tilting my head upwards to get a better angle. My toes curl, and I cling to his T-shirt as I struggle to hold on to my sanity.

When he pulls away, his breathing escalating, I follow, swaying towards him like two magnets drawn together that never want to part.

He rests his forehead against mine, his eyes squeezed shut as he tries to get himself under control. I love this position and have come to call it *our* position. I like how close he is, how intimate we are when we stand like this. It makes me feel special, whereas to some, it's insignificant.

My entire body is still trembling with the effects of those lips, my fingers still gripping his T-shirt. The tips have turned white I'm clinging to him so hard.

"You drive me crazy," he rasps, his voice low and husky.

I shiver, blinking up at him. "That's good though, right?"

"I'm never letting you go," he whispers fiercely.

He says it like I'd have a problem with it or argue. But there aren't any arguments here. I'm not one to play games, to mess around with his feelings whilst trying to figure out what it is *I'm* feeling. I know what I want and it's him.

Jaxon, from the very first moment I laid eyes on him, has been different to everyone else around me. I told myself I didn't understand, but I guess my conscious didn't want to admit what it was I felt for him.

Over time, though, I've watched him protect his family, be there for his sister and cherish her like she was a glass slipper. It broke down my walls. It's why I've never freaked out over him being close, being drunk or touching me.

He brings peace to my mind, whereas before there was nothing but chaos and bad memories.

My feelings, however, come from our time spent together. Not just the brief eye contact we've shared over the years, but from the moment he burst into my house to rescue me from a burst pipe.

The invisible band that was pulling us together for so long, snapped. We didn't need it anymore. It was like it had done its job, bringing us together. We had that push we both needed to realise we wanted to be in each other's lives. Even if, at the time, I didn't fully understand just how much I would come to want him in my life, and how much he'd mean to me.

It's funny how life can turn out in a stroke of a moment.

Our time together has only made my already growing feelings explode for him.

I don't remember a time he wasn't in my life, that's how long the last few weeks have felt for me.

Jaxon chuckles, and I look up, blinking. "Did I kiss you senseless?"

I nod, a lopsided smile on my lips. "You did."

Amused, he shakes his head. "Let's go get your present. It's in my drawer in my room."

I take his hand and follow him out. The sky is darkening, and I can smell rain in the air. The walk isn't far, and by the time we get there, I'm practically skipping with happiness.

He grins down at me as we reach the bottom of the steps to the front entrance. I follow him up, waiting for him to key in a code and unlock the door.

"Come in."

We walk inside and I notice he looks uncomfortable. "Are you turning red?" I ask, peering closer.

He chuckles, but it's not the same as his usual chuckle. Hmm, something is going on inside that mind of his.

"Um, I've kind of been busy lately."

My brows scrunch together. "I know. You really do need a break."

Rubbing the back of his neck, he looks to the floor. "I mean, um, I've not really done much here. I've come back, dropped onto my bed and gone to sleep. Then woke up and got ready for work."

Ah. I smile, stepping closer to him. "I don't mind you having a messy room, Jaxon."

He laughs, his lips twisting in amusement. "It's not always messy. Why don't you go sit at my desk while I grab your things?"

"Please don't be embarrassed," I tell him gently. I never want him to feel like that around me.

He kisses me on the lips before leaning back so our eyes meet. "Perfect." He blinks, shaking himself out of it. "Let me just go clear some things away and you can come see where I sleep. Please keep in mind that Harry Potter's crib is better than mine."

I roll my eyes and gently nudge him away whilst laughing. "Go."

"Bossy," he mouths, walking backwards with a huge grin on his face.

Once he's gone, I walk over to his desk, the one I saw him sitting at the day I came over to say thank you for all he's done.

It feels like a lifetime ago now, but it wasn't that long. I'm so lucky to have him in my life. And I'm glad I braved my choice to come see him in person to say thank you. It makes me sad to think I wouldn't have been here otherwise.

A car door slamming makes me jump, and I peer outside through the tiny window on the door. A woman in tight leather trousers and a low-cut, glittery top steps towards the building, her hips swaying.

I step back as she reaches the door. I must scare her because she looks surprised to find me here. I giggle, giving her a wave. "Hey, I'm sorry if I scared you."

"Um, hey." She doesn't seem happy. I really hope she isn't here to complain. Jaxon has too much going on right now.

I bite my lip, giving her a smile in the hope of relaxing her. She looks tense and still kind of mad. When I'm having a bad day and someone smiles at me, it brightens my day. I guess it doesn't work for her because she's still frowning at me.

"Jaxon is just in the back, but if you'd like to take a seat he'll be out in a minute," I explain so she doesn't think everyone is slacking off.

She laughs and it's sultry, sexy. She pulls her fur coat tighter around her body, eyeing me up and down. "Yeah, sweetie, that's where he always is."

Confused, I look at his desk then back to her. "He's been working really hard."

"He always does," she mutters, her lips twitching.

Why does she make it sound like a bad thing?

"He's not skiving off. He's dedicated to his business, I promise. He'll be a minute longer, I'm sure."

"Girl, I'm not here to do business," she laughs, looking at me differently now. It's the same look people give Charlotte, and I hate it. I hate it when they do it to her and I hate that this woman is doing it to me.

"I'm sorry, are you a friend? I thought you were here for work," I explain, forcing a small laugh as I remain polite.

"I'm here to fuck," she drawls.

"Oh fuck," rumbles behind me.

I'm so dumb.

Jaxon is the only one here. He told me all his brothers are working non-stop all day. It could only be him she's meeting.

Tears gather in my eyes as I turn back to Jaxon. His face is pale, eyes wide. Oh God, she really is here to meet him.

My heart pummels my throat and I struggle to breathe. *No! My chest hurts so bad.*

"Is t-that t-true?"

He doesn't look at the girl behind me, only at me. He softens his expression when a sob rises in my chest.

He's going to tell me it's over. He's going to break up with me. I gasp for air, bending forward a little, resting my hand against the table and using it as leverage when I feel my knees begin to buckle.

"I-is—is that t-true?"

He takes a step forward, but I take one back, shivering. I feel cold all over, dejected. I can't believe this. I can't believe he'd do this to me. I don't *want* to believe it. But she's here, standing plain as day in front of me. I look at her again, finding her the total opposite of me. She's sexy where I'm shy. She's flashing skin in a way I tried once and felt like I was completely nude and on display.

Everything about her is everything I'm not. How do I compete with a girl like her? *Is this who he's wanted all this time?*

I look up at him, pleading with him to talk to me, to tell me the truth. I need to know. I feel like my world is being ripped out from beneath me.

"No, Lily, it's not true. And you know it's not," he coaxes gently, taking a smaller step closer.

"What?" the girl behind me snorts.

"Kim, you've not been here in months. Don't make it sound like you come here every week. I heard some of what you said, and you made it out like you're here when I call or when you're in the mood. It isn't like that at all so don't talk crap in front of Lily."

He turns back to me as the first tears begin to fall. She shrugs. "You've never turned down a fuck before. I was in the area."

I inhale sharply, feeling a pain in my chest. I knew he had girls before me. I did. But hearing it is like a slap in the face.

I thought I was different.

"We live miles away from town for you to just happen to be in the area," he scoffs out. "Now get the fuck out."

I can't keep the hurt out of my expression when I turn back to him. I feel like my heart is being ripped out of my chest.

This isn't happening. Not to us. Not now. Not when I'm in love with him.

"J-Jaxon," I force out, feeling my throat burn. I need him as much as I want to leave.

"This isn't what it looks like, Lily. I promise. I'd never do that to you, ever. *Never* to you."

"Y-you haven't?"

"No, baby. I haven't," he declares, sounding pained. He's a step closer now. *When did that happen?*

"It h-hurts," I choke out, rubbing at my chest. I'm frozen to the spot, struggling to breathe.

"Get out," he snaps to the girl behind me before engulfing me in his strong arms. I collapse into him, clinging to him like he can breathe life back into me. "Now, Kim. And don't come back."

"Hey, I'm sorry. I—"

"Get out," he yells, making me jump.

"He's right," the girl says quietly, sounding remorseful now. "We've not slept together in months."

I begin to shake harder, a choked sob rising up my throat. "Now!"

I feel the cold breeze blow across the nape of my neck as she leaves. "Lily, baby, look at me."

"You didn't sleep with her?" I ask, needing him to tell me. He wouldn't lie. Not to me. I know that much. "She wasn't here because you invited her?"

I can't be that dumb, can I?

He kisses my forehead. "I've slept with her, yes, but not for months. Way before what me and you started. And no, Lily, I've not been with another girl since the day your sink broke."

"And if I wasn't here?" I hate asking. I feel sick in the pit of my stomach for even hinting that he would do it.

He shakes his head, his lips tipped down. "One, I probably would have locked the door before she could get inside. I found out she was sleeping with Maddox, and you know how I feel about that."

My nose twitches. "Ew."

He chuckles. "Yeah," he breathes slowly. "And if the door wasn't locked, I would have kicked her out and told her I was with someone. Happily with them. Lily, I'm not a virgin."

I feel my cheeks flame. "I know. I just… We haven't…" I inhale, clearing my throat before trying again. "For a moment there, seeing her, I thought that maybe—"

"Hey, I know what that looked like, and believe me, I've been a dick in the past, but you need to believe you are everything to me, Lily. You're my world. You've been different from the beginning. I'd never do that to you."

"But we haven't—you know."

He grins, pulling me closer. I relax into him, breathing in his woodsy scent. "I know. But we will. We have all the time in the world, and I know you aren't ready for that step yet."

"I'm sorry for overreacting," I whisper.

"I never want to see that kind of pain on your face again. Always believe in me, Lily, like I believe in you."

"I will. I do. I promise," I tell him truthfully. "It was a shock. For a moment there, I thought—I thought bad things. I thought I lost you."

"You had every right. But you stayed and we spoke it out. You didn't freak and run. Thank you."

I relax more against him and a yawn slips free. "Why am I tired?"

He chuckles, kissing the top of my head. "I'll drive you home. I'll ring Wyatt to put him in charge. We can spend the rest of the day in bed at yours."

A small smile lifts at my lips. "Can we watch Heartland?"

He frowns, a frustrated noise bubbling up his throat. "No."

"No?"

"I'm not going through that again."

"Going through what?" I tease gently, feel much lighter.

He grabs his keys from the desk and swipes up a gift bag. "You know what. I can't stand to see you cry like that."

"Hey, you were crying at that scene where Amy is shouting at the horse."

He arches his eyebrow. "Beautiful, I was not crying. When you were wailing, you threw that Minnie Mouse teddy at my face. The nose got me in the eye."

My mouth drops open. "I'm so sorry, Jaxon."

"We're not watching it. We need something happy."

"But it has happy moments too," I remind him.

He gives me another one of those looks, making me giggle. "You cried at those too. You said your heart was filled with too much happiness."

"It was."

"Something else, Lily."

I smile as we head towards my car, me wrapped in his arms. "Oh, all right."

CHAPTER TWENTY

JAXON

The entire room stands in ovation; Lily and I are no different. When Lily suggested the pantomime last night after the Kim drama, I didn't think it would be my cup of tea. But for her I'd sit and watch Aladdin. I'm glad I did. It was a new experience for me, one I've enjoyed.

Watching Lily laugh and sing along has to be the highlight of my night, though. I think it was best spent watching her reaction. She's loved it. And I'm glad I could make up for what happened yesterday in the office.

When I walked in to find Kim there, I panicked. It wasn't news that I'd often call her to come over when I had a break. She was easy and a great fucking lay.

But I wasn't lying when I told Lily I never called her. I don't even have her number in my phone. I deleted it months ago when I had been told she slept with a Carter. It wasn't until we went to The Ginn Inn that I found out it was Maddox. My brothers might not care if their bed partner has fucked one of them, but I do. I don't want to stick my dick in anything one of them have been near.

So last night, I asked Lily if there was anything she wanted to do that she hasn't done for a while. She mentioned a pantomime and said she really wanted to see Aladdin. We don't live far from a theatre, so I went straight online and booked us tickets.

She links her arm through mine as we file out of our row of seats. How I managed to snag such good seats at the last minute was pure luck. I thought we'd be in a cinema type room with those uncomfortable chairs that you spend the whole time trying to get comfortable in. I prepared myself for a night of trying to look through some woman's hair or hear over screaming kids.

It wasn't like that at all. We were led to a small seating area upstairs, away from the main floor. We could see everything perfectly from where we were, and the bonus of it, we were grouped with around twenty people or so in our section.

"That was incredible," Lily shouts over the background music and people chatting. I lean down to her as we reach the bottom of the stairs, waiting behind the forming queue of people heading out.

I throw my arm over her shoulder when I notice her become tense at the people pushing close to get out. I tuck her back to my front and walk with my arms wrapped around her stomach. She leans back into me, relaxing.

"It was pretty good."

"Pretty good." She tries to look over her shoulder, but with how close we are, she can't see me. "It was amazing. All those songs, the costumes, the choreographs. All of it was superb. We have to go see the movie when it comes out. I heard Will Smith is going to play Genie. I love Will Smith."

I chuckle as we finally get outside the theatre doors. There's three exits and people are piling out of them.

"Yeah, baby, we will. You going to go the loo before we leave? You didn't move from your chair once and you had that extra-large Coke."

"I'm too hyped up to go the loo. That was just so good. Can we do this again?"

I chuckle at her excitement. "I'm glad you had a good time, and yes, we can come to another. Just let me know which one."

"Thank you. I really have had a good time."

"Bye, Cinderella," is shouted from close by. Lily and I turn to the girl we met queuing to come inside earlier.

I chuckle, waving at her.

"Bye," Lily calls out, her cheeks turning pink. I tuck her into my side and head for the main doors. "I still can't believe that little girl thought I was Cinderella."

Her giggle is infectious. "I can. It's all that blonde hair and fair skin," I tell her. The girl had been with her parents and brother. She had let go of her mum's hand and run over to Lily, tugging on the end of her blue coat.

"Are you Cinderella?"

Lily bends down in front of the little girl, zipping her coat closed to shield her from the cold. Always thinking of others.

"I'm not, but I heard there's going to be one here tonight."

"But you look like Cinderella or Elsa, but I think you're too young to be Elsa," the girl tells her, twirling a piece of Lily's hair between her fingers.

Lily's grin spreads wider. "And you look like Rapunzel with your long golden hair."

"I do?"

"You really do. You even have a pretty flowered hairband in your hair like her."

The girl touches the hairband, a smile slowly spreading across her face. "Yes!"

I chuckle at the fist pump she does before running back to her parents.

"Thank you for getting us the tickets. When I mentioned it last night, I thought you were asking what we should do in the future," she tells me, something I already know.

However, I wanted to make her happy, especially after yesterday. And whether she knows it or not, I've seen how much she is hurting inside, even if she doesn't show it. Not telling people about us is making her physically sick.

"I wanted to spend time with you. I don't care if it's watching men in tights sing and dance or cuddled in your bed, as long as you're by my side."

She melts into me, hugging my waist. "You say the sweetest things."

We head towards the carpark and pick-up point, arms around each other.

Lily's phone beeps with a text, and I pull away a little so she can grab it out of her pocket.

Seeing Maddox's name, I tense a little. She doesn't hide the screen from me so I'm able to read the message.

MADDOX: Where are you again? Have I done something to annoy you? I know I can be a little much when I've had a drink. If I did something that offended you, please, just tell me so I can fix this. I can't deal with the distance anymore. Everyone is getting worried now. But I feel like this is aimed at me. You've even started putting the chain and stuff on your door. I want to make this right between us. You're my best friend. I love you, Lily. Call me. Madz. X

"Who is it?" I casually ask, pretending I haven't read it.

She quickly pushes her phone back into her pocket. "It was Maddox."

Looking around, I see the fountain people were sitting on earlier, empty. "Come on, let's sit down and talk."

"I thought we were leaving," she tells me, looking confused.

Sighing, I pull her over to the fountain and we sit down on the stone edge. "You're sad."

Her knees lock together, tilted to the side as she faces me. "I'm not sad because of you."

I tuck a strand of hair behind her ear when the wind blows it in her face. "I know you're not. But this secret is killing you on the inside."

"I want to tell Mum and Dad after Christmas. I think it's best that we do. I know we've spoken about it before, but I don't like keeping you from them. I want to talk to them about you. I want them to meet you."

"What would you tell them?"

She gives me a small smile. "That you're amazing and make me laugh. That you make me happy all the time. I want to be able to talk to my mum about the things we do. I nearly told her about the ice-skating the other day."

When her expression falls, I push closer to her. "Okay, so after Christmas we will tell them. But what about Maddox?"

"Once my parents know, everyone will know. Faith already knows. It's nice talking to her about it, but it's not the same. I'm so happy I could scream it from the roof tops. But it's lying to them. It turns my stomach upside down."

"Is he mad at you?"

Her eyes water when she blinks up at me. "That's what hurts the most. He thinks *he* did something wrong, and he hasn't. I don't want to outright lie to him. And if I reply, he'll ask me questions and want to know why. I just... I can't. So I've been avoiding them all. I'm scared they'll take one look at me and just know. I have nightmares about it."

"You have nightmares?"

This is the first time she's mentioned nightmares. When we speak in the mornings over the phone, before we even get out of bed, she always tells me she's had a good night's sleep.

"It's nothing. If I'm honest, it's a nice break from my other nightmares."

"Lily, let's just tell them tomorrow. You're going to work yourself into the ground if you keep stressing out over this."

She takes my hand, and I frown at how cold she is. I pull her closer, giving her my body heat.

"I want a few more days. I just... Every time I picture telling them in my mind, it goes badly. That's not like me. I always think positively."

"All right. How about instead of setting your goals high, why don't you set them low. In your mind, picture us telling them and them all reacting badly."

"But that's what I'm picturing anyway," she mumbles, pouting.

I chuckle, pecking her on the lips. "No. What you're doing is setting yourself up to fail. You want them all to accept me. You want it to go okay."

"Of course I do," she tells me, fire in her tone.

I grin, arching my eyebrow. "I know. Which is why it keeps playing on your mind during the night. So tell yourself it's going to be bad at first, but everyone will have a chance to calm down and everything will be fine. Don't expect them to accept me right away. That is why it's constantly playing in your nightmares. It's probably your body's way of tellin' you not to set yourself up for heartbreak."

"You're right. Thank you, Jaxon. I'm so glad we spoke," she whispers softly, staring up at me with those doe eyes of hers.

I cup her face, tilting her head to meet mine. I kiss her, licking her bottom lip and tasting the chocolate she was eating inside.

It's hard to pull away when things begin to heat up. My lips are buzzing from the feel of hers. But when a kid's laughter echoes through my ears, I slowly pull away, inwardly groaning at how awkward I feel for getting a semi when there are people milling around.

"Jaxon, tonight—"

The alarm programmed into my phone to alert me of someone being on the property, blares from my phone.

Lily's eyes widen, looking down at my phone that I pull out. "Fuck, two alarms triggered."

My phone rings.

"Wyatt, please tell me you are home."

"We're just heading back now. Is everything okay there? Whoever this is doesn't have a clue about our new security system. If they did, they'd be gone by now. I can't even access what alarm they triggered, just that's it's on the outside. You need to be careful."

Lily follows when I stand up, sensing my panic. "What do you mean here? And be careful? I'm not fucking there."

"What do you mean you aren't there?" he yells.

"I'm out with—" My eyes widen as I stare down at Lily. She looks frightened, and I pull her head against my chest. "I'm out."

"Why aren't you at the office?"

"Why aren't you? It's your turn," I snap, squeezing the phone.

"No, it's fucking not."

"Yes, it is, Wyatt. We take turns on a Saturday. The rotation has you on."

"Yeah, and I covered your shift yesterday 'cause something important came up. You said you'd do mine."

"Fuck!" I snap, grimacing when a young mum covers her child's ears, glaring at me. "Who *is* there?"

"Just Mum. Not even Paisley and Landon are at the bed and breakfast. I saw them earlier as I was leaving, and they said they were spending the night at Charlotte's."

I curse, running a hand through my hair. How did I let this happen?

"I'm fifteen minutes away. I'm coming now," I tell him, but it might not be any use. There's no telling what the person is doing on our property.

"Hurry, we'll probably make it at the same time."

He ends the call and I look to the sky, groaning.

"Is everything okay?" Lily asks on a shaky whisper.

"Someone's on the property, near Hayes Removals. We have sensors near the building."

"Oh my God. You need to go," she tells me.

I take her hand then pause. I'm going to have to drop Lily off first. If she comes, they'll see her, and I know if my brothers find out first, it will make everything worse. They love me but they wouldn't keep this a secret for me, not when it's a chance to kick it to a Carter.

"Lily, I'm going to have to drop you off first."

"No!" she orders quietly, letting go of my hand.

"Lily, I don't have time. If I take you, my brothers will see you. You don't want everyone finding out before you've had a chance to tell your family, do you? And I don't know what is going on there. There is no way I'm taking you and putting you in potential danger. I can't."

"I live twenty minutes away from you, Jaxon. Add in the time it would take you to get from here to there, then from mine to yours, you'll take nearly an hour. I've got money to get a taxi."

"You aren't getting a taxi," I tell her, cutting right to it.

Her gaze softens and she places her hand on my chest, above my heart. "Yes, I am. Your family needs you. After, come back to mine."

"I won't be able to. It could be late."

She pulls away, searching through her bag before she pulls out a key. "Here. I—I was going to a-ask you before. To sleep over. Not to, um—you know, but to sleep. I want to sleep next to you."

Her entire face is bright red, and if I weren't in a rush to get back, I'd be saying fuck it and leaving with her right now.

I'm speechless. It wasn't something I thought she would want just yet. Every night it's killed me to leave her, wanting to spend the night with her in my arms.

"Y-you don't h-have to."

"I'd love to," I tell her, my voice hoarse. I clear my throat, then look around, seeing a taxi pull up close by. "All right. Come on. There's a taxi."

She beams up at me and heads over to the taxi. "Call me to let me know everything is okay," she orders.

I kiss her lips, wishing I didn't have to leave. I hate that she's getting a taxi back. This is how she must have been feeling these past few weeks. Torn between me and the family she loves and adores.

"Text me when you get home. As soon as you're inside the door and it's locked. Okay?"

"I will. And you'll do the same?" she asks, blinking innocently up at me.

I tuck her hair behind her ear. "Yeah."

I help her inside then reach for the passenger side, giving the bloke her address and thirty quid.

I tap the roof of the car before stepping back. I watch her leave before moving my arse to the carpark and getting out of here.

My brothers are going to kill me. I can't believe I let this happen.

I slow my speed once I hit the road leading up to the farm. I don't want the intruder alerted, but mostly, I don't want Mum coming out to investigate. All I need is for her to lose her shit while someone is here.

If they are still here.

She would just draw attention to the fact that we know they are here, and we might not find out who it is or what they are after this time.

This has Black written all over it. We've not had one problem in all our time running Hayes Removals. Then this tosser comes along and begins to fuck things up for us. It didn't matter we spent a year upgrading our business when a Man with a Van began. No, now we have to fight some rich fucker who probably eats money for breakfast.

Wyatt's car is just coming to a stop outside Mum's. I look up to the house, seeing a few lights on so I know she's awake. We've come and gone as we pleased since we were old enough, so she won't bother coming to the window to check who it is.

Wyatt, Reid and Eli step out of the car, just as the twins, Theo and Colton, walk out the house, their heads bent to the tablet in Theo's hand.

Wyatt glares at me when I get out the car, heading over to me. I feel like shit for letting them down. This isn't just my business. It's all of ours.

I take a quick glance at the twins, groaning when they both share a panicked look before heading over.

"Where the fuck were you?" Wyatt snaps.

"I know I fucked up," I admit, rubbing the back of my neck.

"What's going on?" the twins ask, stepping up to us.

"Shush," Eli whispers harshly. "We've had an alert on our phones that someone is on the property."

The twins' eyes light up. "Please tell us we can torch the fucker."

I roll my eyes. Sometimes I worry that the twins' intelligence will get them locked up. Other times it's their crazy antics.

"Who are you fucking? Must be good pussy for you to bail on work all the time. We've hardly seen you. And mum was acting all prissy yesterday, all tight-lipped about something. But we know she knows something," Reid says.

I take a step forward threateningly. He might not know he's talking smack about Lily, but I do.

"Not one word, Reid. I mean it," I warn.

His eyes round. "Holy fuck. You are fucking someone. Who?"

"Shut the fuck up," I growl, looking around to make sure no one is here.

"Way to go," Colton cheers quietly, grinning like a damn fool.

I scowl at him. "Not now."

"We made a stun gun. Can we use it on this guy?" Theo asks. "We've been wanting to try it out, but we aren't sure just how strong we've made it."

"Yeah. We can't test it out on animals. That would be sick."

Reid looks at the twins, disgusted. "But human trials are all right?"

Colton nods like it is. "Well, yeah. Fucker deserves it. It's not like he doesn't know whose land he's on."

"We'll go scout."

The only reason I nod is because I know they won't do anything without telling us. And they're good. Freakishly good with getting in and out of places undetected.

"Are you going to tell us who?"

"No," I snap at Wyatt, but the way he's looking at me is like he already knows.

"We deserve to know why you fucked up. No pussy is that good," Reid says.

I take another step towards him when something falls at the back of Hayes Removals, the sound echoing through the air.

I point to Eli then Wyatt before nodding to the left side of the building. Me and Reid head to the right. Hopefully the twins are somewhere close and won't let the fucker move.

It's time to show this guy just what kind of crazy he's messed with.

CHAPTER TWENTY-ONE

JAXON

Hot air blows out of our mouths as we duck behind one of the vans, peeking around the corner. Someone is definitely here; we can hear them dropping something on the floor. We move closer, careful not to tread on anything that will give us away.

Another noise echoes into the night as we make our way slowly down the side of the building. A male curses, and Reid and I move quicker, Reid going to the right while I keep to the side of the building.

My back goes rigid when the distinct smell of petrol fills the air. "Fuck!" I hiss, moving quicker. If he lights that before we can get to it, we'll be fucked. We have materials and chemicals in the back of the warehouse that are both ours and what we store for Mum.

Seeing a light flicker, I don't think. I rush forward, my heart racing when I see something light up in flames. I'm closer now, and the bloke turns, sensing me, and panics. He goes to throw whatever he's set on fire to the ground, but I'm on him, pushing him away from the building and falling on top of him, pinning him to the ground when he begins to struggle.

He dropped whatever he was holding on the way down, and when I turn back, my eyes widen, seeing small flames flicker towards the building.

"Reid, get the hosepipe," I yell, just as he runs near. He tries to stamp it out, but it follows the line of where this dickhead has poured petrol.

"Fuck," Reid yells when the wall begins to light up, the flames flickering. Wyatt and Eli come running around their corner, panic in their expressions. They know what's in there too.

I turn back to the dickhead beneath me, seeing his face now.

Seth.

I lean up, giving myself room to do what I should have done that day on the front garden of Blanche's home.

His attempt to block me when I lean up and punch him in the temple, is lame at best. He's out cold in a second, and I go to help Reid and Wyatt.

"Got it," Theo yells, and I look around, not seeing him.

"On three," Colton yells, and I'm wondering what the fuck is going on.

"Where the fuc—" Reid starts, but is cut off by water splashing him in his face from above.

"Sorry." Colton winces, holding onto a hose. Theo is beside him, holding one of the fire extinguishers, his face alight with glee.

"This is so cool," Theo yells, hooting.

I dust the dirt off my jeans as I get up, relaxing when I see the fire go out.

"I think you've got it," Wyatt yells, glaring at the twins. "Now get the fuck down before you break your necks."

"What a way to invite them to do it," Eli grumbles, watching the twins high-five each other.

"Yeah, you know what they're like. You tell them not to do something and they want to do it. Remember that time you told them they'd break their arms if they tried riding the pigs, that they weren't horses?" Reid asks.

Wyatt groans, scrubbing a hand down his face. "It was actually Jaxon who told them not to."

Looking up at my baby brothers, I start to count to ten in my head. "Cole, Theo, if you don't get the fuck down here right now, I'll be coming up there and breaking your fucking necks. Don't test me, either, because I'm not in the mood."

I see both visibly swallow. "We've got homework anyway."

"You were on your way out," Eli argues.

"We're doing anatomy in biology."

"And that involves leaving the house?" Wyatt asks sarcastically.

"Yeah, we're doing the female body. We've got a date with Helen Cox to examine hers in the flesh."

"What?" I rumble out, glaring up at them.

Theo holds his hands up. "We like learning with first-hand experience. Don't know what to tell ya'."

Reid laughs. "You aren't a gynaecologist, dude."

"And you've already passed biology," I remind them. They've even done their A-levels since they are so advanced in most of their subjects. The headteacher felt the GCSE level wasn't enough so gave them harder work.

Colton grins at me. "We know. She doesn't though. She's willing to check our anatomy out too. Later."

"Fuck me," I mutter, before staring down at Seth on the floor.

"Hey, I recognise him. *Why* do I recognise him?" Wyatt asks, disgusted.

I can see what he means. Seth isn't exactly someone we'd want to remember. He looks like he hasn't eaten in days, and I can see the track marks on his arms. The fucker hadn't even bothered to put on a coat.

Eli wasn't there that day, and I don't think any of us said anything as it was the day we found George. I run down everything, and when I'm finished, Eli is spitting on the bloke. "Piece of fucking shit."

"But why?" Reid asks. I look over at him, confused. "He didn't even catch your name. Yeah, the van was there, but I doubt this piece of shit can read."

"Let's find out." I grin evilly, pulling Seth up by the scruff of his T-shirt.

"Fuck yeah," Eli hoots, moving to the back of the building. We actually have a floor light there since we have a back entrance. Eli steps up onto some crates and switches it on, disabling the sensors.

The area around us lights up, and I throw Seth against another set of crates. He groans, coming to. He's out of it for a moment, groaning about something under his breath. But then I see the moment everything comes back to him, because he shuffles further back, his eyes widening as he takes us all in.

"Fuck!"

Eli steps over and Seth actually whimpers. We might all look intimidating, but Eli looks downright scary with all his tattoos and piercings. His jaw is clenched as he bends down, clasping his hands together in front of Seth.

"Do you want to leave?" Eli asks, his voice is soft.

"You aren't going to let me go," Seth bites out, scratching at his arm.

"Why would you think that? Maybe we should get to know each other," Eli suggests, and I lean back against our fire bin, grinning.

"Fuck you!"

"That's not nice, now, is it," Eli tells him gently. He's bringing him into a false sense of safety, and Seth is anything but safe right now. I'm barely keeping it together. Not only did he hit the woman I love, but he nearly burned down my livelihood. That shit could have spread and hit the barn. Or the house.

"There's something you should know about me. I'm the quietist of my brothers. I like the simplest things in life; music, art, women." He tilts his head to the side, gauging Seth's reaction. He's cowering, looking between us like one of us might help him. But Eli's expression has changed and there's no stopping him. "I also love pain. I love inflicting it, receiving it. It makes me feel alive."

"Shut the fuck up, you freak," Seth spits at him.

Eli's jaw hardens, and he reaches forward quickly, squeezing Seth's cheeks together. "Make no fucking mistake; I will fucking end you and wake up tomorrow feeling fresh as a daisy."

"I'm phoning the police," Seth yells.

I laugh, stepping forward. Eli nods to me, getting up. I know where he's going. We all do. I watch him head around the corner before addressing Seth.

"You've made him mad. It takes a lot to do that. He wasn't wrong in what he said. He's the laidback one. So, before he comes back, I want you to tell me why the fuck you just tried to burn down my warehouse. Maybe, just maybe, I'll talk Eli into going easy on you."

"I'm not telling you shit," he yells, and I reach forward, grabbing his wrist and snapping it back. He howls, clutching it to his chest.

"Try again," I bite out, standing up.

"Fuck you. I'm not telling you shit."

I smirk, bringing the heel of my foot down on his knee, hard. I feel his knee pop out and revel in his screams.

"You think someone will hear your screams? They won't. The nearest neighbour is a mile out. Scream all you like. It will only make this more fun. Now, tell me who the fuck sent you. I know it was you who vandalised our vans. I want to know why."

"You think I'm going to tell you after this," he yells, tears streaming down his face.

"Yes, I do."

"Then I want money. If you want me to tell you anything, I want money. Or a fix. I'm not telling you shit before."

I bend down in the same position Eli did moments ago, tilting my head at him. "It's funny you think you have a choice. Things aren't going good for you. It's going to get a lot worse when my brother comes back. There are things we do to people like you, people who think they can fuck with us, with our family. They all get their own special treatment. The last one got lucky; Eli wasn't with us."

"I know people," he sneers at me.

I cock my head to the side, trying not to laugh at how pathetic he sounds. "Yeah, Rory Jenks one of those people?"

His pupils dilate, his body trembling with fear. "H-how?"

I smirk. "I make it my mission to know everything about the people fucking with me. I looked into you. You owe Jenks a lot of money. Money he doesn't mind losing if it means he has the pleasure of taking your life. I can call him." I pause, letting him stew on it before adding, "After we've finished with you, of course."

"I'm as good as dead anyway. I'm not going out a rat."

Ah, now we're getting somewhere.

When Eli rounds the corner with his bag in hand, I smirk over at him. "I have the perfect idea."

"You do?" he asks, playing along.

Reid laughs behind me. "If he's thinking what I'm thinking, then yes, he really fucking does."

"Pass us the extension," Eli orders, and Wyatt moves away from the wall and unlocks the steel doors leading to the back of the warehouse. He reaches inside, messes around for a few moments, before coming back out with the extension lead.

Seth, for the second time tonight, tries to flee. Reid moves quickly, pinning him to the crate on one side, while I hold the other.

The buzz of the tattoo gun vibrates through the air, causing him to kick out. Reid is the tattooist in the family, the one with the extraordinary talent for it, but Eli loves to do it as a hobby when he has free time. He's good. Really good. And often takes jobs when he's at a gig and some punk wants a tattoo after getting shitfaced. Music is where Eli's love lies.

"You can't do this to me. I'll tell you anything you want if you get me a fix."

I tense, glaring at the son of a bitch. "We hold the power. Not you. Unless you have something we want to hear, I wouldn't open your mouth too much. Movement might fuck up his work. He's still practicing."

Eli finishes putting on his gloves and shuffles forward, leaning into Seth. "Are you sure you don't want to speak to us?"

Seth's lips tighten but there's no mistaking the stench of fear. He struggles and opens his mouth to scream, but I grab a rag off the floor and shove it in his mouth, muffling his screams.

The buzz of the gun draws closer, and he looks ready to pass out, his breathing escalating.

"Wait!" I call out, reaching into Eli's bag for a pair of gloves. "He clearly likes needles. He'll probably get off on you doing it. So why don't we let me?"

Eli grins and the buzz cuts off. "Yeah, you'll probably press too deep, probably scar him for life."

Reid chuckles behind us. "Personally, it's a waste of ink. I'd just get a knife and carve into him."

Seth's eyes widen, looking over my shoulder at Reid. His muffled screams behind the rag go ignored.

I grab the gun, moving forward and bringing it to his forehead. It's barely touching his skin when all of a sudden, the sounds he's making change to something else, his body tensing but no longer fighting.

Wyatt leans over from where he took over holding him down and rips the rag out of his mouth.

Seth gasps for air, his movements frantic and eyes wild. "I'll tell you. I'll tell you everything."

"You're speaking but not telling us shit," I spit out, moving the gun back to his forehead.

He screams like a banshee. "I will. I will. It was Andrew Black. He was following you the day I went to that old hag's house with that slut there."

I press the needle to his skin, just pressing it there while he screams. Hearing him mention Lily makes me want to rip his throat fucking out. I couldn't give a shit about Blanche, but Lily is where I draw the line. No one talks shit about her. Ever.

Blood drips down his face, leaking into his eyes.

"Get to the point," I growl, feeling the heat of Wyatt's stare.

"He was there. He followed me to where I hid in town and offered me a lot of money to fuck with your business. I needed the cash and you needed to pay."

Even with a needle pointing at his head, squirming like a baby, he tries to talk big. "What did he want you to do?"

He shrugs, but when I move my hand, he begins to shake again, rushing out, "He said to make sure I cost you money, to ruin anything I could get my hands on. Once I had proof I did something, he'd pay me."

"And?"

He catches his breath, scanning us one by one, before shrinking into himself. "Then he got mad, said what I was doing wasn't enough. He said he wouldn't pay the money I owed to Rory unless I did something to end your company. I needed that money."

"You were being played," I scoff. "He wouldn't give you shit. He just wanted some low-life to do his dirty work."

I can see the denial about to roll off his lips, but then something must hit him because he sags against the crates, looking defeated.

"I needed the money."

"Do you know why he asked you to do it?"

He shakes his head, not looking at us. "No. He never told me why and I didn't care. I wanted you to pay."

"Looks like it's your turn," I whisper, before nodding to my brothers. They rip his T-shirt up, exposing his chest. I grimace when I see his rib cage.

"W-what?" he yells, but before any more words can slip past, Wyatt shoves the rag back in his mouth, and I get to work on his chest, pressing hard enough to draw more blood than necessary.

Eli and Reid grin, looking down at my handiwork. "Nice."

Rat.

Adrenaline pumps through my veins as I take a step back, looking to Eli and Reid. "Can you two get him somewhere the cops will find him?"

Reid snorts, grabbing an unconscious Seth from the floor. "Yeah, but you're paying for my car to be cleaned. I think he's shit himself. Literally. It's kind of getting old now."

I chuckle, wiping my hands on my jeans. Wyatt steps closer as we watch them drag Seth away.

"Are you going back to the mystery woman now it's sorted?" he asks quietly.

I glance at him, the accusation there on the tip of his tongue. He wants to know, wants it confirmed. And he can keep wanting because until Lily has told her family, no one else is going to find out. Not by my lips anyway.

"I'm going to take a shower," I tell him honestly, stepping through backdoor to grab some fresh clothes.

"Is she worth it?" Wyatt calls from behind, his tone resigned and wary.

Facing him, I give him a tight nod, knowing it's not what he wants, but it's the truth. "Without her, there is no me."

I leave him with those parting words. He must know who we're talking about. I guess asking me outright would make it real.

He doesn't want to hear me say her name. He knows how this is going to end. He knows it's inevitable that the Carter's will come for me. And he knows I don't care.

After all, actions have consequences.

I'm just willing to face mine.

Loving Lily as much as I do is worth the price.

I've loved her since I was twelve years old. And for twelve years since then, I've had to live with her close yet so far away.

I'm not going back to that. I'm not going back to being a hollow shell of a person. She's the other half of my soul. She completes me.

And not even Wyatt can talk me out of giving that up.

I USE THE KEY Lily gave me, letting myself in through the front door before taking my shoes off. It feels weird. Ever since we started dating, I've been going through the backdoor.

I stroke Willa under her chin when she greets me on the stairs.

I showered before coming, washing away my bad deeds. I didn't want the stench of what I did tonight anywhere near her.

She stirs in bed when I enter. "Jaxon?" Her voice is soft, filled with sleep.

I take off my coat as I answer. "Yeah."

"Is everything okay? You didn't text me," she asks, clutching the sheet to her chest.

I pull my T-shirt over my head before unbuckling my jeans and stepping out of them. I get into bed, pulling her to my chest.

"I'll tell you everything tomorrow. Tonight, I just want to hold you."

I might not feel remorse for my actions—I'd do them again in a heartbeat—but it doesn't mean it doesn't affect me. And for the rest of the night, I want to forget.

All I want to do is hold Lily in my arms all night for the first time. I want to treasure it, not tarnish it with memories of earlier.

He had what was coming to him.

Now it's all about Lily. About us.

She places a kiss on my chest, her lips warm before she yawns. "Okay. Goodnight, Jaxon."

"Night, beautiful."

I stay awake until she falls asleep, and I watch her until my eyelids begin to droop and I'm falling asleep myself.

CHAPTER TWENTY-TWO

LILY

A SMILE SPREADS ACROSS MY FACE and my chest fills with warmth when I feel Jaxon's strong presence behind me. His arm is curled over my stomach, and his hand under my silk night top, and I realise I'm not wearing a bra. Tingles spread all over my body at the feel of him touching me so intimately, and it's only his thumb pressed into my breasts.

And he's hard. His erection presses into my arse, and my stomach swirls in excitement.

What has me smiling is waking up to him in my bed. I've been wanting this for ages, but I never knew how to ask him to stay. I would have spoken to Faith, but I didn't know how to ask her about it either.

The sun is barely up, so I know it's early, and glancing up at my clock confirms it. It's only half seven. It looks like we're in for a dreary day if the skies are still this dark.

Slowly, I turn around, scanning Jaxon's face. The creases of worry and turmoil are smoothed out. His dark, long eyelashes rest against his cheeks and his lips are parted slightly, his breathing deep and relaxed.

I run my fingers over the slight stubble on his jaw, amazed by how good it feels to touch. I follow the path of my finger into his thick, dark hair. It's one of my favourite things to do when we're lying down, watching television. He loves it when I run my fingers through it.

Butterflies swarm my stomach at the thought of him leaving soon. I know he'll want to go before anyone has a chance to see him. I don't want him to go, though. I want him to stay, to stay here with me. He's become the light at the end of the tunnel.

For all the darkness I've endured, ending with him feels like coming home. It's a similar feeling to the one I got when Mum and Dad brought me home to stay that first night. It felt right, warm. I was loved.

I'm different with him. I'm more of the person I aspired to be growing up. I can talk to him, whereas I can still shy away with family—accept Maddox and my siblings. It's like being heard for the first time.

I never want to let go of this feeling.

I never want to let go of him.

Jaxon completes me in a way I never knew I needed.

I startle a little when I look back down at him, seeing him watching me with a soft expression.

"Were you watching me sleep, princess?"

A light giggle slips free as I snuggle further down into the blanket next to him. "I was." He grins at that, and I like it. I love his sleepy expression. "I was worried about you last night. You didn't text."

"Before I get into last night, kiss me good morning," he rasps, cupping my jaw.

My stomach flutters, and I lean forward, pressing my lips to his.

Yep, I really don't want him to go. I could wake up like this every morning for the rest of my life and still get this same feeling.

"Good morning," I whisper breathlessly, blinking up at him.

"Morning," he smirks, our heads pressed together.

"Are you okay?" I ask, watching him carefully. Last night he seemed lost, which is why I didn't pressure him to talk to me. I know him enough to know he just wanted to hold me. I could hear it in his voice when he asked to hold me and go to sleep. It came out as more of a plea.

He sighs, his hand running across my hip. "Seth Merin tried to burn the warehouse down last night."

"What?" I screech, sitting up in the bed. "Are you okay? Did someone get hurt? Did you lose the whole factory?"

He takes my cheeks in the palm of his hands. "Breathe," he tells me, inhaling one deep breath before exhaling, letting it out slowly. I copy, slowly coming down from my panic attack. "We got there just in time. He spent too long making sure we weren't there then went back to his car for the petrol. He was an idiot."

"No one was hurt though, right? *You* weren't hurt?" I ask. I was afraid that was why he was so quiet last night. That he was hurt. I check him over, and for the first time, notice his chest is bare. He has tattoos everywhere. Over the right pec and shoulder is a dragon. The shading looks perfect behind it, giving it a smoky and flame affect. On his left pec and shoulder is a tribal tattoo, but on this one it has 'Family, Loyalty and Honour' written on it.

I become tongue tied when I cast a look at his ribs. In the perfect shade of black and grey blended into his skin tone is an angel. Her perfectly bowed lips are parted slightly, her wings spread out behind her, and I think she's on her knees. The tattoo only begins from her waist, but from the way it's drawn, I can just tell. The angel is on her knees, her head tipped up, looking towards his heart. The suffering yet hope that glistens in her eyes catches my breath.

She looks just like me.

However, it's the way the artist has presented the strength in the photo. I feel it inside my soul when I look at her. Nothing is simple about the drawing. This was designed by a talented person, someone who could draw everything from expression to feeling.

Underneath, 'Soul of my Soul' is scrolled in italic.

I look back up at him, seeing his lips move yet not hearing those words. I focus on what he's saying. "...fine. They took him to the police station."

"Your tattoo," I whisper quietly, a heavy feeling in my chest.

He looks down, seeming uncomfortable. "Um…"

"Is that me?" I ask him, finding my voice.

Looking at me dead on, he doesn't mess around. He's honest; however, I can tell he's nervous, guarded. "Yes."

Looking back down at the tattoo, the back of my eyes begin to burn, and my throat tightens. I reach out, running my finger over the lines of her delicate face. I feel overwhelmed.

"I-is this how you s-see me?" I manage to get out.

Gulping, he nods. "Yes."

"She's beautiful," I whisper, mesmerised by my finger running over his warm skin.

"You are beautiful, Lily. The tattoo doesn't do you justice."

My breath falters when I look up. His gaze falls to my parted lips, and I dart my tongue out, running it over the bottom of my dry lips.

He eyes fall shut as a groan slips past his lips. My skin burns, with what, I don't know. Something. I reach forward, coming up to my knees in front of him. My legs feel like jelly and my hands shake when I bring them up to his shoulders.

His eyes fly open, our gazes locking as heat passes between us. Slowly, in case this isn't something he wants or in case I'm doing it wrong, I lean forward, flicking my tongue against his top lip.

His hands fall to my hips and a moan slips free. He lifts me easily until I'm straddling him, my core pressing against his groin.

This is different from all the other emotions he evokes inside of me. This is raw, and I feel exposed.

My eyelids flutter shut when he grazes his lips across my jaw. I arch my neck, my fingers digging into his shoulders.

"Lily," he whispers, his fingers pressing into the side of my neck. I can feel my pulse beating hard, erratically, and I open my eyes to find him watching me, his expression intense.

Did I do something wrong?

His hand slides around my neck, tugging my head down to meet his. He kisses me, and I melt into him, relaxing once again.

One hand goes around his neck, my fingers twisting in his hair, but I keep the other on his shoulder, needing that support. The world around me might have disappeared, but I'm still aware of everything Jaxon is doing. And what he's doing is driving me wild with a feeling I'm not accustomed to.

I'm startled when he suddenly moves, keeping his arms around my waist as he lowers me to the bed, coming down by the side of me.

"You're beautiful," he whispers, his voice filled with need. "I've always wanted you, Lily. Always."

Tingles spread through me. I trust him. Whatever happens between us right now, I trust him.

Losing my virginity, although hasn't been something I've stressed over, was something I wanted to be special. I didn't mean the whole, no sex before marriage. I just knew it was going to be with the man I loved and would spend the rest of my life with. It meant everything to me that it was with the right person.

And there isn't a man who I could love more than Jaxon. It's impossible. I've always been a firm believer that there is more than one person out there, that you have more than one soul mate.

I couldn't have been more wrong. The connection I feel when I'm with Jaxon can't be duplicated. What I have inside of me, whether it's my soul, my essence, my spirit; it belongs to him and only him. No one else can have a piece of that. My family have my heart and my love. Jaxon, however, has all of me. Every single part.

And I know there's no one else on this earth who could love him the way I love him.

"Jaxon," I whisper, feeling so many emotions tears begin to burn the back of my eyes.

"I've got you," he whispers back against my lips. "I'll always have you."

He runs his finger down my chest, over my silk top and over my erect nipple. I gasp into his mouth, my back arching off the bed.

I lay still when his finger begins to roam over my stomach, unsure of what to do. Even my hands lie by my side, twitching to reach out and hold him.

I'm so nervous I'm shaking, but I've never wanted anything more in my life.

"Kiss me," he rasps against my lips, and I realise I'd stopped kissing him.

Letting my body do the work instead of letting my mind take over, I run my hand up his arm, over his strong, broad shoulder and up his neck until I'm cupping his jaw. I kiss him, our tongues entwining.

I stiffen a little when his hand slides under my pyjama shorts and into my knickers. I moan when his fingers run through my wetness, and I feel my entire body flush.

"Fuck, you're wet," he whispers hoarsely. "God, Lily, you feel so good."

"Jaxon," I cry against his lips. My hips buck when he presses down on my clit, making smooth, small circles. I can feel the wetness between my legs, feel it soaking my knickers.

He covers my mouth with his to swallow the moan escaping. I cling to him, feeling his fingers slide back down to my opening. A shudder rakes through me when he dips his finger inside, not all the way, but enough for me to feel the pressure.

"Oh God," I whimper, my toes curling into the mattress.

He smiles against my lips before pumping his fingers inside of me again. Our kiss starts to become uncontrolled, just like his movements as he moves back to rub my clit. He's driving me wild. My body is building up to something, something explosive, but every time I think it's near, he stops, sliding his fingers through my heat before entering me.

"Oh," I moan, arching my hips a little.

His fingers keep pumping inside of me, slow and steady before coming out to swirl around my clit. He continues to do this until it becomes too much. It's torturous but thrilling at the same time.

My breathing is shallow, my entire body is flushed, and a sheen of sweat glistens between my breasts.

I feel alive.

"Jaxon," I breathe.

"God, you're so tight, so fucking warm. You feel like silk around my fingers," he groans into my neck, his breathing just as hard as mine. "Do you like me finger fucking you?"

I flush at his words yet find myself nodding. "Yes!"

He grins, looking down at me as he speeds up his movements. He thrusts another finger inside of me, causing flutters in my lower stomach.

"Please," I beg.

"I can't wait to taste you, to lick that pussy," he rasps, and for good measure, licks up the side of my neck.

I cry out, my eyes slamming shut as the strongest sensation runs through my entire body. My back arches off the bed, my toes curling into the blankets, and I cling to Jaxon, afraid this feeling will stop.

His fingers slow, and I can feel and hear how wet I am. I blink up at him. "W-what was that?"

"That, baby, was an orgasm."

"I want another," I blurt out, and he chuckles, leaning down to kiss me.

"You'll have plenty more, I promise. But first, I want to make you breakfast," he tells me.

I look at him, feeling something sink inside of my stomach. "We're not, um—y-you know…"

"Lily, as much as I'd love to take you right now, I won't. You deserve for it to special, like it is in the books."

I scrunch my eyes up at him. "I don't think you should use books as an example. You should read the books Charlotte gives me. I don't know what it's like for other girls but losing your virginity after signing a contract isn't really romantic. More like a transaction."

He takes one look at my face to see that I'm serious. He bursts out laughing. But I'm not joking. All the books Charlotte gives me are quite raunchy. And if the female lead is a virgin, she isn't by the first few chapters.

"How about I plan it the way I feel you deserve, then?"

"Like what?" I ask, really wanting to know.

His smirk is dangerous to my hormones. "How about you let me worry about it. Just know that when we do, it will be special. It will be us and everything you deserve your first time to be."

I melt against him. "But we can still do that again, right?"

My cheeks heat at the look he gives me. "We'll be doing plenty of that. I can't wait to feel your hand wrapped around my dick."

I grip his arm, wanting that. He kisses me again before rolling off the bed. "I need to go to the bathroom for a minute."

Not understanding his sudden departure, I get out of bed too. "I'm making you breakfast. You're always doing everything for me. I want to do something for you."

He grins over his shoulder. "Baby, any time you want to cook for me, feel free. You're the shit in the kitchen."

I smile, giddy over the compliment. I nod, grabbing my Tinker Bell dressing gown before heading downstairs.

I feel like I'm on cloud nine. I've never felt anything like that in my life. I'm twenty-four years old and still a virgin. I know nothing about sex other than what I've read or seen on television. It's something I've always shied away from.

I fought for my independence when it came to my parents. First with my job and then when I moved out. I wanted to feel grown up.

But until I started dating Jaxon, I never really understood what I was looking for. It's insignificant to others, but for me, this morning was everything.

It made me feel like a woman.

I head into the kitchen, grabbing bacon, eggs and sausages out of the fridge. I'm going to make him a full English, the entire works.

The door knocks, and because I'm so lost in my happy place, I walk down the hall to the front door and open it. It's quarter to nine in the morning, so I don't know who would be coming at this time.

My blood runs cold when I figure out too late what I have done. My dad, uncle Max, Myles and Malik stand in the doorway with Maddox. Max and Maddox are staring at me accusingly. I know they're doing it in the hopes I will spill everything before they have to ask. The rest watch me as if I'm going to break any second.

Jaxon.

Oh my God. Jaxon is upstairs. The palms of my hands begin to sweat as I try to pull the door shut a little. How could I be so stupid, opening the door. I don't even know if Jaxon heard the door knock and knows to run or hide.

"Dad," I greet, forcing a smile. My throat begins to swell and my eyes burn with unshed tears. I'm going to have to lie to their faces. "Hey, everyone. Is everything okay?"

Dad places a hand on my stomach, pushing me back into the house. I squeak, looking to the stairs and back to them as they all pile into my house, leaving the door wide open.

"No, it's not. What's going on, Lily? You said you'd come to me."

I glance at Dad, hurt. He told them what I told him. Or if he didn't, they know now. "Dad."

He shakes his head. "Enough is enough. I want to know what's going on. Why are you avoiding your family? Did something happen? You need to talk to us, princess."

"Dad," I start again, trying to come up with some excuse, but the tears gather behind my eyes.

They're going to hate me when they find out I lied to them.

"Whose are those shoes?" Maddox asks, his voice deadly quiet.

I jump, looking down at the shoes, feeling like my world is slipping out from under me. I don't know what to do or what to say. I feel like I can't breathe.

"Whose fucking shoes are they?" he roars. "Is some fucker taking advantage of you?"

"I'll fucking kill them," Max agrees to Maddox.

"Lily, princess," Dad pleads.

I step back near the stairs, my back hitting the wall. The hallway is closing in on me and I can't breathe. *Why can't I breathe?*

"I-I…" I stammer out, closing my eyes tightly when all five sets of eyes glare at me expectantly.

"They're mine."

CHAPTER TWENTY-THREE

LILY

MY EYES WIDEN WHEN JAXON takes the first step down the stairs. "Jaxon," I breathe out, panicking. I can feel the tension in the air, and I try to step between him and my family.

"You've got to be fucking kidding me," Dad roars, taking a step towards him. "What did I fucking tell you?"

"Dad, please, just listen to me. You promised," I remind him. "You said you'd hear me out."

"That was before I knew this player sweet talked his way into your bed."

Bile rises in my throat at the way he looks at me. With disappointment. Maybe? Tears are streaming down my face as I keep my hand up.

"Dad!"

"Don't speak to her like that," Jaxon growls, and the tension in the room spikes.

Dad looks up at him, daring him to say something else.

I look to Maddox, who hasn't said anything. His hands are clenched into fists at his side and he's breathing hard. He looks to me, and I take a step back at the blank look he gives me. It hurts, hurts so much I feel the walls closing in around me.

"Why would you let him use you? You know what he's like," he warns me. "Is this why you've been avoiding me? Did he tell you to?"

I shake my head, wiping under my eyes. "He didn't. Please, calm down and let me explain."

He laughs with no humour before his eyes land on Jaxon behind me. "I'm going to fucking kill you. You've been playing her against us."

"No!" I scream, just as he comes at us. Jaxon's hands around my waist lift me off my feet and to the side. Dad grabs my arm, pulling me away as Maddox grabs Jaxon around the throat.

"No!" I cry out, struggling to get out of my dad's arms. "Stop it!"

"You fucking prick. Have you been fucking her this whole time?" Maddox roars in his face. "Did you think you were a big man, fucking sweet Lily Carter? We warned you time and time again to stay away from her."

"Fuck you, Maddox. Never speak about her like that again," Jaxon spits, ducking his head when Maddox goes to punch him.

"She's our fucking family and you think you can use her?" Maddox fires back.

My legs collapse as they fall into the wall, Maddox throwing punch after punch. Jaxon's bleeding. He's hurt and this is all because of me.

He's not even fighting back. He's trying to dodge the hits, but that's it, yet Maddox keeps hitting him, knowing that fact.

"Stop. Oh God, stop!" I plead, the sickening sound of flesh hitting flesh bouncing off the walls. My pulse begins to beat erratically, and I feel like my heart is going to explode in my chest.

Jaxon pushes Maddox off him, breathing heavily just inside the door. He looks over Maddox's shoulder to me, and I try to relax in the fact he doesn't hate me. Not yet. But it will come. My family are hurting him.

"It's okay," he mouths.

I scream so loudly it echoes around the house when my uncle Malik tackles him to the ground outside.

"You're fucking sick preying on innocent girls," he growls, punching Jaxon in face.

"She's a goddamn grown woman who can make her own choices," Jaxon snaps.

My sobs shake my whole body and I have to look away. I want to run, hide, but I can't leave Jaxon to face them on his own.

"Dad, stop them, please," I beg, digging my nails into his arm that's pinning me to his chest.

"No," Dad rumbles, not looking at me as he pulls me outside to follow them. "He's using you, Lily."

"No, Dad. No! He's not," I cry.

"You can't see it yet, Lily, but he is. Men like him always do," he rumbles.

I look outside to where they're all standing now, circling Jaxon. Another sob slips free at the sight of him. He isn't wearing shoes and the ground is frozen. He never even had time to put on a T-shirt before coming down to step in for me. He already has a swollen eye and blood dripping from his lip and eyebrow. My stomach turns seeing him like that.

How could they do this to him?

"I'm going to fucking kill you, Hayes!" Maddox shouts in Jaxon's face. I hiccup, digging my nails into the palms of my hands, feeling blood begin to drip where I've cut through skin. When Maddox looks up at me, I flinch. "Did he take advantage of you?"

"No! No, he didn't. Please, please stop this," I beg once more, trying to shove Dad's hand off me.

"Do you know who she is?" Max growls, taking Jaxon off guard and punching him the gut. Jaxon doesn't even fight back, clutching his stomach.

Why isn't he stopping them?

"Max!" I look up at my dad, seeing his hard expression set in stone. "Please, Dad! Please don't let them do this. I'm begging you."

He looks down at me, unblinking. "He shouldn't have fucked with you, Lily. We wouldn't have liked anyone who dated you, but this prick has it coming. He knew to stay away from you. We know what he's like."

"Dad, please, just hear us out. You don't need to do this," I plead, clinging to him as fresh tears stream down my lips. "He's not hurt me. He hasn't used me. We want this. Both of us. It's real. Dad, please!"

His jaw hardens and he doesn't answer, looking away from me. When I turn back, Jaxon is on his knees, breathing heavily, and Malik is standing in front of him. Bile rises in my throat at the sight of his swollen face. I barely recognise him. My knees give out completely, my entire body like jelly, and if it weren't for Dad still gripping me, I'd be on the floor.

"She's not just our niece," I hear Malik growl, bending down to Jaxon's ear. "She's our fucking sister."

"I know," Jaxon croaks out, trying to open his eyes.

I sob, clutching at my chest as I fight harder to get out of my dad's hold. "Let me go, Dad, now."

"No, Lily. He needs to learn. You deserve better than him. Way better. You deserve the world, not someone who is going to break your fucking heart."

I look up at my dad, barely seeing him through my tears. "He *is* my world."

His breath catches and he loosens his hold. I use it to my advantage and slip out of his arms. I run to the ground just as Maddox kicks Jaxon in the ribs.

"Stop! Just stop!" I scream, falling to the frozen grass on my knees. I can't catch my breath. It feels like the world has stopped spinning and the air is being sucked out of me.

One of them goes to pull me back, but I push them away from me, screaming at them from the top of my lungs. "Don't touch me!"

I move closer to Jaxon, our gazes meeting. I can see pain in them, and a flood of agony hits me.

"I-it's okay," he croaks.

I reach out, going to touch his face that is covered in bruises and blood, but I pull back at the last second, not wanting to hurt him. Instead, I take his hand in mine, resting it in my lap.

They did this to him.

They did this because I fell in love with him. Because he fell in love with me. They didn't even give us a chance to talk to them, for us to show them this is real. I knew they would be mad, react badly, but this is beyond my worst nightmare. And I had plenty of them over the past few weeks. None turned out like this. It was meant to be me they hated for keeping this from them. Me. They were never meant to hurt him.

"I'm so, so sorry," I sob out.

"Lily," Jaxon croaks, clutching his stomach.

"Lily, get away from him," Maddox snaps, shocking me. He's never spoken to me like that. Ever.

He hates Jaxon. He hates him that much he's willing to do this to him. And I can't have them hurt him. I can't. Not again. Not ever.

I know what I have to do.

"Don't touch me," I snap, flinching away from him.

"Come on. Give her space," Myles says gently from beside me, and I hear Maddox step back.

"I'm so, so sorry, Jaxon," I choke out.

He places his other hand over mine clutching me tightly. He's shaking, his hand cold, and I give it a gentle squeeze, letting him know I'm here.

"I-it's not y-your fault," he gets out through clenched teeth, trying to breathe through the pain.

My heart is bleeding and my entire body is shaking seeing him suffer like this. My throat tightens from the sob I swallow down.

"Lily," Malik warns.

I can feel them behind me, watching me, but none of them make a move to touch me again. I look behind me, feeling nothing but the loss I'm about to endure. To everyone and everything else, I feel numb. I'm so hurt and angry with them.

With Jaxon, I'm feeling everything.

I've spent my whole life wishing I could numb certain feelings or memories. I felt everything my mum and her boyfriends did to me. Enough so that I still remember the entire time when most kids don't even remember their life before their fifth birthday.

But right now, I just can't muster up anything. It's like my soul knows it's about to be shredded and doesn't want to part with the person it belongs to. It's being ripped out of my body, piece by piece.

Jaxon.

"Don't come near me," I rasp out to Malik, no longer recognising my own voice.

"What on earth!" I hear boomed, and more tears gather behind my eyes at the sound of Barry's voice. He's going to hate me now too. I shut my eyes tightly. "Is that my Jaxon?"

I look up at Barry, feeling my vision blur. Myles steps in, stopping him, and I look to Jaxon again, his heavy eyes on me, barely focusing.

I did this.

Me.

I can't let this happen again.

I reach forward, running my fingers through his hair, swallowing the lump building in my throat.

"I love you," I whisper, feeling everyone's attention focus on us. "I'll *always* love you. I never knew you could love someone the way I love you. I didn't think it was possible. I never *knew* something that powerful even existed."

"Lily," he rasps out. His voice is filled with pain and not because of his injuries. He can see it in my eyes. I know he can. The way he's watching me, reading me… He knows. And my heart breaks a little bit more when he grips my hands tighter, shaking his head.

I blink up at him through wet lashes. "Don't. Please. Don't." I pause, trying to control my breathing as my body shakes with sobs.

"Lily," he pleads, lifting my chin to look up at him. "You don't have to do this. You don't have to choose."

"Jaxon, I—I…"

"Lily," he pleads one more time.

I shake myself out of it, needing to be strong one last time to get through this. It's the only way I can guarantee they won't hurt him again.

"Don't. This is the hardest thing I've ever had to do. Don't beg me. I can't take any more. I can't. I can't be the reason you're hurt. I love you too much. I love you so much I'm willing to let you go."

He rests his forehead against mine, and I close my eyes, feeling weight bear down on my chest.

I don't want to leave him. He's mine.

"You'll always be the one for me. The one who made me free. The one who made me forget where I come from and made me see where I was going. You made me feel whole for the first time in my life."

He grips my arm when I go to leave, sobs raking through my chest. "Don't leave me," he rasps out. "We can get through this."

I try to pull harder without hurting him. "Jaxon, please."

"You promised, Lily. You promised you wouldn't leave me."

I bend down on my knees, gripping the grass. "I'm sorry. I'm so sorry."

"Come on, Lil," Myles whispers, helping me off the floor.

"Lily, no. You promised." Jaxon breaks, and the strong man I once knew is gone. I cling to Myles, looking away from Jaxon on the ground, resting against his granddad who kneels beside him.

"Jaxon," Barry whispers, and I hear a struggle. I feel numb, staring at the ground.

"I'll help you get him inside," Uncle Myles whispers, and he lets me go slowly.

"You can't leave me," he rasps out, and I glance his way. The pain and sorrow in his eyes is nearly my undoing.

I rub away the pain in my chest, finding it harder with each second to breathe. It's like shards of glass are cutting me up from the inside.

I suck in the air, but it's too thick for me to swallow. My heart is slowly being shred to pieces. I can feel it inside of me, tearing me apart.

I feel like I'm going to throw up.

"I'm doing this for you. Please don't make this harder than it already is," I sob out, stepping back. "You'll be okay. I promise."

"I won't. I won't be okay without you," he chokes out, his arms over Myles and Barry's shoulders, both of them supporting him.

"This is the only way," I whisper brokenly.

I turn on wobbly legs, and I crumble inside with each step as he calls my name, his voice getting weaker and weaker.

"Lily," my dad whispers when I reach my door. I look up at him blankly, feeling nothing.

"I hope this makes it better for you. For all of you," I say, speaking up for the first time in my life. I look at my uncles who have the nerve to look shame-faced. I can't even look at Maddox right now, knowing he inflicted most of the injuries. He's the reason Jaxon is suffering behind me. "While you can all go home and feel better about chasing away the big bad wolf, know that I'll be in there," I tell them, pointing at the door, "with a shattered heart. I've endured pain. A lot of it physical." I watch as my dad flinches, but I keep looking at him dead on. "None of that compares to how much I'm hurting right now."

"Lily, he was using you," Maddox spits out.

"Like you use women?" I ask, ignoring the pang in my chest at using hateful words. But I'm angry. So incredibly angry at him. "He has a past like the rest of you. But with me," I tell him, slamming my hand on my chest. "With me he was different. He was mine and we had a future." More tears flood my eyes, and I find it hard to concentrate. "I love him. I love him so much I could tell him anything. He knows about my past. Everything. More than I've ever shared with anyone. It didn't matter. He still wanted me for me. Me," I cry out, slamming my heart with my fist. "He wanted me. We joked about a future, but deep down, I knew he was serious. I could feel he wanted that with me. He trusted me enough to want to have kids even given my past and the way I react in certain situations. And five minutes ago, you ripped that away from me. From us. You robbed us of a beautiful life."

"You can have that with someone better," Maddox mutters, looking unsure now.

I shake my head, feeling sad that he'll never understand. "No, I won't. Because he was it for me. There isn't anyone else."

I stand inside my door, trying my hardest not to look next door, where I know Myles is helping Barry take Jaxon inside. Even now I want to run to him, to help soothe his pain. But I can't. I can't risk my family getting angry again.

What happens when the rest find out and react the same? I choke on a sob at the thought, grabbing the edge of the door.

"Lily," Dad tries again, and when he goes to step inside, I look up at him.

"I want you to leave."

"I'm not leaving," he says, shaking his head.

"You don't have a choice," I whisper, slamming the door in his face. I make sure the bolt is pulled over before resting my back against the door and sliding down. It won't keep them out—I'm not that stupid—but at least it gives me time.

I crumble, loud, heavy sobs heaving through my body.

I begin to heave, gagging as I try to get up. I grab onto the bannister, gagging once again as bile splatters all over my stairs.

Oh God, I'm going to be sick.

I rush up the stairs as quickly as my legs will take me, my hand covering my mouth as my chest heaves. I reach for the sink just in time, throwing up everything inside of me.

I DON'T KNOW how long I'm in the bathroom for. The banging on my door stopped not long ago.

Finally getting up from the cold, tiled floor, I make my way into the bedroom.

Tears gather in my eyes as I take in the rumpled sheet, remembering what we shared this morning.

God, this morning. It feels like a lifetime ago that we were lying on that bed, him touching and kissing me.

Jaxon's T-shirt lies on the floor, and I hiccup out a sob as I pick it up and bring it to my nose.

It smells like him.

I crumble to the bed as a fresh wave of tears begin. I lie on the side he slept on, still smelling him on my sheets.

It feels like hours pass, my mind torturing me with images of Jaxon hurt and in pain. It could have been minutes ago. I don't know.

"Lily."

I sit up and gaze to the door when Mum calls my name. "Mum?" I call, in case this isn't real.

"Oh, sweet girl," she whispers, coming to my side.

"Mum?" I croak out, feeling that weight on my chest again.

She lays down on the bed, and I turn, shoving my face into her stomach. "He's gone."

"He's not gone, Lily. He's still here."

I shake my head, clinging to her harder. "I can't be with him. They hurt him, Mum. Really hurt him."

"I know. I'm so sorry, Lily. It's going to be okay. It will be okay. I promise."

"I don't know how to live without him. He made me feel whole. How can I go on living knowing I'll never feel that again?"

"Lily, please don't talk like that," she begs, tears in her voice.

"I can't help it. It hurts so much, Mum." I take in a deep breath. "We weren't doing anything wrong."

"I know. Why don't you wait for the dust to settle? I'm sure Jaxon will understand where they were coming from."

She can't be serious.

"No. What they did was horrific, Mum. There was no need for it. And I'll never expect Jaxon to forgive me for it. You didn't see him. He could barely look at me his face was that swollen."

She sighs, running her fingers through my hair. "Your dad has always held onto his guilt for not being there for you."

I blink up at her, confused. "What?"

She forces a smile down at me. "He's always felt guilty for not being there. They never once thought to look for their mum. To them, she abandoned them and left them all with a monster. They didn't know she was the devil's wife." She pauses, taking a breath to compose herself. "He's never forgiven himself for it. He kept asking himself why he didn't, that maybe if he had, you wouldn't have been hurt. He had his brothers growing up; you were alone. When you came to live with us, he wanted to make sure you never felt unsafe again. He vowed to protect you against anything and everything, even if it meant going to school with you every day."

"It doesn't excuse what they did," I whisper, looking away. I don't like that my dad has lived with that. He could have spoken to me though. I've never once resented him for not being there. How could he have been? He didn't even know about me. I didn't even know about him.

"And your uncles. They might act like big uncles, sign cards and presents as your uncles, but in their hearts, deep down, you are still their baby sister. You are the only sister those five boys have. They'd die for any one of you, but you, Lily, are special to them. You hold a place in their heart that their own kids and nieces and nephews don't hold. Because you are more to them."

"Mum," I whisper painfully, gripping the blanket on the bed.

"And Maddox. He loves you like a sister. You're his best friend. He needs you to keep calm. He visits you so often because you make him feel like a better person. You calm the beast inside of him that he gets from his father. He might act like your uncle Max, but believe me, he has his father inside of him too. He feels protective of you."

"He hurt him badly, Mum." I sag against the bed, wishing she wouldn't twist it all up inside of my head. She makes it sound like Jaxon was taking advantage of me, but he wasn't. "I'm not a child. This isn't a crush. I loved him and they didn't even care. They didn't care that hurting him was hurting me."

She pulls me into her arms when I begin to sob. "No, you're not. But they wanted more for you, Lily. They didn't want someone like Jaxon around you."

"He's not who you think he is," I argue, crying into her neck.

"I believe you. I do. But they don't. And hearing you've had sex… it's a lot for them to handle."

I pull away from her, wiping under my eyes. "We didn't have sex."

"What?" she asks, clearly shocked.

I let out a dry laugh. "Yeah. He didn't want to have sex with me. He wanted to make it special. He told me I deserved it to be special, like in the books. That was all him, Mum. This might be new to me, but I would have said yes at any point in the past month. From our very first time spent together, I've wanted him. I'm drawn to him like no other person. He accepts the good, the bad, and the flawed when it comes to me. He takes me as I am. And now I'll never have that again."

She's looking at me differently now, like she's looking for a tell that I'm lying.

"Why don't you talk to your dad? Sweetie, I believe we can work this out. They just need time to cool off."

"You don't get it," I whisper.

"Get what, sweetheart?"

I hug my knees to my chest, staring ahead. "I chose him out there, Mum. I chose Jaxon. He never wanted me to pick between him and my family. He knew what it would do to me and told me he didn't want me to go through that. I couldn't choose. Any time I imagined being put in that position, I would die a little inside because I love all of you, but I love him too. But outside, when they were beating him, I chose Jaxon. I chose him."

"I still don't understand," she tells me, keeping her voice low.

I tilt my head, resting my cheek on the top of my knees, letting the tears stream down my face. "I knew deep down they wouldn't accept him. I had nightmares that they would keep him away or they'd force me to stay away from him. Outside, I chose Jaxon over my family. I chose to let him go in order to keep him safe. With us apart, they have no reason to hurt him again. You have no idea what it was like to see him like that. I can never sort that out. I can never make it right." I pause, taking a breath. "I've lost them, too, in a way. I'll never be able to forgive them, not fully."

"Lily, they didn't—"

"And you're my mum," I say softly, tears still falling down my cheeks and dripping onto my knees. "I thought you'd be on my side."

"Lily," she calls softly, tears falling down her face. "I am always on your side. I am your side. I know what they did was wrong. They shouldn't have touched him, sweetheart. I just wanted you to understand their side of it."

"They don't have a side," I snap out, feeling angry now.

"Lily," she murmurs.

"They don't. They've not lost anything. They don't feel dead inside. I've never asked for anything. Not once my whole life. I've never wanted anything. I never felt worthy of anything." I pant, breathing heavily now. I hate myself. I hate that I'm spitting all these spiteful words out. "I've tried so hard my whole life to be worthy of the life you and Dad gave me. She made me feel worthless and pathetic. She made me feel like there was something wrong with me. Then you and Dad came into my life and I didn't want anything else. I just wanted you. I was too scared that if I hoped for anything else it would be taken away. Until him. Until Jaxon. And I was right. I was never worthy of anything more than I was given. It was me who didn't deserve him."

"Baby," she chokes out, pulling me into her as sobs wrack through my body.

We stay like that, crying together while she holds me, running her fingers down my back. She holds me until someone clears their throat at the door.

I look up, seeing my dad there, and I look away. *How long has he been there?*

"Lily," he whispers, but I turn away from him and Mum, curling into a ball.

"Maverick, we should let her get some rest."

"I'm sorry," he rumbles, sounding broken.

"I can never forgive you for taking him away from me," I whisper.

"I didn't know," he whispers painfully.

I shove my face into Jaxon's T-shirt, feeling my eyes begin to droop.

Dad didn't believe in me when I really needed him to. Faith has Beau, and he never did anything. Aiden has Bailey and Sunday, and although he was mad about him being a single father at first, he still accepted his choices.

But with me, he couldn't let me be happy.

I'll never forgive him for taking that away from me.

CHAPTER TWENTY-FOUR

JAXON

MY ENTIRE BODY THROBS WITH pain as Granddad and Myles take me straight inside Granddad's house. "Let me get dressed and I'll take you to the hospital," he tells me, dropping me down on the chair next to the kitchen table. I groan, reaching for the table to steady myself. "And you can get the fuck out of my house."

"I just want to speak to Jaxon," Myles tells him, his voice calm.

Granddad snorts. "So you can beat him up some more? Gang up on him? My girl, Paisley, said Landon was in hospital not so long ago because a group of men attacked him. You didn't like it much then. I heard the tales from my grandsons on how he dealt with them. Do you think it's okay to gang up on someone like that?"

"No, sir, I don't. I might not be able to stand here and justify their actions, but I won't listen to you belittle my family. Jaxon knew exactly what he was in for when he went after Lily."

"Did my boys treat Landon like that?"

"Granddad," I groan, just wanting them to leave. I need to get to Lily. I need to see if she's okay.

She didn't mean what she said. It can't be over. We've barely even begun. It can't be.

The absolution in her eyes flashes through my mind and a wave of pain hits me. It's like a knife is being twisted in my heart.

I lost her. I saw it. I felt it. I heard it.

I clench my fists as a lone tear slips free. I need her in my life.

"No. Don't give me that tone, Jaxon Hayes. And don't think I won't be phoning the police."

"No!" I shout before falling into a coughing fit. I clutch at my ribs, the sharp pain like needles in my skin. Fuck! "No police." I couldn't do that to Lily. She's hurting enough.

"Look, I just want to speak to him."

"No," Granddad snaps.

"She's my sister," Myles blurts out to him. "She's not biologically our niece; she's biologically our sister. Our only sister, and the baby of the six of us." He scrubs a hand down his face, looking tired and worn out. He pulls out a chair next to me but keeps his distance. "Our parents were fucked up. We thought our mum left our abusive dad, but it wasn't the case. We were sold. She gave birth to us and then gave us to him so he could use us as he pleased. We all had different roles. All of them sucked. Just a little over twenty years ago, our mum came back and blackmailed us. If we didn't do what she wanted, she was going to sell Lily to anyone."

I hear Granddad sit down and feel something cold placed in my hands. I squint my eye open as far as it will go, seeing a pack of peas. I hold them up to my face, wincing at the pain.

Myles clears his throat before continuing. "Long story short, our mum ended up having Malik and Harlow's wedding bombed. That night, we met Lily for the first time. She was skinny, malnourished, and so tiny you wouldn't believe she was four."

My mind flicks to Star, and I know now that when Lily looks at her, she's sees the girl she used to be. He's just described Star when I first met her, perfectly.

My hands clench, already knowing all of this but hating the fact I'm hearing it all over again.

"She told me," I croak out, holding the peas higher.

He forces a smile. "I heard. What you don't understand is that the day Maverick decided to adopt her, we didn't. We may have agreed for Lily's sake, but we were always her brothers. We just had to be her uncles first. But it's never stopped. If she's told you then you know everything she went through. How she was beaten and left with broken bones without any medical care. We were given a copy of the report and it was sickening. Even in all my years as a social worker, I have never come across a case that severe. She went through hell. We are just protecting her."

"From me?" I bite out, forcing a bitter laugh, even though my ribs hurt from it.

"You didn't fight back," he notes, changing the subject.

"Why would I? Lily was there and you guys were hurting her enough. Do you think you've won? Because you haven't. No one won out there. You saw her; she's fucking broken inside, and it's not because of me. It's because of you and your family."

"We are trying to protect her," he tells me, harder this time.

"Not from me you aren't. I'd never do *anything* to hurt her."

"So this wasn't some game to you? You weren't trying to get in her pants so you could later throw it in our kids' faces?"

I twist my face up in disgust. "Get out!"

"Answer me."

"Do you even know Lily? *Really* know her? Because I can tell you for a fact that she can see when people are playing games. She can sense when someone isn't being sincere towards her. It's like a sixth sense, probably something she got when she was a child to protect herself. You fuckers put one and one together and got zero. Being with Lily wasn't about anyone else. It was about her." I take in a calming breath, knowing if I lunge for him, it will do more damage to me than him. "You all treat her like she's broken, and she's fucking not. She doesn't need you fighting all her battles. She has a spine. She just needs the space and courage to use it. Yeah, she's fragile, but with that comes a heart of gold, a soul so pure it could make grown men bow down to her. She can make her own life choices. She can make her own fucking mistakes. But I'm telling you right fucking now, I wasn't one of them. Now get the fuck out before I change my mind and call the police."

Slowly, he gets up, heading for the door. "For what it's worth, I'm sorry you got hurt. But we love Lily. We've seen people try to take advantage of her and you've got quite the reputation."

"I *love* Lily," I bite out, looking away. "Just get out."

The door shuts quietly behind him, and I look down at the table, finding it hard to swallow.

This can't be it. It wasn't meant to end like this.

"I'll get changed and call your brothers."

"Don't," I croak out. "I don't want them coming and causing shit. Lily doesn't need that."

"I don't care," Granddad snaps. "Look what they've done to you."

I look up at him, feeling pathetic when my eyes water. "Granddad, please, don't. She didn't ask for this. I bet she's punishing herself over there because of it. She wouldn't have wanted this."

He sighs, knowing I'm right. "I'm sorry. I won't call them, but they're going to find out eventually. I'll call a taxi to come pick us up and have one of your brothers drop me home later."

I close my eyes, giving him a small nod. I'm hoping I have enough strength inside of me to persuade them not to go after any of them. I didn't want any of this to happen. I knew it wasn't going to go down well. In fact, I dreamt of them murdering me so many times it's untrue. But I never once factored in Lily and her reaction. I could see she was torn. It was her family, and I could understand that. I'd never let her make such an impossible decision.

But she didn't break up with me because of them. She broke up with me thinking it would help me.

"All right, let's go. I'm pretty sure your nose is broken," Granddad mutters, getting down on his knees to put some socks on me. When he pulls on some old trainers, I almost groan in disgust. "The taxi is outside."

With help from my granddad, I get to my feet, wheezing when my ribs protest. I would've fought back, but I didn't want Lily to witness that, and her screams were my undoing. It was killing her to see us fight.

I can still smell her on me, still feel her in my arms and how good she felt coming all over my fingers.

A pang hits my chest, and I close my eyes to shut off the pain.

For twelve years I've built Lily up in my mind. I've gone from the school boy who didn't fully understand the meaning of love, to a man who can't live without the love I share with Lily. I'd spent so much of my life fantasising about her, but nothing could ever compete with the real thing. Now that I've gotten to really know her, to truly have her in my life, I can't lose it. What I felt all those years ago is nothing compared to what I feel now. I can't keep living without her in my life, in my arms.

A hoarse laugh escapes me. I stayed away for so many years when we were teenagers, giving her the space I thought she needed. She was untouchable to so many. And I was always scared that if I approached her, I'd never get my shot when the time was right. So I waited. And waited. Still, the timing was never right.

By the time I turned fourteen, I had messed around with some girls, but I was always saving the real thing for her. I was saving my heart for her. I kept telling myself she'd be mine. There was never any doubt.

The day I pulled her out of the bathroom at school was the day I realised I didn't deserve her. I felt unworthy. I knew no amount of time would make me worthy of someone so innocent and pure. I got so angry at myself. Angry I couldn't have her but wanted her so badly.

I fucked a lot of girls that year. All of whom I wished were Lily. They didn't even come second. Being with them wasn't special. It was a moment of bliss when I got my release and then it was over.

What I felt with Lily on that bed this morning will last a lifetime. It wasn't just a moment. It wasn't just one of many. It was my life with Lily and every second counted.

And now she's gone.

"Fuck," Granddad barks harshly under his breath.

"What?" I ask, looking up and finding everyone still outside. My heart races as I scan for Lily, but she's not there. They're banging on her door, calling her name.

Maddox swings around when he sees me.

"Are you fucking happy?" he roars, stepping over. Myles blocks his path, and this time I notice Maverick step in too. "You think you've won?"

"Won?" I rasp out harshly, my throat burning. "You think this is winning? Do you think she's winning? Nobody won today, you fucking prick. You're just too fucking shallow to see that. You might have broken us up, but you haven't won. You've just torn her to pieces."

"Fuck you."

"No, fuck you, Maddox."

"You turned her against us," he bites out, trying to push his uncle off him. "You've brainwashed her into thinking what you had was real. You've broken her fucking heart."

I shake my head, wishing I had the strength to lay into him. He needs his arse kicked and his head banged up a wall a few times.

"What we had has fuck all to do with you, but I will tell you that it was real. It had not one fucking bit to do with you or anyone else. This was me and Lily." I control my breathing, leaning against Granddad when it becomes too much. "And you turned her against you all by yourself. But she's Lily. She'll forgive you eventually because that's just who she is. She doesn't have it in her to stay mad at anyone. But I'm warning you, I'm not giving up. I won't. She's mine."

"You'll stay the fuck away from her."

"Maddox," Myles snaps.

"No. I'm not having this. He's a fucking player. He'll break her heart and just leave once he gets what he wants."

"You really are as dumb as people say you are," I growl. "The only one who has broken her heart is you lot."

"This isn't the end of it," he bites out.

"No, it's really not," I warn. I look up to where her bedroom window is, feeling her up there. When I look back down at the Carter's, they're all watching me with hard expressions. "I won't let her go."

I step into the taxi, ignoring Maddox cursing me to hell. The minute my head hits the back of the seat, I pass out, and it's a welcoming relief.

My body protests as Wyatt helps me down onto my bed. I got back from the hospital less than five minutes ago. Once I told Mum I wasn't staying at the main house, she rushed off inside to make me a cup of tea and something to eat.

I had a slight fracture on one of my ribs, the rest were just swollen and bruised. Everything else was superficial and would heal over the next couple of weeks.

Mum, however, acted like I was on the verge of dying when she saw me.

"I'm going to take Granddad home. When I get back, I want to know everything, and I mean fucking everything," Eli growls.

Wyatt takes a step back, watching me closely. I haven't told them who hit me yet. Granddad promised he'd keep it quiet until he was back home and my brothers were away from the house. The only worry we have is Eli running into a Carter outside Lily's and him putting two and two together. I don't want them kicking off or retaliating. And I'm not in the fucking mood. I'm tired, in pain, and I feel hollow inside. I just want to get the bottle of Jack out of my drawer and drink myself to sleep.

I don't want them here. As close as we all are, all I want right now is to be alone. My phone is in my car, where I left it in my coat last night. I can't even text her to beg her to change her mind. I want to hear her voice, to check she's okay.

"You didn't fucking listen, did you?" Wyatt growls.

Everyone stops what they're doing, turning to me. I glare up at him as I get more comfortable in my bed, leaning against my bedframe.

"Not now."

"What's he talking about?" Luke, one of the triplets, asks.

"Please don't tell me this is over a chick," Reid growls.

"I said, not now!" I snap, wincing at the sharp pain in my ribs.

"I can't believe you. What did I fucking say?" Wyatt scowls, stepping close. "She was off limits. We all knew something was different about her. All of us. And we didn't all go to school with her."

"School?" Colton asks, stepping further into the room.

I narrow my eyes on Wyatt, warning him to shut up. "Yeah, this dickhead went and fucked Lily Carter."

I reach out to grab him, but he steps back out of reach.

"Way to go," Reid hoots, but then sobers, stepping towards the edge of the bed. "Hold the fuck up. Are you tell me *they* did this to you?"

"You've got to be fucking with me," Isaac, the third of the triplets, hisses.

"After all we let go with Landon? We could have fucking killed him, but you sat us down and warned us not to touch him, that you were watching them closely," Reid yells, pacing the room.

He's right, I did warn them all to leave them alone. When I found out it was Landon who was the father to the baby she lost, I went postal. It confirmed everything I ever believed when it came to them. I was so angry at Paisley that I lashed out. I hated that I wasn't there for her. Instead of standing beside her when Landon outed them in front of us, I lashed out. Seeing the emotional damage I inflicted had been excruciating. I knew she loved him. We all did. We watched her pine after him as a teenager.

I sat all my brothers down one morning and told them how it was going to be. It was the morning after I found Landon sneaking out of her window. We couldn't interfere; however, it didn't mean they couldn't give him hell.

"I'll fucking kill them," Reid begins.

I sit up straighter. "No, you fucking won't."

"What do you mean we won't?" Wyatt yells at me. "Look at what they fucking did to you."

"Yes, to fucking me. Not any of you. I can deal with this."

"All this over some fucking crazy chick?" Luke spits out.

I grab the glass left on my side table and throw it at his head. My aim is perfect, and he staggers back, clutching the side of his face. "Don't ever fucking speak about her like that again. Do you hear me? Ever, Luke. 'Cause brother or not, I will rip out your fucking spine."

"Are you hearing yourself?" Wyatt continues to yell, making my headache throb. "If this were any of us, would you be doing the same thing? Would you be holding us back?"

"Which one did it?" Reid asks, throwing a T-shirt to Luke to stop the bleeding.

"It doesn't fucking matter," I snap at him. "I hear any of you did anything, and I mean anything, I'll be done with you. I'll leave this place quicker than you can blink. I fucking mean it."

"All this over Lily?" Wyatt asks, his tone wary yet hard.

"Wyatt, please don't fucking lecture me. You have no idea what I feel for Lily. You've never even tried to feel it with a girl, so don't give me that look."

"You can't seriously mean any of this," Luke argues, throwing his hands up.

"I'm deadly fucking serious. I love her. She's my world, and I will get her back."

"You're saying she broke up with you?" Reid spits out, and I turn my lethal glare to him.

"Yes, to fucking save me from her family," I scoff. "She thinks she's doing the right thing."

"Well at least she's got something right," Luke snarls.

"I swear to god, Luke, one more word," I bite out.

He throws his hands up in the air. "I just don't get it. She broke up with you. You couldn't have meant that much to her in the first place if she let it happen. She has every single one of them wrapped around her finger. She let them do this to you for fuck all. She didn't even stick by you."

"It wasn't like that," I whisper, feeling myself weaken.

"It's exactly like that," Wyatt yells, slamming his fist against the wall. "Fuck, Jaxon. How can you ask this of us?"

"Because you're my brothers. Because I'm asking, for the sake of the woman I love, to not go in guns blazing. It would destroy her, and she's hurting enough right now. She left me for a reason. She sacrificed her own happiness to make sure they wouldn't keep hitting me."

"They can't get away with this," Reid warns me.

"I meant what I said, Reid. I'll do it. I'll do it because I love her. One day you'll get it, but until then, shut the fuck up."

Wyatt opens his mouth, his face red and filled with anger. Theo and Colton step closer to the bed. "Can we just do something little?" Colton asks.

"You heard your brother," Mum states calmly as she steps into the room, her skirt swaying from the breeze flowing through the open warehouse doors.

"Mum," Wyatt starts.

"No. He's been there for every single one of you. He's let you deal with stuff on your own when you've asked. He's watched you grow and helped raise you. If he wants you to leave the family alone, you will leave them alone."

"You knew?" Reid gasps accusingly at Mum.

She rolls her eyes at him. "Yes. And I've not seen a love like that in my life. She adores him. So you will leave him to deal with this. If I hear one of you have gone there, I will tan your hides, do you hear me?" When no one speaks, she arches her eyebrow, raising her voice. "I said, do you hear me?"

"Yes," they all say.

"Good," she snaps. "Now go into the house. I'll be there shortly to make dinner. You will not leave this property, and if Eli gets back before I do, you will make sure he knows not to do the same. Am I making myself clear?"

"Yes, Mum." Reid pouts, shuffling out the door with the twins.

When they're gone, she walks over, resting the tray on the bed. "I poured you some orange juice to take with the prescription the doctors gave you. I think you should try to eat some of this soup first, though."

"Mum," I rasp out when she doesn't look at me.

"You shouldn't take them on an empty stomach."

"Mum," I call, taking her hand.

She looks up, tears in her eyes. "I'm sorry. I'm being silly. I just don't know how to fix this."

"I'm fine. The doctors said I'll be healed in a few weeks."

She waves her hand at me, controlling her emotions. "No. I know that, darlin'. It's your broken heart. I don't know how to make that right."

My stomach sinks. "Mum, I'll make it right. I'll get her back. I will. I just need her to speak to me."

She shakes her head, looking sadly down at me. "Not yet you won't. I don't want you going near her family. I don't want them near you. Give it a few weeks, Jaxon. Please, for my heart, give it a few weeks."

"I can't promise you that."

"I need you to."

I sigh, not arguing any further. "Can you do me a favour? Can you get Paisley to go around Lily's to get my car? It's parked around the corner."

"I will. Is there anything else you need?"

To restart the day. To hold Lily again one more time. To have everything perfect again.

"No, Mum, I'm good. I just need to sleep."

"All right. I'll be over later to check on you."

CHAPTER TWENTY-FIVE

LILY

I'T'S CHRISTMAS DAY, AND I DON'T feel like celebrating. I feel lost and so alone. Everyone is laughing and sharing their gifts around me, but I take no notice, my mind flashing back to a few days ago when my world ended. I no longer feel like I can't live in a world where I'm not with Jaxon, but I know in my heart, my life will never be the same without him in it. It still hurts. Deeply. I don't want to be surrounded by people who are deliriously happy.

We're at Dad's this year, a place I don't want to be. Once we've spent the morning together, we'll all separate then go to eat dinner. This year we're having dinner with my uncle Malik and aunt Harlow. Since we're such a close, big family, there isn't room for all of us in one house to eat, so they've closed the restaurant for the day.

Which means I've to endure everyone. My mum wouldn't let me stay home. When Faith and Beau walked in with their arms wrapped around each other, it was like a knife twisting in my heart.

It got worse when Aiden walked in with Sunday and Bailey. They looked like the perfect family, and immediately, my thoughts drifted off, wondering what could have been.

Seeing Landon walk in with Paisley was just another knife to my chest. She looked so much like her brother that it killed me. I could tell she knew everything; it was in her eyes. She avoided looking at the men in our family, knowing what they did. I wanted so badly to ask her how he was, but I was scared of the answer. I was worried he was still in pain. Was he missing me like I was missing him?

It's been days since my breakup with Jaxon. Mum had stayed with me at mine, but I don't know who else stayed. I didn't want to know, but people were always there. Sometimes it felt like it was to make sure he stayed away, sometimes it felt like they were worried I'd do something stupid. I was hurting. Grieving a loss of someone who hadn't died, and it was killing me inside.

Today is the first day I've left my room. I tried to force a smile for my mum's sake, but I was beginning to feel guilty. She looked sad, tired, and that was my fault. So this morning, I got out of bed and got dressed. I forced a smile and faked the happiness I didn't feel, but it's becoming too much. I feel drained, and it isn't like they can't tell I'm a fraud. I can tell by the way they're all watching me, hovering too close.

I want to breathe again.

I hate myself for disliking my family. I don't hate them, but I'm dying inside, screaming in mind at them for life being unfair. *Why* do they get to be happy? *Why* do they get to cuddle up to the person they love, and I don't? Is there something so wrong with me that I don't deserve to have that? I had that. I didn't have it for long, but it still made a huge impact on my life.

Tears gather in my eyes as I sit on Dad's sofa, staring blankly at nothing. I don't like feeling like this towards them.

I don't like the burst of energy inside of me that wants to scream and yell at them.

I don't want to resent them.

But I miss Jaxon so much. And I blame them for their part in why I left him. It's like a piece of me has been torn inside and there is no way to fix those broken pieces. I feel everything. I feel it deeply. Strongly. And this new kind of heartache is new for me.

Jaxon has tried calling me. I've wanted so badly to read his messages, to hear his voice, but I knew it would only hurt me more. In the end, I let my phone run out of battery and haven't touched it since. It's been sitting beside my bed, taunting me.

"Lily," Dad calls softly.

I jump, looking to the side. I hadn't realised he'd come to sit down next to me. I look away, keeping my expression blank. It still hurts to look at him. He promised to always protect me, to make sure no one ever hurt me, and he stood there and held me back while they hurt the person I love.

"Lily, please talk to me or at least open your present me and your mum bought you."

He holds out a large package wrapped in shiny gold paper. Mum clearly wrapped this with the pretty red bow on top. Dad's wrapping looks like one of my pupils have done it.

"Yes, open it. You're going to love it," Mum gushes, sitting near the fireplace with Faith. I force a smile, taking it from Dad.

"Thank you," I whisper, my voice still broken from all the crying I've done over the past few days. I unwrap the paper, not feeling the same excitement I used to when I opened presents.

Not even the large shoe box stirs anything inside of me. I just feel dead inside. I lift the lid and lift the tissue paper off.

My heart squeezes painfully in my chest, and I struggle to catch my breath. My mum takes it as something else.

"There's a new ice rink that has opened up. We know you don't like driving to the one in Telford by yourself. We thought you could start up again. You loved it as a kid."

A tear spills down onto the tissue paper. "You don't like them?" Dad asks.

I run my finger over the white, glittery skates. "They're beautiful," I tell them. And they are. But my mind goes back to mine and Jaxon's first official date and a flood of memories hit me.

I can't do this. It hurts too much.

I hand Dad the box and get up. "I'm sorry. I can't do this. I need to go."

"But you've not had dinner," Mum states, sounding sad.

"Yeah, stay," Hayden tells me.

"Lily," Maddox starts, and a sob rises up my throat. I can't even begin to forgive him. I thought he was my best friend, someone who understood me. I thought he loved me, and he went and betrayed me.

"Leave her alone," Madison orders, getting up. "I'll help you find your coat, Lily."

"Thank you," I whisper.

"Wait, it's Christmas," Mum cries, and I hear a shuffle behind me, and I know she's getting up.

Everyone has gone silent, making me feel like I'm on a stage with a spotlight on me.

I pause at the door, turning to her. "I'm really sorry, Mum. I don't mean to ruin your Christmas, but I just want to leave."

"Lily," she murmurs.

"He's just a man," Maddox argues.

He really doesn't get it.

"I trusted you," I tell him, my voice stronger. "I trusted all of you. I thought you had my back. You promised to protect me. And you have. But I didn't need protecting from Jaxon. You might not like him and that's your prerogative, but I loved him. I was happy. Blissfully happy, Maddox. Why couldn't you want that for me? Because you don't like him?"

"I'm not sorry for what I did, Lily, but I am sorry you're hurting," Maddox tells me, tears in his eyes. "I miss you so fucking much. I miss my best friend. My cousin. My family. I can't stand seeing you like this. You aren't eating, you've not been sleeping, and I hear you crying. I hear you crying all the goddamn time, and for that, I'm truly fucking sorry. I don't know how to make this right," he tells me, rubbing a hand over his face. "Don't leave. It's Christmas, and you love Christmas."

I shake my head. "Not this Christmas. I'm not feeling very festive," I tell him sadly.

"Please don't go," Dad chokes out, looking broken. "It's ripping me apart to see you hurting like this."

"I can't stay here, Dad. I'm sorry. I need time alone. I love you all so much, but I can't pretend to be happy after everything that's happened. And I don't want to ruin your Christmas any further. It will be better if I'm not here."

"Don't say that. Ever," he tells me sharply, before exhaling. "I don't understand, princess. You were doing okay before. You looked happy."

Faith leans over to look in the box with the skates Mum and Dad got me. "Your first date," she whispers, looking up at me.

Dad looks at her, his eyebrows scrunched together. "What?"

She looks at her lap, realising she just dropped herself in it. As far as I know, she hasn't told anyone that she knew, and I haven't offered that information. They didn't deserve it.

"He took her ice skating for their first date. It was closed for a private party, but a little girl let them in anyway. Jaxon gave her money for her birthday."

"Are you talking about the girl with cancer?" Paisley asks, shocked.

My pulse beats rapidly. Does this mean they called? "You know about her?"

Turning to me, she nods, her expression sad. "Yes. Jaxon has booked them a room for the end of January. The doctor gave them the date treatment will end. They said it will help boost her spirits."

I smile a real smile for the first time in days. "I'm glad. He really did make her day. All of her friends loved him too."

"Wait a minute, you knew?" Dad asks Faith. "And you didn't tell us?"

"This is just fucking great," Maddox growls. "We could have stopped this before she got hurt. Why didn't you fucking tell us?"

My breath hitches. It wasn't Jaxon who hurt me, it was them. He'll never get it. Never understand how much I'm suffering right now until he falls in love himself.

"Wait a minute," Faith argues, standing up now. "You didn't even give him a chance. You're so pig-headed you can't actually see that he really does love her. I've seen him with her. He was gentle, caring and so torn the day Seth attacked her. He didn't want to leave. He was different with her. You might not like him, but Lily was never asking *you* to date him."

"She's right. You are all overprotective and we love you for it, but you've known from the beginning that doing that to him would force Lily's hand," Hayden pipes in. "You knew she wouldn't want to see him hurt and what she would do so it never happened again."

"But I—"

"But nothing, Maddox," Madison snaps. "Sometimes I wonder if we're actually twins. How did you think she would react? Did you think she'd go back to being best friends with you? It backfired, and one day, when you fall in love, you'll understand exactly what you did to her. Until then, sit down and shut up."

I lean into Madison, grateful she's speaking up for me.

"Yeah, she's put up with a lot from you, Madz. A hell of a lot," Hope begins. "She's had girls show up at her door thinking you're cheating on them with her. And she never says anything. Never speaks up when you crash at her house, invading her space."

"Or when you eat all her food," Ciara, another cousin, says.

"Or when you locked Peggy in the downstairs toilet," Charlotte adds.

"That was you," he snaps, looking to the ceiling.

"Well, you did something," Charlotte mutters.

"What we're trying to say is you can't control everything. None of you can. One day, we will find the person we love, and you are going to have to trust us enough to make that decision. We aren't little girls anymore," Hayden tells them.

"Who are you dating?" Max bellows, and I take a step back.

"No one," Hayden snaps at her dad.

"Then why bring all that up? I swear, our family is big enough. We don't need any more adding to it."

"I'm not pregnant," she yells at him. "Jesus. Get a grip, Dad. You had three kids. Maverick has more than you and he's fine."

Max rolls his eyes. "He didn't have triplets. You don't understand what that did to my sex life."

"Ew, gross," Aiden yells, covering Sunday's ears.

"Thanks for that," Landon mutters, eyeing his dad with disgust.

"Just saying. I loved you kids, but you seriously knew how to time it. I don't want you having kids yet. Your mum will want them and that takes our sexy time away."

"Max," Lake snaps.

"Well, it's true," he tells her, holding his hands up.

"We didn't need to know though," Hayden snaps.

"This conversation just took a turn for the worse," my aunt Denny mutters. "I need a glass of wine." She squeezes my shoulder as she passes to go to the kitchen, and I force a smile.

"Please stay," Mum pleads, walking up to me.

I wipe under my eyes. "I'm sorry, Mum. I just need some time alone. I just don't have the energy to pretend."

"All right, but I'll be around later to stay, and I'll bring you a plate of food."

I hug her to me, grateful she's letting me go without another scene. "Thank you."

"Try to get some rest. You're exhausted."

I nod, stepping out of the room while the rest argue about who had the naughtiest kids. "It will get better you know," Madison tells me.

"Will it?"

With a dark cloud in her eyes, she nods. "Yeah. It just takes time. I'm still routing for you though. Hopefully the men in our family bang their heads together and see sense. Maybe then you can sort things out with Jaxon."

She looks like she's talking from experience—the heartache part—but I know enough to know that she won't talk about it to me. We're close, but she has friends and our cousin Hope, who she's closer to.

I shake my head sadly. "No. I don't believe in two miracles happening to one person."

Her eyebrows pinch together. "What?"

I shrug, forcing a smile. "I got my miracle the day I was freed from my mum and the abuse. To get another miracle is impossible. And for my family to accept Jaxon, it would have to be one."

"Lily," Dad chokes out.

Madison jumps, looking to the side where Dad is standing in the doorway. "I'll, um… I'll see you later, Lily. Merry Christmas." She leans over, hugging me before rushing off into the front room.

"Dad, I'm tired," I tell him, grabbing my coat from the door rack.

"Do you honestly believe that?"

"What?"

"That it was a miracle?"

I look up at him, feeling tears pool in my eyes. "Yes. I thought the only way out was my death. Even at a young age I knew what it meant, that it was how it would stop." I take in a deep breath. "I never told anyone this, but I often prayed for it to end. I would wish for it to end."

"Lily."

"I don't mean to upset you. I truly don't."

"I know," he tells me softly.

"I really did love him. He centred me. He soothed my mind enough that I stopped having nightmares all the time. He made me believe in more. And for the first time in my life, I *wanted* more. I clearly don't deserve it."

"Lily, don't—"

"I'm going," I interrupt, feeling a ball in my throat. I don't want to break. Not here. Not now. Then something comes to mind. "You said you'd do anything to make this right?"

"Yes," he answers, not blinking. "Anything."

"Someone is giving Jaxon trouble with his business. He's losing customers because of it." When his jaw clenches, I swallow past the lump. This isn't easy for me, but for Jaxon, I'll do it. "When you sell a house, recommend Jaxon's company. Ask Maddox to do the same when he's working in one. It will help him."

"Did he ask you to do this?"

I shake my head sadly. "He's never asked me for anything, nothing other than to promise to not leave him. I've broken that promise already, Dad. With this, I can help. Will you help him? For me?"

He sighs, slowly nodding. "Yes."

"Thank you."

"Please stay," he pleads one more time.

"I can't," I tell him, feeling my eyes begin to burn. "Thank you for my present. I really do love it. And Merry Christmas."

I rush out of the house before he has a chance to hold me. It was always in his arms I felt the safest, but it changed when Jaxon held me in his car that first time we went out together. He became my safe place.

I don't know how I make it home. I can't even remember crossing roads. It was a blur, and I was glad Mum decided to drive us this morning.

CHAPTER TWENTY-SIX

LILY

*S*HE WAS BACK. *I COULD HEAR HER OUTSIDE.*

Mum had left with her friends after breaking up with her boyfriend earlier. She left in a bad mood, blaming me for it. Leaving me alone was a punishment. I was scared of being alone in this cold, dark house. The neighbours were always screaming, and I didn't like it when Mum's friends turned up.

I hear the front door open and loud voices follow. I shiver between the sofa Mum had shoved me by, cowering in the corner, out of sight.

She said she didn't want to look at me anymore. Her boyfriend had bought me a book and a rabbit. She ripped my book up and threw my rabbit in the bin. She got mad and shouted at him to leave. I was scared to leave the spot, but I wanted my rabbit. I got her out of the bin before hiding back in the spot she threw me in. She was dirty and smelly, but I liked her soft ears. They felt nice.

The music turns on full blast, and I cover my ears when it hurts them.

"You have a kid?" a lady asks, and I shiver back between the sofa and the wall, trying to appear as small as possible.

"Leave her," Mum barks, and I shiver. She blocks everyone from looking at me and bends down, slapping me around the face. "Don't fucking move from this spot, Lily. Don't bother my friends. They don't want a worthless little bitch bothering them."

"Hey, baby, why don't we go to the bedroom," a man says, and Mum smiles, leaning back against him.

I whimper when his eyes meet mine. He looks mean, and I don't like the way he's looking at me. "You can bring the girl if you like."

Mum laughs loudly. "No. I have plans for her. Big plans. She's going to get me everything I want."

I don't like the way she says it.

"But we could have fun," he whines.

"Yes, but she'll be worth more intact. Not a bruise on her. Either her brother is going to pay good money for her, or someone will. Either way, Mummy's getting paid."

"I have the perfect buyer," her friend tells her.

"Who?" she asks, her eyes glazed over. She always gets like that when she drinks those blue cans.

"Come with me."

"Where?"

"I know someone who can make you an offer you won't be able to refuse. He'll pay good money for a girl as pretty as Lily."

Mum squeals, jumping up his body and wrapping her legs around him. I look down at the floor when they start kissing.

"Let's go then."

I wake up with a start, breathing heavily. After that night, none of mum's boyfriends touched me. They stopped hurting me and Mum seemed happy all the time.

Then I was left there with her friend and things got bad. I didn't see my mum again, and not long after, the social workers walked in. It takes me a moment to shake off that same feeling I got that night. I knew something was going on. Men would come and go, but she'd always make me stand in the middle of the room naked until they left, saying they'd be in touch. I never knew what it meant back then, but now I do, and all the missing pieces of how it started sneak up on me in my dreams.

I want to text my dad, to tell him I love him, but I don't know how to right now when I feel like this.

I get out of bed, and although the house has warmed up since I returned, I still feel cold to the bone.

I glance at the time and notice I've managed to get a few hours' sleep. Mum will be dishing out dinner right about now, and a pang of sadness hits me.

Making my way downstairs, I pick up Peggy, hugging her to my chest. She begins to purr, rubbing her nose along my jaw.

"Merry Christmas, Kitty," I whisper, placing her back down on the ground. There's a knock on the door just as I'm about to enter my living room.

My eyes draw together, wondering who it could be. Opening it and seeing Star and Miah was not what I expected.

"We got loads of presents," Star shouts. "Santa loves us. He put us on the good list."

My heart hurts for the little girl who believes she was even on the naughty list. I bend down, forcing a smile. "You're always a good girl. Never forget that. And people love you."

"Are you okay?" Miah asks, sensing my mood. I stand back up, wrapping my dressing gown tighter.

"Just feel under the weather."

"We got you a present," Star tells me, still filled with excitement.

"You did?" I ask, surprised.

She hands me a wrapped gift, and I take it. A lump forms in my throat when I see what they've made me. "We were going to do handprints like Mummy did for Grandma, but Miah's hand is way too big."

"It's beautiful," I whisper, running my finger over their thumb prints. Star has painted hers in pink glitter and Miah's is blue. Carved underneath it reads, 'You made a difference'.

"Miah wrote that. I wanted to say Merry Christmas."

I look up at Miah, shocked. "You did?"

He clears his throat, shifting on his feet. "You did. We have better lives now. I'm sorry for how I reacted at the beginning. I was scared. And you might think what you did was small, but it made a difference. You saved us. And we're grateful," he tells me, looking away briefly. "Dad was arrested yesterday morning. He won't be able to hurt us ever again."

I sag with relief. "I'm glad. I'm so happy for you."

"We got Jaxon a gift too," Star announces, holding another small gift up.

My heart lurches, and I swallow down the pain. "He's not here. But I'm sure if you drop it off to Barry next door, he can give it to him."

"Why can't you?" Miah asks accusingly.

"I—I just can't," I tell him quietly, and his eyes harden.

"All right," he says, but I know he's still watching me knowingly. "We'd best be getting back. What do we say to Lily?"

"Thank you for all our gifts. I love my hair doll. I've been braiding her hair all morning."

"She has. And thank you for the different gift cards."

"It was my pleasure. And thank you for mine. I'll treasure it forever."

Star beams at me before hugging me around the waist. "Thank you, Lily."

I wave goodbye to them, watching them until they reach Blanche's to make sure they get back okay. After, I take my gift and head into the front room, hanging it on the tree.

Seeing a bag under the tree makes me pause. It's the gift Jaxon gave me before everything happened.

I reach down, taking it over to the sofa. I stare for a few moments, wondering if I should even open it now that we aren't together. I can't return it though. I don't think my heart could handle seeing him right now. However, I know I want him to keep the gifts I got him.

Seeing a card with 'open me first' written on the top, I pull it out and open it. It's not actually a card, it's a letter, and I slowly peel back the envelope, my heart racing.

Dearest Lily,

I'm not good with words. Speaking them that is. And around you, I always seem to lose them. I thought I'd be different, romantic, and write you a letter. I mean, I didn't get to do this for you at school and you deserve to experience everything. And I want that to be with me.

From the moment I first laid eyes on you, I felt a connection to you, to your soul. It called to me on a level I never truly understood.

I just remember seeing you in the hallway at school and thinking you looked like an angel. Immediately, I knew you were the one. For boys my age, we didn't want that. We wanted to party, to get drunk, to make out with girls. But I took one look at you and I knew there'd be no one else who could make my heart race like you could. Who could make me imagine a future at such a young age. You changed my world that day. You made someone who never wanted to be one of those boys in a relationship, become one. I wanted to be that person. For you.

So many things got in the way of us finding each other. My dad dying, raising my sister when Mum checked out and making sure my brothers stayed out of trouble.

Then there was you.

I didn't know someone so beautiful existed. With each passing year we shared together, I still couldn't believe it.

You were kind and attentive, yet distant and fragile. You held a pain inside of you that I wanted to soothe. I wanted to be the one you ran to when things got tough. I wanted to be the person you whispered things to in the dinner hall. I wanted everything I could get from you because I'm a selfish bastard.

Wiping under my eyes, I take a moment to compose myself. Reading this, I can hear him speaking. I can hear the words on the page as if he's whispering them in my ear, and my heart is breaking all over again. I want to go to him. I want him to hold me.

Switching to the next page, I continue to read on.

Really selfish, because I will never deserve you. Today probably isn't the best day to unload all this on you, but I want you to know me before you get to the next part of the bag. The best part. Wink, wink.

I've done things you'll never understand and agree with, things that will make you look at me differently, and Lily, I never want you to look at me like that. Because when you look at me, I feel like I can walk through walls. I feel like I can do anything.

I've had my fair share of women in the past, but none will ever come close to you. I don't mean to be a jerk, but with you, everything has meaning. With them, it was meaningless.

The day you said yes to me going to the cinema with you, I felt like I had won the lottery. I was in there. You gave me a chance. Me.

You don't understand how lucky that makes me.

Getting to know you better over the past few weeks has been nothing like I have ever dreamed. The reality of you is far beyond my expectations. You were always special, Lily. Always. But getting to have the real you, the one you bury deep down for only your family to see, has been a string of moments I never want to give up. You are beyond my wildest dreams. I never want to give you up.

I told you I was selfish, right?

I know I am. I know I shouldn't be with you. I know you deserve to have someone who is clean, worthy, who gives a shit about other people. Someone who your family will approve of.

I'll never be that guy.

And I don't care.

Because that guy could never love you the way I love you. It's impossible. That guy wouldn't stop at nothing to make sure you were always happy and safe. That guy wouldn't make sure you had everything your heart desired.

And you deserve to have everything.

You deserve the world.

For the past twelve years I have loved you, but these past few weeks I have been so hopelessly, deeply in love with you, I don't think I'll survive without you.

I love you.

Now go to part two of the present before turning the page.

Tears spill onto the paper as I place it down, reaching for the bag. Inside is a small wrapped box, and with shaky hands, I pull it out.

Unwrapping a light blue box, I pull open the lid, and my hand covers my mouth when a sudden gasp escapes.

Tears continue to spill as I stare down at the beautiful silver ring with two heart cut stones on a band overlapping each other. One stone is blue, the other is clear. *One for me and one for him.*

I hold it up closer when I notice it's engraved inside. A sob escapes me as I read, "Soul of my Soul."

I keep the ring clasped in my hand, but needing to hear more of his words, I turn the page and keep reading.

This ring is a promise to you.

It's a promise of our future, of our lives together.

It's a promise to be the best boyfriend/fiancé/husband I can be.

It's a promise to be the best father to our children.

But most of all, it's a promise to love you even in death. A promise to be the best man I can be for a woman worthy of so much more.

I love you, Lily. I have always loved you, and I will continue to love you even when our souls have moved on to the next life.

I might not believe in God, but I believe in that. I believe that we were always meant to be together.

Merry Christmas, Lily.

Yours always,

Jaxon.

I slide the ring on my finger as loud, heaving sobs tear from my chest. I fall down, clutching the papers to my chest and curling up on the sofa.

He was so wrong. So terribly wrong.

It was never him who never deserved me. It was me who never deserved him.

CHAPTER TWENTY-SEVEN

JAXON

THE PICTURE OF ME, LILY, ALEX and her friend burns a hole in my desk drawer. I want to get it back out, to stare at the picture she had framed for me for Christmas, anything to see her face again.

Our time apart is tearing me up inside. I don't know how much longer I can wait. I miss her company, her smell, her voice. I miss *her*. I miss what my life had become with her in it, and I miss how she made me feel when she was with me.

Hiding the picture away in the drawer just seemed easier. It wasn't out of sight, out of mind. She was always on my mind. I want to know how she's been doing, if her family is supporting her or making her feel like shit. I pray to hold her, even if it's one last time.

Hiding the picture though, was more to do with my brothers' actions over everything that had happened. They're still sour they can't retaliate and opt to take little digs at Lily and the Carter's. Luke is still sporting a black eye from his last dig.

It's been over a week since I last saw or spoke to her. I've called and text so much I've lost count. I've not had one message back, not even to say if she's okay, and the silence is deafening.

And Paisley, my own flesh and blood, won't tell me anything either. I knew she had spent Christmas morning with the Carter's, and when she got back, she was tight-lipped, telling me she didn't want to get involved, that it was for us to sort out. I only wanted to know if she was okay. The only reason I didn't lose my shit was the warning glare Landon had thrown my way.

It was killing me inside, the not knowing.

Turning up at her house has been a bust too. I was hoping to get her to open the door, see her through the window, but I got nothing. She's constantly got someone there, and I didn't want to make matters worse by causing another fight. And that's what will end up happening, because I'd plough through them all to get to her. That's how much our time apart is affecting me. She's like a drug I need to take one more of, an addiction I can't shake and don't want to.

She's my world.

I slap the file on the table, leaning back in my chair to stretch my back. It's New Year's Eve, and so far, my evening has been spent filling out our tax forms, ready to submit in the new year. It looks like I'll be doing it through the night since none of us kept on top of it. It was normally Paisley's job, but since she left to start the bed and breakfast, we've fallen behind.

Wyatt and Eli are the only ones who've stayed back to help me. The rest are getting ready to go out and spend the night bringing in the new year with alcohol and their pick of women.

The drink sounded good, but the thought of being around happy, cheerful people made me want to slit my throat.

Wyatt shoves away from his desk, scowling. "I can't fucking take any more of this. We need a receptionist, Jaxon."

"Then fucking get one. You don't need me to hold your hand to do it," I snap, getting up from the chair I've been sitting in for hours.

"You know what, I'm getting fucking sick of your attitude. It's been fucking over a week, bro. Get out your mood or leave, 'cause we're all sick of it. You're blowing up at us every minute and we're tired of it."

"If you don't like it, why don't you fucking leave? I'll do this my fucking self. It's better than listening to you whine at me like a girl." I turn towards my room, but stop, looking back at him and Eli. "And I swear to fucking Christ, you mention her again, name or not, then I'll lay you out."

He shoves his cup off the desk, letting it smash to pieces on the floor. "Fuck you. We're meant to be a family and you're treating us like the enemy. Get your head out of your arse before it's us who lay *you* fucking out. There's only so much shit we're going to take."

Eli gets up too, grabbing his coat. "While you're going into the back, we fixed your shower. Fucking take one, because you stink, bro."

I wait until they leave before leaning down and smelling my T-shirt. He's right, I do stink, but taking a shower has been the last thing on my mind.

I run a hand down my face, feeling weary. I have blown up at them a lot. In my defence, I've wanted to be alone, and it's hard to do when you sleep where you work. When they couldn't keep it down after Christmas, I ended up getting out of bed and catching up with paperwork, trying to figure shit out. We also had a number of calls from people booking removals come out from nowhere. Things were picking back up, and I couldn't even muster up the energy to care.

I pull my shirt off as I walk down the hallway, grimacing at the slight pain in my ribs. I'm still healing, and most of the bruising has gone down, yet it hadn't completely healed. It will take a while before I can look in a mirror and not see the bruising, even if it has begun to fade.

All of it is superficial. It was the damage done inside that's irreparable. I could live a thousand lives and without Lily, I'd still be a broken man, a man without a soul.

Because the person who held it, who brought it to life, wasn't in my life anymore.

And some days, it feels like I'm suffering a loss, a death. But she's here. Alive. I just have to find a way to get her back, to make her believe again.

THE ROOM IS filled with steam as I finish drying myself off. I'd been in my head so much I hadn't even realised my brothers had fixed the shower. I either went to Mum's to shower or took a cold one here at the warehouse. I feel like a shit brother for the way I've been treating them lately. They did something nice, and I've done nothing but throw it in their faces. And it's not just the shower. They waited on me hand and foot while I recovered.

I need to make it up to them.

Pulling on some joggers and a clean T-shirt, I step back into the hallway. I guess I may as well finish off the taxes since I sent them away. No point in all of us spending the night miserable. It's not like I have anything better to do.

I pause when I step into the room, startled for a moment to see all the Carter brothers in my office. I mask it just as quickly as it appeared, stepping further into the room to show them their presence doesn't affect me. It does, and I'm wary of why they are here.

"Come to give me another beating?" I drawl, scanning each of them for weapons. They don't have any, but then again, they don't need any.

Mason, the second eldest of the family, is leaning back against the wall next to the door, his arms crossed and one leg bent with his foot leaning against the wall. He looks casual, like he's waiting on an old friend. And we've never even spoken a word to each other.

Malik stands in a similar position on the other side of the door, like he's guarding it. I raise my eyebrow at that.

Myles is sitting in Wyatt's desk chair, relaxed and cool as always, while his twin brother, Max, twirls in circles in Eli's.

Maverick stands from my desk, watching me carefully. "We aren't here to hurt you."

"Then why are you here?" I sneer, hating each of them for taking Lily away from me.

"We're here because my daughter is hurting. She is dying inside and there's nothing we can do can fix it. But you can."

"Is this some sort of joke?"

"Believe me, if it was, we'd already be laughing," Max drawls, stopping to rest his feet on the desk. "But we're not. I can't stand to see the pain in her eyes.

She's not been this way since she first moved in with us. It's like her body is there, but what made Lily, Lily, is gone. She even put us in our place Christmas day."

Hearing about her sends a sharp pain through my chest.

"She loves you," Myles tells me, more gently.

"I know," I tell them, nothing smug about my answer. "What I want to know is why you're here. What's changed?"

"We've changed. I wasn't there that day, but if I was, I would have reacted the same way as these. I've got two daughters and I'm overprotective with them. With Lily, it's something else, it's another level of protectiveness. Because when I look at her, I'll always see the four-year-old girl who was scared of her own shadow," Mason tells me, and I look to the floor, seeing the torment in his gaze. "I'll always see the sister I never got to save."

"She deserves someone who is going to treat her like the princess, like the precious human being she truly is," Malik adds. "She's too kind-hearted to be with someone as rough as you."

"No one could love her like I love her; I can promise you that. I might have a shady past, but who in this room doesn't?" I ask, looking at each of the men.

Max holds his hand up. "Me. I'm a fucking golden boy."

I snort. "Right! And I'm a virgin."

"You fucking better be," he replies snottily. "Nothing but the best for our Lily."

I roll my eyes. "I don't even know what this is. Is this permission to date Lily? Because I wasn't going to ask for it."

Maverick's jaw hardens. "No. Not entirely. This is us coming to make peace so that you can finally man up and go to her."

"She's over at Faith's New Year's party," Mason adds.

This has to be a joke, some sort of set up to get me alone. "You're going to kill me, aren't you, and hide my body. That's what this is."

Max snorts. "You'd already be dead by now, chopped up into pieces and fed to your pigs. Did you know they eat anything?"

Disgusted, I look away, watching the one man I want answers from. I raise an eyebrow at him.

"I'm not going to stand here and pretend that I want you with her. But I love her too much to see her hurting like this. She thinks this happened because she isn't worthy of happiness. She thinks coming to live with us was her one and only miracle, the only good thing that will happen in her life. I don't want her to live another day feeling that way because my girl deserves everything her heart desires. She deserves to be loved."

At least we can agree on something.

Hearing she's hurting so much is a stab to the chest. I lean back against the table, pinching the bridge of my nose.

"I know," I whisper.

"So what the fuck are you going to do about it?" Malik asks.

I look up, scowling at him. "I've been waiting for you guys to give her five minutes alone so I can see her."

"We can't leave her alone right now," Maverick whispers, and it sounds like it pains him to do so.

My gaze shoots back to him. "What do you mean by that?"

He shrugs, looking to the floor. "It means she's fragile. She's not herself right now and we can't trust she won't do something stupid because of that hurt. You're her first love."

"And last," I interrupt, glaring at him.

He sighs, shaking his head. "What girls as teenagers feel when they break up with their boyfriend is everything she's feeling right now as a grown woman. She's can't see past that stabbing pain her heart, the hollow feeling in her chest. We're not saying her love for you isn't real—we know it is—but this is all new for her."

"That can't be the only reason," I state, knowing by his flinch that it isn't.

"She said some things that had us watching her more carefully."

My shoulders sag. "She's not going to take me back. She won't believe you're serious about it."

"Then make her," Malik snaps, his tone filled with disgust. "I thought you loved her. Fucking hell, this was a waste of time."

I take a step towards him, but Maverick's hand pushing back on my chest stops me. I glare at Malik behind him. "I fucking love her. But you know her. You know she'll do what she feels she must to make everyone else happy. She left me to save me from you guys. But deep down, she also left me because she doesn't like you being angry at her."

"I was never angry at her," Maverick bites out.

I scoff. "Could have fooled me." I pace the floor, gripping the strands of my wet hair. "All of this is pointless if you aren't all on board with this. And I can't see Maddox giving me his blessing."

Malik stands away from the wall, smirking now. He reaches for the handle, opening the door and letting the cold breeze blow through. I shiver for a second, but then my body heats when Maddox walks in, and anger fires in my veins at seeing him.

"Why the fuck did you bring him here?" I accuse Maverick.

"This is the last place I want to be," Maddox answers for everyone. "But I miss her. I didn't realise just how much she loved you until Christmas day. I didn't realise what you had together until then either."

"You didn't exactly stop to ask. We would have told you that morning," I tell him, feeling my hands ball into fists.

He sighs, throwing his hands up. "I know. I fucked up and I can't even blame being drunk. I hate seeing her like this. She's not eating. She's lost so much weight I'm surprised she can stand. She's not sleeping, and we hear her crying every night. And when she does sleep, she wakes up from nightmares, calling out your name. She's my best friend, not just my cousin, and if it means I have to welcome you to the family, then I will."

I stare open-mouthed, pinching inside of my elbow to see if I'm dreaming. Nope, wide awake.

I want to gloat, to smirk and goad him, but my priority is Lily right now. "You can't blame me for this," I tell him hoarsely.

She wasn't hurting, she was fucking dying inside, and I wasn't there for her.

"Look, my five minutes is up," he says, glaring at his dad over his shoulder. "But before I go, I want to tell you I'm not going anywhere. I'll make it up to Lily, even if it means I spend the rest of my life doing it. I'll always be her best friend. And just because she's with you, don't think you can change shit. I'll still crash at her house, and when I do, you'll keep it PG in the bedroom. You won't come between our friendship in any way, because that beating will seem like child play."

I sneer, shaking my head. "Trust me, Maddox, the next time you touch me with intent to harm, I'll rearrange that pretty little face of yours. You need to remember, I didn't fight back. I won't do that again."

"Aww, you think I'm pretty," Maddox teases, but it doesn't match his expression.

Max puts his hand up, stopping mid spin in the chair. "Anyone else freaked out over that comment?"

"What comment?" Myles asks, then groans. "Why did I ask?" he mutters.

Max grins at him before facing the room. "He said: 'Next time you touch me with intent to harm'. I'm just saying, we aren't like that. We don't keep it in the family."

"What the fuck are you yapping on about?" Mason snaps, looking exasperated at his brother.

"Well, if he was to touch him with kindness, it sounds like that will be okay."

"Seriously, you had to bring them?" I ask, looking at Maverick.

"Leave!" he calls out, and everyone looks up.

Mason nods, then looks to me with a warning glint. "Hurt her, and you're dead."

Malik stands to leave next, pulling Maddox with him. He doesn't say anything, just gives me a death glare before leaving behind Mason.

Myles gets up, straightening his coat. "Welcome to the family."

He looks down at Max when he doesn't leave. Max groans, jumping up from the chair. "You're no fun anymore," he tells his brother before looking at me. "Make sure you make plans for a funeral. You know, just in case."

Once they leave, the room fills with silence. Maverick moves to take a seat on the edge of Wyatt's desk while I do the same on mine.

"This is killing you, isn't it," I remark.

He looks up, a flash of surprise at my statement. "Yes. I've only ever wanted her to be happy. I didn't want someone like you for her. But it's what she wants. And I was stupid to think she didn't know who you were. Right now, she needs to know you aren't going anywhere."

"I'm going to marry her," I tell him, waiting for his reaction. He doesn't disappoint when he goes pale. But it's like he expected it, because he nods.

"I can't even yell at you for wanting it. I want to knock you out so bad, but it will get me nowhere. I can't even blame you. It's just hard to see her take the next step in life."

I don't think he understands. As the plan forms in my head, I get up from the table, feeling more optimistic about getting her back.

"You don't understand."

He looks up at me, his forehead pinched together. "What?"

I tell him my plan, and once I'm finished, he nods with approval. "I want what's best for her. I'll see it happens."

"Thank you," I choke out, feeling my palms begin to sweat.

I'm going to get her back.

I take a seat at my desk, ready to get the number I need, when he stops, walking back over to my desk. He places his fist down on the desk, leaning down so we're face to face.

"Just one thing before this happens. My family, they're lethal, but they're more bark and no bite compared to me. You won't need to plan a funeral if you hurt Lily. You won't even need to make sure you have pigs on the farm. Because I'm warning you, you hurt Lily, and I'll kill you. I've got blood on my hands and more for the sake of my family, and I've never lost sleep over it. And mark my words, when I'm done with you, they'll never find your body. Do we have an understanding?"

I take a deep swallow, feeling like the teenage boy who walked home all those years ago, afraid for his life. It was in that moment that I remembered why I thought he was the deadliest. He's like me in a way. The oldest. The one who protects his family at all costs. So I know he means every single word he just said, because I'd do the exact same thing when it comes to mine.

"I do."

"Good. Then you'd better hurry up. You've got over an hour before New Year."

CHAPTER TWENTY-EIGHT

JAXON

Panicking, I pace the front room at Mum's house, pulling at the tie around my neck. "Are you sure he's coming?" I ask her for what must have been the tenth time.

"Yes. Now here," she says, handing me the piece of jewellery I thought was long gone.

"Are you sure?"

Her watery eyes meet mine as she cups my face. "Yes. Your father would be so proud of you. He'd want you to have them."

A car pulling into the drive has me diving to the window. "It's him."

"Isn't this pointless?" Eli asks behind me, but I ignore him, rushing down the steps and pushing the man Mum had dragged out of bed back into the car.

"We need to go. It's nearly time," I tell him. "Follow us."

We all rush into the cars and drive quickly down the lane and straight over to Faith and Beau's lane, heading up to their house. When I see the massive marquee outside, my stomach swirls with nerves. There's a fifty-fifty chance this could go wrong.

No one blinks when they see me, which is how I had planned it. We have seconds before the firework display is about to go off and Lily has yet to see me.

Just as planned, she's now wearing a dress and a long black jacket. She's looking up at the stars, still yet to hear the newcomers.

Maverick gives me a chin lift, just as the shouting begins.

"Five."

She's got her arms folded across her chest, her expression so sad it breaks my heart.

"Four."

People part to let me through, but I don't give them a glance, wanting to get to her.

"Three."

Faith looks over her shoulder, spotting me for the first time.

"Two."

She whispers something to Lily, stepping away as I come up behind her.

"One."

I wrap my arms around her waist, startling her. "Happy New Year," I whisper in her ear, kissing her neck.

"Jaxon?" she whispers hoarsely, sagging against me as fireworks explode around us.

I grin, turning her in my arms, and her tears undo me. "It's me."

She looks around, her eyes wide with panic. "You can't be here."

I take her face gently, getting her to look at me. "Lily, I love you. I've loved you for so long, but these past few months have made me truly fall in love you. I can't go another day without you. I could live a thousand lives and not want to live a single one of them if meant you weren't in it. You mean everything to me. You are the air I breathe, the blood that pumps through my body. I love you."

I wipe at the tears that stream down her face. "But my family," she chokes out.

"Look around, Lily. What do you see?"

Her nose twitches as she pulls her gaze away to look around her. Her mouth opens, astonishment written all over her. "What's happening?"

"Do you love me?" I ask her, keeping my voice low.

"More than I've ever loved anyone. I need you like I need my next breath," she whispers.

Getting down on one knee, I take the ring Mum gave me out of my pocket. It's the ring she got when she married my dad. I had thought they were buried with him, but Mum said their plan was always to hand them down to me. I was glad. I wanted Lily to have this.

Lily gasps, covering her mouth with her hand. "Lily Carter, I promise to love you every day for the rest our lives. I promise to take care of you, cherish you, and protect you for as long as we live. Will you do me the honour of being my wife? Will you marry me?"

Through her sobs, she cries, "Yes," wrapping her arms around my neck.

I lift her up, swinging her around, smiling when cheers of celebration break out. I place her down, pushing the ring on her finger, grateful when it fits.

When she rises to her tiptoes to kiss me, I have to pull back, and it's the hardest thing I've had to do tonight.

I shake my head, finding her pout cute. "You can't kiss me before the wedding."

Her eyes widen. "But that could be months away."

"Nope. It's happening right now," I tell her, letting Mum's priest walk to the front. Everyone gathers behind us, smiling.

"B-but," she stutters, looking around in confusion.

"It won't be legal. We'll have to do the paperwork when the offices open, but I can't wait until then. David is a long-time friend of my mum and dad and happily agreed to marry us. He'll help with the paperwork too."

Mason steps up beside us, taking Lily's hand away from me. I let him, watching as she struggles to control her emotions. "Be happy, Lily." He kisses her forehead, stepping aside to let Malik through.

"Proud of you," he whispers against her forehead.

Myles is next, his watery eyes shining. "Always and forever, married or not."

Lily chokes on a sob, struggling to stand up when he steps aside, letting Max through.

"Give him hell, baby girl."

My fingers dig into my palms when I see she's barely holding on. I take a step closer in case she falls when her dad says his piece, Teagan, Lily's mum, by his side.

"My baby girl getting married. When did you all grow up? I wish you many years of happiness, Lily. I'm so proud of the woman you've become. Truly. I love you."

"I love you too, Mum," Lily whispers, hugging her mum back.

Teagan walks back over to where Faith, Mark, Aiden and his tribe are standing, leaving Maverick to have a moment with his daughter.

"You look beautiful," he tells her, lightly pulling her hair out of her face. "I love you, Lily. From the very first moment I laid eyes on you, I loved you. You were ours. Mine. Tonight, you will become a wife, but that doesn't change anything between us. I don't have to let you go. I'm not going to lose you. I promised you then, and I'll promise you now, I'm not going anywhere. I'll always be here for you. You'll always be my baby girl," he chokes out. "Now go be happy."

Lily begins to cry, throwing her arms around his neck. "I was so mean to you. I love you so much, Dad."

He holds her just as tightly, closing his eyes. "It was nothing I didn't deserve," he says, opening his eyes to look at me. He pulls back, cupping her face. "I love you more, princess. Always."

The priest clears his throat. "Are we ready?"

I give him a dry look before taking Lily's hand. She grips my fingers, looking to the crowd at where Maddox is standing. He gives her a warm smile, putting his thumbs up. She giggles before turning to me.

"We're really doing this?"

"Yes, we're really doing this. I want you to know that I'm not going anywhere. I want you to know that my love for you can overcome anything, even a family feud. I can't go another day without you being my wife."

"I love you," she whispers, wiping under her eyes.

"I love you too," I tell her, before we both turn to face the priest.

LILY

I'M MARRIED. I'm really married to Jaxon, and I couldn't be happier. I feel like I'm in a dream. Earlier, I was so down I didn't want to celebrate the new year. I didn't want to start it without him. It didn't feel right.

Then Faith dragged me to the farm, and it was all I could do not to go see him. He was so close, yet so far away.

The countdown began, and all I thought of was him. It wasn't on what Faith was talking to me about, or how Maddox and the other men were acting weird. I wasn't even angry Maddox spilled his drink all over me so that I had to borrow one of Faith's dresses. I didn't even know you could wash every pair of jeans or leggings at the same time with the amount Faith had.

It didn't matter. I didn't even feel the cold anymore.

Then I turned and saw him. I thought I was hallucinating, but there he was in the flesh. At first there was panic. I was terrified of them hurting him again. He still looked worse for wear.

But no one moved. No one looked angry he was there.

"Am I dreaming?" I whisper to my husband as the priest finishes announcing us man and wife.

He smirks down at me, resting his forehead against mine. "Baby, every day I'll be with you is a dream. We'll dream together."

I melt against him, cupping his neck. "Forever," I whisper hoarsely.

"Kiss me, wife," he orders gently, and smiling up at him, I bring his lips to mine, sealing our fate together.

He is mine.

I am his.

Forever.

Married.

MAVERICK

SHE'S MARRIED.

My baby girl.

She has come so far. So fucking far.

She's no longer the broken angel that clung to me at night, who wouldn't leave my side.

She's no longer just a woman who had moved out.

She's married. And before long, she'll have children of her own.

Our lives are changing.

Our kids are evolving.

Faith, who is tucked under Beau's arm, leans up to kiss him, trying to hide her own emotion at seeing her sister marry.

Aiden is taking turns on who's face he's going to pepper with kisses, alternating between his daughter and the love of his life.

It won't be long until Mark finds his person, just like me and my brothers did so long ago.

"This is it," Malik says quietly so no one else can hear him but us.

"It's really starting," Mason agrees. "They're all finding their happily ever after."

"We did good," Myles chokes out.

"We really did," I rasp out, watching my daughter shine with happiness as she clings to her new husband. "We really fucking did."

When Max doesn't say anything, we all turn to him, arching our eyebrows. "What? I was letting you guys take the credit. I was being humble. But who am I kidding? I raised great fucking kids."

Myles looks at his brother. "You're planning to keep Hayden single, aren't you?"

"Until my very last breath," he whispers, before walking off.

I roll my eyes before stepping over to Lily, pulling her attention away from Jaxon.

"You're really okay with this?" she asks me, not a flash of pain in those beautiful brown eyes of hers.

"I wouldn't have gone over to make peace if I wasn't," I tell her, wrapping my arms around her. "I've only ever wanted you happy, Lily."

"I am," she tells me when she pulls back. She flicks her gaze up to her husband, smiling wide before looking back to me. "So happy."

"I love you."

Jaxon finally turns from his Mum, giving me a chin lift. "Lily, Paisley kindly offered us a room at her bed and breakfast."

"She did?"

I don't need to hear this. I inwardly groan. I glare at Jaxon, but he takes no notice, wrapping his arm around my daughter.

"Yes. As much as I'd like to celebrate, it will have to wait for another day. Maybe when we make this legal, we can throw another party, but right now, I just want you to myself. It's been too long."

"I really missed you," she whispers up at him, tearing up again.

"Not as much as I missed you," he admits in front of us all.

"Seriously, get out of here before I change my mind," Maddox mutters.

I watch as they say their goodbyes, taking one of the cars they drove over in. Teagan walks up beside me, taking my hand.

"She was always going to grow up," she tells me, resting her head on my shoulder.

"I know, it just feels like it's too soon. I won't be the one she turns to anymore."

"She's stronger than you give her credit for."

I look down at my wife, the love of my life, and I soften my gaze. "She's always been the strongest of us all. She just couldn't see it."

"Something tells me she will now," she whispers back.

As much as it kills me to admit, I have to agree. Jaxon brings it out in her.

"I love you," I tell her, pulling her into my arms.

Her entire face lights up. "I love you too. You gave us a beautiful family."

"Pretty sure you did all the hard work," I tell her through a chuckle.

"No, we did. Together."

"Together," I whisper back, before taking her lips in a heated kiss.

When Wyatt hires the new secretary, he
gets more than he bargained for.
She gets under his skin like no other, and it's driving him crazy.
But something is holding her back from becoming his.
She's keeping a secret. A huge secret.
He'll stop at nothing to get answers.
An Eye for an Eye.

If you want to find out what Black does next,
stay tuned for Wyatt's book.

KEEP READING FOR A SNEAK PEEK AT WRONG CROWD

wrong
Crowd

Chapter One

MY MUM HAD BEEN BURIED TWENTY-FOUR hours, and before I could even let it really sink in, to mourn the mum I wish she was and the person she *really* was, I was being carted off into the unknown.

I glance over to my aunt, Nova, my mum's twin sister, someone I didn't know about until two nights ago.

I take a moment to take in her appearance. She couldn't be more different to my mum if she tried. In her fancy clothes—pink silk top, loose and flowing, and beige suit trousers—she reminds me of a teacher or someone official. Someone I didn't like at my old school. I think it's why I don't trust her. The flashiest thing Cara Monroe owned was her heels. Her clothes screamed slut and were beyond tacky.

Although the two had similar features, Mum had looked ten years older than her age. Her face had weathered and wrinkled from all of the drugs and alcohol she pumped into her body. Nova's skin was smooth and looked soft to touch. It makes me wonder if Mum had been that pretty at one point.

A lot of men would comment on her looks, giving her advice on what do with her hair, her makeup, her clothes. It never made a difference though. She had abused her body for far too long.

Who knows why.

Mum also had bleach-blonde hair, whereas Nova's is dark, yet lighter than my jet-black hair which almost looks like it has a blue tinge to it.

The other thing that cuts the two apart is the fact my mum was dirt poor and Nova is clearly rich if her handbags, car and clothes are anything to go by. She has this presence that screams money. My mum couldn't even claim benefits; they cut her off after she refused to get another job last year—not that she could get a job most of the time. We've been squatting in our flat ever since, scrounging by, using food banks and homeless shelters to eat, and she'd always screw men to get her money or fix. They didn't even know what they were in for before coming inside most of the time. Not until she had robbed them clean and threatened to tell loved ones what they got up to behind closed doors.

Why did she make us scrounge for leftovers if she had a twin sister who was rich? It was the one thing that seriously bothered me. It made me hate her.

"Ivy, I can hear you thinking. You can ask me anything, you know," she says, her voice sweet, soft, nothing like my mum's scratchy voice. I avoid her gaze and look back out of the windshield.

"Why didn't I know about you?"

"Your mum didn't want you to. We tried to see you as a baby, you know."

News to me. I didn't even know we had any family, but according to this lady, I have an uncle and grandparents. None are here in England. Apparently they're in the States on business.

When I don't ask her anything else, she takes a deep breath. "I had my housekeeper go out and get you some more clothes."

My stomach bottoms out, and I look at her in horror. "I am not wearing your fancy as shit clothes," I snap. I like my jeans, my tank tops, and my boots. They are the nicest things I own, and only because one of the ladies at the food bank took a liking to me and offered me help where I needed it.

A small smile plays at her lips, but I don't know what she finds funny. "There's going to be rules."

"Let's go back to the clothes," I order. Fuck the rules. I've raised myself for as long as I can remember, and rules didn't come into the equation. Mum never set any. She never cared enough about me to do it.

"Don't worry. I told her to get whatever she wanted with underwear and pyjamas, but for clothes, I did inform her you liked jeans and jackets. I'm not saying there won't be anything fancy when you get home, but there will be something you like."

"It's not my home," I snap defensively.

"It is for as long as you want it to be."

"I turn eighteen in a month."

"I thought we had a deal," she murmurs, and I sink further down in my chair.

I hate my mum. I hate that she died and left me. She left me with a debt owed to a drug dealer and with no money to pay it, no home, and a bag with a few items of clothing. I'm stuck. And getting a job with the state my clothes are in would be impossible in our area. I had tried many times before, fed up of starving and freezing to death. They took one look at me and decided there and then that I wasn't worth it. They probably thought I would steal from the cash register or bring trouble.

When Nova found all of this out, she tried to talk me into going back with her, informing me I was family and she wanted to get to know me. I said no, not trusting her. But then she made me a deal. I could go live with her, get a part-time job so I could save my money up, and have somewhere warm and safe to sleep. As long as I agreed to try school for a year. If I made it the full year, she would give me ten thousand pounds to start my life with. And on top of all that, she would give me an allowance monthly.

I wanted to say no at first, wondering where this woman got off on throwing her cash around. But I'm not stupid, far from it. If I want to get out of the life I'm in and away from the exact path my mum made, I need out. If she wants to waste her cash on me, go for it. I know I'd survive without it, but I'm tired of surviving. I want to finally live my life.

"We have a deal," I tell her. "But I told you, there is no way I'm getting in to that fancy as fuck academy, college, or whatever it is."

"Language," she scolds. "And you already have. It's a private academy. It will give you choices and it's different from other colleges. And I'm good friends with the family who own it, so stop worrying."

"Whatever," I mutter, looking back out the window.

The dirty streets littered with rubbish and women hanging on corners left us hours ago. Now we're driving down roads with houses bigger than my old school.

When Nova pulls up outside a huge gate, I can't help but freak out a little. She really is rich. Even though I knew it, seeing it is another matter altogether.

She waves to the guy sitting in the small building beside the gate. He leans out the window. "Good evening, Nova."

"This is my niece, Ivy," she tells him, her voice cheery. "She's coming to live with me."

I watch the guy bend down to see into the car where I'm sitting, and I can see the surprise written on his face. I snort, looking back out my window.

"Nice to meet you," he says. Fake. All of them are fake.

Nora ends their little chat. "Have a good night."

The gates open and as we pull back off, I look at her. "You have your own security guard. *Who are you?*"

She rolls her eyes. "No, I don't. This is a gated community, Ivy. They are there for all of us."

"All of you?"

"Yes. The two houses there at the top of the hill, one is Monroe Manor and the other is Kingsley Manor. Our families are the ones who bought this land and built on it. Over time, more people built and here we are. A small community for the rich."

The houses we pass are huge, yet when we weave up the curvy hill, two large houses, built side by side, come into view, and there is nothing to stop my eyes from bugging out.

"Holy fuck!" I gasp.

"Language," she scolds.

A lady in her fifties is waiting inside the garage. She's wearing a grey polo shirt and black suit trousers. Her hair is pulled back in a tight bun. She steps forward the minute Nova shuts her car off, and I follow her as she heads to the back of the car. I quickly get out, moving around and snatching my backpack from her.

"I can take your bag, Miss Monroe," the lady greets me.

"No." It's all that I own. I'm not optimistic about this working out. I don't belong in a place like this. I feel like dirt they trod in through the door.

She goes to take my bag again. "It's perfectly fine. I'll take it straight to your room."

I take note of what is in my bag, and although none of it's valuable, it's all I have, and she's not taking it away. The house feels like it's getting bigger as I take another step closer. There is no way I am going to make it here. Nova might dress me up, but it will only take another of her kind to take one look at me and realise who I am.

"Ivy, this is Annette, our housekeeper. She has her own home at the back of the property but is here from five until six."

I don't say anything, and when she sees that, she blows out another breath and gestures for me to follow her. I do, taking in everything as I go. I didn't know what to expect when she told me I was going to live with her. I met her the day before yesterday and I still don't know what to think.

This house is really something though. She told me she lived alone, so why would does she want all this space? There are open rooms everywhere. We walk through the kitchen, and I marvel over how clean it looks. I bet there's food in those cupboards too.

"Down there we have a cinema room and a games room. Feel free to check it out tomorrow," Nova explains as she points to different doors. "We have an outdoor pool that's heated throughout the year. You'll find swimsuits in your bedroom. Living room, dining room, another living area and the conservatory," she adds, and walks me to a set of stairs. "The other rooms down here don't get used. "We have seven bedrooms. Mine is on the other side of the house along with my office. I've kept you on this side to give you more privacy."

I have to stop her there. "More privacy? I could walk around this place naked and not even risk bumping into someone."

Her face scrunches up. "Do not walk around here undressed."

I smirk, hiking my bag up higher on my shoulder.

She opens a door to the right, letting it swing open, and takes a step back. She looks at me, and when I don't move, she rolls her eyes. "Go. This is your room."

I try to hide my nerves as I take a tentative step inside. Two lamps on either side of the bed have been left on, casting a warm glow around the room. I swallow, taking in the clean sheets and fluffy pillows. It's also a king, something I've never seen before. I had a single-sized bed that was held up by some old library books.

The walls are cream, and Nova has kept them plain. There's a huge window with a reading nook underneath it. The chaise will come in handy when it rains, which is meant to happen over the weekend. There's a huge seating area to my right, a table next to it with a vase of flowers.

There's a desk next to the window and my eyes bug out at the laptop, mobile, and a set of keys.

"The mobile is under contract and my numbers are programmed into it. Laptop is all set up to the Wi-Fi and is yours to do schoolwork on. The keys are for the front door, garage door and backdoor. If you are ready to start your driving lessons, I do have someone who can teach you within a week so you can take your test."

This sounds too good to be true.

I step back over to the bed, running my finger along the soft cotton sheets. When my gaze finds two doors on the other side of the room, I look at Nova over my shoulder questioningly. She takes her first step into the room, pointing to the first door. "That's the bathroom. It's yours and yours alone. Second door is your wardrobe. Would you like Annette to fix you something to eat before you go to sleep?"

My stomach grumbles, but there's no way I could eat right now. I'm too nervous, and if I'm honest, I miss my mum. No matter how shitty she was or however fucked up, she was still my mum. I knew what to expect and that was nothing. With Nova, she has the power to give me more than I ever dreamed of having and take it away in her next breath without a care in the world. We don't know each other. We have no emotional ties. Yet even though I'm not completely convinced I won't end up going through life along, she's here and she's family. I might as well suck it up. The minute she shows me a different side to her, I will be gone and she'll never see me again. I might not understand why she is doing this for me, someone she doesn't know or has cared to know, but she is. I don't ignore the hurt I see flash in her gaze when she's watching me either. It's there, even when she tries so hard to hide it. I just don't know why.

"No. I'm good, thank you."

"If you change your mind, head down to the kitchen and help yourself to anything. In fact, I'll get her to make you a sandwich and pop it in the fridge."

I nod, not feeling my confident self right now. She must see it because she only nods. "All right. I'll let you get some rest."

I hear her reach the door and let out a breath I didn't realise I was holding. I feel tears gather in my eyes, but they don't fall. I didn't even cry when they announced my mum was dead. I didn't feel much of anything. I did get a sense of relief, and with that followed guilt. Even at her funeral I didn't cry. I couldn't. I just felt helpless.

Sighing, I look around the room once more. Even the carpet looks expensive. It kind of makes me angry, but I don't know who at. At Mum for knowing she could have this or for an aunt who had it and didn't share it. It's just seems unfair that this was here. Hell, I would have been happy to sleep in the garage.

I have so many questions, but I don't know who to trust. Mum isn't here to answer them and there has to be a reason she lived in shit and didn't come crawling back. She had no problem when it was one of her male friends, so why not her own twin sister. It wasn't a pride thing. My mum never had any.

There are secrets here. Secrets that can explain why I only found out I had an aunt two days ago. Nova hadn't explained anything to me, just said Mum disappeared.

So whether I can trust Nova or not, still has a big fat question mark around it.

I can't help but compare the room to our flat. It's bigger than our entire flat, that's for sure. However, it's how clean and well-kept it is that makes me feel uncomfortable. I'm not used to it. And I guess a part of me is scared to in case it's ripped away. You can't miss something you never had, which is how I spent my whole life.

Fuck it.

I'm here and I don't have anywhere to go. By now, the council have taken over the flat and are gutting the place. Nothing inside was worth saving, not even the bathroom tiles that were thick with grime because we couldn't afford cleaning supplies.

Heading over to the door, I quickly take a peep up and down the hallway to make sure she isn't hovering before shutting the door quietly behind me. I survey the room in all its glory and drop my bag down by the end of the bed.

The bathroom door is my first stop, peering inside and gawking at the magnificent marble. Everything shines, even the ceiling with its spotlights poking out of the ceiling. It has a huge walk-in glass shower that has a bench inside. Looking closer, there's a box with a million buttons and dials inside. It better come with a simple hot or cold button otherwise it will never get used. It has a huge white cast iron bath to the left, not too far away from the his and hers sinks. Bottles of stuff are set in place on the counter top, along with fresh towels and dressing gown hanging up on the back of the door.

I quickly do my business before heading over to the sink. As I wash my hands, I examine the countertops for a toothbrush and toothpaste. There's nothing. Only bottles of hand wash, shampoo, conditioner and body wash.

I dry my hands with the hand towel hanging over the edge of the sink and notice there are drawers to the side of the sink. I go to pull it but it doesn't move, so I shove it. "Damn thing!" I curse. Something clicks and it slowly falls open.

Mouth agape, I notice more toiletries inside, along with a toothbrush, toothpaste, moisturisers and, thank god, a brush. I've had to use my fingers for the past few weeks since mine completely fell apart on me.

It doesn't take me long to wash up. I had a shower this morning in the hotel

Nova made us stay at after the funeral. I think she wanted me to say goodbye to it all after Mum's funeral, which is why we didn't go back to the flat. Not that I'm complaining.

Heading back into the bedroom, I go to grab the over-sized T-shirt but something stops me. I like my things. They're scraps of cloths to other people, but to me, they are the best things I own.

Sighing, I head over to the wardrobe. There's no harm in finding out what damage her housekeeper did.

I have to step back when the doors open.

Holy fucking shit.

"This isn't a wardrobe. This is a fucking bedroom," I murmur, wide-eyed. In the middle of the room is a massive white, suede, round pouffe. "No, it's a fucking clothes shop."

To the left is a row of T-shirts and tops. I run my fingers through them, my nose scrunching up at the pink blouse.

Never going to wear that.

Most are black tank tops, a few T-shirts and other tops that I kind of like but would show too much skin and look ridiculous with my skinny body. My hips might flare out a little but there isn't any meat on them. My mum gifted me with her large breasts, ones that have gotten me into trouble with the men in our block of flats a few times. In my defence, I was a kid and they were staring. It was only fair they got a black eye or a knee to their balls.

The row of tops stop, and in the middle are shelves filled with trainers, some white as snow, some black, some pink, and some cool as fuck boots. I pick up the black pair with laces to the ankle, admiring them. I might have had doubts but I know there is no way I'm going to pass up wearing these.

On the other side is another row of clothes, these ones coats, jackets and other stuff. I say stuff because I ignore the row of handbags on the thinner set of shelves. I do, however, see the backpack shoved at the bottom, like someone was trying to hide it out of sight. I reluctantly grin. Continuing to walk around, I come to some drawers. Opening them the same way the bathroom one opened, I flick through them. Bra's and underwear are in the first one. Bikinis and swimsuits in the second. In the third and fourth is a bunch of sleepwear. I ignore it for the moment, knowing I'll be going back to it for something to sleep in.

There's another set of drawers next to it, but I don't bother looking through it.

The right wall is stacked with jeans first, all in different shades. They look too neatly stacked for me to pull a pair out to check if they are okay or not. I skim past the dressing table, even though the girl inside me does want to see how those skin products feel. I also see another brush.

I roll my eyes when I come to the next row of clothes. It's all dresses. Yeah, I won't be wearing them either.

I head back over to the drawers and push the drawer with the nightwear in. Most of it's thin silk. I pull out the first set; a burgundy colour with black lace on the edge. I hold the silk top up, biting my bottom lip.

What the hell. I've got nothing to lose. I quickly change, marvelling at the feel of the material against my bare skin. The shorts fit snug over my round arse.

I yawn, but I know I won't be able to sleep. It was hard at the hotel last night with no noise whatsoever. I even tried to turn the television on for some white noise, but it wasn't the same.

I have a book shoved into the bottom of my bag that I can read until I'm sleepy.

I pause when I walk past the mirror, doing a double take of the girl staring back at me. My black hair is tied back in a bobble, but even I notice it has a shine to it that it never had before.

The pyjamas make me groan and aren't something I'd ever pick out for myself, but I can't help but think I look good. My cleavage shows and my legs look longer.

After ten minutes of figuring where the light switches are and then turning them off in the wardrobe, I head back over to my bag. I grab the old, withered book I got for free at a carboot sale before flicking one of the lamps off and leaving the other one on.

I grab the throw from the end of the bed and drag it over to the chaise. I stack the pillows against the wall and get comfy, wrapping the blanket over my legs, even if the night air is stifling tonight. It's another reason I'm glad it's meant to rain over the weekend, not that I believe it will happen. They've been saying it for weeks. We're having one heck of a summer.

I'm barely into the new chapter when a squeal gains my attention. I jump, looking through the window at the manor across the way. Most of the lights are out, but one is on in the bedroom opposite.

I shouldn't look, I know it, but when two bodies—two very naked bodies— come into view, I can't look away.

Holy shit!

The guy's headboard is up against the window, so although the girl's back is to me, giving me a good view of her arse, he's facing me. I could get caught.

If he didn't want someone watching, he should have shut the fucking curtains and turned off the fucking lights.

From what I can make out, he has dark hair…

Oh my God. He lifts the blonde by her hips and throws her down on the bed. I gape at the quick glimpse I get of his athletic body. I'm sad when he crawls up over her, wanting to check him out a little bit more.

A small puff of air escapes between my lips when he grabs onto the headboard with one hand, his other still somewhere on her, and begins to thrust, hard. I can see the bed shaking from here.

My cheeks flame watching them, but I can't look away. I don't *want* to look away. I've had one sexual partner in my seventeen years, and although I have nothing to compare it to, it was good. The guy had experience and knew what he was doing. This guy though… he looks like he mastered in sex.

Heat pools between my legs, and I take bets on which one lives there. With my luck, it's the girl who doesn't mind people watching her while she gets fucked.

Or…

I freeze when he lifts his head, and although it's too far to tell, I know he's looking at me. He could be looking at his reflection in the window, but I'm not that lucky. I can feel the heat of his gaze all over my body.

My lips part, and after a moment, he smirks, then thrusts harder inside the girl. Her scream echoes through his open window and my eyes widen in shock.

Quickly, I throw the blanket off me and run over to my bed, facing away from the window.

Knowing my luck, the hot guy who just caught me watching him have sex lives there.

Crap!

Chapter Two

THE NEXT MORNING, I TAKE A long, warm shower and grab some clothes out of the wardrobe. Annette either has good taste or she got a sales lady to help her, because most of these clothes are the shit.

Instead of my usual jeans and T, I grab a pair of denim shorts that come to mid-thigh and pair them with a T-shirt that has 'New York' written across my chest area. It looks good. Real good. It feels foreign to have options, to have something that feels so nice against my skin instead of the usual rough material that scratched me.

I didn't see them before, but I grab the closest pair of flip-flops. I've never worn them before, but they're actually comfy. And it's not like I can wear my ratty pumps with clothes this nice.

After what happened last night, I couldn't sleep, so I went mooching through the rest of the drawers. I mostly found girly shit, which is why when I found the dark purple nail polish, I sat and painted my fingernails and toenails. I never understood why the girls at school would do it until then. It made me hate my mum a little bit more for taking another thing away from me. It made me feel feminine, something I never felt before in my ratty clothes and lack of girly products.

It's nine, too early to be awake when I was up most of the night, but I woke up with a feeling of someone watching me. I could feel the tingle down my neck. As I rose from the bed, there was no one in sight. It still made it impossible for me to go back to sleep.

I retrace my steps from last night and, thankfully, find the kitchen with only one mistake. The voices echoing outside the entryway have me pausing.

"Why is she here?" the menacing voice asks. "Did you learn nothing from your sister?"

What?

I take another step forward, but Nova's words stop me.

"She's my niece. I don't want her anywhere else. She's nothing like Cora was," Nova argues.

"What about the money? She has rights to that money," the man tells her. "Does she know?"

"She doesn't know, and even if she does, why would I care? She can have it."

"You really have a problem with boundaries, don't you, sweetheart?"

I jump at the raspy voice in my ear. A startled squeak escapes me and I turn to face the guy from last night. Don't tell me how I know, I just do. He's more handsome up close. Strong jawline, perfectly shaped lips and dark green, smouldering eyes that girls could get lost in. However, peering closer, I see a void in them I hadn't noticed at first glance.

I can see why the blonde didn't have a problem fucking him with the lights on and curtains open. I'd want to see him too. He has broad shoulders, and his black T-shirt clings to him, giving me a peek of a tattoo wrapped around his bicep. I'm willing to bet my soul his bad boy physique looks better up close and personal.

"Who are you?" I ask.

He looks over my shoulder, pasting on a fake smile. "Nova, morning."

"Ivy, you're up." She sounds surprised and looks kind of fidgety, which makes me question what I just heard even more. Why were they talking about me? And why would he be worried about money? I don't have any. "Morning, Kaiden. I see you've met Ivy, my niece."

"Or she met me," he replies sweetly. He stands so close to me his shoulder is touching mine, and I can smell his woodsy scent. It's enough to make a girl drop her panties. "Isn't that right?"

"Um…" I struggle on what to say, his presence making me dizzy. I've never had this problem before. The old Ivy would have snapped some snarky comeback and walked out of the room. Not this Ivy. She got hit with his beauty and lost how to speak.

"Annette is making breakfast. Come on in and take a seat."

I go to follow her inside, highly aware of the large figure looming next to me. I'm pulled back by the hoops of my shorts. I glare up at the handsome devil but don't make a sound, wanting to escape Nova's attention.

He scrutinises every inch of me, his top lip curling in disgust, yet his actions show something different when he runs his finger down my neck. I try to swat him away, but he chuckles low and deep, moving his finger back as he runs it across my cleavage.

My chest rises and falls, whether it's from fear or want, I don't know. I try to take a step back, his presence doing too much for my libido.

"Get off me," I hiss, glaring up at him.

"Don't think I don't know you were watching me last night. Tell me, did you enjoy the show?"

"Get off me," I hiss louder when he doesn't let go of the loop in my shorts.

He shakes his head, like he's disappointed in me for speaking. "Never forget your place, Ivy."

The way he says my name sends a shiver of fear down my spine, like he knows exactly where I come from, *who* I come from. I watch him swagger past me, his stride assertive and dominant, and the deviant in me wants to lash out, kick the back of his knees or something. Anything to wipe that smug swagger he's got going on.

Even with the bad vibes coming off him, I can't help but glance down at his denim covered arse. I'm a girl after all. All plump, tight and round. He really works those jeans.

Yum.

Shame he's a fucking jackass.

I follow him into the kitchen, and the second I do, Nova tenses, her gaze briefly going to the other man in the room. I ignore Kaiden, eyeing the man watching me with disdain. He's older but looks good for his age. He has light brown hair and dark, soulless eyes. They're almost black and it creeps me out.

"Ivy, I presume."

"Yes," I reply, not bothering to ask who he is. His eyes flare with annoyance, but I don't care.

"As I'm sure you know, I'm Royce Kingsley. I live next door."

I inwardly snort at the entitlement rolling off him. He really believes I should know who is and either be impressed or awed. I'm neither.

I'm bored.

I ignore him, turning to Nova. "Can I go into to town to apply for a job?"

"A job?" Royce asks, like the world is foreign to him. My gaze flicks to Kaiden, and I notice he's just watching me, something working behind those eyes.

"Yes. *A job.* It's where people make money."

"We don't work low-paying jobs," he shoots out snottily. "And I doubt you have the expertise to get anything better. We will not have you ruining our reputation by getting a job as a cashier."

Is this guy for real?

Nova looks uncomfortable about the subject, and I know what dickhead just said is true. "Nova, you said I could," I remind her.

"Maybe you should take some time to get caught up with studies. We could go to the academy, take a look around."

I raise my eyebrow. "I'm free to go out, right?"

She sighs, not looking at dickhead. "Yes."

"I'm going out."

"Wait! I have something for you," she tells me, running to her bag sat on the side. I watch as she pulls out her purse, then walks over to me, handing me a bunch of twenties.

What the fuck does she think I need this for? I have clothes upstairs, food in the cupboards, and right now, that's more than I've ever had in my life. If she thinks she can buy me, she has another thing coming. I'm getting a job. She promised.

"Take this until your debit card comes. I ordered it yesterday," she explains, and I take the cash, not wanting to refuse in front of strangers. I can feel my face flame with heat. "Kaiden, would you be a dear and drive Ivy into town?" Before he can reply, she continues. "Make sure you have your phone, and when you're ready to be picked up, call me."

Wait, what?

"No. I can walk," I tell her, my voice rising a little too loudly.

Her expression can only be one of horror. "No. One: you don't know where it is, and two: it's a little bit far to walk."

"I'll run," I deadpan, not wanting to be alone with Kaiden.

"I'll take her," he says, his voice scratchy.

"Where are the boys?" Royce asks.

"Out," Kaiden replies shortly before looking at me. "I need to be somewhere, so you should go get your phone. I doubt you've got it on you."

I shiver from the way he looks me over, like he's picturing me naked.

I go to refuse, but Nova pushes me back towards the stairs. "Go. Have a look around in town, then come back and I'll show you around the property more."

Mutely, I nod and head back up the stairs. I grab the new phone I turned on last night and head back down. Kaiden is waiting for me, charming Nova like the devil isn't inside of him.

She can't really believe his act, can she?

"Ready?" he rumbles. I nod, then give Nova a chin lift before following him out. He walks across the gravel road, over to his house, where a sports car beeps from being unlocked.

I don't even know what kind of car it is, but I know it had to have cost a mint. Up until now, Kaiden didn't scream rich, just an entitled prick. Even the way he dresses is normal, not what I thought someone with his money would dress like. He seems just like the lads I grew up with, except he clearly knows how to shower and dresses like he owns it.

"Get in," he demands, and I quickly shove myself inside, strapping myself in.

It has that new car smell, and apart from a pack of cigarettes in the compartment under the touch screen tablet, everything is clean.

Probably hires us poor folk to clean it every day.

I'm pulled out of my musings when he gets into the car, his movements graceful and fluid. He pulls his Ray-Bans down, covering those forest green eyes so I can no longer get a read on him.

He turns the music to a rock station before wheel spinning out of the driveway. I cling to my seat, my heart racing.

Mum never had a car. The first and only car I got into was Nova's. I flinch when he drives too close to the fence bordering the road.

We pass more houses bigger than the school I went to. They get smaller as we get closer to the gate, and I wonder if that was intentional on the architect's part. Most likely.

He doesn't waste time by chatting to the new security guard, just drives on past like he owns the place.

He kind of does, I remind myself.

As he drives, I glance at the scenery. It's green, lots of trees and more pretentious housing. I've not seen any run-down houses at all. Not long into the drive, he pulls over onto the side of a dirt road in front of a gate leading onto a field.

"What are you doing?" I ask, glancing around. There's no sign of civilisation and a shiver of fear runs down my spine.

"What are you doing here? What's your game?"

"In this car?" I ask, dumbfounded.

I can't see his gaze, but I know it's on me. I can feel the burn on my skin. "No, here with Nova. You're what, eighteen soon? You didn't have to come with her."

Not liking his tone, I sit up straighter in my seat. "It's none of your business."

He smirks, leaning forward in his chair. "That's where you're wrong. It is my business."

I tilt my head, meeting his gaze with a challenge. "How's that?"

"You want money, princess, I'll give it to you. I'm sure I can think of ways for you to pay me back," he drawls.

I lean forward until I can feel his hot breath on my face. The nerve of this guy. "I don't know who the fuck you think you are, but you don't fucking know me."

"I don't?" he asks, not pulling away. I don't either, not wanting to give him the satisfaction.

"No!" I snap. "How dare you!"

"No, how dare you think you can come here. *You.*" My back straightens at the way he says 'you', like he knows me. Which is weird because I've never met him before. Pretty sure I'd remember. "Daughter of a whore. You should know, whatever fucking game you're playing, you won't win. I'll fucking destroy you, ruin you."

"Game?" I ask incredulously, not denying my mum is a slag. She was. "I'm not sure what Nova told you, but she wanted me here."

"Yeah, and you came willingly, wanting to sink those fingers into money that isn't yours. But we both know why you're really here," he tells me cryptically.

"Fuck you," I snap, having enough of talking in circles. I feel like I'm missing a crucial part of the story. Before I have chance to argue any further, he leans closer, his lips a breath away, and I freeze, my mouth going dry.

"Great arse, great tits. Might even be able to get past the rest of you for just those. I think I've even got enough change on me to pay you." He slides his Rays up on his head and glares at me with disdain.

My lips part at his words. Pretending he isn't getting to me isn't going to work much longer.

The moment he touches me, my skin begins to burn, and I try to move back. I'm frozen to my seat when he brings his nose to my exposed neck, running it along my jaw and up to my ear.

"You'd like that, wouldn't you? Do anything for a few quid," he whispers harshly. I jump when he cups my breast, and I slap his hand away.

"Get the fuck off me."

He chuckles dryly, eyeing me up and down, making me feel naked and exposed. "Yeah, money hungry slut. Get out."

"What?" I gasp, trying to wipe off the effects of him touching me has left. I meet his gaze to see if he's being serious, but he's showing nothing, his expression blank.

"Need me to dumb it down? I said, get the fuck out. I said what I needed to." Short, curt, and he means it.

"You're gonna leave me here? I don't even know where *here* is," I screech at him.

He sighs, turning the car off and opening his door. I panic when he walks around the other side, and I'm almost tempted to lock the doors and jump in the driver's seat. But I have no idea how to drive.

He can't really be doing this.

He opens the door and leans in to unclip me, his fingers purposely brushing my breasts, before dragging me out of the car. I'm in a haze so I don't fight. He really is going to leave me here, wherever here is. On my own.

"Kaiden, let me go," I start, coming to terms with what's happening. I'd beg, but that's one thing I'll never do, especially not to him.

He slams the door shut behind me before pushing me against the car. The car, hot with the summer heat, burns into my back, and I wince.

"Listen. Know your place when you're here. You don't belong. Never will. Don't go snooping into things you have no business being in. And last warning; we'll be watching you."

"Are you fucking serious," I yell.

He stares at me dead on, no emotion behind those forest green eyes as he replies, "Deadly."

"Wait," I yell, going to grab his arm. He shoves me off and I trip, falling to the floor. My arse and palms sting and almost bring tears to my eyes. *Almost.* I've not cried since I was little and learned that it got you nowhere. I didn't even cry when they told me my mother died, or the day she was cremated.

"Never touch me," he snaps, looking deadlier than I've seen him yet. I knew he was dangerous, but this is more, and I know I'll have to watch my back if I'm to stay here. "Just like your mum, down on her back."

His leaving comment hardens another part of me inside, and I get up from the floor, dusting myself off. I lean down, picking up a rock, and before he can pull off, I aim at his back window and throw. It smashes from the force, and I grin to myself before picking up another and walking over to it.

I reach the back of the car with a smirk on my face, and slowly, I dig the stone into his red, flashy paintwork and run it along. The door opens and he slowly gets out, and my back straightens. I expected him to get mad, to yell at me, but this seems much worse. I don't cower, instead I stand taller, showing him I won't be pushed around like some new toy Daddy bought him.

"Never, and I mean, *never*, lay a fucking hand on me again. Never speak to me that way either. Stay out of my way, and I'll stay out of yours. I'm here a year. I'm sure someone like you doesn't feel that threatened by a nobody like me."

His glasses are back on, so I can't read what he's thinking. Even his body language isn't giving anything away, which makes it all the more worse.

He takes two steps to reach me before leaning down in my face. "You'll regret that, princess."

He doesn't say anything else to me. Just folds himself into the car and screeches off, his tyres kicking up dirt, so stones hit the bottom of my legs.

My hands shake as I sit back on my haunches, wondering what the fuck I just did. He's not like the guys I'm used to. He's in a league of his own.

A dangerous one.

And I just seriously pissed him off.

Shit!

Chapter Three

I'M FUMING BY THE TIME I make it into town. My feet are killing me. I'm pretty sure my blisters have blisters.

He wasn't just a jerk, he was a fucking wanker.

And to make matters worse, this isn't a town. It's a few shops in a small area surrounded by a few town houses. It's like I've hit a place where there is zero population in the middle of nowhere. There are no charity shops, no banks, no take-out joints, nothing. Just a corner shop, a flower shop, and a couple of others that hold no appeal to me.

The amount of horse shit I saw on the way over made me want to puke. It was worse than the dog shit that would litter the streets where I lived before.

I sit on the steps of the church, eating a breakfast bar I grabbed from the corner shop. A corner shop that literally sells fags, booze, and a few bits and pieces. When I asked where a Tesco or a Morrisons was, the guy looked at me and laughed. Actually laughed. He said folk—yes, he actually used that word—had their shopping delivered.

I guess rich people didn't want to get their hands dirty by going to something as small as a grocery shop. Heaven forbid they get caught in the condom aisle.

Grabbing the phone Nova bought me, I flick through the contacts and decide to text her. If I speak to her right now, I'll lose my mind. She let me go with that—that… moron, and what's worse, she acted like the sun shone out of his arse.

I'm thinking a year here is going to be harder than I thought. There is nothing here. Nothing I can do to keep my mind off things. There isn't even a skateboard park—not that I have a skateboard anymore. The one I snatched after finding it abandoned at the park near me, broke last summer. This was an endless place of nothing. I might die of boredom.

Nova texts straight back to say she's on her way.

I wait, watching the few people walk by. This is nothing like the place I lived. There're no bags of rubbish outside on the pavement, no gangs of kids on the street corners causing mayhem, and everything is clean. I swear, the pavements are cleaner than the carpet in our old flat.

I've never seen anything like it. Hell, I didn't think a place like this existed. I kind of miss the noise of traffic, kids causing trouble and couples arguing. Silence isn't something I'm used to.

And then there's Kaiden, a new brand of male. I've never encountered a jerk like him, and I've met plenty.

"Are you lost, dear?" I turn to the old lady walking her two beagles. She has to be in her fifties or sixties, easily.

"Depends who you're asking," I mumble, taking a swig of Coke. It's getting hotter and sweat is running down my back.

"Ah, I've been there. You don't live around here," she states, and I guess I have a plaque on my forehead that screams, 'Doesn't belong'.

"Nope. I just moved in with my aunt. My mum died," I tell her.

She walks up the steps after tying her two dogs to the end of the rail. "You don't look too upset about it."

Is she for real? Why is she talking to me?

"I'm not."

"Weren't sad to see my mum go either. Best thing to ever happen to me."

That piques my interest. "How's that?"

She helps herself to one of my chocolate bars, peeling off the wrapper. I fight the smile threatening. She really gives no shits. I kind of like that about her.

"Was a mean woman. Should never have had kids. Couldn't hold a job neither, not that I think she ever had one."

"You don't look like someone who grew up poor," I murmur bitterly. In fact, she's dressed in a pantsuit, even though she's only walking her dogs. You'd think she was on her way to a wedding, which she could be for all I know.

She laughs. "I was. I just didn't let that control my life. Most people who grow up in poverty feel like they deserve to be there, so they never try hard enough to get themselves out."

Her words hit me like a train. It wasn't too long ago I was thinking the same thing. I don't fit in here and to be honest, back home, I was settled. I knew my life was never going to get much better; the most I'd get was a job that paid a good wage.

"What if that person really does belong there?" I ask curiously. I've got no idea why I'm talking to her, but it's not like she's given me a choice. That and she's the only one I've seen today who hasn't given me side-eyes or watched me like a hawk. One woman pushed her kid in a pram to the other side of the road when she saw me coming.

"That's BS."

"BS?" I laugh. The words leaving her mouth are hilarious.

"No one belongs in a life like that. Is that what your life was like before your aunt?"

"I guess, in a way. I've only been here a night," I confess, still wondering what the fuck is wrong with me. Usually, by now I've told the person to fuck off and leave me alone. I'm not really social. My mum, on the other hand, was, and I think that's why I'm not.

"Where are you staying?"

"Anyone ever tell you you're nosey?"

She laughs, finishing her—no, *my* chocolate bar. "You seem like someone I can be around."

At her shrug, I watch her for any catch. "What, you want to be bingo buddies?" I snark.

"Testy," she remarks. "No. But when I see a beautiful girl looking sad and lost, I want to brighten her day."

"So, you feel sorry for me?" I didn't mean for it to come out so harshly, but it does. "Sorry."

"It's fine. I am curious though... Why hang out here?"

I sigh. "Like I said, I've been here a day. And my aunt Nova said it was a town."

She laughs at my expression, patting my knee. "If you want shopping malls, cinemas and all that, it's another thirty-minutes' drive. There is a bus that runs every twenty minutes going to and from," she informs me. "Wait, by any chance are you talking about Nova Monroe?"

"Jesus, it really is a small town. And yes," I inform her.

"Bad time of it that one," she murmurs.

"What do you—"

"Ivy. Mrs White," Nova calls through her open window.

"Your aunt has my address. If you want, you can come help me on the weekends."

"Help with what?" I ask, holding my finger up to Nova.

Mrs White grins at me. "Strawberry picking. My husband's arthritis is acting up so he's not been able to help me much. I could use a young, fit girl like you. Wouldn't be able to pay much, but you have to start somewhere."

I have so many more questions, but Nova calling my name again has me standing up.

"I'll ask her. Thank you. My name's Ivy by the way."

"You're welcome. And call me Elle. Mrs White makes me feel old."

"You are old," I tell her without meaning to. I groan. Did I mention I was dragged up, not brought up?

"Call me old again and I won't invite you to bingo night. It can get rowdy, I tell ya."

"Take your word for it," I tell her, and this time I can't help but grin.

As I reach the car, Elle calls me back. "If you do turn up Saturday—early—you might want to wear different shoes."

At that, the throbbing comes back, and I wince. I nod. "Will do."

"That was quick," Nova comments as I get back in the car, pulling the belt across me.

"There's nothing here," I whine.

She chuckles. "What was you talking to Mrs White about?"

She tries to act natural, but there's something else there; worry maybe?

"She asked me to help her Saturday."

Seeing her visibly relax in her seat has me raising an eyebrow. Yeah, definitely hiding something from me.

Which reminds me of Kaiden.

"Nova, what is Kaiden to you?"

"What do you mean?" she asks, looking briefly at me.

"Just… you seem pretty close."

"I've watched him grow up. I'm his godmother," she tells me, and I all I can think is, 'great'. There's no way she'll take my side over his when I tell her what the jerk did. Might as well keep it to myself. "Which reminds me. He came back after dropping you off." I snort, interrupting her. Bet he didn't say *where* he dropped me off. "What?"

"Nothing, carry on."

"He and his brothers—"

"Hold the fuck up. He has brothers?" I ask, wondering which one is more of a nightmare; my old life or this new one.

She laughs, nodding. "Yes. Twins; Ethan and Lucca. They are your age."

"Oh God," I moan, resting my head back against the seat.

"Anyway, they came over earlier and Kaiden made a good point. He said it would be good for you to get to know them since you are practically living on top of each other and will be starting Kingsley Academy come September. The twins are having a party Saturday night and will have a few friends from Kingsley Academy attending. They want you to go."

"They actually said that?" I ask, not believing a word. She's clearly pushed them into it. Or paid them. And twins… God, what the hell am I gonna do if they're bigger dicks than their brother?

"Yes. They popped by as soon as Kaiden arrived home. They seemed excited."

"I bet," I mutter. "I'd rather not."

"Ivy," she warns. "It won't hurt you to get along with them. Please, just try. If you don't like it, come home. You'll only have to walk across the garden."

"Can I think about it?"

I notice we're getting closer to Nova's housing community. I'm hoping I can relax in my room or maybe somewhere in the garden. Alone.

"No."

The kick out of it? If I want a better life, a start to get me somewhere, then I need her. I'm not naïve enough to say otherwise. I know I can make it on my own, but it comes at a cost. It comes with being scared to go to sleep at night, too hungry to even think about food because it just makes you hungrier. But I'll do it if I have to.

Right now, I don't, and I will take the help she's offering, just as long as she knows I'll never ask for anything.

"Oh, I had Annette's husband grab an old bike out of the garage. If you want to use it to get into town, feel free."

"Where does Mrs White live?"

"Did you see the house we past five minutes ago?"

"The one near the field with all the horses?"

"Yes. She lives there with her husband. She used to own the land the horse are on, but they gave it to their son and daughter-in-law when it became too much for Mr White. She has her garden though, and it's famous for her strawberries."

Since that house was only a few minutes away, I could use the bike to ride there. Because one thing is for sure, I'm not hanging around in that house all day.

"I'll use the bike to go there then. She said she couldn't pay me much," I tell her, but it's better than I've had.

"You don't need to work there. I thought you were just helping her out, which is great."

"You said I could get a job," I remind her.

"I didn't think you would. You don't need to. I can give you money while you concentrate on school."

"Kingsley Academy hasn't even started, and I want to make my own money. I'm appreciative of your help, Nova, I really am, but I'm not some money grabber."

We pass the same security guard as earlier, and he waves us in.

"I didn't say you were. I'd never think that."

I look out the window, not looking at her. "But I would."

"Just think about it," she tells me, but it sounds like an order, one I won't follow. She'll learn that quickly.

We pull up outside her garage and, unconsciously, I begin to exam the house next door when I get out. Unlike the other houses in the gated community that are spread apart, these two are close together, like the occupants, at one point, were best friends and it got passed down through generations.

But it's not just that. Nova's, although clean and pretentious, is nothing like the one next door. You can see there have been updates made, and the stone pillars just make them look more snobbish. I mean, who do they think they are? Royals?

"Still got a problem with minding your own," a deep voice rumbles.

I startle at Kaiden's voice yet narrow my eyes when they land on him.

"What did you say?" Nova calls out, bringing her head out of the back of the car, her hands filled with a small laptop case.

"I said, mind your feet. They look sore," he calls back, stepping closer.

Nova looks confused for a moment, staring down at her feet before looking at mine. "How long were you gone? Your feet look sore, Ivy."

No shit. And it's all thanks to that arsehole.

I smile sweetly at him. "They'll be fine. Thanks for your concern." I peek behind me and a sly smirk reaches my lips. "Nasty work someone's done on your paintwork. Pissed off the wrong person?"

"Ivy," Nova gasps, before looking at Kaiden. "Sorry about that."

"Don't apologise for me," I bark snottily.

Kaiden just smiles, and it's so fake I want to puke. "It's okay, Nova. Clearly someone mistook me for someone they could fuck over."

Nova looks unsure. "Don't go getting into trouble, Kai. I'm sure the police can handle it."

"Where's the fun in that?" he tells her, but his gaze is burning into mine.

"Right, I need to get some work done. Ivy, if you want a late brunch, let Annette know. I'll be in my office."

I watch her leave before turning to Kaiden. "You're a dickhead for leaving me there on the side of the road. It took me an hour to get into town because I didn't know the way," I snap.

"Keep running your mouth and I'll find something to fill it."

The calmness in his voice sends a shiver down my spine. I straighten, stepping away from the car.

"*Find* being the key word, right?" I say, looking down at his crotch to emphasise my meaning.

"Oh, I'm going to enjoy breaking you."

He walks off, leaving me standing there breathless. After a minute of him being inside, I stick my middle finger up, feeling pathetic. He's not even there to see it.

WHEN FOOTSTEPS NEAR, I look up to find Annette walking towards me with a tray of food in her hand.

After staying in my room for two hours, I got bored and decided to check the place out. After getting bored of that, I grabbed the tatty book from my room, a seat cushion from a deck chair in the garden and headed outside to sit under the tree.

The place really is beautiful. Even the air smells different here. It feels clean, fresh, something I've never smelled before.

Nova mentioned last night that Annette lived at the back of the house with her husband. She was right; the small bungalow sat just to the side of the property once you came out of the main garden. Which has a freaking pool. I ventured further, stepping through the arched, freshly trimmed bushes and into a clearing where a massive pond was. I was far enough away from the house to not feel like an unwanted guest and far enough out of the way of the deep, dark pond.

"Ivy, I brought you out a sandwich. I wasn't sure what you'd like so I just went with one turkey and one cheese."

"Um, thank you." I take the tray from her, and I thought she'd leave. Instead, she grabs a blanket from the bag I hadn't seen she was carrying, laying it out on the ground.

"I wasn't sure if you had anything to sit on. I can see you have. I was worried about you sitting in an ants' nest."

Wouldn't be the first time, I muse as I place the tray on the blanket, grabbing a turkey sandwich.

"How did you know I was here?" I ask curiously.

She smiles gently. "I saw you head out this way. It's a beautiful spot."

"It is."

"I'd best be going. I need to take Miss Monroe her lunch."

"Thank you—for the sandwich," I tell her, holding up the sandwich higher.

I take a huge bite whilst trying to get back into the book. It's boring as hell, but it's the only thing I have. Maybe when I get paid, Nova will take me to the library.

If they have one.

I've not even finished the first sandwich when more footsteps near. I look up, scrunching my eyes up when two identical looking lads walk towards me with so much swagger it's almost cringeworthy. They work it though, both hot as hell.

I guess this is Lucca and Ethan, Kaiden's brothers.

Both look like the man I met this morning at Nova's breakfast table. They both have light brown hair, unlike Kaiden's dark hair, and the same facial features as their father, just younger and better looking.

I can't see the colour of their eyes because both are wearing shades. I do scan their physic over once again. They're in shape, both have a good amount of muscle.

Yet they seem more laid back than Kaiden in their shorts and tank tops.

When they get closer, both of them grin at each other.

"Lucca and Ethan, I take it?" I mutter when they're closer enough to hear.

Their grins spread wider. "She's heard of us already," the one wearing the red shorts chuckles.

"Something like that," I tell him, trying to figure them out.

They might seem friendly, but they look unpredictable.

"Thinks she wants a go?" Blue shorts says to his brother.

"Slags always want a go," Red shorts replies.

"Would you like me to leave you two alone?" I ask sarcastically, deciding to get up and head inside.

I begin to shake off the grass that has somehow managed to get on my legs when they step closer.

"W-what are you doing?"

They begin to circle me, and I start to feel dizzy.

"What are we doing, Lucca?"

Ah, so red shorts is Lucca and blue shorts is Ethan. Good to know. Let's hope they keep to the colours every day.

"Having some fun," Lucca replies.

I go to step forward when they give me an opening, but Lucca pushes me against Ethan.

"I heard she likes it rough," Ethan whispers in my ear.

I jump away, glaring at him. "Fuck off."

"Tell me, little one, just how rough do you like it? Because we tag team. Although, someone like you is probably used to having every hole used."

"I said, fuck off," I snap, yelping when Ethan pushes me into Lucca.

I try to shove off, but Lucca grabs me around the waist, holding me to his body, his one hand grasping my tit.

Another hard body steps up behind me, pressing his dick against my back, and butterflies flutter in my stomach.

"Go, now," I yell, trying to get free, but with another pair of hands gripping me in place, I have no hope. Ethan's fingers run along my stomach where my top has risen up and my mind begins to race. I've encountered assholes before, even fought off advances from grown ass men Mum brought back with her, but this… this is something else. I wasn't expecting this.

"No!" I yell, trying to fight them off.

"Do you think it's passed down?" Ethan asks cryptically.

"You wondering what makes *her* special too?"

"Must have a magic pussy. Wonder if her daughter does too," Ethan drawls, his fingers now running over my denim covered sex.

I squeak, getting pissed off with all the cryptic comments going back and forth. Both have charming characteristics and confidence with a big ego that would make people believe them over me if I said they were terrorising me. Not that I'd grass. But you can believe your sweet arse I'd get revenge. And if I get caught, no one will believe me over them.

When he moves his fingers back to my top, exposing more of my midriff, I slap his hand away and shove it back down.

Wrong move.

Lucca is drawn to my cleavage that has popped out more from shoving my top down.

"We should have a taste."

"Kaiden would be pissed if we played with his new toy," Ethan replies, but doesn't sound upset over it.

"Fuck this," I snap, and before Lucca can get any more handsy, I knee him in the balls. He falls down to his knees, grasping his junk.

"Fucking bitch," he wheezes.

Ethan begins to laugh, helping his brother back to his feet before they both turn to me.

"You're tougher than we thought."

"You think this is a fucking joke? You just sexually assaulted me," I snap, grabbing my book from the floor. Annette can get the rest of the shit herself. I storm off, ignoring their laughter.

"Love, we did you a favour."

I spin around at Ethan's voice, and I know it's his because his is deeper, whereas Lucca's is raspy.

"Did me a favour?" I ask in disgust. God, I need to get drunk.

He grins, eyeing me up and down. "You need to be strong for what he has planned for you. We were checking if you were—that and we're assholes."

"What are you talking about?" I ask, gripping my hair from my face.

"Kaiden," Lucca tells me, still catching his breath.

"Are you fucking kidding me? This is about your brother?"

Ethan laughs. "Love, you have no idea. We were going to fuck with you either way, just the usual, but you pissed off our brother. And when he gets mad, he gets even and then some. I'd watch it if I were you."

"Why can't you all just stay out of my way?" I snap.

He shrugs. "You don't belong."

Oh, no, not this again. "You guys need to grow the fuck up. You make it sound like I bribed my way here and am holding Nova under protest. I'm not. She invited me here."

"You really don't know, do you?" Ethan asks, scanning my face closely.

"Know what?" I yell, throwing my hands up. "I've been here a day."

Lucca looks at Ethan and shrugs. "If I were you, I'd keep it that way."

I scream in frustration when they walk past me.

"Oh, and Ivy... great tits."

"Fantastic arse," Ethan finishes.

Anger boils inside of me and I storm in the direction of the house. There are secrets here, and I intend to find out why. There's no guessing it has to do with Mum and why she isn't a part of this life. It's also the reason those boys have gone out of their way to make my life hell.

If they think I'm going to roll over and cry, they're wrong. If Kaiden wants to fight, he's got it. I'll fight back.

First though, it's time to find out who my mum really was.

ACKNOWLEDGEMENTS

Before I start, I think we can all agree on how beautiful the cover is, right? Thank you, Cassy Roop, @Pink Ink Designs, for bringing another cover to life. I love it.

And thank you, Stephanie Farrant, for editing another novel for me. Thank you for being the friend I needed over the past few months, and thank you for always being there when I needed advice and support during difficult parts of the book.

Thank you for always steering me in the right direction when I go wrong.

Just, thank you. Thank you for completing the book.

I want to finish by saying thank you to the readers who continue to read my novels. It means so much to me, more than you'll ever know.

To all the reviews given, I read them. I see you. I see what you loved, and what you didn't, and your words mean everything to me. It gives me the drive to keep writing, to keep going, and for that, I'll always be grateful that you take the time to type one out.

So, what can you expect next from me…

Well, as you know from above, Wrong Crowd will be coming soon. I am hoping for a June release.

I'm looking forward to releasing Ivy and Kaiden's novel. It's something

I've wanted to write since I published Malik. If you didn't get to watch the live video on my author page, then I'll explain. Malik was originally going to be the snippet you just read, Wrong Crowd. I've made a few minor adjustments, but I finally got the setting I'm in love with, which is perfect for their story.

But I know you are all dying to know who is next. Will it be a Carter, will it be a Hayes brother? I don't know. I'm holding my hands up right now and telling you I don't know.

I have Maddox, Charlotte and Hayden all screaming at me to write their story. All for different reasons.

Then I have Wyatt's story.

It's a hard decision to make, especially when I've been dying to write two of the books since I began Faith's.

I will always keep you updated though. If you don't already, follow me on Facebook @AuthorLisaHelenGray

I love hearing from you all, so keep in touch.

Wishing you a happily ever after,

Lisa.

OTHER TITLES
BY LISA HELEN GRAY

FORGIVEN SERIES
Better Left Forgotten
Obsession
Forgiven

CARTER BROTHERS SERIES
Malik
Mason
Myles
Evan
Max
Maverick

A NEXT GENERATION CARTER NOVEL SERIES
Faith
Aiden
Landon
Soul of My Soul 3.5 (This is the first book in the spin of series for the Hayes brothers, but I would read after Landon and before the next book)

TAKE A CHANCE
Soul of My Soul

WHITHALL UNIVERSITY SERIES
Foul Play
Game Over
Almost Free

I WISH SERIES
If I Could I'd Wish It All Away
Wishing For A Happily Ever After
Wishing For A Dream Come True – DATE TO BE ANNOUNCED

KINGSLEY ACADEMY

Wrong Crowd – Release date to be announced.

Printed in Great Britain
by Amazon

21089085R00194

The first time I met Lily Carter, I thought she was an angel. I'm still convinced she is.

She was pure.
She was kind.
She was Lily.

Everything about her captivated me.
She called to my soul.

Being with her broke an unspoken rule between the Hayes' and the Carter's. But they broke it first when one of them started dating my sister.

Now, all bets are off.

Lily may be fragile, but she's not broken, and it's time people stopped treating her like she is. I'm making Lily mine, and there's only one thing that can stop me:

Death.

And I wouldn't put it past a
Carter to go to those lengths.
I'm willing to pay that price.

Because without her, without that piece of my soul I know she holds, I'm dead inside.

ISBN 9781092760829

9 781092 760829

90000